THE LAST DAYS

OF OSCAR WILDE

a novel

by

John Vanderslice

THE LAST DAYS

OF OSCAR WILDE

Published by Burlesque Press

www.burlesquepressllc.com

ISBN: 978-0-9964850-9-8

Book design by Daniel Wallace

Cover photo originally taken by Nil Castellví

Dedication

This book is dedicated to the memory of the late
Patricia Horstmann Vanderslice.

Much love, Mom. And endless thanks.

I am going under, the Morgue yawns for me. I go and look at my zinc bed there.

After all I had a wonderful life, which is, I fear, over. But I must dine once with you first.

-- Letter from Oscar Wilde to Frank Harris, winter 1897.

Dying in Paris is really a very difficult and expensive luxury for a foreigner.

-- Letter from Robert Ross to a friend, December 1900.

I Must Dine With You First

Paris. 20 October, 1899.

The day, at last, was clear, the sun breaking hard across the striated tops of the shops on the Rue Saint Honoré, where Armstrong sat outside the Café de la Regence celebrating the arrival of true autumn with a full bottle of white wine and a three course dejeuner: escargot, half-lobster, and roasted potatoes followed by a dessert. He'd just finished his tarte aux fraises and was convinced it was a revelation, possibly the single best thing he'd ever put in his mouth. Armstrong had been in the city almost a week and until this day he'd been served nothing but uncomfortable rain—the measly, pestering kind; a harbinger of winter—along with drowsy Parisians shuttling through the wet streets with their shoulders lowered, their heads huddled under black umbrellas. But on this day he'd finally witnessed the Paris he'd been told to expect from the francophiles he'd encountered in Arkansas, those men and women—usually non-Arkansawyers passing through Hot Springs on their way to St. Louis or Fort Worth or Salt Lake—who claimed to have visited all the great capitals of Europe and ranked Paris as the most beautiful and most easy; certainly the most welcoming to Americans. Find a café on a sunny afternoon and sit with a bottle of wine. Take your entertainment from the street for an hour, and you will not need a museum or an orchestra again for as long as you live.

So far, at the very start of his six month Grand

Tour—requisite polishing before Armstrong assumed a lifelong place at his father's law firm—their advice had proved less than useless; in fact, a lie. He hadn't been able to sit outside a café even once. Meanwhile, the insides of the cafes were jammed with people trying to get out of the rain, and tables were nearly impossible to snare, especially for a polite foreigner whose French could stand considerable improvement. He'd gotten flustered several times already when giving addresses to impatient hack drivers and had settled for walking everywhere, even in the drizzle. His hotel room was comfortable but not entirely restful. For two straight nights he'd been beleaguered by the noise in the next room: grunting and yelling in a language that sounded like Polish, a language he'd recognized because he'd heard it spoken by a group of farmers in the Marche when he'd paused there during a trip to Fort Smith three years before. Armstrong hadn't tried the theatre yet because he was afraid he would not understand half of what he was seeing, despite the French-language instruction he'd received for six years when he was younger. The museums and concert halls had been his only places of refuge. Armstrong had started to believe that, despite that romanticized claims of the travelers he met, sunshine never came to Paris, at least not in autumn.

But then came today and this afternoon, and a sky so hard and blue that it reminded him of the sky above his uncle's farm in Bismarck, Arkansas; along with a sun so auspiciously bright that it seemed to remonstrate Armstrong for his sin of ever doubting it. Armstrong hardly minded the reproof. He mostly ignored the men at the tables near his: small-faced, hungry-looking types bent over chessboards. Instead he focused on the Rue Saint Honoré, leisuring in his unguarded view of the faces of the ladies passing by: their clear skin, their angular noses, their ponderous green and hazel and charcoal eyes no longer stuffed up under umbrellas but out in the open, for everyone to see. He smelled the musky cab horses as they trotted by; he watched the concentrated world weariness on the faces of the workmen and the hurry on the faces of chefs who, boxes and baskets in hand, were intent for les Halles and supplies for that night's dinner service; he studied the shoes and the canes and the coats of other men who meandered more slowly and more happily, often with women beside them in long, narrow dresses and small, tidy hats. Once in a while he glanced up higher and across the Rue de Rivoli to spy the exquisite monstrosity of the Louvre, that converted palace that ruled the streetscape of central Paris like a citadel. Two days earlier, he passed an entire morning and afternoon in the museum. Seven hours total—and he barely scratched the surface of its holdings. Today, however, he would rather look at living men and women, and so he dropped his glance back to the street before him. Living men and women, he decided on the spot, were far more entrancing to observe than any still piece of art, no matter how carefully rendered.

Armstrong was finally alive and outdoors in the middle of it—Paris city center—only a few minutes' walk from the Siene. As soon as he finished this last glass of wine, he would wend that way, cross at the Pont Neuf, which was sure to be crowded now with thriving, shining bodies. Today he would stop at those stalls on the other side of the bridge and inspect all the wares for sale. It didn't matter if they were useless, because he didn't need anything at all. Or, rather, what he needed was to be outside in the City of Light, with the sun turned on.

He remembered at once the cigar in his jacket pocket, what he'd intended to smoke as soon as he'd finished his tart. How could he forget? He'd brought the thing all the way with him from Hot Springs—1500 miles across the eastern quadrant of the United States, another 3000 miles across an ocean, and then the 140 miles from Le Havre to central Paris—all for the sake of enjoying it after his first real café meal; what months ago he'd promised himself when he bought the cigar, the most expensive he could find in the tobacconist shop back home. "I'm not going to smoke this," he announced to his father and mother, "until I am sitting outside a café in Paris, a little street side table, with a full belly and sunshine above me." In his four days in Paris he'd eaten at plenty of cafes, but he'd kept the cigar stowed in his coat pocket, waiting. Even today he'd waited, deciding that with the fine weather he would take a much longer morning constitutional: hiking all the way from his hotel on the Rue de l'Odéon up to Montmartre, around the curving streets there, then back down again. He passed by the Café de la Regence shortly after one, so famished at that point that he could not help but stop and order what, based on his rudimentary French, seemed to be the most substantial repast available, replete with the tart and the bottle of wine.

He clipped the cigar and brought it at last to his lips, only to realize that he had no match. Armstrong laughed. He'd lugged the damn thing all the way to Paris but forgot to bring matches? Sometimes, in odd moments like this one, he wondered if he really was fit for a law career after all. Sometimes, his mind seemed altogether too foggy. A man two tables away eyed him with a look that Armstrong could not decide whether to interpret as concern or disapproval. A stony penetrating stare coming from dark eyes set inside a wide, pasty face. This stranger had lips more prim than normal for a male; and yet the delicacy of those was offset by an overbearing nose and a broad chin. He was wearing a light brown coat that appeared a bit worse for the wear, perhaps one could say fusty; also a black bowler. The hair that stuck about from beneath the bowler seemed mismanaged, as if he were weeks overdue for a trim. Yet the impression the stranger's stare gave off was not so much tawdriness but a penetrating, possessive intelligence. A discriminating and scrutinizing air. Armstrong wondered if he had accidentally dribbled a bit of wine on his collar or dropped crumbs from the tart onto his sleeve, some violation of decorum that revealed him as a novice.

Rather than suffer the stranger's scrutiny, Armstrong looked again at the street, tried to fix his attention on some particularly glamorous or ridiculous figure. But there was no one like that at the moment, only ordinary Parisians going about their business. He was wondering whether he should just abandon that last glass of wine when he sensed someone nearing. He turned his head and saw that it was the stranger, standing now at his table as stolidly as if Armstrong had summoned him for an errand.

"I see," the man started, "that you are unable to light your cigar. May I offer you a match?"

Armstrong laughed—so that's what the man's stare was about. He nodded. "I was hoping no one would notice. I don't know how to ask for one. Kind of embarrassing."

"No reason to let ordinary embarrassment keep you from enjoying a good cigar." The stranger reached into his pocket, removed a matchbox and struck one. He leaned in closer, putting the little flame at Armstrong's service.

Armstrong took the initial puff and felt the heady rush of smoke, so long anticipated, into his mouth, over his tongue, into his brain. Indeed, this would be a very good cigar. He leaned back, blew out the mouthful in a rush. He closed his eyes. He opened them. The stranger stood there, regarding him with an envious smile.

"Thank you," Armstrong said. Then: "Please." He gestured to the open chair on the other side of the table. The stranger nodded—a small, grateful motion—and sat. "I'm sorry to say that this is the only cigar I have. I brought it from home to save for just a day like this one."

"A subtle gesture," the stranger concurred, "and apparently a wise one—given how much pleasure it affords you."

Armstrong smiled. He didn't know what to make of this English-speaking stranger, one who had so easily pegged him as another traveler from the Anglophone world. On one hand, the man seemed perfectly harmless, even gracious, and certainly graceful. He spoke with an aristocratic pronunciation and syllabic emphasis, as if he went home each night and performed in front of a mirror. But no, his sonorous speech rolled off him too easily for that; he seemed born to it in the way that British speakers so often do, in a way that Americans for all their colorful bravado and New World slang could never hope to equal. This aspect of the stranger was flawlessly polished and not a little intimidating for the twenty-five-year-old Arkansawyer; but then again, it was quite at odds with the threadbare coat, the untrimmed hair, the tint of despair accenting the corners of the man's eyes. Was he an underemployed scholar, badly in need of new pupils? Or a gentleman who had suffered some catastrophic financial downtown, something so awful it turned him out of his comfortable Paris apartment and into the streets? Or was he simply a charming hobo, surviving on his wits in one of the world's busiest cities? Armstrong could not know for sure, but he sensed that the stranger was not trying to sell him anything or take anything from him. Instead the man just seemed in need of company.

Armstrong spoke. "How about I tell the waiter to bring another bottle of wine?"

The stranger almost grimaced, but then the expression relaxed. "I would be in your debt. And thankful. But that's not why I offered you the light."

"I know. But it's the least I can do for someone who rescued my plans."

"Rescued?"

"I've owned that cigar for nearly five months. I've been waiting for just the right time to smoke it. It would have represented quite the overthrow to have had to leave here today without enjoying it."

A slow nod of recognition from the stranger. The waiter noticed Armstrong's gesture and came over.

"May I?" the stranger said. "I think there's a variety you might like even better."

"Please," Armstrong said, "but let me pay."

"Of course," the stranger said and proceeded to address the waiter in a French so natural that Armstrong wondered if this was the man's real speech and the English a magnificent put-on. Even if Armstrong lived a whole year in this city he could not speak French that well. Two years. Hell, five.

"You've been in this country a while," Armstrong said, when the waiter left, "from the sound of it."

"I have been a bit of everywhere, actually."

"Your accent is impeccable. I mean your French accent."

The stranger smiled wryly. But the longer the smile remained the more it turned down at the ends, like an emotional pointer his face could not resist. "Accents are a simple matter. A bit of rudimentary acting."

"But it's not just the intonation. You know the language itself so well."

The man made a dismissive gesture. "Not so well

as you think, according to some people."

Armstrong was about to ask *which people?* but the waiter returned with uncharacteristic rapidity, a sign Armstrong interpreted to mean that the period for dejeuner was fast closing down, and that les hommes were expected to be gone sooner rather than later. And yet here was the bottle. The waiter had not tried to talk them out of it.

"When one is raised in England—or Ireland—or Scotland—and if one attends a passable school—learning French is practically an automatic affair. It is right from the start."

"Well, for me too—me too. I mean, my father paid for private tutors. There was never a question. But I haven't got half your accent, or your fluency."

The stranger offered a languid, distracted shrug. He'd become bored with this subject, or embarrassed by it. Armstrong couldn't tell. For a few moments the man's face closed down; he looked at the street without quite registering what he saw there.

Then he took a sip of wine and started talking: "You said that you brought the cigar from home. May I ask where that is?"

"America," Armstrong chirped.

"Of course, America," the stranger said, as if insulted. "Where in America?"

Armstrong told him, and the stranger looked surprised. "Now that may be the only place in your country I have not visited."

"I don't know," Armstrong said. "Doubt that. My

country is mighty spacious. Many corners."

Meager smile from the stranger, a smile that acted like a lockbox. But then the stranger gave him the key.

"Years ago I traveled for ten straight months across your country."

"Ten months! Where did you go?"

"Everywhere. Without exaggeration: everywhere. Except for Arkansas."

Armstrong chuckled but said nothing; instead he waved for the stranger to continue.

"New York, of course," the man said. "Several times. But really the full extent of the land. Every direction, big cities and small. Chicago. Baltimore. Philadelphia. Boston. San Francisco. Denver." As the list went on, he slowed, thinking harder to pull out the names. "Fort Wayne. Racine. Cincinnati. Where else? Houston. New Orleans. Vicksburg. Richmond. Dozens of others, large and small."

"The South too then."

"As I said, every direction. Even a bitty little community in Rhode Island, rarely visited by anyone I dare say."

"Which?"

"It's called Pawtucket."

Armstrong nodded heartily. "I've heard of it. Couldn't tell you what it's about, however."

"Nor could I. It was just the one night, more than fifteen years ago." His voice trailed off wistfully.

"That's a nice bit of wandering. But how did you cover your expenses? They must have been titanic. What did you do?" A startled grimace crossed the stranger's face. Armstrong remembered too late what he'd been told several weeks before he left home: Europeans do not like to talk about money and how they got it. Either they have it, or they don't. That is all you need to know. This was hard for Armstrong to understand, and even harder to accept, because in America money talk flowed as freely as money itself. People were not only willing but eager to explain to you how they'd made a buck, especially if it was a buck more than the next man. Such talk was part of the fun of being rich. When Armstrong expressed his incredulity about this advice he was told, "Chances are it goes back to some quirk in the family tree. Somebody married someone they shouldn't, and whether it made them rich or poor they don't care to have the secret history discussed." So it must be with this stranger, Armstrong thought. There's a story he can't tell, and yet I'm trying to force it out of him. He was about to apologize when the man answered his question.

"That's just it. All that traveling was for the sake of earning money. It is how I covered the expenses."

"What did you do, perform in a circus?"

Now the stranger laughed. Not guffawing, not with hilarity, but with something broader and sadder and more important behind it. "Yes, that's exactly what it was. Every night. Three rings. A strongman. Dancing animals. Many bearded ladies. And I myself was the acrobat."

Armstrong could tell, of course, that the stranger was talking sarcastically, but at the same time, the man's voice carried no malice; he spoke without bitterness. He was not trying to make fun of Armstrong, even if he was lying to him. But what was he trying to make fun of?

At that moment Armstrong saw another stranger approach his table. This man looked at least ten years older than himself, with shredded strands of gray in his otherwise dark sideburns and a look of moral severity in his expression, an urgency in his eyes, as if he'd just recognized Armstrong as the one who, a few years earlier, had poisoned his dog, and now the man wanted to give Armstrong his due. Armstrong cut off the conversation with the polite stranger at his table and raised himself slightly in his seat, to get ready for whatever this new man had to say. It was then he realized that he'd seen this man before. When Armstrong had first taken his table, this severe-looking gentleman had been sitting at a table further down the sidewalk, a woman across from him, fingering menus. Armstrong had not tried to catch the man's attention, and Armstrong hadn't spared a glance that way the whole time he devoured his meal; yet here was the selfsame gentleman approaching him with an intentional look.

When the man was only a step or two away, all of Armstrong tensed and his right hand curled into a fist. A bad habit, perhaps, leftover from a Hot Springs childhood, but a habit nonetheless. It turned out the man did not slow and did not stop; he did nothing threatening. He did not, in fact, say a single word. What he did was to flip a small white card onto Armstrong's lap as he passed. Armstrong looked down, confused. What just happened? He saw the card, bright against the black of his trousers.

He read the words that were written there in thick gray lead, a hurried slovenly cursive: *This man is Oscar Wilde.* Armstrong looked up and into the face of the disheveled stranger, the charming hobo, seated at his table. The stranger's face had changed drastically, as if he had been able, from where he sat, to read the card and precisely interpret its import. As if he knew everything about it. Now that Armstrong considered it, the man at his table did look like an older, oversized version of the famously scorned aesthete, whose trial in 1895 had caused such a scandal in the American papers, and who was known now to be shambling through a variety of European cities, disgraced and practically in hiding. Wilde looked disconcerted, maybe even abashed. He stared into Armstrong's eyes for seconds as if hoping to find mercy there, but then he looked away abruptly, as if certain he would not.

Armstrong didn't know if Wilde should feel disconcerted. He didn't even know how he himself felt. He seemed to feel three or four things at once: honor and disgust; astonishment and rue; incredulity and a queer kind of joy. The man sitting across from him—the man who had chosen to sit across from him—was, only five years earlier, one of the most lionized, recognizable men in the western world, the new king of the London stage. Of course, the same man, as if overnight, had become toxic goods: preached about in pulpits; defamed in the press and on college campuses; on the losing end of so many strident public attacks. The last time he was in St. Louis, Armstrong had seen in the window of a bookshop a volume titled *The Sins of Oscar Wilde.* He hadn't bought it. And now here was Wilde himself, sharing his bottle of wine. One thing was sure: The strained moment had gone on too long. Armstrong needed to say something; he needed to set the atmosphere right. But his tongue stayed heavy, unwilling to move.

A curtain fell over Wilde's face. He looked at Armstrong directly: dark eyes level and set with resolve. "I remove the embarrassment," he said, and stood. With that, he took one step to his left and surged forward: past Armstrong's right shoulder, headed west on the Rue Saint Honoré, as if he had a mind for the Tuileries. Ironically, the same direction the man with the card had gone. Armstrong was so flustered and guilty and angry—at whom he wasn't exactly sure—that he forgot to ask the waiter for l'addition. Instead he blindly cast down scores of francs and stood. By the time he'd gathered himself sufficiently to look over his shoulder, Wilde was a dozen steps up the street, surging on, as if his feet were on fire. Armstrong didn't think about chasing the poet down, about asking him for his side of the story. Instead he stepped on to the Rue Saint Honoré and started off the other way.

PART ONE

CHAPTER ONE

CHAPTER ONE

Paris. October, 1898.

"Are we going?" Ross said. "Or are we just going to wait around until they start hounding you about your bill?"

Wilde laughed. He'd only just then, at 3:05 in the afternoon, finished dressing for the day. He might have been delayed longer if Ross had not shown at 1:40 and knocked like a hammer out of hell on the door of his tiny room in the Hôtel de Nice. It had started Wilde out of a groggy yet fitful sleep, one brought on by having lapped up entirely too many of the sweet advocaats the night before at the Café de Flore. Now he was pleasantly surprised to realize that his skin felt better and the headache of doom he'd woken with had evaporated. He wondered if such an easy recovery from a night's drinking was a sign of alcoholism. Probably, but he was not going to let himself feel anxious over it. He'd suffered enough anxiety, god knew. Perhaps, he thought, he should trim back on the liquor and get serious about opium.

"You're such the pragmatist," Wilde said to Ross, straightening his defeated collar one more time before turning from the shabby mirror on the far wall. "How come you and Frank aren't better friends?"

Ross was seated in the chair closest to the door, poised to spring up at any moment. He started at Wilde, his delicate eyebrows forming a crucifixion above the cloudy blue eyes. "Frank Harris?"

"Of course. Who do you think?"

Ross blinked. "It's next to impossible, you know, to keep an inventory of your acquaintances, Oscar. Even now." Wilde saw some unarticulated decision cross Ross's face, and then the man stood. "For all I know, there might be two dozen Franks with whom you are on a first-name basis."

"Not anymore. Certainly not here. The only Franks in this city are leftovers from the ones who chased out the Romans."

Ross dropped his stare and clucked, shaking his head.

"What?" Wilde said.

"Your mind. I would not have put Frank and Franks together."

"Yes, you would. You just did. In any case, I would hardly rank Frank Harris as an 'acquaintance.' That's an insult to us both."

Harris, currently living in London and supervising the *Saturday Review*, a paper he not only wrote for but owned, was one of Wilde's more reliable sources for emergency financial rescue, especially necessary after Wilde's wife had died and her lawyers had refused to continue the stipend she'd been clandestinely sending him. You broke the agreement regarding Alfred Douglas, they said to him in a final communication. Hence, you will not, and do not deserve to, receive a farthing. Since then, Harris had sent Wilde at least £15 on three different occasions. However, the last time Wilde had seen his journalist friend, during one of Harris's frequent Paris stopovers, the man had turned hectoring. "What are you working on now? What will be the follow-up to *The Ballad of Reading Gaol*? Now that you're back, you know, you have to keep going." Not for nothing did Frank Harris—born in Ireland to Welsh parents—spend the better part of his youth and young adulthood in America. "Now that you're back, you have to have a follow-up" might have been the most American thing Wilde had heard since his tour of the States back in the early 80s. Harris's Americanness was endearing actually, but Wilde worried it might become hard to keep the well-meaning busybody at bay. At least he kept sending money.

Ross sighed. He raised one hand, a gesture of futility.

"Whatever you say. But, for the record, Frank Harris and I are on passably good terms. I'm as friendly with him as I can be with someone who is not one of us."

An interesting expression, Wilde thought. Not one he'd ever heard Robert Ross use before. It also suggested a bias he'd heretofore not witnessed in the man. Wilde looked at his friend, as if to check to see if a stranger had entered. But, no, there he was. Good old Robbie. Same as ever: nattily attired in a gray suit and waistcoat; competently and quietly handsome: his small face, his clear eyes, his sharp bones, his penetrating analytical intelligence. A man who looked like exactly what he was: never not in control of a situation, no matter how chaotic; a person immune to panic; a person whose reaction to any awful development was not to blubber—not even for a moment—but to strategize a way out. This was a talent Wilde himself could admire and rely on but never understand, since he had none of it himself. Whereas Wilde felt himself at all times to be sloppy and needy and surging, Ross was absolutely steady, impossibly sane, as shrewd as any advisor could be.

If one didn't know better, one could easily take Robert Ross for a lawyer; which, ironically, is what Frank Harris had once been. A natural born psychologist and mind reader, Ross could interpret any situation, particularly situations between people, with exacting accuracy. The underlying truth of any case came so easily to him that it had nothing really to do with analysis but just observation. As a result, Ross usually had firm ideas about the appropriate way Wilde should handle this or that person, this or that crisis. Wilde sometimes took his advice, but usually he didn't. And when he didn't, he always regretted it later.

Wilde went for his walking stick—an ordinary derby cane, at least ten years old and found for next to nothing in a secondhand shop on the Rue de l'Odéon—currently propped against the miniscule set of drawers the hotel had provided him. He took it in hand and squeezed. "Have I ever told you that, to be terribly frank"—at the word he flashed Ross a coy smile—"I think you're the smartest person I know. Of course, sometimes, you're the dumbest too."

He was also the most generous. When Constance's lawyers had told him not to expect anything more from her estate, Ross had quietly stepped in and offered to take over the payments Wilde's wife had been quietly sending him; at the same amount: £150 a year. Wilde was so grateful he kissed his friend full on the lips, out in public, at a café. Ross offered to divide up the sum the way Constance had: one remittance a month of more or less equal value. Yes, Wilde had said, that is the way we must do it. The one nagging, continuing problem was that Wilde had the worst time not spending any money he possessed. Ross's stipend was usually gone after one week's time, leaving Wilde to scrounge and beg and put off and con for the next 20 days. At this point, he was getting rather good at it.

Presently, a fragile smile hung suspended on Ross's face. Wilde thought he might have seen in Ross's eye the movement of a tear—an actual tear from the unemotional Robert Ross. "My god, Robbie, you're not going to take hurt from any of the rubbish I say, are you? I was trying to be kind."

"But it's true. I am dumb—in my center. It's only the outermost part of me, the least important part, that thinks and moves quickly."

"That's true of everyone."

"No. It's not."

"It is. It's true of me."

Ross chortled. "You," he said.

Wilde started for the door. "We should leave this minute. Bosie is waiting, and you are being ridiculous."

Wilde took a first firm step toward the door and with it came the resurgence of his headache. He stopped and breathed. His eyes cleared. Better. A kind stranger at the café had covered the cost of the drinks. At least

Wilde thought the man was a stranger—he could not remember having ever met him before—until the man explained, altogether too late in the evening, that he was one for whom Wilde and Alfred Douglas had helped procure rent-boys over the course of 1894 and 95. In fact, right up to the week that the Marquess of Queensbery, Douglas's father, had left a note in Wilde's club accusing him of being a sodomite, the fatal action that set so much in motion and made impossible any further involvement by Wilde in the renter trade.

"You were both so fair to me," the man said, sadly, a lordly-looking fellow, several years older than Wilde, with a gargantuan walrus moustache and a new, clean-smelling suit. The man had had one too many drinks and looked in the moment as if he might weep. "And perfectly discrete."

Wilde felt taken in. He and Bosie's dedicated assistance to urbane gentlemen like this one, who both were desperate to satisfy their Unitarian tendencies and avoid exposure, was as an aspect of his London life—and his relationship with Bosie—that he preferred to forget. It was probably the most devastating evidence presented against him by Queensberry's lawyers during the trial. Barely a restaurant in the city was willing to seat him when word got out about the testimony. It would be like accommodating some East End pimp. Well, actually, not like it at all. Not merely like. Even now he could not think about the disgrace without wincing. And here at the Café de Flore was this half-drunken lord who kept throwing an arm around his neck and fulminating about gratitude.

Wilde would have left sooner except that every time he tried, the man—what was his name anyway?—kept insisting that the poet enjoy another drink, on his bill. How could Wilde refuse? Given how clotted his head felt upon waking, how tightly his skin clung to his skeleton, how sweaty his nightshirt was and how dry his mouth, Wilde knew he should have refused the last few drinks. He most certainly should have. But he also knew that he could not have, and never would, turn down free alcohol.

"I'm not sure I even want to go now," Ross said.

"Bosie is waiting for us," Wilde repeated, but Ross's only answer was a disgusted glare.

It was not precisely true that Lord Alfred Douglas was waiting for them. More like the opposite, actually. Yes, Douglas was headquartered in Paris now—living in an apartment Wilde had alerted him to on the Avenue Kléber—but while Wilde dropped in semi-regularly to catch up with his old flame, Wilde could not know for a fact that Douglas was there at the moment. And Douglas could not be anticipating the two of them because he did not even know that Ross had come to Paris. On a moment's inspiration the evening before, Wilde had scrawled a quick note to Bosie—I will drop in on the apartment tomorrow afternoon, yes?—and then paid a boy ten francs to carry it to the Avenue Kléber. He'd had no verification that Douglas had actually received the note, much less read it. He had even less verification that Douglas would be enlivened by the message.

Wilde hoped to bring his two old Uranian friends together at long last. At one time in London Ross and

Douglas had been his most regular companions and trusted confidantes, though they were usually not in the same place at the same time. It was evident from both—it had been evident since before Wilde even went to jail—that they did not like each other—not at all—a situation at once heartbreaking and exhilarating. Once upon a time, Wilde would have had to admit in his most private of hearts that he enjoyed thinking that their mutual animosity was on account that they were fighting over him. But that particular set of emotional facts was long gone. Doulas would not fight anyone for Wilde now. So the two men might as well become friends again.

"You should have brought More with you," Wilde said. "This visit might go easier."

Ross looked at him carefully, but said nothing, as if on purpose.

"Or Reggie, for that matter. Reggie would be even better. Reggie can talk to anyone."

"He's busy," Ross grunted.

"Is he?" Of course, Wilde considered. Their mutual Unitarian friend Reginald Turner was becoming quite the item in the London paper scene, with his new idea of a gossip column for *The Daily Telegraph*. From what Wilde had heard, now that Turner had a trumpet, the whole city wanted to talk to him. "I suppose. But wouldn't he be just the thing to negotiate between you and Bosie?"

"I hadn't planned on needing a negotiator, Oscar," Ross fired back. "Because I hadn't planned on seeing Douglas at all." Ross paused. "This visit is your idea, remember?"

At the door now, Wilde hesistated, perplexed. Yes, it had been, hadn't it? Funny how he'd forgotten.

Out on the Rue des Beaux-Arts, Ross surged toward the Rue Bonaparte, his head down, his shoulders squared, his steps as efficient as pins. Wilde had no choice but to follow as best he could. They reached the intersection. Without hesitation, Ross turned right. On to the Seine. As if he'd just thought of it, Ross paused suddenly to check to make sure Wilde was there. Wilde was, but only barely. "Robbie," Wilde said, "aren't we getting a cab?"

No change of expression; the familiar, determined look. "I thought I'd rather walk," Ross said bluntly. "If you don't mind." The Robert Ross who had almost come to tears back in the hotel room was gone. This tone of voice belonged to another, more determined, and perhaps very annoyed person.

"Of course I mind. It's quite far."

"I know where it is. And it's not that far at all. Nothing's far in Paris."

Wilde could have treated his friend to a long disputation about how far apart Paris neighborhoods could be, but fact was Wilde was fifteen years Ross's senior. Wilde had almost reached the mid-point between forty and fifty—that is, firmly into middle age—while Ross was not even out of his twenties yet. So of course nothing seemed far to him. Nor did it help that Wilde had developed a long and mysterious pain in his right leg, which made him walk like some fairy tale villain. Most observers, Wilde knew, would think of him as an ogre. Strike that. He was an ogre.

Wilde shrugged with theatrical fatalism. "If you say, Robbie. I'm just afraid your feet will hurt."

Ross blinked. "My feet never hurt."

Wilde sighed. Of course they didn't. He bowed his head. "As you wish."

The two walked in silence for a time. When, after a few blocks they reached the Siene, they did not cross at the first available bridge, but instead continued along the Quai Voltaire, hugging the riverbank. Ross, hands in pockets, face caught in thought, spared few glances upon the smooth, gray waters, or the boats that idled by, or the tradesmen selling wares at stalls. "I have to tell you," Ross finally offered, "that I think it's a very good thing you and Bosie live in separate flats."

"Bosie's living in a flat. I'm crammed into that breadbox of a hotel." Wilde didn't actually mind the size of the room. It was the room he could afford, when he paid for it. And it was a clean enough space. He just didn't feel like being obliging right now. This unnecessary walk was making him testy.

"You know what I mean," Ross said.

"I know what you mean, and I partially agree."

"Partially?"

"What you need to understand is that Bosie and I are never actually apart. No matter whether we are speaking or not, or living together or not, or chasing the same men, or even in the same country. It doesn't matter if we never kiss each other again or whisper in each other's ear.

Our connection is well beneath all that; beneath it and broader. It's eternal. It is outside of time."

To his shock, Wilde saw Ross clench at these words. His hands dug deeper into his pockets, his shoulders came up around his ears, and his chin drooped. Ross bowed his head; his eye roved in little blue chits.

"Oh goodness," Wilde said, and despite himself he placed a hand on Ross's shoulder. "Really, Robbie?" At one time, over a dozen years before, Ross had been a spry and daring teenager, frightfully thin but ridiculously energetic, not beautiful but passably handsome and charmingly cocky, a boy who lived in London, harbored literary pretensions, and came from a good if uninteresting family. Wilde had been an arrogant poet and man about town, with a mane of hair and deliberately dandyish, no longer young but flaunting a young man's confidence. He also was a married man and a father, but one who had begun to recoil at the strictness of his bonds, who only was starting to realize what it meant to be obliged to a woman and to her offspring for a lifetime. He had experimented twice or thrice with illicit encounters. These were less important for what technically happened than for what Wilde decided he must do as a result of them.

The two met at one of Wilde's lectures—at this long remove, Wilde could not even remember which one, what the subject had been—and Ross had forced himself on the older man, engaging Wilde with a series of questions and counter-questions, a contest of wits so exhilarating it ended with the two kissing in the deserted, darkened foyer of the lecture hall. Wilde proceeded to pay for a hotel room, and the encounter they both longed for happened. The first of many surprises that evening was that the skinny and boyish sixteen year old was as knowledgeable as if he'd slept with dozens of men already—maybe he had—whereas the older poet was noticeably nervous and unglamorously clumsy. But when the ferocious part was finally over, Wilde had learned more than a little about what he did and didn't like when it came to physical contact with a man: an encyclopedia upon which he drew in all the years that followed. It was an education for which he was always grateful; and yet one night was the extent of their sexual relations. Neither Ross nor Wilde felt compelled to arrange future clandestine meetings, and so none happened.

At the touch of Wilde's hand, Ross's shoulder spasmed and then, of its own accord fell away. Wilde did not place it back on the shoulder. Ross walked on, face straight ahead. "You have no idea," Wilde said, "how little I deserve your friendship. To say nothing of your devotion."

Ross's heels clicked angrily against the white sidewalk: snap snap snap. For a few seconds, it looked like he intended to push far ahead of Wilde, who with his poetical shamble could not hope to stay abreast. Ross called over his shoulder. "That's where you're wrong. I know exactly how little you deserve me."

Wilde paused. His legs were in pain, and his head suddenly felt too light to hold in place. But laughter surged out of him. "You're a wonder, Robbie."

Ross looked back and stung Wilde with an angled

glance. The blue of his eyes had turned darker and angrier in the sunlight—scratched somehow, mineral hard. More animated, more exasperated, and somehow more honest than the rest of Ross's glances.

Wait, Wilde asked himself, when hadn't Robbie been honest with him? And if so, what did that mean? For years he had been telling people that Robert Ross was the only perfectly honest man he'd ever met. So did he believe that or not? Were there coarser, vengeful, nastier feelings in Robbie that he'd never expressed?

Wilde didn't think he wanted to know. It might be too much for him to grapple with, especially now, with the way things were. He didn't know how long he would be permitted to stay in his hotel, or or if the pains in his legs were nothing at all or the beginning of an end. Most of all, he didn't know what to make of Bosie. Everything he had said to Robbie about he and Bosie's permanent communion was true—after all, one does not throw off one's marriage and one's public identity on a lark—but truth was the two men were as distant now as they'd ever been, despite living inside the same city. There was an increasing air of tedium about their conversations, as if they were beginning to carry on a friendship out of rote memory and nothing more.

Despite the many months Wilde and Douglas had spent sharing rooms in London and in Algiers, then later in Naples and in Rome, the idea of he and Bosie occupying the same living space now was unthinkable. Wilde knew exactly how badly that would go; how easily conversations would turn into arguments and inquiries into accusations. They no longer had the patience with each other that they'd once had. Despite their soul-communion, they no longer saw the other as the height of romantic glamour. Neither was inclined to kiss the other, or even slap his shoulder. Douglas especially felt this. Wilde knew that Bosie could not just ignore the shabby state of his clothes, the punishing settlement from his wife, the atrocious, under-furnished room he somehow survived in, the disgrace with which his name was repeated from person to person, even people who still loved and sympathized with him. For Bosie to really and truly love anyone, to remain fascinated with anyone—be they a man or woman—that person would need have some glorious position in life: money to burn and the willingness to burn it.

And yet... and yet... they still laughed sometimes, didn't they? When he showed his face at Bosie's door unannounced, didn't Bosie sometimes smile and welcome him in, introduce him to others? Hadn't they passed several hours in recent months reviewing the latest releases from London, and agreeing on almost all of them? Didn't Wilde sometimes mutter "dear heart" to the boy? And Bosie did still seem like such a boy: impulsive, needy, mercurial, a collection of so many different people and energies inside one body, some smiling and platonically pure, others demanding and devilishly selfish. Strange to say, Alfred Douglas was both the most pure-hearted friend Wilde had and the vilest of opponents.

Ross's face relaxed at the sound of Wilde's laughter. He waited for Wilde to catch up to him. "We don't need to linger in his flat if you'd rather not," Ross said.

"Why would you think I would not want to linger?"

Ross glanced away toward the river, then back. "You know how I feel about him. How I've felt about him."

"Robbie, you and Bosie are my oldest friends in all the world. You should find a way to get along. It would be an immense relief to my mind."

Ross nodded once: a short snapping motion. He was about to say something, some counter, but Wilde cut him off, switching subjects.

"How is More anyway, Robbie, speaking of dear old friends. I never see him."

Ross, with a bitter glare, closed his mouth, sealed inside whatever he had been about to say. Then he opened the mouth again. "He's fine. We're all fine."

"Tell him I want to see him again. I'm hurt that he never comes."

"I'm sure he's busy enough. With his own life. We have those, you know."

Ouch. Robbie was even more bothered than Wilde realized. Thing is, he did want to see More Adey. In prison, Adey, an astute art critic, had been one of his most frequent visitors. More had been there when he'd gotten out. For months before that, More had even agitated for Wilde's early release. Wilde had once counted More Adey as a better friend than Robert Ross. Once. But ever since he'd left England and moved to France, Adey had kept mum. And he never visited.

"I just never see him. I'd like to see him."

"I don't think More passed those petitions around, and argued so hard to get you out, only to see you leave the country. I expect he'd hope you stay on and be a shining example."

"Of what? A whipping boy? A scapegoat? A masochist?"

He was hoping to prod Ross into revealing himself. Did Robbie think he shouldn't have left? Did Robbie think he should have remained in England and let himself be cut and despised, spit on and made fun of—even worse than he was in Paris? The English in Paris treated him more venomously than than any other group. He literally could not imagine spending every waking hour surrounded by those people.

But Ross said nothing. He kept his eyes on his feet and proceeded along the quay. After a minute, he spoke. "I can get along perfectly well with Bosie, Oscar. I always have. Because I never expect anything from him, except maybe loutishness. And I never ask anything of him either, so I'm never disappointed. But I don't know if you can say the same."

Wilde, mildly stunned by the attack—when they were on their way to visit the man, after all, when Wilde had deliberately tried to get them talking about someone else—didn't know what to say at first. He tried to decide if Ross's description amounted to jealousy or insight. Both, he decided.

"He's a lovely boy," Wilde finally muttered, and realizing the extent of the non sequitur, he grimaced. He shivered inside his own skin. A terrible embarrassment.

He looked ahead down the quay—all the way to the Palais Bourbon—for something to distract him, something else to talk to Ross about.

"Bosie Douglas is twenty-eight years old," Ross said bloodlessly. To make sure the point bore home, he added: "He's one year younger than I am." He raised his hand, showed an index finger. "One."

Wilde nodded: slowly, dumbly, and abashed. He hadn't actually realized this fact. Indeed, it felt completely wrong. Robbie—self-sufficient, competent; worldly and so canny—with his fearfully receding hairline and the middling-quality business suits he wore, looked entirely the part of a man whose youth was over. A man who had become a man, and didn't mind it. But Bosie? Would Bosie—the gifted, gilded one—the eternal child—would he ever become a man? Wilde was not sure he wanted to live to see that. He was not sure that Bosie, who had worn youth so brilliantly well, could wear manhood well at all. Wilde lowered his head, lost in the fact.

"Look," Ross said, a new gentleness in his voice, "look, Oscar." Wilde looked up, thinking that Ross was trying to point out someone on the street ahead or perhaps some craft on the river. But when he looked at the river, he saw banal, metallic colored currents; when he looked at the street he saw bodies in overcoats and hats moving ahead in silence; a wordless, workaday immolation. "You look terrible," Ross continued. "You were right. Perhaps we should get a hansom."

"Robbie wants me to lunch him today," Wilde said. "Very

urgent, he says."

Douglas shivered, as if a cold wind had struck him between the shoulder blades although it was perfectly warm in the house, and Douglas himself, after entering without knocking, and then charging up the stairs, should feel anything but cool.

Douglas's blue eyes narrowed to slits. "What's it about?"

"He didn't say, but I suppose we can guess."

"Yes," Douglas said with a low rasp, "I can make a pretty good guess."

Wilde nodded numbly and stared down at the top of his writing desk. He was in his study in his home at Tite Street, attempting without much success to pen a breezy letter to Sarah Bernhardt. He still had hope that Salome could see the English stage, and with her as star, as they had planned all along.

"I'm coming with you," Douglas said.

Wilde's head shot up.

"Don't worry, I won't order anything on Robert Ross's tab," Bosie explained. "I just want to hear what the little man has to say. I have a feeling it won't be any good."

They decided to take the lunch at the Albemarle; Douglas's idea; as both an assertion of innocence and act of defiance against his father. Indeed when the waiter had tried to seat them at a booth against a wall, Douglas had pestered the man to put them at a center table. The waiter sent a dreadful glance across the dining room. On seeing an open table almost exactly at the center of the room he turned to Wilde with an imploring look. Wilde was about to declare the booth just perfect, when Douglas strode menacingly to the table, turned, and signaled to the two others. Wilde looked at the waiter. The man shrugged and started toward the table, his shoulders sagging worse with each step.

After they had ordered, Ross began his planned recitation with the obvious: There had been suspicions about Wilde for years, since the early-80s at least, suspicions that cooled but did not exactly disappear after the poet's marriage to Constance Lloyd. And everyone knew Queensberry's attitude toward dandies. They especially knew how he felt about the fact that his son was seen in the company of Oscar Wilde every night of the year. Ross, who had not been happy at all to find that Douglas was at Tite Street and determined to accompany Wilde to this lunch, stared hard at the both of them, undeterred. "The note he left here about you should not have been surprising to anyone, especially not to either of you two."

"What are you saying?" Douglas said. "It was grotesque. Abominable." Ross did not react. "Oscar was perfectly right to feel outrage. Anyone would have."

"I'm not defending the note. I'm just saying it should not have been a surprise."

"Well, it was," Douglas spat.

"What are you saying, Robbie?" Wilde tried. "I mean really."

"What I'm saying is obvious. I'm saying you should have stayed cool then—and you should stay cool now."

"And what the hell is that supposed to mean?" Douglas said, louder than he should have, his nostrils wide, his pale face reddening.

"Bosie," Wilde intoned.

"You don't need to do anything about this," Ross said to Wilde, "except maybe make a joke of it. Anyone who knows Queensberry knows not to take anything he says seriously."

"But don't you think this is beyond the pale?" Wilde argued. "Making it a public matter? Calling me a sodomite? If I

don't take him on, how can I show my face in this club ever again?"

"You can't," Douglas said.

"Couldn't it turn on you though?" Ross countered. "How is it going to go with you if you lose? Have either of you thought of that?" He spared a glance at Douglas then focused again on Wilde. "What if Queensberry's lawyers are able to make his charge stick? It's not as if you and Bosie have been up to nothing. And isn't that exactly what they'll try to prove? If they tell the jury what you've been up to, his insult won't seem so heinous after all."

Wilde could feel Bosie beside him almost hopping with impatience. He wanted, he needed, to reach over and pat the boy's thigh. Just stay calm. For now. Please. *But of course he resisted the instinct. Ross continued: "Queensberry is a rube and a hothead. No one likes him and no one listens to him—except those who have to listen to him. If you let this go, people might write it off as just more of his misplaced bluster."*

Misplaced bluster *was a brilliant phrase, one that captured virtually everything John Douglas, the Marquess of Queensberry, said or did in his life. It had not occurred to Wilde that he could actually lose the libel case—what were Queensberry's solicitors going to do, drag male prostitutes into court?—but he saw the sense of Ross's advice. Wilde grew quiet. He could almost be convinced to follow the path Ross was setting down, but it would certainly be a turnaround. It would certainly...*

Douglas, who had been surging and bristling for minutes, could not contain himself. He stood up in the middle of the dining room and announced: "You're a coward, Robert Ross; you're a simpleton. And you're a traitor. Now is not the time to be giving Oscar doubts. Now is the time to buck him up, get him charged for court. Now is the time for anyone who says he's a supporter *to be firing at the enemy. Because we are going to win this case; as long as wets like you don't get in the way." Douglas was literally red in the face. He kept clenching and unclenching his fists as if ready to murder the other man. Then he turned to Wilde and shouted, "You have to do this!"*

Wilde glimpsed apologetically around the dining room. They were fortunate to have arrived just as the luncheon high tide had passed. Presently, the room was only a third full. At least half those people, Wilde noticed, were now staring purposefully at the white linen on their table, or the article of food in front of them, or deliberately away: at the deep brown walls, lacquered to a high polish; at the bright chandeliers overhead;at the ponderous mirror at the far end of the room. As for the rest of the diners, they stared—nearly every one—with contempt at the figure of Alfred Dougas; and the few that weren't were staring the same way at Wilde.

At that moment, Wilde gave up any idea of not proceeding with the libel suit. No matter what Ross said, there was something else more important and more abiding to consider: He could not go through life as the man who refused to deny Queensberry's scandalous charge, as the man too cowardly and too guilty not to refute it directly, not to clear his name. He just wanted to clear his name. And too, it was not far from his thoughts that there was no greater gift he could give to Bosie than the sight of his father—the man who'd cheated on and then divorced Bosie's mother; the man who'd roundly scoffed at all three of his "poofter" sons—bound in cuffs, led away to prison after a verdict of guilty on the charge of libel. Bosie would be delirious with joy; Bosie would be stratospheric. Wilde desperately wanted to be there for it, indeed to enable it. And he wished to be able to stare back hard at all these righteous clubbers and say through his eyes: What are you looking at?

We're innocent, or haven't you heard?

"Hello," Douglas called jauntily when he opened the door of his apartment and found Wilde outside. Then he caught sight of Ross, a few steps back, reclining against the wall of the hallway. Bosie's eyes dimmed considerably. But he recovered, nodded, and said, "Bonjour, Robert," pronouncing the name in the French manner.

"Afternoon, Bosie," Ross said and straightened. "Kind of you to let us in." He proceeded to walk around Wilde and into the apartment. Douglas's mouth tightened into a querulous grimace, but he said nothing.

"Bonjour, *mon cher ami*," Wilde offered quickly. "Charmed, as always. As you see, Robbie has showed up in Paris. But he's only in town through the weekend, so I thought I ought to bring him along. Did you get my note?"

It took Douglas a second, but finally he nodded, a slow and distracted motion. "I did."

The apartment was as fastidiously kept as ever. But it was not just the state of cleanliness that was impressive. Wilde saw a couple of new pieces of furniture since last he'd visited. Against the far wall of the sitting room was a salmon-colored, Rococo-revival sofa. A stunning showpiece. Compared to the length, bulk, and splendor of that sofa, the three walnut chairs near it—upholstered in gossamer white fabric—looked less than ordinary. When Douglas had first moved into the apartment that spring, Wilde had used £70 donated to him by Frank Harris for the three chairs and a green bed. If the boy were going to stay in Paris and occupy the apartment—an apartment

Wilde had recommended to Douglas after hearing about it from Jean-Jacques Renaud—he would need chairs and a bed. But at the time Douglas claimed abject poverty, so loudly Wilde thought he might actually give up this rare find of a flat—with its spaciousness and good floors and tolerable proximity to the center of Paris—and move into a hotel in Tunis or Algiers or, spare the thought, back to England. So he offered Frank Harris's £70 and together they disposed of it in an afternoon at Maples.

Douglas had promised to pay Wilde back as soon as new money came in. Clearly new money had come in. That was obvious looking at the sofa; but too the marble-top table around which the other pieces gathered: dark, heavy, and ornately carved wood underneath, glittering white on top with agile veins of blue and silver running through the stone.

Spectacular.

Expensive.

"Those are charming pieces, Bosie," Wilde said, pointing toward the sofa and the table. "Where did you find them?"

Ross, without express permission, had seated himself on one of the walnut chairs. He glanced around the room with a look that might have been innocent or might have been amused. Wilde couldn't tell. Robbie was excellent with a poker face. Douglas, meanwhile, had moved barely a step from the doorway. He hovered there uncertainly, as if he might have to go out at any minute, although he'd already told them the opposite.

Douglas pointed toward the sofa. "That one," he

said slowly, as if struggling to remember, "came from a dealer on the Avenue de l'Opera."

"New?"

"Last week."

"Beautiful," Wilde said. "Truly." He did not want to ask Douglas how much it cost, although the question resonated at the front of his mind. He wanted to know how Douglas could have afforded that sofa but not the repayment of £70. But it would be pointless to put Alfred Douglas on the defensive. Wilde would never get an answer out of him that way. Not any Wilde would want to hear. He tried a subtler opening. "Did your mother buy it for you?"

Douglas' face looked stricken; then he blinked. "Indirectly, I suppose."

"I'm not sure what that means."

"It means that she is partially responsible." There the explanation ended. A heavy silence settled on the room.

"Sounds like there's a story," Ross said cheerily.

Douglas's lips formed a purse. He rolled his eyes. "Not much of one, actually. The facts are banal."

"Try us," Ross challenged.

Douglas's cheek heated a noticeable measure. "My mother loaned me a couple hundred pounds, as she does on occasion. To do with as I will." He leaned into those last words, firing them at Ross; then he glanced at Wilde. "She wants me to be relaxed here, after all. She wants me to enjoy myself."

Wilde felt himself grow warm and faint at the same

time, and not a little stomach-sick. "So she did buy it for you," he said quietly. "More or less."

"No, she didn't," Douglas said, in a tone that suggested he was tired of this game. "She gave me the money to do with as I pleased, and I pleased to take it to the Longchamps." Wilde's stomach dropped now almost to his knees. The horses? "It was what I pleased," Douglas reminded.

"But you never win," Wilde managed to say.

"Sometimes I win."

"Bosie, you lose. You lose every time."

"I won this time," Douglas shot back.

"You did?"

"I did."

"What did you do with the winnings?"

Douglas waved toward the furniture. Of course.

"And that used up all of it, I suppose?"

"No, not all of it. I had some left over. In fact, I had more than a two thousand francs left."

"Two thousand."

"Yes, I bet well."

"And what did you do with the two thousand?"

"I bet them, of course. The next time I was at the track. What do you think I'd do with them?"

"All right," Wilde said softly, trying his best to cover his hurt. It did not help that he could see, across the room, Ross regarding Douglas with abject dismissal.

"What do you think I'd do," Douglas repeated. He was almost shouting. "It's not as if you are the only person in this city to whom I owe money, Oscar. I actually owe quite a lot of money. To people that are more important, and significantly more nasty than you are. And when I have a chance to turn a mere two thousand francs into enough to pay off everything and everyone I owe— including you—what do you think I'd do? What do you think I should do?"

If you'd never started betting in the first place, you would not owe most of that money.

If you'd not bought an imperial sofa in the first place, and instead given me my seventy pounds, you would have plenty of money still to bet with.

Or with which to pay off your other creditors.

Or just buy some champagne.

"Do you know that one day at the Longchamps I saw a man begin with twenty-five francs and by the time he left he was carrying over forty thousand?"

"I'm sure that's true, but—"

"And that is hardly a once-upon-a-time circumstance. I see it almost every time I go."

Wilde nodded slowly, a show of agreement with no conviction behind it. He could forgive Bosie the past; but he struggled with forgiving the present. It did not help his feelings that he knew to open his mouth would be to ruin any hope of getting his money back.

"So... is there any of it left?" Wilde asked. He tried to sound jaunty but instead heard in his voice a hope so hurt and so pointless he almost shrunk inside his shoes.

"Of course not. When I bet, I bet until I win, or until there's nothing left to bet with. You should know that by now."

Wilde nodded again. Indeed, he knew this too well.

"How long did it take you to lose it all?" Ross asked, without any of the padded gentleness with which Wilde had tried to lob his questions.

Douglas's eyes turned newly hard, guilt-free. "We're not talking about this anymore. You are, after all, a guest in this place. If you intend to sit there and insult me, you can leave."

Ross raised an amused eyebrow at this. He looked at Wilde. "Oscar?"

"I think what I want, Bosie," Wilde said, "is to sit on this splendid new couch of yours. Unless you'd rather I not."

"Go ahead," Douglas said, and jabbed a bitter arm at the piece, his head still too full of the recent unpleasant discussion. "No, wait. Sorry. Sit there instead." He pointed at one of the chairs Wilde had bought for him. "I have someone coming in a few hours."

Wilde paused over this. "Someone?"

"Some people."

"When?" Ross said.

"Later. Nine o'clock."

"That's five hours from now," Ross said.

"So what? A stain just doesn't come out in five hours. Sometimes it never comes out at all."

"What stain?" Wilde cried. "How do you expect that I would stain your couch?"

As much as he would have liked to, Wilde could not forget a piece of testimony offered during the first trial: a housekeeper at the Savoy Hotel claimed to see fecal stains on Wilde's sheets. This on top of testimony from a chambermaid and a masseuse of seeing teenaged boys sleeping naked in Wilde's bed. Instead of saying out loud what he knew to be the truth, Wilde had tried to simply deny the housekeeper's memory, to suggest she must have misunderstood whatever stain she saw. It was a thin defense and everyone in the courtroom realized it. Who knows stains better than a housekeeper? But he refused to state the truth he knew: that the stains were not his nor the result of any lovemaking he had made with young men. The stains occurred when Bosie climbed into the bed and enjoyed those young men in a different way than Wilde himself was inclined to. Wilde's own fixation was almost entirely oral. Bosie's not at all. But he could never have said this in a courtroom. Never. He was trying to avoid jail himself, why would he have wanted to incriminate the man who was his virtual spouse?

He lowered his head and emitted a slow stream of a sigh. No matter how much he tried, details from the trials had a way of returning and scratching him, especially when he had the least of his defenses up.

"I don't expect you to stain my couch, Oscar," Bosie said. "I don't expect anything of the sort. I am just being careful. One never knows what can happen. Until it's too late."

"Isn't that the truth," Ross tossed in.

Douglas concentrated testily on the other man, as if reading his statement over again carefully, hunting for an insult. Ross just smiled.

"I guess you've never had any decent furniture,

Robert," Douglas said. "Otherwise, you'd understand what I'm talking about."

"Well, no decent furniture like that," Ross said, pointing. Another smile.

Douglas stared hard at Ross; he pressed his lips together. His thin, blonde-brown brows lowered a fraction of an inch. Then Wilde saw a visible relaxing, a relenting of the prickliness. The skin at the sides of Douglas's eyes pulled back. His nose no longer looked like a fist. "No, I guess not," he said quietly. Douglas appeared to have interpreted Ross's comment as a straight one. Thank God for that, Wilde thought, although it seemed clear to him that Ross's sentence was every bit the insult it sounded like. Sometimes Bosie did have a tin ear.

"Do you gentlemen want some tea?" Douglas asked all of a sudden.

"Desperately," Wilde breathed, although champagne would have been far far better. Or any alcohol at all.

"Yes, thank you," Ross said neutrally. Maybe Robbie was finally giving up the game.

With no little showmanship, Douglas stalked further into the apartment and to the right. A few seconds later, Wilde heard a muted but distinct low-level explosion of flame. Ross turned in his chair, craned his neck to look. "Is that gas?" Ross said.

"It is," Douglas chirped.

"And you bought that?"

"No, it was here. Oscar can tell you. It's quite the new thing. With this around, I actually don't need to hire a girl." A bad joke occurred to Wilde, but he didn't even consider uttering it. "But I still do anyway," Douglas said. "For the mornings. And for tidying." Then, to Ross: "You don't have a gas stove? In London?"

"I do. But nothing like that one. Most of the time I let it alone."

"I cannot imagine that," Douglas said. "I am an Englishman, and this is tea time. I do what I must."

"Yes, well," Ross muttered. Wilde could tell he felt the sting of that last comment. Born in France to Canadian parents, but having spent less than two years in Canada before his family moved permanently to England, Ross was by any meaningful reckoning more an Englishman than a Canadian—there was nothing in either his accent or his habits to suggest otherwise—but when push came to shove anyone who wanted to could turn him into a provincial on a technicality. "Tea time is valuable for anyone, I'd say."

Douglas nodded and showed a hint of a smile, as if he'd scored a point. Then he turned back to the stove. While the water in the kettle came to a boil, Wilde and Ross kept quiet, in an awe of wonder at the care Douglas took in assembling a tea service: teapot, cups and saucers, pot of milk, pot of honey. Then his delicate pouring of the hot water into the pot; his scrupulous addition of tea leaves, counting each scoop silently with moving lips. Doing this, Douglas looked more content, more at ease than Wilde could ever remember. All that angry-frantic-sexual-demanding energy had dissipated. "Just a few minutes, gents," he said.

When the tea was through steeping, Douglas carried the service to the drawing room table. He proceeded to pour tea for each of them, and even prepared the cup as each man preferred. Then he handed the cup, on top of a saucer, to its rightful owner—without a single drop spilling over the rim.

"Splendid, Bosie," Wilde breathed and drank from the cup. In these moments of abject selflessness all of Douglas's beauty returned. Wilde's heart surged with a renewed love.

"If this aristocrat thing doesn't work out," Ross joked, "you should consider household service."

Douglas chose not to play along. "I've heard that before," he grumbled. Then he sat and enjoyed his own first sip. Wilde saw him nod at the cup with affection, as if to say, Well done. In the moment, Wilde had a frightful, oppressive thought. For so many months when he and Douglas had been inseparable—a kind of divinely sanctioned, even mythic, pair of exalted lovers—Wilde had given control over to Douglas on so many matters, great and small: choice of restaurants, choice of hotels, choice of boys, choice of carriages and liqueurs and Piccadilly openings; he had opened his bank account and practically poured it into Douglas's lap to do with as the younger man had insisted. In some fundamental ways he had become Douglas's servant, thinking the whole while that the secret to their exalted relationship enduring was for him to keep Bosie happy. But now, seeing the calm on Douglas's face, seeing the measured way he talked, Wilde wondered if he'd taken the completely wrong tact. Maybe he should have set Douglas to work. Maybe he should have ordered the boy around. Maybe if he'd done that, they never would have separated.

Wilde blinked. What was he doing? He already had enough past regrets to surmount. What was the point of inventing more? Their lives had gone the way they had. He was the Oscar Wilde he was now; and Bosie was the Douglas. There was no way of really knowing if anything could have been different. And yet here was the evidence of his own eyes: Douglas sipping his self-made tea, smiling with satisfaction, casting questioning glances to both himself and Ross as if to ask if they found the concoction suitable too. More blonde and more beautiful now, perhaps, than when Wilde had first met him at age eighteen. Beautiful because more pure, in the way a saint is, or a Buddha. The beauty and purity and infallibility of the seasoned soul, the one who had survived a harrowing fire. Well, was not Bosie a seasoned soul? He was a poet, after all.

"How is your writing coming, Bosie?" Wilde asked, a surprise almost to himself. Lately Douglas and he did not talk at all about poetry. Ever since Wilde had given up the pen, he'd not been inclined to either deliver or listen to earnest sermons on the art of literature. It made him feel uncomfortable and too vulnerable. But with a fierceness that overcame any of his normal reservations, now he wanted to know what Douglas was doing and why. Was this spoiled but delicate young man still able to pen spiritualized verse on paper? He used to—oh, how he used to. He used to write so beautifully. This more than the sex, even more than Bosie's born-with beauty, had made Wilde love him.

Douglas frowned. "It goes," he said. "More slowly than it used to, but... yes, it goes." Douglas was uncharacteristically reticent; abashed even. Why, he'd just blushed. Was he ashamed of what he'd written, or that he'd not written more?

"I'm glad," Wilde said. "I really and truly am."

"I hope to come out with another volume soon, a bigger one, and in England this time." He'd published a slim volume of verse, simply titled *Poems*, in France in 1896, while Wilde languished in Reading. No one in England paid any attention to it. Wilde, angry then at his former lover, said repeatedly that if he were ever given book privileges he would deliberately not read Bosie's. Later, he was granted book privileges. And later still, he did relent to read the volume. The worst he could say about it was that it was a young man's work. The best is that it contained moments of genius.

"I am an English poet," Douglas continued. "By every conceivable measure. I deserve to be published in my home country."

"How much bigger?"

"Bigger?"

"You said it should be bigger."

"Yes, by a couple dozen pages, at least."

"A couple dozen. My." Wilde shook his head. "In that case, young man, do get going." It was the kind of thing to say, and the tone of voice to say it with, that if he'd said it a year earlier, Douglas would have been sitting next to him and Wilde would have pushed his hand against the man's knee. But now a heavy table and months of renegotiation separated them. Wilde raised his cup and took a drink, as if in salute.

Douglas offered a small, shy grin. Then a new, more confident look came into his eye. "I have written a few new things. Things you have not seen."

"Is that so?" Wilde took another sip. Where in all the world had Douglas learned to prepare such a cup? It was so good he almost overcame his longing for something stiffer. "I feel like I've read your full corpus. The whole of it."

"No," Douglas said.

"No?"

"No, you haven't."

"Well, show me then."

Douglas smiled. "Perhaps I shall."

"And while you're at it," Wilde said, catching the mood of rapprochement, this approximation of their old, loose way of being together, "bring me a real drink for God's sake." Douglas looked stricken; then his cheek burned a shade of nauseous crimson. A wave, an actual sickness, appeared to pass through him, head to toe as he sat absolutely still, watching Wilde with blank eyes.

"Not that this tea isn't lovely," Wilde rushed to say. "God no. It's beautiful. It's brilliant. Honest." But the moment had passed, and words were pointless. "Listen, why don't you get some of your recent ones and perform them for Robbie and me? Let us be your audience."

Douglas was obviously alarmed by the suggestion:

most likely because of its inclusion of Ross. But that was too bad. Robbie was here. He'd come all the way from London. Wilde was not about to allow Douglas to exclude him.

Douglas glanced at Ross, then momentarily down at his feet. Then he set his teacup and saucer on the table, put his hands on his knees, and with visible effort pushed himself up. "All right," he said quietly with all the enthusiasm of a man abutting his eternal doom. Douglas straightened his shoulders, rotated, and walked in new direction, to a room opposite the kitchen, the door of which was closed. This was the bedroom, Wilde knew, because he'd asked Bosie weeks ago if he could take a look at the monstrosity of bed he'd paid for at Maples; how Bosie had arranged it. Wilde had looked and Douglas had waited silently, several steps behind. They proceeded to do absolutely nothing on the bed. Wilde had not expected them to.

Presently, Douglas opened the bedroom door, stepped through, and fastidiously closed it behind him. A minute later he reappeared with a familiar burlap suitcase. Wilde had seen this suitcase in Naples and in Algiers, in Rome and in Venice, in Nice and in London and in Oxford. As long as he'd known Douglas, the young man had traveled with the case. He'd seen Douglas stuff it full with too many tailored shirts and pants and leather shoes, toss it under this bed and into that wardrobe and onto to that carriage. He rammed it and let it be rammed, so much so it was polluted with age-old scratches and sores and dents. The edges of it were severely worn and there was even a small burgeoning rip.

So long ago now it didn't seem to matter, Wilde had wondered why Douglas had not upgraded to a sturdier or more elegant model. Everything about him, after all, was elegant. No, pristine. This was the same Douglas who discarded clothes after a single wearing, who turned down cab rides because he wanted a better-looking carriage, who dropped friends and family members so instantaneously it was as if they'd fallen off of the end of a square planet instead of still living on this round one. The same Douglas declared his undying love for the ragamuffin piece. He would not buy a new one until this one's locks were rusted and its straps worn to strips, its side unable to hold anything in anymore. "This case is like a brother to me," Douglas said once.

Douglas set the case on the floor, opened it, and pushed his hands inside. He shoved notebooks aside and sheaths of uncollected papers. Wilde spied dozens of lines in Douglas's boyish, vertical cursive. A whole lifetime's output? Yes or no, Bosie had produced more than Wilde had ever credited him with. Wilde made a mental note to correct that reckoning. Finally, Douglas located whatever poems it was that he had in mind. He carefully extracted the sheets, lowed the lid of the case, and then the tapped the paper's on the case lid to put them in crisp order.

"God, Bosie," Wilde said, "how many of those are new?" He pointed a finger at the case.

Douglas shrugged. "I don't know. I haven't counted. But this is one."

"You've been busy, I say."

"I don't know," Douglas repeated. "I don't count them. But this is one."

"Yes. Sorry. Good. Read it for us, won't you?"

Douglas glanced uncertainly at Ross and then again at Wilde, who made a wide, welcoming gesture that he had hoped would seem conducive but which he instantly knew looked asinine. A grown man patting a little boy's head. Douglas would not appreciate it. Except Douglas did not react in any noticeable way. His face remained flat, even foggy, as if the better part of him were lost in invisible rumination and his vision canceled. He lifted the top piece of paper and began to pronounce.

> There is an isle in an unfurrowed sea
> That I wot of, whereon the whole year round
> The apple-blossoms and the rosebuds be
> In early blooming.

Douglas's reading voice was breathy and too high-pitched to claim authority over an audience, but it was not without precision, not without a certain natural music.

> Thither death
> Coming like Love, takes all things in the morn
> Of tenderest Love, and being a delicate god
> In his own garden takes each delicate thing.

After a while, it became difficult for Wilde to listen.

He thought the lines were good, quite good in fact. But it hurt Wilde to think that Douglas had accomplished them on his own, with no input or example from Wilde himself. Not like the old days when they used to lounge about, pontificating and shouting poems across a room to one another. Inspiring one another, challenging each other to do better. The old irresponsible, impossible days. At the same time it seemed bitter and broadly unfair that a beautiful and vibrant young man like Douglas could spend out his poetic energy rhyming about death. Why would Alfred Douglas have to worry about death? Bosie was indestructible. The boy would probably live to seventy-five. Maybe one hundred-and-five. And in any case why fall in love with dying, of all realities? Why when there so much excitement to wrench from life?

> Young animals, young flowers, they live and grow,
> And die before their sweet, emblossomed breath
> Has learnt to sigh save like a lover's. Oh!
> How sweet is Youth, how delicate is Death!

As soon as he had stopped, Douglas looked up, hungry and feral, spying for a reaction from the listeners. The fear was naked on his face.

"That's wonderful, Bosie," Wilde said with as much effort as he could summon. In fact his body suddenly felt so enervated, and his mind so distracted, it was hard for him to summon anything at all. He'd not even heard the final lines.

Douglas's face hardened, and his voice snapped.

"Do you actually think so—or are you only humoring me?"

Wilde was stunned. Is that what Bosie thought of him? A doddering and genial Grandpa, someone who offers undeserved kindnesses to young fellows? No wonder he wanted no part of sex anymore.

"Of course I'm not humoring you. I think it's very good. That is the truth."

Douglas visibly relaxed. He even smiled. There it was. That golden expression Wilde had not seen in so long. In fact, he didn't know if he had ever seen Bosie this happy. Douglas's mood was so improved he even turned to Ross and said, "Robert?"

Ross nodded for a second or two, with absolute precision. Wilde's heart clutched. He held his breath. If Ross said anything cheeky or underhanded, if he played for a comic moment, Douglas would blow up, and this new mood would be ruined. Please, Wilde thought out to Ross. Don't. But to Wilde's eternal gratitude, Ross said, in a clear and neutral voice, one stripped of all irony, "It's profound."

Douglas beamed, all teeth and eyes and hair. "Thank you," he said. "Thank you, gents." Then, immediately: "Okay, so here is another." He shifted the papers he held. "I only wrote it last week." He tipped his chin upward showily, then began:

> Thou that wast once my loved and loving friend
> A friend no more, I had forgot thee quite.
> Why hast thou come to trouble my delight

With memories? Oh! I had made clean end
Of all that time, I had made haste to send
My soul into red places, and to light
A torch of pleasure to light up my night.
What I have roven hast thou come to rend?

In silent acres of forgetful flowers,
Crowned as of old with happy daffodils,
Long time has my wounded soul been a-straying,
Alas! it has chanced now on somber hours
Of hard remembrances and sad delaying,
Leaving green valleys for the bitter hills.

Before Douglas even reached those final lines, Wilde's felt his heart ache with a renewed, eternal love; so tidal his eyes filled with tears. So many tears he could not even see Douglas anymore. He had had no idea: He could still affect Bosie this way, and Bosie could express it so? Good lord, what an amazing person this boy was. Always amazing.

Douglas was speaking. "What? What, Oscar? What?" Wilde's eyes cleared enough for him to see Douglas's look: half-worried, half-impatient. Then Wilde remembered. Bosie had wanted them to comment.

"Nothing," Wilde said. "It's a fine poem. It's an extraordinary poem."

Quick smile. A confirmation. Douglas had known it was a good one too. "It's called 'To L—,'" he said. "I wrote it for my cousin."

Wilde's body surged; his neck became iron straight.

56

"Your cousin?"

Douglas nodded.

"You wrote that for Lionel Johnson?"

"Yes," Douglas said, nonplussed. ""To L—"" he re-minded Wilde.

"Lionel Johnson is the subject of that poem? Is that what you're telling me?"

"Yes. Because it's so."

How? How could that possibly be so? And if it was, Wilde wanted to scream, why read it aloud? Why here? And to me? It was unspeakable.

"I—I guess," Wilde managed to say, "I find that hard to believe."

Douglas tilted his head slightly. He looked at Wilde with a blank expression, genuinely confused. "Why? He's not only my cousin. He's one of my oldest friends."

Wilde stood up straight out of the chair. His head was clear, his eyes dry. "It's a beautiful poem, Bosie. You should feel proud. And Lionel should feel honored. Give him my best, will you? It has been a very long time since I've seen him. All right, Robbie. Let's along with us. We have tarried too long, I think, imposing on poor Bosie."

Douglas wore a new look of alarm—and conster-nation. The too familiar cross expression. "Where are you going? You only just started listening. I have others I could read. Where are you going?"

"Nowhere," Wilde protested. "We are not going anywhere that matters."

"So why leave then? What's the trouble with you?"

It was then that Ross intruded. "All right, Oscar,"

he sang. "I am ready to leave when you are." Wilde was astonished to realize that Ross was standing right beside him, next to his elbow, as effortlessly as if he'd been there the whole time.

"It's really... nothing," Wilde managed to say to Douglas. Then he could say no more.

"Oh," Douglas said, his head rearing, eyes darting back and forth between Ross and Wilde. "I see. I see how it is." He showed a smile as menacing as a shiv. "No surprise on that score."

Wilde's head was moving in what he meant as a shake, a rebuttal, but felt out of sense altogether. He was sure it communicated nothing and only made him look like a spastic. He pushed blindly through the door of Douglas's apartment and poured himself into the hallway. At some point, somewhere behind him, the door slammed. He was still standing up on two legs, although he didn't know how; all of him felt like water, or like fire, or like water and fire, like a puddle in flames, not able to walk so much as flow or rock or ripple or leak. Or burn. Ross was somewhere behind him. Somewhere.

After the door slammed, Wilde flowed backward, blindly, to grab his friend's clothes. And cry. And cry. And cry.

CHAPTER TWO

Paris. January 1899.

Wilde walked the bicycle slowly through the alley. Another six or seven steps and he would reach the openness of the Boulevard Saint-Germain; then he would be more than visible. He needed to be especially careful now or risk savaging his surprise altogether. His new beloved—the soft-shouldered soldier boy with the round cheeks so redolent of baby fat and his eyes of such a pure charcoal color that his stares lasted for eons—was just around the corner waiting for him outside of a café. At least that had been the plan, and if Wilde knew anything at all about Maurice Gilbert it was that Gilbert was dutiful to a fault. Not for nothing had he settled into a more or less content life as a member of the French army. Wilde had suggested three o'clock as the time, an approximation at best; but he'd learned, after five weeks of knowing the boy, that Gilbert would arrive at the Café Belisle precisely at three p.m., not one tick sooner or later. Gilbert would be standing there stolidly, waiting. He would wait for hours if Wilde made him; but for that reason alone, Wilde did not want to make him wait.

"So we will celebrate my birthday with a meal at the Belisle?" Gilbert had said, in French, the evening before, stopping in at Wilde's hotel on his way back home from duty. Home was his mother's apartment on the Rue du Four. Gilbert's smile had suggested that he could think of no other restaurant in the whole of the city that would be more appropriate. But he would have shown the same smile if Wilde had suggested catching dinner at the circus—or taking a picnic.

"Not exactly," Wilde said, "but I do want to meet you there, and then we can go somewhere else."

"Okay." Gilbert nodded. "But why there?"

"I can't tell you."

"Why?"

"Maurice, think about it."

Gilbert had frowned and looked down, his eyes scanning the room's terrible maroon carpeting.

"What day is it tomorrow?"

"My birthday!"

"And what do you think I'm going to give you on your birthday?"

"A gift, I hope."

Wilde chuckled. "That is all you need to know."

"So... in order for you to give me my gift I need to waiting outside the Cafe Belisle?"

"Something like that."

Gilbert shrugged. "You don't really have to give me a gift, Oscar."

Oh, yes, he did. For weeks now Wilde had been planning this one, ever since he'd casually asked Gilbert one day what he would like if he would be allowed to ask for anything. Anything at all. From anybody. Wilde had always found this to be an excellent barometer of a person's character, a picture into their deepest aspirations. He had a feeling Gilbert would not disappoint, and Gilbert didn't. "That's easy," the soldier had replied at once. "I have always wanted a bicycle, but my parents refused. They were sure it was not worth the money. Then I saw one just yesterday, at Augustin's, that would be the one bicycle in the world I would buy, if I could. It had nickel-plated handlebars. They shined like water. Like fish in the water. You know?"

Wilde had been so touched by the simplicity of the request, and the ingenuousness of Gilbert's simile, that he'd determined to buy the bike at once, as soon as he could locate it, even if he had to steal the money. In the pretend-casual conversation that followed, Wilde managed to extract from Gilbert that Augustin's shop was on the Rue Benardines, only a few streets from their present meeting place; and the price for the bike almost exactly matched Wilde's monthly stipend from Robbie Ross, due any day. So he would just not pay his rent this month. At least not yet. And he would have to beg meals. Not much change there.

He gently set the bike against the outside wall of the café and stepped ahead, closer to the corner, his heart beating more heavily with excitement. For several days he'd been terrified that some other person would have bought the bike already before he had the cash in hand. And then yesterday, when he finally was able to complete the purchase, he'd had to ask the shop to hold it, since he did not dare store it in his hotel room. Might they have shoved it into some back corner, only to bang up against a pipe and get scratched? Might someone have pushed it aside and bent a spoke? Or lanced the tire? But no, the bicycle had been there and had been brilliant as ever.

Now Wilde couldn't wait to hand it off, to see the happiness on his beloved's face, and his dark eyes sparkle with the sunshine of affection. He anticipated what came later: Gilbert's moist, fawn-like kisses, his strong arms, the sloping muscles of his rump. In his own idiosyncratic way, Maurice Gilbert was the most beautiful man Wilde had ever met, even more beautiful than Bosie Douglas. Well, a different sort of beauty, so much more Mediterranean in tone, darker than Bosie's British schoolboy pallor. Yes, he said to himself a moment later, Gilbert was actually more beautiful than Bosie. Not just different but more. Because he was so much more pure than Bosie. More soft—in spirit, that is. Because he had no guile in him—none—nothing to keep Wilde's heart from blooming fiercely with a love so profound, so all-encompassing, and so many-sided, paternal and fraternal and romantic all at once, that it sometimes scared him. And sometimes it even saddened him. Because as a soldier Gilbert would inevitably be called away; he would always be called away. And Wilde worried that fate was setting a deadline on their romance.

The odd thing was that he'd felt all of this the very first time he'd ever seen Gilbert. It was outside Maire's restaurant. Wilde had been hurrying to make a dinner appointment with Frank Harris, who had arrived just that evening from Calais and was set to leave the next morning. Wilde was so late he'd decided to pay for a ride in a victoria. Just as he'd been stepping out of the car, a soldier passed on the sidewalk and their eyes met. The boy was outfitted for the evening in his uniform: the sparkling blue coat with silver-colored buttons, and those bright red pants. But it was not the clothes the soldier wore that held Wilde's attention; it was his face. The dark eyes and soft cheeks, the compact body. He looked like a Florentine bronze by some anonymous master, or like Napolean when he was first Consul. Except there was none of Napolean's imperiousness about the boy, and none of the Little Colonel's war-mongering spirit. He was simply a devastating beauty with a sweet soul resonating in his eyes.

Wilde had read the soldier's character in a moment, and every part of him had responded. He'd felt so compelled by the sight of Gilbert that he immediately put aside his dinner plans and instead followed the soldier down the sidewalk. When he caught up to him, Wilde offered to buy the boy a drink. The soldier stopped, thought about it for a second, and this whole face opened in a smile. "That sounds too good to refuse!" Wilde just about fell on his knees and worshipped him right there. They found a café and shared conversation for an hour. The soldier told Wilde about the mother he still lived with and the father who had died while serving in Algeria. Not in battle, but in a knife fight. Nothing he heard or saw that evening overruled his first reading of the boy's character, but most important was finally finding out the soldier's name: Maurice Gilbert. It was the perfect appellation, almost a holy one; those two successive iambs with the rhyming assonance at their center made such a mystically sonorous sound it might be the name of an angel. Well, in fact, it was.

About to turn the corner at the Café Belisle, it occurred to Wilde that he could have simply asked Gilbert to meet him at the bicycle shop, but that would have ruined the surprise. Better this way. On a Paris boulevard. With Gilbert not even able to guess. It was too important an occasion to diminish with foreknowledge, not with Gilbert set to leave the following week for an indefinite stay in Tunisia, with this birthday—which luckily fell on the boy's day off—the last significant event they could share before Gilbert left and whatever happened to him in Africa happened; and whatever happened to Wilde did here.

Wilde stepped out on to the Boulevard Saint-Germain, and there was Gilbert, not ten yards away, leaning against a tree planted in the sidewalk, dressed not in his uniform but in an ordinary overcoat and dark pants— his hands in the pockets, his gaze tilted up at the sky, a faint almost unconscious smile on his face. As if this were even possible, the simplicity of Gilbert's expression made Wilde fall in love with him even more. Wilde brought up his right arm and waved. He should call, he knew, but he hated these days to call attention to himself. He waved again. Soon enough Gilbert would feel his presence, lower his gaze. But Gilbert didn't, not for several seconds more. Wilde was tempted to look up to see what could possibly fascinate Gilbert so, but he knew if he did that he would only see an ordinary January sky, clouded over and speaking of eventual rain. The kind of sky one can see over Paris any day of the week. But that was the most wonderful thing of all about Gilbert: toward the most ordinary stuff of life, what would bore 99% of the human race, Gilbert felt nothing but active fascination.

Wilde tried waving one more time. This time, Gilbert's chin came down slowly, then his eyes. His head turned. He saw Wilde and his smile went from dream-laden to animated.

"Hello, Oscar. I am here, as you asked!"

People passing on the street turned to see to whom such a happy, charming lad might be signaling.

"Come over here, Maurice," Wilde said, in French. "I need to show you something."

Gilbert opened his mouth as if about to speak. Then he closed it. He pushed off the tree and started to trot over to Wilde. Wilde laughed. "Slow down. No hurry."

Gilbert stopped. "But what is it?" He put his hands back in his pockets.

"It's your birthday, you know that."

"Of course. So?"

Wilde chuckled. How quickly Gilbert forgot. "Don't you want to know what I got for you?"

"Oh, I'm sure it must be good, Oscar. Because you are so good."

Wilde felt a surge through his chest, and he almost couldn't breathe. He would have almost called it pain, except it did not feel painful; he would have called it a tearing in the structure of his heart, except that sounded unfortunate. Truth was, his heart was breaking apart because it could not contain any more love for this sweet man-child.

A thought crossed Gilbert's eyes. "But what did you get me? I don't see that you are carrying anything."

Wilde signaled behind him; then he turned and began walking toward the outer wall of the café, against which was set the bicycle with the nickel-plated handlebars. He waited to hear a scream from Gilbert. Hearing none, he turned and saw that the boy was standing in the same place, watching him.

"Maurice," Wilde said, and pointed directly at the bicycle. Only then did Gilbert's eyes move to the wall of the café. He saw. It took a moment, but Gilbert emitted a choking sound; then he put his hands on his head and spoke a wet, breathy "Ay yai yai yai yai." Wilde could not help but smile. He could not help but rest on his heels.

"You did it. I cannot believe that you really did it."

Wilde laughed. Against his better judgement, he walked up to Gilbert and wrapped an arm around the boy's waist. Together, they took in the sight of the bicycle.

"It's beautiful!" Gilbert said. "How did you find it? How long do you have it for?"

"How long? It's yours, you dear man."

Gilbert put his hands on his head again. Even though his mouth was open in an O of delight he was unable to form words. Then he pulled Wilde closer to him; he dipped his head closer.

"It's mine?" Gilbert whispered with disbelief.

"Mine alone? You bought it for me?"

Wilde clapped his hands together. "Who else would I have bought it for? Don't you remember asking me for it?"

Gilbert's huge dark eyes clouded, his brows crossed. "I never... I do not think..."

"I asked you if you could have anything in the world what would it be. You told me you wanted the nickel-plated bicycle you had seen the night before."

Gilbert was shaking his head now, slowly, numbly. "But you only asked. I never—never—thought you meant to get it for me." He pushed his face closer now and secretly kissed Wilde on the neck. "I never thought that was possible."

They were lying on Wilde's bed. Both men were naked and crying.

Wilde said, "Why can't you simply say no to them?"

"But how?" Gilbert said, his arms stretched to the ceiling.

"How? N-o-n."

Gilbert shook his head vigorously. Like a ten-year-old. "Stop it. Please."

"What?" Wilde said.

"I cannot do that. I have signed the paper."

"It's a paper," Wilde said. "It's not as if it has arms and legs to track you down and tie you up."

"But that's the thing. It does. It has the law behind it. This is a scary thing in France."

"Don't tell me about the law, Maurice. Especially

not a scary law. What do you know about scary laws?"

Gilbert's face broke open with a horrible expression: half embarrassment, half dread, and full amazement. "My god. I am sorry. I am sorry!" He reached across and grabbed Wilde's chest. "I am sorry!" The display was so genuine, so not strategic that Wilde forgave the boy immediately, without hesitation. Then he realized he had nothing to forgive, because Maurice had not sinned. Wilde joined the embrace. "Don't apologize. It's me. My need. I don't want you to go."

Gilbert pulled back. "That's the thing, Oscar. I would like not to have to go too. But I cannot think of any way to do that. I am sorry."

"There isn't a way. I'm just being stupid in my old age."

Gilbert shook his head. "No, you are never stupid. You are amazing. You are generous. You are funny." Gilbert rolled into Wilde's boy and rested his furry black head on Wilde's chest.

Wilde sighed. He could not help but hear the note of sadness in his sound, which made no sense, because possibly he had never been happier than this moment.

"What if you meet some handsome, older man in Tunisia, a man who falls in love with you?"

Now Gilbert laughed, even as his eyes remained shiny wet from the guilt and tears of before. "I have a handsome older man in love with me. I do not want any other. There is just sweet Oscar, who buys me bikes." Then he turned his head upward and kissed Wilde on the mouth. Wilde felt a revelation of lips: demanding like a man's; soft like a woman's; all genders in one person; all sex too. A beautiful, sexualized baby, big-eyed and solemn about its needs. Wilde had already exercised himself upon Gilbert's penis twice; Gilbert had exercised himself on Wilde's once; but Wilde felt himself rise and quicken regardless, newly earnest. He withdrew from the kiss and let his breath fall full upon Gilbert's cheek.

"Did you know," Wilde said, "that Tunisia is the site of the founding of Carthage?"

This brought out a shy smile from Gilbert. Then he shrugged. "I think you know everything."

"My god," Wilde said, "how can you not know that and yet... be so perfect."

Gilbert moved his head back to Wilde's chest. For half a minute he said nothing. Then: "I will take my bicycle with me to Tunisia, and I will ride it everywhere. And I will tell everyone who bought it for me."

Wilde coughed. "Maurice, you can't possibly be allowed to bring a bicycle on an Army mission."

"I can ask. It is my bicycle."

"Yes, it is."

"Besides, what else can I do with it?"

"You should leave it with your mother. That way it is safe."

Several seconds passed and Gilbert did not respond. He only frowned, more deeply than ever. Then he sat up on his elbow. "Actually, I should leave it here with you. My mother will not understand."

"Oh, no. I am not about to start riding a bicycle across the city."

A turn of a smile appeared on Gilbert's face, a thought in his eyes. "You don't know that. It is an extraordinary machine. Very easy on the legs."

"Maurice, I love you, but I will never ever ride a bicycle, no matter how much you try to charm me into it."

Now Gilbert smiled so widely his dimple appeared. "Okay! I don't care! As long as I know you have it. That is what matters. It will make me feel good while I am in Tunisia that this beautiful velo is waiting for me. And, even better, I will have reason to rush back to your hotel and find you when I return."

"But you don't know when that will be!"

"Yes, but whenever it is, the velo will be waiting."

Wilde shifted on bed. "You do not need the excuse of the bicycle to come to my hotel. I want you to come to me no matter what. The very hour your train pulls in. The minute you are free of it. The whole time you are away I will not be thinking of anything but that day, that hour, that minute."

Gilbert's dark eyes fulminated with a shivering silver light. "I love you, Mr. Oscar."

Wilde sobbed. It came, and it came, and he could not hold it back. It came from out of the dark well of his chest. His upper body shook; his head bowed; his shoulders vibrated. He hated—hated—how this must look, to the young and optimistic soldier. Stop—stop—stop. But he could not stop.

Gilbert ran a soft hand along Wilde's arm. "I do not understand," Gilbert whispered. "I said I love you. Why are you crying?"

"Because I have not heard those words spoken to me for what feels like a lifetime. And after you say them to me, you have to leave for Tunisia, of all places."

Gilbert settled back against the pillow. He spoke so gently, with barely any breath. "It is just a country. It is not you."

Now Wilde laughed. He laughed and shook his head. This boy! He saw that Gilbert was looking at him now as if worried about his emotional stability. "That is right, Maurice. Tunisia is a country, but I contain multitudes."

Gilbert studied him out of the corner of his eye. "You do?"

"That's a line. From a poem. 'I contain multitudes.'"

"A line of yours, Oscar?"

"No. Someone else's. A man I met, long ago. A man I kissed on the lips when we parted."

"Is this man famous?"

Wilde paused, considered. "Yes. He is. Quite."

"Maybe you should write him a letter," Gilbert said. "And tell him that we discussed his poetry, you and I."

"Should I tell him we were naked and in bed at the time?"

Gilbert thought for a second. "Yes!"

Wilde chuckled. He rubbed Gilbert's knee. "He would have loved that. But, actually, he's dead now."

"Oh. So sad."

Wilde shrugged. "He died at his home. In the company of friends and admirers. An exuberant icon. It is said that a thousand people came to view his body."

Gilbert nodded. "A great man always has many devoted friends. You can tell this way that he is great."

Wilde started. "What did you just say?"

"You can tell—"

"No, the first thing."

"We should write him a letter?"

"No, after that, what about a great man?"

"A great man always has devoted friends?"

"Did you think of that yourself?"

Gilbert looked confused. "Of course I did. You heard me say it."

"My," Wilde said, shaking his head. "You are a wonder."

Gilbert, obviously unsure of what to make of this summation, was not quite smiling. "Why?"

"Because none other than Samuel Taylor Coleridge once said, "'Hath he not always treasures, always friends, the good great man?'""

"And that's what I said!"

"Have you, by any chance, ever read Samuel Taylor Coleridge?"

"I've never even heard of Samuel Taylor Coleridge. Is he French?"

Wilde laid his head back and roared. "There's a bust of him in Westminster Abbey!"

Gilbert frowned; his huge dark eyes were much smaller now. "And where is that?"

Wilde laughed again. "You are a force of nature, Maurice!" He leaned in and kissed the Frenchman full on the lips. His hand went greedily for Gilbert's penis.

"And you," Gilbert offered, "are a great good man."

CHAPTER THREE

Above the Gulf of La Napoule. France (Côte d'Azur). January, 1899.

"My god, Oscar, what a night this is," Frank Harris said.

Wilde could see Harris's eye alight with the primal beauty of the evening: the litter of dirt and leaves across the path ahead of him, the subtle substance of the forest, the silver cast of moonlight, the tepid coastal air. Harris's face, always pale, was shining like a lantern. His grin threatened to break his square bony chin, and his moustache, waxed to fine points, was as vibrant as a tusk. He looked like he might strip off his jacket and howl at the moon. Naturally lean, at thirty-two Harris showed no evidence of a coming middle age. If anything, he seemed more energetic every year. He could stroll briskly for hours, talking and pointing and debating the whole way. Wilde wondered if Harris, as a boy in Ireland, had ever tested himself in running contests. Surely he would have conquered the competition.

"Shall we?" Harris said with a hiccup of tentativeness in his voice, and an uncertain gesture of his hand toward the path, as if to reassure Wilde that he did not expect him to run the hill to the sea.

Wilde was glad to feel how mild the winter air remained—or was he simply numb from the drinks?—and how lit by the effort of full moon. But looking ahead at the leaf strewn path that meandered in curving fashion and downwards, hundreds of feet, through an avenue of forest and finally to the shore by the Bay of La Napoule, he worried about the possibility of tripping. He was old and fat and drunk. And he'd never been very coordinated in the first place. He wished he had not left his cane at the hotel, but that had been at Harris's insistence: "No need, Oscar. We're only going for a little stroll."

A little stroll. Wilde should have known better than to trust that statement from Frank Harris. Harris was endowed with the Celts' impatient energy, which America had only encouraged and taught him to put to practical use. That energy accounted for most of Harris's charisma, all of his professional success, and a good deal of his unapologetic fucking of women—whether single, married, divorced, or barely of age—on both sides of the Atlantic. It could also, once in a while, turn him into a complete pain in the arse. "You don't need a cane when you have legs," Harris had remonstrated. "Make them move for once in your blasted life." Wilde had tried to remind Harris that his legs were not presently any good, still hurting as they were from their expedition of the day before when, after Wilde had suggested they take a bottle of champagne at a café with a terrace view, Harris had insisted that they first cover the stretch of seashore that ran in front of the hotel.

"We shall," Wilde said presently and took the first step. It was a firm step, unproblematic. He followed it with others. Indeed, in no time at all Wilde was feeling—after complaining in his mind so long about Harris's vitality—oddly animated. Both men fell silent, during which time a pattern of smoky clouds drifted across the face of the moon and then finally, reluctantly moved on; the path was cast anew in a brassy, luminous splendor, even brighter than before. Wilde looked up. In the moment, the moon had never seemed so forgiving or so purposeful, so much like a sentient being of the heavens.

"Do you remember that phrase from Virgil, Frank, *per amica silentia lunae*? That's always seemed to me indescribably lovely, the most magical lines about the moon ever written. I love that amica silentia. What a beautiful nature a man must have to feel the friendly silences of the moon."

Harris nodded noncommittally. For a moment, Wilde was not sure his friend had heard. Then something occurred to him. Was it possible Harris had never read the Aeneid? Self-starter and man of the people that he was, maybe a gap that large could exist in his unsystematic literary education. For the first time in years, he felt a twinge of pity for Frank Harris, that most decidedly non-Oxford scholar.

"What do you think?" Wilde prodded.

Harris shrugged. "I have to admit that as far as literature goes I am a partaker of the modern world. I like to think that literature evolves just like the human soul does and human culture, that the here where we are now represents the ultimate flowering of human potential. At least until the next flowering."

Wilde felt himself almost drawn to a stop. "You cannot be serious."

Harris chortled. "I cannot? I cannot? I'm perfectly

serious. I refuse to discredit the world as it is precisely now. I won't hamper my brain with my disingenuous nostalgia for a past that never existed. Life was never more than it is now—even with all the rot around us; hope was never higher than it is now. At the very least, the now is no worse, even if it is not in all ways superior."

Wilde laughed. Once more he was face to face with it: the many-sided man that was Frank Harris. How could someone who'd just uttered such a thing about the modern world have wanted to visit a monastery in the hills above the southern coast of France, and not just visit but lounge, linger, share an old-fashioned meal with a man in that most old-fashioned of positions: abbot. When Harris had harried Wilde out of their hotel, insisting that Wilde stop clinging to the chaise like a sloth to a tree branch, Wilde had assumed it was to run by the town hall or the offices of the local newspaper or, god save them all, some seaside factory whose methods Harris thought wickedly instructional. But no, instead they'd walked for nearly two miles, hugging the beach, Harris saying very little, and finally—after a period to let Wilde rest—up the slope of a wooded hill to a monastery. Not an old one, but one constructed according to old ideals of community and mutual responsibility. Harris had introduced Wilde to the abbot, a further surprise, because it was instantly clear that Wilde's Welsh/Irish/American friend—that determinedly cheerful agnostic—had visited with the abbot not once but several times before.

Four hours later, Harris and Wilde left the monastery with their stomachs too full for comfort and their brains soaked with both red and white wines and a variety of home-distilled liqueur dense with the flavors of bitter and sweet oranges. The abbot had certainly been most kind. First to set aside his duties for the day to show Harris and Wilde around the monastery, the construction of which he had personally supervised. And then to insist that they stay on for dinner, which the abbot had told a young novice to bring to his office, so that the three men could enjoy some privacy.

When Wilde had asked if the abbot did not prefer to eat with the other monks, the man raised his hand. He was younger than Wilde expected an abbot to be, with a full head of hair, gone only partially gray, and a seething glint of irony in his eye. No wonder he and Harris got along. "I can always eat with them tomorrow," he said. "I can eat with them any time I please." Wilde laughed but appreciated even more the abbot's next comment: "I can only eat with you gentlemen tonight." And eat they did: a subtle *tourin d'ail doux* with black bread, followed by richly buttered haricots verts, and then boar, and then three different cheeses. Along with the food and the wine they shared cordial chatter about Nice and about Paris and about Balzac—the abbot was a literary man!—and about chickens and about money and about prayer and even about Jesus. When Wilde admitted that at university he'd strongly considered converting to Catholicism, the abbot smiled and nodded, as if he would have guessed as much about the corpulent and highly mannered man with the unusual voice. It was such a knowing look that Wilde felt obliged to add, "When I lived in Berneval-le-Grand I went to mass everyday." It was an exaggeration, but not by much.

"Why did you stop?" the abbot asked. Wilde could not answer him because he began to cry. Harris had kindly reached over and put a hand on his shoulder, but it didn't really matter. The tears still came. "Mon Dieu," the abbot breathed, but instead of pursuing this line of inquiry he decided to bring out the after-dinner liqueur, which indeed put all of them on a much better footing.

Now, against the fact of Harris's outrageous estimation of the modern world as superior to the classical, Wilde forgot his legs altogether, as well as his drunkenness and the eternal sickness of heart. Now, Wilde laughed, with deliberately accented mockery and more force than he'd had in a long time. He did not intend to sound cruel, but he couldn't help it. Harris's position was so preposterous Wilde could barely keep from dancing over it. "'Not in all ways superior'?" Wilde gibed. "How about, 'In nearly all ways inferior'? Are you honestly going to tell me that there is anything in the culture of contemporary England that cannot be shamed by the beauty of the classical world? Are you actually trying to argue that?"

"Yes, I am. And I can." The fight was on and Harris was warming to it. "I have nothing against Mr. Plato or Mr. Sophocles. But I believe there are a hundred writers in Britain today as talented as any one in old Athens."

Wilde hooted. His head felt even clearer, his step quicker. "Really. Really now. So what giant of letters in contemporary England do you credit?"

Harris considered the question for a tortured moment, the rosy and waxen glow of inebriation burning on his cheek. There was that curious fact about Harris: for such an energetic and animated man, drunkenness showed on him like a calling card. Wilde knew—because others had commented on this frequently—that after four or five straight hours of consumption his own cheek looked as pristine as at the start of the day.

"Well . . ." Harris started. "Arthur Symons for one. He is about as modern as one can get, and in touch with what is happening in France, which is more than I can say for most of his generation."

"Arthur Symons," Wilde sighed. "All egoist and no ego."

A fresh spark of anger rose in Harris's cheek. "All right, then. What do you think of George Moore? One of your own countrymen, and like you an expatriate."

"Really, Frank. George Moore? The man has carried out his education as a writer entirely in the public eye. He published three books before he knew there was such a thing as an English grammar. A few years later, he'd learned that sentences had to build into paragraphs and paragraphs into chapters. Maybe by the time he publishes his final book he'll reach the level that most writers start from."

Wilde could see he'd landed a blow there. Harris looked honestly stung. So George Moore was a hero to Frank Harris? Amazing. Wilde could see Harris mulling over more names, more wary now, seeing how this game was wending. Finally, he said, "Bernard Shaw?"

Wilde coughed. "Yet another Irishman. I thought we were discussing English letters."

"My point's the same," Harris said.

Of course it was. Wilde was merely delaying. The truth was he admired Shaw. After Wilde's sentencing, Shaw—resisting the tidal wave of Londoners' angry recriminations—had publically supported him. But then again, Shaw always did love to play the contrarian. And, before, in Wilde's glory days, he'd never been sure whether Shaw actually liked him or only held his nose and tolerated him. He suspected the latter and thus had never felt completely comfortable around the man. But however complicated his feelings about Shaw, this game with Harris had gone too far for him to pull back now. "Real talent but a bleak mind. Wintry sunlight on a bare landscape. Shaw has no passion, no feeling. He loves nothing and believes in nothing."

Harris was smiling now, catching the spirit of the conversation. "Care anything for Thomas Hardy?"

"Hardy only recently discovered that women have legs underneath their dresses. And this discovery almost wrecked his life." Harris laughed uproariously. Wilde pushed on. "He also writes poetry, I'm told. That must be very hard reading."

Harris half-nodded, and smiled, but offered no comment. They were almost halfway down the path at this point. Here and there, as the route turned, openings appeared in the trees. The beautiful night-black water of the coast shimmered like a new gossamer reality. They

slowed almost to a stop. The view was so stunning neither of them could talk. But step-by-step they proceeded, and eventually Harris said, "Why do I have the feeling
that no matter which writer I name you will profess to
despise him?"

"Oh, it's not a matter of despising. Only aesthetical
analysis."

Harris clucked, his sharp chin rearing. "Yes, sure.
Merely analysis." He made a bitter noise in his throat.
"So, let's see, who have I failed yet to name?"

"There are plenty of others, Frank. You may name
as many as you like. Name them all."

Harris paused. "Oscar Wilde," he said. "How
would you rank him?"

Now that was unexpected. But typical of Harris:
trying to put Wilde on the defensive, trying to remind
him that at one time he was named in the same breath
as those other men. Perhaps even in a finer breath. Maybe the wine and liqueur really were wearing off, because
Wilde couldn't pick up this joke. In fact, he didn't feel like
playing anymore.

"He has suffered enough notoriety," Wilde said. "I
think we should let him go from the world if he wants.
In pace requiescat."

Harris's face moved and then finally shuttered. He
lowered his head and looked at nothing but the ends of
his shoes as the trees on both sides of them grew thinner,
the Gulf of La Napoule even more obvious. "If you say
so," Harris said. Then: "But that would be a mistake."

Wilde's anger flared. Jesus, the man can't leave it

alone. He was about to say something, about to yell—this was his own life Harris was dissecting, after all, as if Harris owned it, when no one owned it, no one owned it but him—but he finally decided to let it go. For now. Yet again.

Wilde knew that his resentment toward Harris could fairly only extend so far, because it was Harris who was footing the bill for this three-month vacation; a vacation Wilde had agreed to, and gratefully. Flush from his sale of the *Saturday Review*, Harris offered Wilde an escape from the winter gloom of Paris and his broken heart. Wilde had been all too happy to say yes.

Maurice Gilbert's leaving had just about been the death of him. For two days straight, Wilde had stared at the bicycle with the nickel-plated handlebars and cried and cried some more and drunk champagne and developed a bad body stink. Worried that if he did not leave the hotel soon he would never leave, Wilde had gotten up on the third day, washed, changed clothes, and proceeded to push the new bicycle all the way to Gilbert's mother's apartment. There he paid a boy to carry it up the stoop and inside, then up a flight of stairs. He knocked on the woman's door and was surprised to see, when the door opened, a hard-looking person with penetrating eyes. Eyes as dark as Maurice's but with none of Maurice's sense of wonder or his gentleness. The eyes of someone who has decided that life's essential lesson is never to trust. A narrow, angry person. Also, Wilde had to admit to himself, a person who was not in any noticeable way physically attractive. This was the woman who had birthed that beautiful, sweet boy?

"I am a friend of your son's," Wilde started, in French. The woman looked suspiciously, even hatefully, at him. All right, Wilde thought, so that's it then. But he was used, at this point, to dealing with hateful people. He was efficient in the business of getting on. "Maurice left this behind at my hotel the other day—accidentally of course."

"My son owns no bicycle," the woman countered, practically through bared teeth.

"Madam, I know what I saw. I was present. You were not. Your son was upon this bicycle when he approached my hotel." This much was true. Gilbert, stupidly giddy at the sight of the thing, had mounted the bike and immediately ridden it all the way to the Marsolier; then he'd circled back to find Wilde proceeding slowly along the sidewalk, not even that far yet from the Café Belisle. So Gilbert rode again to the Marsolier and back. Then again. Until Wilde had finally made it home. "He called it 'his bicycle.' He told me in no uncertain terms how much he liked it.'"

"This is not possible," the woman replied.

"Not only is it possible; it is in fact true," Wilde said. Then he shoved the bike forward, forcing the woman to step back. He would not tell her he had bought it for Gilbert; he would not tell her a single thing more. But it was Maurice's, and so this is where it belonged.

"Bonjour," Wilde said. He tipped his hat, turned on his heel, and left before she could even get hold of the disputed vehicle. When he'd descended as far as the front door, he heard the apartment door slam above, and a wail of exasperation.

A week later, Harris had appeared and had talked him into this present escapade to the south. Well... escapade? Not exactly. Wilde would like it to be so, but he knew how badly Harris wanted him to pick up the pen, to avail himself of the time and the place; to make of it a writing retreat. Wilde had been too grateful and too eager for the escape to turn down Harris's offer. But in fact, when, almost as soon as they arrived, Harris absented himself for weeks to conduct negotiations for the purchase of a restaurant in Monte Carlo, Wilde had proceeded to accomplish exactly nothing in the way of literature, unless Harris counted the several adoring letters he wrote to Gilbert.

But he knew Harris would not count those, so Wilde never told him about them. And while he had so far avoided saying so to his old London friend, he did not intend to accomplish anything more just because Harris was back now and griping at him. What he intended to do was enjoy himself. To taste the many comforts of the south. Let others aspire to write epics, let others pen their angry utopian manifestos or socially progressive novels; he would drink champagne, read silly books, watch the human flesh occupying the seashore, and attend plays that made him laugh. Soon enough he would do his enemies the favor of dying—he felt it coming in his bones. But until then he would remember Maurice Gilbert and enjoy himself.

Ten minutes later they were almost at the bottom and nearly level with the shore. To their left, more than a hundred yards off, a short pier stabbed like a tongue into the body of the sea. Wilde spied the bulks of three or four fishing smacks laid up on the sand behind this pier, but no sign of the boys who hours later would push them out into the water for yet another morning of hauling in nets full of mullet and goby and mackerel and bream. He let out a sigh, a louder noise than he'd intended.

"Tired?" Harris asked. "After that short walk?"

"Tired to death," Wilde said.

Harris frowned, but this time with concern. "You want to see if we can let a boat? Get rowed down to our hotel?"

It was a fine idea. A brilliant one, in fact. "That would be splendid, Frank. Thank you. I do not know if there's anyone there to let from, however."

"Of course there is," Harris said. "There always is in a place like this."

They proceeded eastward across the upper portion of the sand, more packed and dingy brown in the moonlight, easier to walk on than the fulvous humped-up white that made up most of the beach. Even so, Wilde could feel each step in his legs; his calves mostly, but too his thighs and his knees. Before their trip south, he had not done this sustained kind of walking for a very long time. Really, not since Oxford. When they reached the pier they saw no one with a boat to rent. "Perhaps if we wait," Harris said, "someone will show." Wilde was relieved to hear the note of disappointment in Harris's voice. "Probably they are going back and forth all night."

Wilde had nothing to say except that he hoped so, and Harris already knew that. So he said nothing, only followed his friend when Harris stepped up onto the pier and strolled to the end. There, they let themselves enjoy a broad blanketing view of the gulf: veiled on its backside by hills, so calm on this unerring, windless evening; black and bright at the same time, opaque as raw steel and yet in the light of the full moon as glittery as a newly christened cutlass. Harris stared and stared at the water and said exactly nothing. He stared for so long Wilde began to worry what words might next come out of the man's mouth. Finally, Harris rotated back toward the shore. His face narrowed. He pointed. "There," he said.

Wilde wheeled. Sure enough, on the shore someone was smoking a cigarette, the orange bulb of the light obvious in the nighttime. Whoever it was must have been there the whole time. And on a night as bright as this one it was not hard to decipher the outline of a human figure: a male, probably young, dressed in sloppy, working man's trousers and a loose, white shirt. He might or might not be wearing anything on his feet. Wilde could not make out any pertinent features of his face, but his hair was as dark and his manner as casual as any of the fishing boat boys.

Harris walked back down the pier. "Excuse me," he called—in his rather untutored French—when they were closer, "could we pay you to take us down the water to our hotel?" He gave the name of the place: the Hotel des Bains. The boy had no immediate reaction. Wilde hoped that meant the hotel was so familiar as to not need saying.

"Oui," the boy said then, tossing away his cigarette. "Je suis heureux de vous emmener." I'm happy to take you. The boy took a step forward and Wilde realized that he knew him. Good heavens, what luck. He'd spent an afternoon, almost two weeks earlier, lounging on the beach near his hotel, laughing and flirting with this boy, meeting his eye, sending him signals that could not be mistaken. The boy had made him work, but in the end it had turned out wonderfully. The boy had not told Wilde his name until they were all done. Léon. What a powerful, sonorous appellation. So male and yet so gracious at the same time, especially when pronounced in the French manner: Léon. He'd seen Léon two more times in the weeks that followed: friendly chatting and a few meaningful glances that unfortunately came to nothing, probably because there were too many other people around to carry off a transaction. But he never felt that Léon minded the attention or wished he would go away.

"Léon," Wilde called. The fisher boy's head stood up straight, and his shoulders; the features of his face narrowed to a point as he stared. Then Wilde saw a smile slide slowly across his face. "Mr. Oscar," Léon said, in English. "Good evening!"

"You know this person?" Harris said. Wilde couldn't tell if his tone was more astonished or disgusted.

"A little," Wilde said. "We've met. Right Léon?"

"Oui. Yes," the boy called.

Harris looked carefully back and forth between the two of them. Whatever suspicions he might have had he put away for the time being in order to move on to the negotiations. Harris knew better than to be duped by the boy's rudimentary English and so spoke in French the whole time. "We need to return to the hotel. We could walk there, of course, but I'm afraid we've done a good deal of walking already. So you can take us?"

"Of course. I would love to." Léon smiled at Harris as if he'd been waiting all evening for someone like Frank Harris to ask him that question. A smile that had a curl on each end. Wilde knew that Harris was about to be asked to pay far more francs than he expected.

"How much?" Harris said.

"Oh, yes, well, let me think." The boy glanced at Wilde, holding the look for a second, as if expecting a message, a crucial answer. Instructions. At the moment, though, Wilde had none to give. Léon would have to work this out on his own. "Let's say—not too bad—two hundred and fifty francs."

"Two hundred and fifty?!" Harris's jaw dropped. His fists might even have curled.

Léon either did not notice the reaction or pretended not to. His smile stayed in place, all beautiful white teeth and Mediterranean ease. "It will not take long, but it is late, and I am quite tired myself."

Wilde almost laughed. Thankfully, he held it in, as the sound would have given Léon away. Not only was it not late in Léon's world; it was almost early. The boy would probably be out here for four or five more hours, giving rides and/or turning tricks as the opportunities presented. A fisher of men, he was. Léon, though charmingly, beautifully young—he could not be older than six-teen—knew his business as well as any fifty-year-old. In this place, on this night, even churlish and pragmatic Frank Harris was no match against him. From the start of his stay here, Wilde had known better than try to bar-gain with these boys. What was the point? Just pay up and enjoy their company. After all, when would he have the chance again?

"Frank," Wilde said. He was about to add, in an artificially weary voice, "it's late," but he didn't have to. Harris's expression closed down and his brows lowered. "Fine," he snapped. "Two hundred and fifty francs. Just get us back. Fast."

Léon offered a bow of perfect courtesy. "Of course. This is no problem at all. Can I ask your name?"

"Biggest Sucker," Harris said bitterly and no more.

Wilde saw the light of comprehension in Léon's eye, but the boy—so smart—merely nodded and smiled. He gestured toward his boat. "If you give me the francs, I will have it in the water instantaneously."

Without a word, Harris plunged a hand into his pocket. He removed a billfold. Almost without looking, he peeled off three paper bills and pushed them into the Leon's hands.

They were close to the stopping point on the beach by the hotel. For the first half of the ride, Harris had stayed silent and simmering, so Wilde had focused solely on Léon, chatting easily with him about his family, about the fishing business, about his boat, about La Napoule.

Once he had reached over and touched Léon's forearm, as if to accent a point he was making, but really to send a definite signal. From the momentary waver in the boy's cheek, Wilde was sure Léon understood. Wilde hadn't told Harris this, but he had more than a hundred francs in his pocket. Léon liked him. He would take one hundred francs or even less, to spend some extra moments with Wilde, whether on the boat or on the beach or in some hidden alcove just offshore. Private moments.

When they drew close to the shore, Wilde looked back at Harris and saw that his friend had finally relaxed. He'd wisely given up worrying about the money and was just enjoying the beatific evening, the moon striking the gentle waves of the Bay of La Napoule. This would make what Wilde had to say much easier. "Don't expect me to go back to the hotel with you," Wilde said. "Not just yet."

Harris looked confused. The tense looks again. "What? Why? We're here."

"I'll be along later," Wilde said. "Don't worry. Not that much later. You go on by yourself."

Something shifted in Harris's eye. He glanced at the fisher boy softly pulling the oars; he glanced at Wilde. A barbed look hung in his eye for a moment, but then he nodded: a grim, sad motion. But he said nothing; he offered no rebuttal.

"We have arrived bonnes hommes," Léon sang, his voice like a bird. A tanned and black-haired, pearly-teethed, supple-limbed creature that could only be found and enjoyed in the environs of La Napoule. That rare; that ephemeral.

CHAPTER FOUR

La Napoule, France (Côte d'Azur). January, 1899.

"That's completely impossible," Harris said. "I don't understand it. It makes no physical sense."

"It makes every physical sense."

"But you know women. You married one—a beautiful one, I might add. At least before her worries beat her down."

Beneath the burden of the comment Wilde collapsed onto the scarlet cushions of the couch. He had thought that they were about to head out from this pampered hotel suite, which had become too much for even him. What with its expansive bedroom, more luxuriously appointed even than Wilde's had been back on 34 Tite Street; an alcove with a lacquered walnut and oak secretary with bookcase on top and its leather upholstered chair with scrolled back and arm rests; and this sitting room larger than three ordinary hotel rooms put together. Harris, though he was paying for it all, had taken the suite on the other end of the hall, the smaller of the two. Wilde wished now the reverse were true. His suite was so large, so devoid of companionship, and so obviously intended, by force of isolation, to drive him to that secretary—which the staff checked every day in order to refill its inkwells or restock its paper as necessary—that he was forced to flee each afternoon to find what was actually pleasurable to him, to what didn't stink of obligation.

Now that Harris had completed that business in

Monte Carlo and had returned to La Napoule for the duration, Wilde was hoping the man might finally relax. Just a half-hour earlier, Wilde had looked forward to luncheon with Harris in the hotel restaurant; perhaps followed by a carriage ride into Nice for an afternoon cocktail. Maybe several cocktails. But then Harris—who sat on the chair opposite the scarlet couch, tilting like a panther set to pounce—had started in on this ludicrous subject: the superiority of women's bodies to men's. Really? Was Frank Harris that socially clumsy, to say nothing of dim-witted? Wilde would not have thought so. And then Harris had gone and made it worse with that last comment about Constance: her beauty and her worries. Well, of course, the whole world knew exactly who had brought on those worries, didn't it? It was a very mean thing for a friend to say, and Harris knew it. It stung Wilde about as deeply as Harris should have anticipated.

"Has it never occurred to you, Frank, that I have already castigated myself for the way I treated her? What do you think I did for two whole years in jail?"

Harris, to his credit, went white for a second. "I'm sorry, Oscar. You're right. Perhaps that was not the best example."

No, it was not. Not anymore, or at least Wilde hoped. He'd made his peace with his now-deceased wife, even while he was still at Reading. He had not been an "Ideal Husband" but a terrible one, and he knew it. He would never have denied it. His only plausible excuse was that he had so much else on his mind, and in his life, then. But in prison, there had been nothing at all. Only time and confinement and the hollows of his own soul. Indeed, in prison the torture of his conscience became a balm that had finally allowed him to settle things with Constance. She'd visited him several times and even expressed to the warden her concerns for his treatment. It was Constance, and no one else, who had made them treat him more like a human being. It was Constance who'd won him the right to books. Also she who had informed him of his mother's death.

He'd apologized to Constance in person repeatedly, and committed himself to living a new life when he was released. Not for the sake of winning her back—although Wilde knew that some, especially Frank Harris, had hoped for that outcome—but for the sake of a new life. A different life than the one in which he'd indulged in 1895. Constance had told him she wanted the same: a return for him and a better existence: active, happy, and unhounded. *I don't want that for me but for you,* she'd repeated. *For you.* She had agreed to withdraw the petition of divorce once it became clear that the divorce would require yet another trial against him—because she would be forced to admit that his "unnatural" desires were the cause of the proceedings—and a likely second sentence. As Constance said, "Neither of us could live through that." So instead they drew up an agreement that they both felt certain they could accept, including the provision that he must never see Lord Alfred Douglas again. In exchange, Wilde would receive an allowance of £150 a year, paid in installments.

Of course, when, the fall after his release from

Reading, he took that trip to Naples and officially re-newed his alliance with Douglas, Constance had been hurt. Well, furious. She'd stopped communicating with him, and her lawyers had enacted the prescribed penalty. For three months, not a farthing came to him from her estate. But then, after a letter from him, filled with much gossip about his state of affairs in Paris, Constance—out of her own pocket—began sending him remittances. *Do not tell anyone I am doing this*, she'd written. *Not even your French friends. Or it will surely get back to my solicitors.*

Constance was always better and more moral than the fierce, conventional morality she claimed to stand for. She loved him, and everyone, better than that—and she showed it. When she died in April of 1898, Wilde had felt the sting, but he also, admittedly, felt relief: the relief of a lingering and painful mistake put to rest. He had been a terrible husband to a woman who had deserved better.

He liked now to console himself with the thought that surely there must have times of sweetness between the two of them—after the courtship, after the heady marriage—he had not always been a terrible husband, had he? Even after things became frayed and tired be-tween them: after the work of restoring the house and hiring servants and starting his career and making money and lanching themselves into the dinner scene; after the lightning bolt of childbirth and the physical changes in her and the sudden role for him of fatherhood and the need then for more money and more servants and more work... Had there not ever been moments of sweetness?

He remembered at least one, come upon unexpectedly.

He had returned far sooner than usual from the West End, just after midnight. Twelve successive evenings of reveling in another performance of A Woman of No Importance, *and then carousing afterwards with Bosie and whomever else they could string along in their tour of nocturnal London, had left him spent. He had begged off from the unquenchable Alfred Douglas—just this once, he pleaded with the disappointed younger man—and paid for a cab ride back to Tite Street. The house, he had assumed, would be dark, all three of its primary residents safely and painlessly asleep, enjoying the dreams of the ignorant. He would make his way as softly as possible up the stairs to the third floor and then along past Constance's door to his own at the back. He would fall into his bed, grateful for it, go off straight to sleep, and not wake until the following afternoon—a sensible plan, if we were to have the energy to keep going like this.*

But as soon as he stepped through the front door and into the hall he heard, from one of the upper floors, someone crying. Cyril. Cyril was crying. Why was Cyril crying? Then he heard Constance speaking strictly. He listened for a moment. He could not make out what she was saying because of a muffling effect—they must be inside one of the rooms—but he could discern her tone. It did not sound like she was addressing the boy with menace exactly, nor with retribution; but Wilde could hear from her the timbre of distinctly strained patience, of holding back—if barely—the torrent she would like to express, her soul hovering near exhaustion and the breaking point. So someone else in the family was tired too.

Constance was a preternaturally calm person, calm even in situations where any other woman, any other wife, any other mother, would panic or shriek. She seemed especially calm with the children, as if she'd decided that acting so and being so was her assigned role in life. She was not a person immune to anger; but she did not take to it naturally or well. When her patience did break, when she finally released a rising torrent, her raised voice, flaring eyes, and jittering, demonstrating hands seemed so peculiar and unbecoming—even inexplicable—that the expressions only reinforced how fundamentally sweet-tempered she was. Anything else was a violation and a divergence. 80% of the English Wilde knew could huff to match any of the world's insufferable populations. But not so Constance. She could not pull it off. And yet presently Wilde could hear how near she was to losing control.

"Constance?" Cyril's crying stopped. His wife went silent. He tried again: "Darling?" He moved to the stairs and pushed aside the white curtain guarding the entrance. "Constance, what's happening?"

"Oscar?" she called. The third floor. "Is that you?" He heard no small amount of surprise in her voice.

He started up slowly, his head drooped, his eyes on his feet. He studied the familiar yellow and gold pattern in the stair runner—his choice during the remodel, like nearly every other aspect of the interior decoration—and it occurred to him that the yellow somehow looker brighter than he remembered, almost lemony; and the gold more tarnished, descending toward bronze. Not tarnished from dirt or wear. The servants cleaned these stairs each day, or at least they were supposed to. But if not, then from what? And if from dirt, how to explain the more exuberantly yellow yellow, brighter than he remembered? The contrast between the two colors was more stark than ever—a starker contrast, he was certain, than when the runner was first installed eight years ago. A contrast he liked.

He heard a scramble of feet from above and looked up. Constance's head—dark hair, thick eyebrows, heavy white cheeks—appeared above the railing. A moment later, Cyril was there, next to her elbow. Wilde could not help but smile on seeing the boy. He only ever smiled on seeing Cyril: his thick head of rangy brown hair, that distinctive nose, those dark penetrating eyes so much like Constance's, and like hers set wide apart on his face. A combination of his parents, and yet completely himself at the same time. Wilde wondered if in the long run what would prove in the boy the stronger inheritance: his own precociousness or Constance's saintliness. At eight years old it was too early to tell. Wilde hoped for the latter and expected that might be it. After all, Cyril's was an impulsive but sweet nature. There was energy but no devil in him. Like Constance, Cyril was smart—even bookish at times—but not exactly clever. He was a good son, and a surprisingly good older brother to Vyvyan. So much a better older brother than Willie had been to me, Wilde thought, with both pride and sadness. And better surely than I would have been if our ages were reversed.

"Hello, daddy," Cyril said, smiling as soon as he saw Wilde look at him.

"Cyril," Wilde said. "How are you this evening?"

The boy glanced at his mother and then said, "Well. Thanks."

"I am most glad to see you, Oscar," Constance offered, "but also surprised."

Wilde held her eye for a moment. "I decided to come home tonight right after."

Constance answered with an uneasy half-smile, one that strained the skin on her rounded cheeks instead of making them lighter. "Happy to see you home," she said.

"I am happy to be here," he answered quickly. "Now, Cyril. When I came in I thought I heard crying sounds. Crying sounds that sounded devilishly like your own. What's this about?"

The boy smiled again. "Mother kept telling me to take a bath and go to sleep. I told her I had to finish first."

"Finish?"

The boy turned without a word, and disappeared. Wilde glanced at Constance; her wan and sulking look told him that whatever this was, it was the crux of the matter between mother and son, and nothing Constance cared to play out on a stairway. Wilde continued up and was almost to the third floor landing when Cyril came back holding a leather-bound book. With both hands he pushed the book toward Wilde.

"Ah yes. Kidnapped. Good old, gruesome, thrilling Stevenson. Do you like it?"

"I'm almost done, like I said. Except mother wouldn't let me. That's why I was crying."

"Because you wanted to finish it. Because you liked it."

"I love it," Cyril offered.

So this was the kind of boy he was, the man he would become: One who finished what he started, no matter what the cost, no matter what was argued by those around him. A quality that could make Cyril dearly loved; maybe even revered. At least among a certain set of humanity; as long as what he started had no darkness about it, but that was impossible to imagine with dear, sweet Cyril.

"What page were you on?" Wilde said.

"Two hundred and seventy-four."

"Out of how many?"

"Two hundred and seventy-nine."

Wilde glanced disapprovingly at his wife.

"It's late, Oscar," she said. "I've been waiting so long for him to be done. Hours it seems. I can barely keep my eyes open."

Wilde nodded. He could believe this was true. "How about this then?" he said. "Cyril, you and I will proceed to your bedroom, wherein I will read the last five pages of Mr. Stevenson's classic— careful not to wake Vyvan, of course—"

"Don't worry," Cyril said, "nothing wakes Vyvan."

Wilde smiled. "So much the better. And when I've finished, you will take your bath as quickly as you can, while I stand outside guarding against the Vandals."

Cyril chuckled. On his young and changeable face all signs of crying were gone. "They aren't coming here," he said

"Do not be so sure. In any case, upon completion of the bath you will dry yourself off, change into your nightclothes, and prompt- ly go to sleep. No more reading." Cyril nodded. "And dear"—he turned to Constance—"I hereby release you from any further re- sponsibility for your son this evening. You may go and enter the land of Nod."

Constance's smile was distinctly happier this time. "That's all right. I'm happy to hear you read to him, if you'll have me."

"Of course, I am," Wilde said. "And of course I will." Oddly, in the moment he meant it.

They proceeded to the first bedroom. The gas lamp was still on, if at a low level. It was bright enough to read. Wilde took the book from Cyril and propped himself up on Cyril's bed, with his back flat against the wall. He patted the open place beside him. Cyril shook his head and instead sat on the floor and crossed his legs. He crossed his hands and rested his chin atop them: a pose of pure concentration.

"You are ready, aren't you?" Wilde chuckled. Constance,

meanwhile, sat in the space next to her husband, her thigh lightly touching his, her hip grazing his own. "Let's see," Wilde said, and started turning the pages to find 274. "Ah," he offered, and then cleared his throat. Constance sighed and, as if involuntarily, her head dipped and fell against his shoulder.

"So," Wilde said softly, "we begin."

* * * *

"Look, Oscar," Harris said. "I didn't mean to resurrect a bad memory. Only to make a point. So let's drop it."

"Good. I'm happy to."

"I mean the example, not the point."

Wilde sighed. "This is nonsense."

"Consider the Venus de Milo," Harris pressed on. "Will you actually try to argue that there is a more supreme example of physical perfection anywhere in the world of art?"

"Perfection?" Wilde said. Wilde found it hard to believe that after everything that had happened Harris thought he could clobber him into accepting such a proposition. Frank—loyal, helpful Frank; the so-prominent journalist who, on the heels of Wilde's conviction, had declaimed against the stupidity of the English and tried to circulate a petition among literary men in London to have the sentence reduced—was acting as 95% of Englishmen would: assuming that one form of love was innately superior to another, that the other could simply be turned from its course by a pretty female face.

"She's a lovely specimen, Frank, I admit—"

"Lovely! Good God. Have you looked at her?"

"I have visited the Musée du Louvre," Wilde said drolly. "One cannot help but look at her." He paused, then added: "It's what everyone else is doing."

"No, you haven't really looked. You've just observed. On your way to something else." Wilde said nothing. In fact, this was true. Why should he waste minutes in front of the Venus de Milo when he could see Antinous? "If you had really looked, you would have noticed how the turn of her hip pushes her lower half right up against the shrouding sheet; you would have noticed the impossible tautness of her stomach—firm, smooth, fatless—and yet not in the least emaciated or starved. You would have noticed her young woman's breasts: evident but not overly so, perfectly in keeping with the rest of her figure. If you had studied her face and her head you would have seen a whole universe: the nose that is long and noble and fearless, the thoughtful eyes full of dreams, the poised lips; and her hair: short but thick and coiled; those gorgeous Mediterranean tresses."

Wilde chuckled. He'd always thought the Venus de Milo's nose to be quite a conk, an actual embarrassment. It never occurred to him that anyone would think differently about it, much less that it was "noble." Dreamy eyes? He'd always thought they looked bored—and boring. Her lips were ordinary. Constance had had better lips. And it didn't help that the Venus's were pursed in an expression of disapproval. Since when was disapproval comely? Who needed that? And as for her hair? "Her hair is a boy's hair, Frank. It's obvious."

Harris laughed. "Oh, stop it."

"A boy's hair would be even better, actually. Especially a Grecian boy's hair."

"Wait, there's more," Harris said. "You can't forget to take a tour around to the back of her. After you've fallen completely in love by gazing at her front, you simply have to go around. There's she's even more magnificent. The naked muscles of her back, all the way from her neck to her waist. I've never seen a more inspiring back on a woman. And then the sculptor astutely gives us only the upper third of her arse; those two beautiful muscles exposed where the sheet drops down. The sculptor knew that to cover the rest of them was to fill the viewer with imagination—and with longing. It is simply an amazing feat that statue. Epochal."

"I had no idea you could become so rapturous about a pile of stone. Maybe you should propose to it."

Harris turned a mild shade of pink. "Oh stop it. You can't tell me you don't understand what I'm saying. You can't tell me that you don't finally agree."

"I can't? Why can't I? I find it amusing that you can sit here and wax romantic about that old woman, when in my opinion she is self-evidently inferior to Antinous." Wilde saw a great pause of an expression cover Harris's face; one could even call it confusion. "Don't tell me you haven't seen his bust in the Louvre."

"I suppose I have," Harris said dimly. "But it must not have made much of an impression."

"Because you probably lingered for five seconds or so, which is what I give to your old maid. Don't talk to me about a noble nose or expressive eyes until you have studied Antinous's. Or the hair. Oh my. The hair on the Venus de Milo is a limp mess compared to Antinous's locks. They rove all over his head like thick, swollen muscles. His cheeks are perfect lines. His skin is godly. And while I am profoundly disappointed that there is no lower half of him to worship, his breasts surpass the Venus's—or any woman's. Beautiful, smooth planes. But you can practically see the muscles inside them demonstrating. I could idle in front of those breasts for hours, Frank. In fact, I have idled in front of them for hours. When I stand in front of the Venus all I can think of is how more impressive she would be if she had arms."

"Blasphemy," Harris spat.

"Arms are really the only graceful part of a woman's anatomy. The only part of her worth looking at. Though I suppose that among the whole of them there is a fancy neck or two."

Now he was purposefully pecking at Harris and delighted to see how it was working. The man—exuberantly masculine—became so frustrated he couldn't sit still. He pushed himself up from the chair and paced away a few steps, as if the exertion was necessary to calm himself. Harris made anxious, chewing motions, his waxed black moustache and dark, slicked hair glinting like pieces of flint.

"Oscar," Harris finally uttered, after he had gotten himself under control, "I confess that I do not understand it. You were in love with a woman once. You know the feeling."

Wilde's hands moved on their own, pinching and jittery; not an unusual reaction when the subject of Constance came up. "Don't use that word. It's not fair to either of us. I admired Constance, certainly, in my chaste fashion. She was a lovely girl with the kindest soul imaginable. When I first knew her she was like a flower: white and slim as a lily. And her laugh was the most distinctive sound I'd ever heard. She laughed very little, but when she did—and I could get her to—it was like a restorative."

He saw Harris nodding with self-satisfaction.

"But that does not add up to love, especially not the physical adulation we are talking about now. Over time, Constance became much unlike a slim, fresh lily. Motherhood, as holy as it is, was not kind to her. She became sad and heavy and eccentric. It became harder for us to communicate. I continued in my kindnesses. I continued to touch her and hold her, though"—he hesitated, knowing how bad this would sound to Harris—"in fact, touching her had become loathsome to me, something I overcame only by an act of will, the conquering of nausea. Physical communion with her was actively disgusting." He was overstating the case now, but thickheaded Frank Harris needed to understand. He had to be made to understand. "Of course, it was not her fault. I am not blaming her. It is simply what happened."

Harris blinked and chewed over his response. Apparently, this was an unusual admission. Wilde knew of course that there were men who found Constance perfectly attractive, even alluring, even after the births of

Cyril and Vyvyan, even after she'd added forty pounds to her frame, and her breasts sagged, and thighs bulged, and her eyes became sunken with sadness. Chances are this was precisely what Harris, caught with that stupid look on his face, was stumbling over. *Oscar, your wife was an angel.* But then Harris, the great seducer, surprised him.

"But wouldn't her sufferings have moved you at all, Oscar? Maybe even to a deeper love? Did you not pity her?"

The proposition was ridiculous. "Pity has nothing to do with love. In fact, pity kills love. You should know that."

Harris's face fell, not just with disappointment but mystification. He turned away for a moment and drifted deeper into the room. When he came back his voice, and his face, was different. "Didn't prison teach you anything?"

Wilde went still. Now that was an unexpected comment too, even worse than the other. The back of his neck went cold, and the edges of his ears numb. A queer tingling sensation enveloped his upper chest and shoulders. "It taught me a great deal. It taught me far more than any idiotic boarding school. And its lessons last."

"It didn't teach you enough. Or not what it was supposed to."

"Which is what exactly?"

Harris's mouth dropped open. "Are you actually going to ask me that? I would think that two years hard labor in an English prison should tell a man what his civilization thinks of his behavior. The behavior that put him there. And I would think that said man upon release would reconsider his choices, and his inclinations."

The tingling became a riot: dry, red, and uncomfortable. His body had known what Harris was going to say before he said it. It had intercepted the words in the air of the man's brain. But now that the words were out and spoken, Wilde felt, even more than anger, blistering disbelief that his friend could be so misguided, could still, even now, misread what Wilde was, what so many others like him were. He remembered that fateful conversation he'd shared with Harris—on the street, coming from the courtroom, in the middle of the libel trial. Harris had been so sure Wilde could continue to fight the charges brought by Queensberry, and ultimately defeat the man. He'd been sure that the statements offered by Edward Shelley, the once upon a time Uranian who had been so enamored of Wilde, and whom Wilde had fatefully slept with—before Shelley's conversion to religion, his veritable mania for it—were without consequence. In the trial it had seemed that Shelley would say whatever Queensberry's lawyers wanted him to, no matter how repellent to an audience. Shelley seemed on a mission to stop the Uranianism he once practiced so fervently.

"Shelly is an accomplice," Harris said, his body bending with the undeniable fury of certaintly, his face leaning toward Wilde. "The man's testimony needs corroboration. I know you don't understand the law, Oscar, but without corroboration those statements need to be and should have been ruled out. His whole testimony should have been ruled out."

Wilde nodded and walked on with his friend, but in his stomach he felt the same sinking feeling he'd felt all morning—all trial really—listening to such brutal and graphic testimony. Nothing any of them had anticipated, certainly not his own lawyers, who seemed, with every hour, increasingly dumbfounded. He had sworn to them he was innocent. All they asked of him before they agreed to take his case was to tell them the truth: in private, for no one else's ears but their own. Could Queensberry fairly accuse him of being a sodomite? Then he gone and lied; denied it all. He'd denied it all, with the force of his life behind his words. And now they were nothing but stunned, shock-riddled. He was all but certain that even they did not believe him anymore. And yet, and yet, Frank Harris spoke as if they still might win. As if such an outcome was inevitable.

"You talk with such conviction," Wilde started, then hesitated. "As if I were innocent."

Harris pulled to a stop. For several seconds he did nothing but scrutinize Wilde, every millimeter of his face, his stare so intent it might have been fueled by kerosene. "But you are innocent. Aren't you?"

Wilde's heart broke. As much for himself as for his friend. Now he would need to explain himself, when he'd begun to believe it was unnecessary. When he'd started to accept, without admitting it to anyone, that of course everyone surrounding him knew he was a liar; when everyone around had to know the truth of the situation, the truth about him. After all, they were hearing it every day in court. "No. I am not innocent," he said sadly. "I am not." He dropped his head. He could no longer hold Harris's stare. "I thought you knew all along."

Harris shifted in place. Wilde could hear the agitation in his feet; he could see with the eyes of his heart Harris's neck grow stiff and his shoulders shift back and his anger—no his loathing—become a visual substance, an extra layer on his skin. Then Harris cleared his throat. He spoke. "I did not know. I did not believe any of the accusations. Not for a second."

Wilde raised his eyes hopefully and spoke like a stricken child. "I suppose this will make a great difference to you?"

He saw a pause on Harris's face, and his heart ticked with new alarm. The moment before, he had hope that Harris might be so good as to accept him, as to defend him afer all. But now he was frightened to hear whatever it was Harris would finally say, when this once-upon-a-time friend finally got his brains around words. Wilde readied for Harris's outrage; worse, the man's disgust. He felt his shoulders turn inward, anxious for the verbal blow. But then Harris shocked him.

"I won't lie, Oscar. This dumbfounds me. But it has no effect on my friendship for you. I just think the battle is going to be a great deal harder now."

Wilde could not see for the tears that started; not tears for Harris' last sentence, but the one before that. Tears from the same instinct that made him want to hug the man, right then, on the street. But he only nodded, said some sort of thank you, and managed to move his feet again, in whatever way they had been ordained to go.

* * * *

How much more frustrating now that it should be Frank Harris ranting at him, Harris claiming that in prison Wilde should have learned to not like men anymore; that he should have internalized society's conventions so completely as to be able to adhere to them without trauma. Frank Harris, who had been so profligate in his pleasure-seeking among women and girls that it was rumored he was a sex fiend. This Frank Harris thought Wilde could and should somehow have turned dry.

Wilde sat up straighter on the couch; he controlled his voice. "So if I understand your position correctly, because the law did not approve of who I admired, I should simply switch my admirations."

Harris looked stung. "Stated that way it sounds flippant. There's nothing flippant about this."

"Of course it's flippant. What else could it be?"

"That you learn from your mistakes?"

"I have learned a very great deal from my 'mistakes.' More than you can imagine. For two whole years since I was let go from Reading I've done nothing but learn about people's low opinions of me. People who've never so much as exchanged a single word with me. As well as people I once regarded as friends. Even close friends. I've learned how easily it is to cut someone when they've already been cut by everyone else. I've learned how easy it is for human beings to toss cruelty on top of cruelty; and how hard it is, apparently, to do the opposite."

Harris said nothing for a moment. He crossed the room with a guilty step and settled again in the chair, his mouth set, his face grim. He took a moment, then said, "I know that all of that is true, Oscar. I know it is. I've witnessed it. And I'm sorry, but I don't know if you've learned enough."

Wilde stiffened. Here he thought he'd finally convinced the hardheaded magazine man. Apparently that was not to be. Well then, make him say it. Make him say exactly what he meant. Every obnoxious vowel. "Such as?"

"Isn't it obvious?"

"Such as?"

"You're being lazy. Mentally lazy."

"You're being vague. So again—such as?"

"Such as your damned obsession for boys!" There it was. Harris stayed in his seat, but his face was newly coiled and his voice thin. "I gave you this escape from Paris. To think. To rest. To start writing again, blast you. In Paris you told me you were too depressed. And too distracted. Too overwhelmed. You said if you could get clear for three months or so maybe you could produce work again." Harris leaned forward. "We're here to give you those months. We're here now—in the south—and as far as I can tell you've done nothing but linger at the docks and try to meet boys."

"And that surprises you?"

Harris stopped; again, his face fell. Even further this time. "Yes, actually, it does."

"Because prison should have cured me."

"I didn't say that."

"But you meant it."

Harris said nothing. There was nothing, after all, he could say, accept to admit that is indeed exactly what he meant.

"A patriot put in prison for loving his country," Wilde said, "loves his country. And a poet put in prison for loving boys loves boys."

He stared hard at Frank Harris, harder than he ever had, because this fact Harris needed to understand, even if it had to be driven in with hammer and nail. If they were to continue to coexist in this hotel, to continue to pass weeks together exiled from their respective homes, Harris had to give up the expectation that Wilde might change. It was true that he was not writing. But to think that he would travel to the Mediterranean and not talk to boys, to think that forbidding him from so doing would make it more likely he could begin to work again... that was laughable. Also an insult.

Harris must have sensed that he lost the point because he began to tick and agitate in the seat, fritter away his glance this way and that, anywhere but Wilde's face, as if looking for something he left behind the last time he traveled to Monte Carlo. Yes, Wilde thought at him, you did leave something behind. *It's called rational sympathy.*

Finally, Harris's head came back. He looked in Wilde's eyes and said, "Then that's your choice, Oscar. You are my friend one way or another. It's your life to spend as you choose, despite everything that has happened."

"When has it not been my choice?"

Harris blinked; in so blank-eyed a fashion Wilde wasn't sure the man heard him. "I just hope—" Harris started "I mean—I wouldn't want to see you get into any more trouble. You've suffered enough trouble for one lifetime."

"No protest from me on that score. But you need to realize that I do not go around deliberately courting trouble. I am who I am, and thus be who I am. Courting trouble is the last thing on my mind. Have I ever struck you as a rebel or a criminal or an anarchist?"

"No, I dare say you're more conservative than I am. Perhaps by much."

Wilde smiled and bowed in recognition of the insight. Now this was the Frank Harris who had been his friend back in London. "On the other hand, I like to think I am also the kind of person who accepts what happens to him with the best of grace."

Harris nodded slowly. "'No protest from me on that score'," he parroted. "But you're also the laziest son of a bitch I've ever met."

Wilde laughed; now he was enjoying this tête-à-tête. "I'm not lazy, Frank, as much as profoundly out of energy. My body feels leaden. My heart is an echo chamber." Okay, so now he was being too theatrical. But the man deserved it.

Harris's hazel eyes went flat, tinged at the ends with disappointment. "I thought if you'd stayed here for a while and rested you would feel like working again. I thought that something must strike your fancy. You almost promised me that, Oscar."

This was true enough as it went. Wilde had in fact been sick of the capital, sick of the constant rejections by Englishmen and Frenchmen he'd once flattered with the designation of "friend," sick of Bosie's distant scoffing, sick most of all at the heart-heaviness that had set in as soon as his Gilbert had left for Africa. Wisely or not, he had confessed his bitter feelings to Harris, declaring that he was too heartbroken to write in Paris. Harris, with typical American pragmatism, had, instead of just listening to Wilde's complaints, which is all Wilde had wanted, immediately declared his willingness to remove Wilde from Paris. Problem solved! Indeed it was a kind offer; Wilde could not deny it. But in exchange for his generosity Harris wanted some output in return. A play or a long poem or perhaps even a novel. *For Jesus's sake, Oscar,* Harris had sawed with his odd combination of vocalizations, *at least scratch out a sonnet once in a while*. But Frank Harris had a lot yet to learn about Wilde's inner motivations.

"Almost, yes. But there's a great gulf between an almost-promise and an actual one. A gulf mostly filled with misinterpretation and coercion."

He watched as Harris's face went sour all over again. The man leaned far into his chair, dejected.

"Actually, something has struck me, Frank. I've got a subject and even some verses."

"What?" Harris came forward, his shoulders alive, his face alert, his eyes shifted in an instant to bright lemony-green. "What is it? Tell me. May I read it?"

Wilde chuckled. It almost broke his heart to see the naked hope in Frank Harris's eyes. All the poor man wanted was for Wilde to scribble some lines again—any lines. And not just that, but publish them. To become *Oscar Wilde* again. But there was no hope. That Oscar Wilde was dead the moment he was told to strip off his clothes at Holloway and let himself be examined. It was a very different, sobered Oscar Wilde who, while still locked up, was able to write a bitter, one hundred page letter to Douglas that Robbie Ross had given the title *De Profundis* and floated as a next, new publication.

There was yet another Oscar who, during a slim period of anti-prison activism following his release, wrote a letter to the *Daily Chronicle* complaining of the state of affairs inside English jails and thereafter started a long, sad ballad about Reading—the poem that was the last piece of literature he'd felt compelled to finish; the poem that in some quarters was being heralded as the latest great poem of the English language but to Wilde was little more than an exercise of funneling his sadness into a fictional episode. As he'd written *Reading Gaol* he'd certainly had ambitions for the poem—high ambitions indeed—but when he looked at it now what he felt so keenly was not the ambition but the sadness. And he knew—although he would never admit this to a soul— that the poem was decidedly not a great one. There were too many passages of naked melodrama and verses that bordered on doggerel. At best—at best—it was only a near-great work; and in that case the world would probably have been better off if he'd never written it at all. Or written a fairy story instead. For nothing is so frustrating as a piece of art that could and should have been of the highest caliber but never made it there, because the artist himself was incapable. Art that was simply bad was, by comparison, a relief.

And since? Since finishing *Reading Gaol* any Oscar Wilde who had an inclination to put pen to paper was a ghost. Or at least a fiction. Certainly not the Oscar Wilde who sat upon this too comfortable couch in an excessive hotel on the Côte d'Azur, watching hopefulness play across the face of Frank Harris.

"Well," Wilde started tentatively, "I think of it as a companion piece to my *Reading Gaol* poem."

"Really?" Harris could hardly contain himself. "Another long one? Will you finally tell the world what happened to you there?"

Wilde picked at his coat for a moment, trying to decide how better to explain this "composition," and how to avoid the masculine wrath of Harris. "I probably should have used another word than 'companion piece.' I mean in my mind they are side-by-side, more for their differences than their similarities. These latest verses are not in any way a continuation of the themes of *Reading Gaol*. Indeed, they are a counterstatement against it."

"I don't understand."

"I've been thinking about all these young lads in the fishing boats who come in off the sea every morning to hawk their catches."

Now Wilde saw cutting disappointment on Harris; perhaps even fear. "What about them?"

"They are free in the broadest sense possible. Nothing is unavailable or inconceivable to them. Their lives exist on a plane of pure joy, pure possibility, pure enthusiasm. They are free from want, free from unhappiness, free from ugliness, free from disapproval. No one in particular is watching out for them, but far from provoking danger this has liberated them; it has made the whole world of experience available to them. They are like a new typological form of humanity: beautiful, exuberant, uninhibited, open-minded."

As he waxed about these boys, Harris's expression turned more and more sour. Now Harris looked positively solemn. Solemn and dour. "They don't charge you money, do they?"

"For?"

"You know what for."

Frank Harris had a longstanding and instinctive habit of cutting to the chase. No wonder he was so indifferent to the law once he received his degree from the University of Kansas; no wonder he earned his success instead as a journalist and businessman. The law was too slow for him and too ornamental. Too many imprecise and debatable shades of meaning. Journalism was far more direct and capable of bringing quick results, quick changes of opinion. But in this instance, cutting to the chase had also led Harris astray. It didn't matter whether he gave money, or some other payment, to the boys for their "attentions." The exchange—and these verses in his head—finally wasn't about the money; it was about the love.

"No, they don't," Wilde lied.

Harris nodded once, glad for that answer. Any money Wilde carried on this trip came from Harris, and Harris, Wilde knew, would not want that money going to renters. But that was just it. These creatures were not really renters; they were just free, beautiful boys.

Wilde cleared his throat. "And I assure you, Frank, I am not the only foreign gentleman here who enjoys their company."

Harris clucked. "Oh, I don't doubt that. Not at

all." His nervous energy was back, accompanying his dislike for the subject. Any moment, Wilde guessed, Harris would be out of the chair again, waving his arms, arcing high-minded pronouncements at him from across the room. Frank Harris was not a lounger. He was a fascinating, intelligent, and good-hearted friend, but he had no capacity for taking a day—or a minute—off. Instead of getting up, Harris changed the subject. "But what about this new poem. Tell me more. Will it be as long as *Reading Gaol?*"

"Remember, it's a counterstatement not a repeat," Wilde said. "Freedom, beauty, hopefulness. Liberty instead of prison, joy instead of sorrow, a kiss instead of an execution."

"Check. And you've started on it already?"

"I have. A few verses."

"May I read them?"

"You can listen," Wilde said. Without explaining, he sat forward, straightened his chest, and tilted his chin, ready to pronounce the verses that had first come to him a week ago while he lingered on the beach waiting for the fishing boats to come in. In the days since—in stray bored moments or in the middle of finishing a bottle of champagne or nibbling on something at a café—he polished them and whittled them, replaced some of the words with others, initiated pauses where before there had been none. Although he had absolutely no ambition for them, he was perfectly happy with the verses now; even proud to let them loose into the open air. It was the first time in almost a year that he'd recited poetry at all.

At first the words scraped against his creaky throat like shots exiting a gun. But within seconds his delivery had loosened and the performance became more sonorous. Like the casings of shells that leave that gun, parts of each word fell through the air of the sitting room. They echoed a second sound to accompany their first. This, Wilde knew, was what great poetry did.

Harris listened with evident amazement and delight, his face beaming, his eyes as light and happy as if he were dancing with a beautiful sixteen-year-old. The instant Wilde finished, Harris jumped up from the chair, this time with quite a different spirit. "Superb! Those are wonderful, Oscar, very worthy of you. It reminds me of Davidson's *Ballad of a Nun.*"

"Oh, please. Davidson is so Scotch. These are not nuns but fisher boys. I am not severe with them at all."

Harris was barely listening. "This poem will need to published," he said, "just as soon as it is finished." Harris's expression was as grateful, and as unbelieving, as a man who'd bet his whole savings—his entire future life—on the number 10 while knowing there was virtually no chance it would hit. Except then it did. "How much more is there?"

"There isn't any more."

"Oh. Too bad. Soon, then? Perhaps?"

Wilde shrugged.

Harris's brows crossed, a momentary expression. "Okay, well then, let's say you give me a written copy of them—I mean what you just recited for me—and I will send them on, stir up some advance interest. If you let

me, I could even get a bidding war going between publishers."

"Frank," Wilde said.

"What?" Harris said, arms swinging. "What now?
What is it?"

Wilde considered what he was about to say and
wondered if he even should. But there seemed no other
way out. "I haven't written the verses down anywhere,
and I don't intend to. I certainly am never going to publish them. At this point in my life, I have published all I
need to and even more than the world wants. The world
is not clamoring for any more ingenious fulminations
from Oscar Wilde. Not about fisher boys. In fact, the
world wants me dead."

"That's absurd. You can't—"

"Frank, listen to me closely. It is enough for me to
have formed those words in my mind and put them in
a certain order. It is enough—more than enough—that
you liked them. I really do not feel any particular need
to go further. And even if I do, I promise you I will not
write anything down."

"But you're a writer."

"I was a writer."

"You *are* a writer. Any time you want to be; if you
will just let yourself."

"What if I choose not to?"

"That's wrong!"

"By what code?"

"By any code. The writer's code."

"It's not wrong by my code, and I'm a writer. Or

so you say."

That was it for Harris. The man's exasperation crossed a fatal line. Wilde actually saw Harris's left cheek tic before he opened his mouth and let loose his blast.

"Then what are we doing here, Oscar? Why I am paying for you to have a respite from Paris—from all that was depressing you there—from the worries and the attitudes that you said kept you from writing. You told me back in Paris that you can 'only sing in the sunshine, when you're happy.' It's been, what, four weeks of sunshine, and you're telling me that not only have you not written anything, you absolutely refuse to?"

"That is so."

"Then what am I paying for! For you to sit around and grow obese again from champagne and slowness?"

Ouch. Wilde lowered his eyes. That one hurt. It hurt because it was true. He couldn't ignore the mirror in the morning. He could not not see the expanding girth of his waist and the horror of his foggy, hungover eyes. He could not not see it. It was just that by midday he always felt better. And he thought he'd been hiding his fat fairly well.

"You can not write all you want in Paris," Harris said. "You can not write and drink too much and borrow dinners and scare your friends perfectly well there. You're an expert at it. But everything we do here is on my dime. And I don't have to pay for it anymore if I don't want to."

"No, you don't," Wilde said, in a tone he made purposefully and disingenuously playful. "That is exactly correct."

Harris collapsed into the chair again, beaten, angry, festering. His attempt at guilt-mongering had obvious-ly not landed the blow he'd hoped for. Now he needed another gambit. Wilde watched him try to find one and come up short. "But I want you to write," Harris whined.

Wilde chuckled. He moved his head. "Oh, dear Frank. You do indeed. And I am flattered."

Harris sat forward. "Don't be flattered, be embar-rassed. Be abashed. Be humiliated. Whatever the emo-tion is that will let you pick up a pen."

"You know, if you could only let me talk instead of bothering me to write I should be quite happy."

"It's not the talk I care about," Harris blurted, but then he seemed to realize the lie in that statement. Af-ter all, what had they been doing for the last four days? "Well, not as much as I care about the writing."

It was not going to end. As long as Frank Harris was by his side and footing the bill, this persecution was not going to end. "Frank, perhaps we should spend the day packing. For the return trip."

"Stop it," Harris practically shouted. "I retract what I said a moment ago. We're not returning to Paris. *You* are not returning to Paris. We are staying here, and we'll have a fine time, and maybe you will want to write again. Maybe."

Wilde nodded, relieved. "Maybe," he muttered, as a gift. He didn't actually want to go back. Not if Gil-bert was not there. If Harris was willing to let him, he'd much rather remain in the south. He didn't want to say so to Harris—because it sounded disastrously melodramatic—but he felt that going back to Paris meant going to his death. He'd spent whole months and even years in that city, on top of all those long visits he used to make in the old, active days. He knew Paris too well, and it him. There was not much left for him to do there but die. And if he were going to die he'd rather do it in Nice or La Napoule. He'd rather do it among these fisher boys.

CHAPTER FIVE

Nogent-sur-Marne. August, 1899.

As he stepped down the hallway of the second floor of the Hotel des Coignard, only yards from the door of the room Douglas had rented for the second half of the summer, Wilde had the vertiginous sense of not knowing what he should anticipate—or, rather, sensing, like a cat hearing things through its whiskers, a coming reaction that could likely be hurtful. Although he had no confirmation of this, he'd had the distinct feeling lately that Douglas was spending so much time at Nogent not to escape the heat of the capital but to hide out from him. A paranoid notion, of course; but in fact Nogent was only six miles from Paris. How much cooler could it be? Not much at all, it turned out, based on the oppression Wilde felt on his skin on his walk here from the train station.

So was Douglas hiding out? Could Bosie really be that brutish? In the first half of the summer, he'd seen Douglas more accidentally than intentionally. There was the occasional visit to Avenue Kleber, the irregular night out. But such reunions had been growing more infrequent for months, even before Wilde's trip to the south with Harris, and when he did happen to see Douglas, what was apparent was that the torrid emotional intensity of their once upon a time life was extinct. More than ever, their meetings were simply strained, as if Douglas had decided he'd been doing nothing but humoring an old man all these years. They did not openly argue, but what they did do was possibly worse: talk about nothing, or sometimes barely talk at all. The £70 Wilde once loaned Douglas for furniture was no longer discussed. Forgotten history. As was the money promised to Wilde by Douglas's mother for "standing up to that monster," meaning her ex-husband, her pledge to restore the substantial amount that the trial and verdict had cost Wilde. No, he'd received precious little from Douglas or his mother, even though all of Europe knew that the Queensberry affair—and the prison sentence that resulted—had ruined Wilde financially, and in about every other way too.

Wilde noted these changes in his relationship with Douglas; he checked them off in a mental chart he kept of the fluctuations in their history. But he did not exactly despair. Not exactly. Not yet. One never knew what the future held, especially with Bosie Douglas. With Douglas, it seemed, as soon as you were certain of the emotional facts, the emotional facts changed. And it was no longer romance Wilde was after anyway. Wilde had a different beautiful young man to fixate on these days; perhaps he could fixate on Gilbert even more with him being absent in Tunisia. What he would have liked—no, what he badly needed—from Bosie Douglas wasn't romantic fervor but a friendship leavened by lifelong and continuing affection, by a mutual love of poetry, and by a common stance against a prejudiced world.

In the beginning of July, Douglas had mentioned he was taking a hotel room in Nogent for several weeks, paid for by his mother when she heard from him that no one who mattered lingered in Paris during the worst of the summer. "I won't be around as much," Douglas had warned Wilde then, "but you can drop by if you care to." Wilde had a hard time reading the sincerity of Douglas's suggestion, but finally he decided to just take it at face value. And thus this morning, for the first time, he'd acted on the invitation. Because, whether Douglas had meant him to or not, Wilde had a pressing reason to seek out Bosie; he had a vitally necessary concern: the soon-to-be return of his soldier boy. It seemed to Wilde that Gilbert had been gone from France for generations, even if it was only six months. On certain days Wilde's longing had been so bad, his pain so acute, Wilde wondered if his body had started to turn on itself. But now, as best as Wilde could tell, Gilbert was due back in Paris any day. In fact, he should have arrived already.

Gilbert's letter in June had predicted a mid-July return. Wilde had written back immediately—a short, bright note that hid from Gilbert the pain he'd been feeling and instead expressed his eagerness for their reunion. But Wilde never received a reply. The same happened with a follow-up letter. At present, Wilde had suffered through six and a half weeks of silence, and he was mortally worried. He had not heard news of any military actions undertaken by the French army in North Africa. But he could not help but wonder if Gilbert had somehow been hurt—perhaps critically—and hospitalized. How else to explain the young man's continued absence—and his silence? It was true that Gilbert was young and naïve in the ways of Uranian love. Conceivably, Gilbert had not realized how the imminence of his return to Paris would set Wilde off in an anticipatory riot: daydreams of assignations, of evenings together and gifts given; a swirling fantasy of sighs and tears and pronouncements about true love. During one fervent week in July he'd had to masturbate hourly to contain his excitement. But then... no news.

It was this dread that had finally driven him to seek out Douglas in Nogent. Douglas, being far better connected than Wilde to the upper levels of British society, including some men in the diplomatic corps, might actually have heard something about French soldiers in Tunisia or elsewhere. If nothing else, Douglas would be able to understand Wilde's predicament. Douglas had met Gilbert before and been impressed. He'd stared hard at the boy—with that keenness only Douglas could summon—and later said something off-hand to Wilde about his "luscious find."

Of course, it was impossible not to be impressed by the sweet-faced, dark-eyed child with a soul far too tender for soldiering. Gibert had no business being in the army, really, except that he took well to duty and seemed to have nothing else to do; and that his mother, according to Gilbert, had felt that he needed "toughening." From his one interaction with the woman, Wilde guessed Gilbert was telling the truth. What Gilbert's mother failed to appreciate was that her son's less "tough" qualities— Gilbert's innocence, his lack of ken—were at the same time his most important and useful and endearing ones. Most of the time, Gilbert seemed not nineteen-years-old but more like thirteen. Or eleven. A more precious and physically beautiful age.

As he raised his hand to rap on the door of Bosie's room, it struck Wilde that maybe Douglas was in Nogent for reasons not of place but person. Some new love he did not want to share with anyone. A poet? Or a painter? Or a dressmaker? Someone full of intriguing and unstoppable artistic promise? Probably not. Bosie had never cared to talk literature with the boys he courted. Bosie more or less just wanted to fuck them. The more of them the better. The only person, in fact, who could ever claim a hold on Bosie's mind was Wilde himself. It was how they came to love each other in the first place, although finally even poetry had not been able to keep them happy. Was it possible that Douglas's escape to so miserably middlebrow and closeted an outpost as Nogent-sur-Marne was because he'd finally found Wilde's replacement? Could it be as simple as that? Dread or no, vertiginous or not, Wilde took in a breath, held it, and knocked.

The door came open almost immediately, as if the person inside had been anticipating his arrival. But what he saw next was no face of welcome or enthusiasm or even affectionate surprise. He saw the pale cheeks, thick nose, and sky blue eyes of Alfred Douglas, his lips pursed and brows raised in a stunned expression.

"Oscar," Douglas said.

It was perfectly apparent that Douglas was not dressed for visitors; in fact, he was barely dressed at all. He wore only a beige dressing gown, not tied off very tightly, so that a large swatch of his chest, almost to his stomach, was exposed. Beneath the gown Douglas was quite obviously naked. Wilde—who had lain next to and lain upon and kneeled before the naked Douglas more times than he could count—could actively smell the man's skin.

"Bosie," Wilde started. He kept his eyes strictly on Douglas's face and pushed the encounter forward. "I'm sorry it's taken me so long to come. Really no good reason for me to put you off. But it occurred to me this morning that it was time to make due. I hope you'll forgive the delay." It was better, Wilde sensed, to withhold the request for information about Gilbert. Keep Douglas off the scent. Besides, Wilde knew exactly how unannounced this visit was. If he couched it as the overdue rendering of a favor, Bosie was less likely to be angry.

Douglas stared at him with a gaze of pure befuddlement that was not like him at all. "Did I ask you to visit me?" A genuine question.

"Of course you did."

"I don't remember that."

"Maybe not in so many words."

"Which words then?"

So Douglas was angry, after all. The signs were all there: the flush in his cheek, the stricture of his shoulders, the way his forehead seem to grow taller and more angular, the light that went out in his eye.

"You gave me the address."

"When?"

"I don't know. Right after you found the place. How else would I have known where to come?"

"I have no idea, Oscar," Douglas said, his voice rising with each word. "Maybe you asked one of those friends of yours that you beg money from? Maybe you demanded from one of them to know where I was?"

Wilde really could not fathom this resentment. "You told me the address. I think I even asked you to write it down for me. And you did—on an envelope, from your brother's letter."

Until that moment, Wilde had forgotten the envelope. In fact, he had no idea where the envelope might be now. He had never consulted it; the address had just stayed etched in his mind from the moment Douglas spoke it, prodding him to visit. Presently, he saw Douglas's eyes cloud; the man was staring over Wilde's shoulder, but not at anything in the hallway, not anything physical at all. "I do remember the envelope," Douglas said, as if surprised by the fact.

"Is Oscar here?" Wilde heard someone say in French, a voice as musical as it was innocent, in fact musical for being innocent. All of his heart surged upward through his throat and dizzily toward his head; until he had the thought that followed his recognition of the voice and simultaneously he saw the telltale barb in Douglas's eye. Like a street tough anticipating a brawl.

"Is it Oscar?" the voice inside said.

"So," Wilde said quietly "that's how it is, is it?"

Douglas stood as tall as his diminutive height allowed. "That's exactly how it is. Do you want to come in and say hello?"

Douglas pushed back on the door and moved to the

side. A portal of space opened that Wilde suddenly did not want to pass through. But Douglas was giving him no choice. He could barely feel the bottoms of his feet and the ends of his fingers as he took his first doomed steps across the threshold. He knew what he would see when he looked to the left, and then he saw it: Maurice Gilbert, naked as a baby, relaxed on the couch, his skin so olive as to be almost negroid, his chest and shoulders bare of any hair except that adorable little growth right at his sternum, his lopsided grin so trusting, his eyes as beautiful as chocolate. Wilde felt a surge of blood in his head, and his vision wavered.

"We were just having coffee," Douglas said behind him, in French. Wilde thought he heard the tone of a taunt. But then he realized that indeed a table stood before the couch and on it was a tray with a breakfast service: a pot of coffee, a smaller pot of warm milk, two porcelain cups, a basket containing two petite baguettes and a few croissants, a porcelain bowl with a thick wedge of morning-softened butter, two knives. Taunt or no taunt, this part of it was true. But the question, of course, was not if they were sharing coffee, but what they were doing before they shared coffee. It was a question that Wilde knew he should not ask himself, because it would come to no good. Besides, just looking at the two men the answer was apparent.

Score another victory for the bitch.

"It is wonderful to see you again," Gilbert said, without irony. He stretched his arms toward the ceiling for emphasis.

"Bonjour, Maurice," Wilde said, but he did not move. He just stood there wavering, until he realized that both Bosie and Gilbert were looking at him as if they expected him to say more. "How long have you been back?"

Gilbert pondered the question strenuously, rubbing his chin. "Twenty days, I think."

Wilde closed his eyes. He opened them again. "Twenty days?"

Gilbert waved a hand. "Plus ou moins."

Wilde had to be very careful about what he said next and how he said it. Douglas already owned the morning's victory. Wilde did not want to pile satisfactions on top of it. He spoke calmly, and in the most indifferent pitch of voice he could muster. "I had thought you might tell me that you'd returned."

Gilbert's silky clear cheeks lined with confusion. "Mr. Bosie told me he would take care of it."

"Oh," Wilde said. "I see."

"Didn't you tell Oscar I was coming back, Bosie?"

Douglas crossed to the couch. With a breezy air he took a place close to Gilbert. "It must have slipped my mind. Sorry, Oscar. As you can tell, Maurice is back. At least for now." Douglas turned to Gilbert and beamed a smile at him. He reached forward then and poured some coffee into a cup, followed by a long pour of the milk. He handed the cup to Gilbert, who nodded his head gratefully.

"For now?" Wilde managed to say. He had yet to move an inch closer to the couch.

"Yes," Gilbert said wistfully. He sipped his coffee. "They have told my company that we will be shipped to Réunion next."

"Réunion?"

Gilbert shrugged.

"Tough duty," Douglas said, smirking.

"When are you leaving?" Wilde said.

"About a week. I must report to headquarters on the 22nd."

"A week?"

Gilbert frowned. "Yes, it is terrible. Tunisia was so long and insufferable. So hot. And now it's off again, away from home."

"For how long?"

Gilbert's frown went deeper, almost to his chin. He raised a helpless hand. "That is the thing. They will not tell us. I am becoming afraid that we may be gone a very long time."

"Yes, to Réunion," Douglas emphasized. Gilbert drank more coffee and smiled.

"I..." Wilde started. Gilbert turned to him expectantly. He was so beautiful, and still so innocent, so oblivious to what was going on, that Wilde's heart surged with affection, despite himself. Despite this. "I thought that when you came back to Paris, you would be in Paris. Not Nogent." He did not check to see how Douglas reacted.

"Me too," Gilbert said gaily. "Me too, Oscar. I had not planned on this at all. But Mr. Bosie wrote me a few days before I left, and he said I should come to Nogent instead. Much more comfortable, he said. More

room than my mother's apartment. And I could be independent, from her, you know. Which is very good. He
would cover all my expenses, and we could still visit all
my friends in Paris, anytime I wanted. Including you."

"Indeed," Wilde mouthed. "How kind."

"Yes," Gilbert exclaimed. "We've been over several
times to try to see you at your hotel. But each time we go,
you are not there. You are never there it seems."

This was unfathomable. For nearly a month, as
he'd longed for and anticipated Gilbert's return, Wilde
had been almost nowhere but his hotel. His new one,
that is: the Hotel de l'Alsace. In June he'd finally been
chased out of the Marsollier for failure to pay his bill;
he'd been rescued only at the last minute by the owner
of the Alsace, Rene Dupoirer, who not only paid off his
debt to the Marsollier but gave him a room at the Alsace
for free. And Douglas knew about this. He'd met Douglas in the city for lunch one day and told him where he'd
moved and why. Douglas had even followed him back to
the Alsace to declaim about its horrible state. How can
you live here? It's abominable. Not twice, but seven times
Douglas had commented about the place. Douglas could
not possibly have forgotten the whereabouts of Wilde's
new residence.

"How many times have you come?" Wilde said.

"Oh, heavens," Gilbert said. "Four? Five?"

"Five? I don't understand."

"I thought it was your place, Oscar," Douglas interjected. "Maybe I had it wrong. I know you've moved. But
you were never there. I can swear to that."

One does not just "forget" where a friend lives. Not in Paris.

"I am sure I wasn't," Wilde said. But Douglas did not catch his tone. He was too busy leaning in toward Gilbert and licking the younger man's ear.

Gilbert giggled and pulled away. He touched Douglas's cheek.

"Not too much tongue among the solider boys, I bet," Douglas said.

Gilbert's face dropped; abashed. "Do not be so certain. More happens in the army than you think."

Douglas chortled and faced Wilde, an old-timey fun-loving look on his face, such as he used to wear when they caroused through the lower end of London together. "Now that's one spot we never thought to look into, Oscar. An army post."

Wilde grimaced a lookalike smile and stared at his feet.

"What matters though," Gilbert declared, "is that you are here. We finally found you. Or you found us. When we gave up looking for you, you came looking for us." The soldier's boy smile was so broad it practically broke Gilbert's cheeks.

Wilde could barely stand to see it: the smile, the man. The beautiful young man sitting there, not even caring to cover up his cock, the cock Wilde had thought about for months but which now belonged to Bosie Douglas. Once upon a time he and Douglas had shared boys. But not in a very long time. Not now.

"How is your bicycle these days, Maurice?" Even

he could hear the hopelessness in his voice.

"Oh." Gilbert frowned. "Bad news, I'm afraid. My mother said it was too big for her to keep, so she set it outside the door, in the hallway." Wilde winced. "Someone stole it the next day."

"Yes. Of course they did."

He had never seen Gilbert act embarrassed, but that was the expression he showed now: palms in the air, a blush in his dark cheek, a bad, failed attempt at a smile on his face. The look did not suit the boy at all. It only made him look a puerile clown.

"I wish I could have brought it with me to Tunisia," Gilbert continued, "but you know in the army they don't just let soldiers keep bicycles."

"I think I told you that," Wilde said. "The first time."

When we were in bed together.

Another queasy smile from Gilbert. "You did?"

"I did."

A guilty shrug. "Anyway—so it's gone now."

"Why don't you have some coffee, Oscar," Douglas said airily, "since you've come all this way. We do have a luncheon date soon, but we can spare a few minutes on you." His smile was so shiny clean it would have been hard for the uninitiated to see the evil in it. Funny, on his way over on the train, he had found himself wondering how Bosie's book project was coming. He had been impressed—shocked even—by the quality of the poems Douglas had read to him and Ross months earlier. But they had not spoken of poetry since. He had determined to ask Douglas about it straight away. Now he didn't care if Douglas's entire literary corpus sunk to the bottom of the sea.

"Yes, come on," Gilbert said. "Please sit down. Tell me what you have been doing since I left for Tunisia."

Wilde sighed and moved to the chair to the side of Gilbert's end of the couch. He looked desultorily at the coffee tray without the slightest desire for a sip. "I went south with a friend named Frank Harris," Wilde said quietly. "He's an American citizen, but he lives in London for now. He comes over to Paris frequently. You don't know him. I've never introduced you."

"Frank Harris," Douglas groaned. "Is he still sounding off to the world?" Douglas reached for one of the baguettes, broke it like someone snapping a chicken's neck. He lathered it with a smear of butter.

"He is."

Douglas bit hard into one end of the roll, while simultaneously he wagged his head up and down. After he'd managed to choke down the mouthful, he said, "Frank Harris always did think he was superior. He used to look at me like he smelled a dead animal at the foot of the wash basin."

Now Wilde could not help but smile. "I wasn't aware of that, Bosie."

"Well, he did."

"What does this man do with himself," Gilbert asked, "that he gets between you and Mr. Bosie, my two closest friends in Paris?"

Looking into Gilbert's ingénue face, Wilde thought

not of Frank Harris but of Ross, traveling at that moment, elsewhere on the continent. Ross had met Gilbert before the solider left for Africa and Wilde for the south. Of course Ross had fallen instantly in love. What unisexual didn't when faced with the dark-skinned beauty, the tender mouth, and sweet simplicity of a Maurice Gilbert? But Ross had managed to keep his dignity. He'd shaken Gilbert's hand with an almost studied indifference and proceeded to ignore the boy for the rest of the conversation. But Wilde knew Robbie. He'd seen the look in Ross's eye, the alarm on his small but expressive forehead. Good god, Ross would be chewing on glass if he knew that Bosie Douglas of all people was sleeping with Maurice Gilbert. Worse, that Douglas had stolen Gilbert right out from underneath Wilde's distracted, pining gaze.

"Frank Harris is completely transparent," Wilde said flatly. "He feels what he feels and says what he believes. No matter how infuriating those beliefs may be, at least they are all out in the open. He has no secret plans or hidden resentments. He does not walk around figuring how to foment separation between loved ones." Douglas made a noise. "So I would suggest, Maurice, that you put Frank Harris out of your mind entirely. Certainly out of your resentments."

"Done!" Gilbert declared, with a broad smile and a wave of his free arm. Then he tipped his coffee cup back and drank the contents as only a soldier could. "That was easy," he said when he brought the cup down.

"He'll never be out of my resentments," Douglas said, tearing off another hunk of baguette. "He was always against me. And he was always trying to take credit for everything."

Wilde looked at his old lover, the object of his obsession, the keeper of his heart, the tutor of his corruptions. He thought to say something to Bosie about charity, but decided there wasn't any point. Instead, he said, "Frank Harris might be surprised at the depth of your loathing. I'm not sure the feeling is mutual."

Douglas's head came up, a fierce bit of questioning in his blue eyes. Then he shrugged. All three of them went silent. In the long pause of the moment, it seemed that even Gilbert could understand how tense, how wrong the air was, how charged with unspoken accusations and particulars of debate. Wilde could swear he heard a ticking noise like an old clock but could see none in the room. Perhaps the very molecules of the air had become so tight as to crack in little pulses. Or maybe he was just hearing the countdown to his doom. He knew that he should go. There was no point in his remaining except to put off the horror of the lonely train ride back. That, he knew, would be nothing but a devastation of tears.

"I should warn you, Oscar," Douglas said in a different voice: more neutral, more clinical. "That I have determined to try a different tack with my father."

Wilde's hands went cold. "Your father?" He really could not imagine what this might mean. For as long as he could remember, Alfred Douglas had despised and criticized his father, almost to the point of derangement. As far as Wilde knew, the two had not spoken since before the three trials in 1895.

"I think it's safe to say that me being unkind to him has gotten us nowhere, either of us. I mean him or me."

"Unkind? But he had me sent to prison."

Douglas actually smiled. "Of course, he did. And I was furious at him afterwards. You know that. You know what I said about him. In public, what I said about him. But it's been four years. And he's actually not in the best of health. And so perhaps I should try to turn the page with the old crank. For my sake—and for his."

It was difficult for Wilde to even speak; he'd gone completely numb, like a man after a paralytic stroke. Maybe he'd just had one. He didn't actually know that if he told his body to move it would obey him.

"I wrote to mother, and she agrees with me. She says it's gone on too long."

"Your mother does?"

"That's right," Douglas said. "So I'm all set. Plans made. After I see Maurice off in a week or so, I'm heading back to London to speak with Father. I'm actually starting to look forward to it."

Wilde's head made a tiny nodding—or was it shaking?—motion. When he realized what he was doing he stopped.

"It has been very hard on him, you know."

"Hard," Wilde muttered.

"The death of Francis made him crazy.. If not for that, I'm not sure he would have hounded us at all."

Wilde had no reply to give.

"Edith says that the one time she introduced her

husband to him, father treated the man so rudely that she refuses to see him anymore. Not that she would be inclined to anyway. And he hasn't been able to talk to Percy since I can't remember when. Those two are on worse terms than even father and I are. Then we ever were. They really cannot stand one another. And you know, too, father's without a woman right now. He's been without a companion since the annulment with Ethel Weeden."

Wilde found that with each successive word from Douglas his left hand jerked with an inexplicable tremor.

"So, queer as it may be," Douglas continued, "it appears that I am all the family he has. And I think that's sad." There was anything but sadness in Douglas's voice. "Besides, what good has it done me to be divorced from him this long? What did I ever get out of that?"

Nothing, of course. Douglas had gained exactly nothing from taunting his father and avoiding him, publically disowning him, virtually egging him on. Insisting that Wilde take the man to court and press a libel case. Expressing as his most sincere wish that his father be arrested and made to serve time. Wilde never understood the point of all that animosity when they were in the middle of it. Predictably, Douglas had received nothing as a result, either in emotional satisfaction, public exoneration, or financial recompense. It had all been a sad tragic-comedy of misfire and bad aim. But Wilde could not help but approach the question differently: What did I lose, Bosie?

Douglas poured himself some more coffee and

milk, reclined on the couch, sipped tidily. "I know this seems like a bit of a turnaround, but the truth is I've been contemplating it for several months. And, like I said, mother agrees with me that it's a good idea."

Wilde found his gaze fixed on the white porcelain coffee pot. Somehow it maintained that fierce, unblemished exterior—so white as to be sunlight—and yet for hours every day it held a steaming liquid concoction; a toxic black color.

"This is the first I've heard of it. Yet you say you've been thinking about it for months."

Douglas smiled, an attempt at easiness, but Wilde saw the barbs at the ends. "Am I supposed to report all my thoughts to you?"

"You don't in any case."

Douglas chuckled. He was about to reply when Gilbert said to Douglas in a loud voice, "If you are trying to be friends again with your father, does this mean you will need to leave Paris?"

Douglas reached a hand over and patted Gilbert's knee. Then he reached in further and gave Gilbert's cock a squeeze. Gilbert chuckled and pulled away. "You stupid child," Douglas said. "Of course I need to leave Paris. Father lives in London. I have to go to London if I want to see him."

"No," Gilbert countered, "I mean, will you be leaving Paris for good?"

Bosie's blinked: once, twice. His face was a blank. "It's hard to say how long I'll be gone. But I expect by the time you return from Réunion—if you return from

Réunion— I'll be back on Avenue Kleber again. I don't have any other place." Douglas spread his smile out wide. "And I will be eagerly anticipating you. All of you." This last phrase he spoke only to Gilbert. Gilbert smiled again, relieved and happy.

Without a word, Wilde stood. He rotated on the balls of his feet, like some dumb industrial machine operating on a timer, and took a halting first step. He had stayed too long, and it had gotten worse. He knew it would, and it did. It had become as bad as his imagination could invent. No, worse actually. These days, the fact of his life put his imagination to shame. No wonder he didn't see the point in exercising it much.

He did not know if either Douglas or Gilbert realized that he was walking away from them. Behind him he heard Douglas raise his pitch and angle his voice so that, whether intentionally or unintentionally, it arched across the space of the room in a killing parabola that ended at the door.

"To be honest, though, Maurice, sometimes I think I am done with Paris. Yes, it is lovely; it's astonishing. The most beautiful city in the world. But, you know, it's also filled with some of the most useless people. Posers and floaters and riffraff. I don't understand where these people come from or where they go. For now I am happy to take this little suite in Nogent with you, among people who actually do things, and only see the people I want to see in Paris when I want to see them."

"Yes, yes," Gilbert murmured unctuously. "I can see that. I can see the wisdom there, Mr. Bosie."

CHAPTER SIX

Rome. St. Peter's Basilica. January, 1900.

As soon as the others knelt, so did he. Having come this far, there was no point in resisting. If the unlikely junket were to have any meaning at all, it would come through submission. Wilde lifted his gaze from the marbled floor of the Gregorian Chapel and offered it instead to the old man. At 89, standing before the group of twenty or so hurriedly assembled devotees, Pope Leo XIII looked like an enchanted being out of a fairy story: a wizened, gently smiling figure, some sweet-hearted, old-souled jinn, one who could not be other than kind to despairing humans; his pointy, octagenarian shoulders disappeared beneath the covering of his cassock and mozzetta; the exaggerated contours of his beautiful bald head made only more apparent by the snow-white zucchetto resting lightly on the back of his skull.

For a moment the spell was broken as Leo proceeded toward them with half-steps that seemed less the carefree gait of a supernatural power, less even than the natural stride of a man in his declining years, and instead like consciously planned movements intended to keep him from falling. Nor was his face that of some ageless god-like spirit: narrow, ghost-bony, so paper-white as to be harrowing, unbalanced by the heft of that wide, prominent nose—the same one he'd had since his name was Vincenzo Pecci and he lived in Carpineto—also by those extravagant ears, uniquely long and attached so far back on his head as to seem inhuman. And yet somehow when one was looking at his face, all one saw was his dark, gentle eyes, beaming with love, beaming more than ever with love, and his smile: that small, knowing, serene expression. A face that signaled both a genie's charismatic abilities and a saint's selfless purity.

Like any faithful priest, Leo had spent his whole adult life denying certain pleasures of the body, with the expected result for that body: a curved spine, a skeletal face, an overly careful walk, a thin and deteriorating frame. Leo's body, Wilde told himself, had had its revenge. At the same time, it was impossible not to recognize what those years of denial had endowed him with: a beatific glow, warm and liquid and benevolent. It blazed through his eyes. Not doddering, no. Reggie Turner, Wilde knew, would call it doddering. But Wilde knew doddering. One could see doddering anywhere, especially in the back alleys of Rome. Leo's softness of expression had nothing to do with an impaired mentality, only spiritual purity. His mind was obviously still sharp. Indeed, when the Pope drew to a stop and gazed out upon them, his face wore a delighted, humorous expression, as if he was geared up for some wisecracking as soon as this solemn ceremony was done.

"*Benvenuti a tutti*," the Pope said. Then he repeated the phrase in French, in German, and in English. "Welcome, everyone." He took two more mindful steps, moving farther from the grand altar behind him—the altar of Our Lady of Succor, embellished with the most extraordinary opulent stone work Wilde had ever seen—and closer to the kneeling group. These people struck Wilde as mostly local: ordinary Romans, obviously devout. Their pinched and frowning expressions, worried eyes, and weathered hair would give them away as everyday faithful even if they weren't dressed in workman's clothes and banal dresses. The women wore black lace veils over their heads; the men had obviously made a point to wash their faces. But otherwise, they looked themselves. Their ages spanned from mid-20s to late 60s. A handful in the group had the whiter skin, colder eyes, more formal bearing and more expensive clothing of visiting northerners: Danes or Finns or Germans or Dutch. But by an easy majority, these people did not seem like tourists. The Pope did not need to extend the courtesy of the four languages; but certain protocols, Wilde supposed, must be inviolate. And of course the custom must have come from a welcoming instinct in Leo's heart.

Who else but locals know that each morning at 8:00 on the Piazza del Popolo, an officious dark-eyed cardinal dressed in a long black robe curtained with dark red accents, a ponderous cross around his neck, and a scarlet zucchetto on his head, would appear out of a curtained black coach with twenty tickets in his hands that he was willing to sell for 200 lira apiece. Not a bad deal at all, considering that the ticket afforded you the opportunity to receive a blessing from the head of the Church of Rome, the most powerful figure in Christendom. The money raised from each day's ticket sales was supposedly distributed to different religious charities throughout Rome.

Wilde himself would not have found out about the eccentric practice if not for the unstopping nosiness of Reggie Turner. He would not be in the city at all if not for Reggie, who, needing companionship on this trip—a long overdue escape from the vivacious yet exhausting social frenzy of *The Daily Telegraph*—offered to pay Wilde's way. Despite the fact that the trip was supposed to be Turner's respite, not just from the social column he wrote but from society itself, the man couldn't help himself. No matter how far from home he ranged, Reggie exhibited the same inclination—more than that, it was a gift—for cozying up to people and for getting them to talk.

It was Reggie, exploring Rome alone while Wilde rested his legs back in the hotel, who had overheard a conversation on the Via Paolina between an old woman and her middle-aged daughter. Reggie heard something about "tickets to see the Pope" and his ears stood up straight. Reggie, being Reggie, did not hesitate to engage the two women, even given his rough Italian; and, being Reggie, he soon found out all about the early morning carriage on the Piazza del Popolo, the cardinal, the necessity to be waiting at the small door on the north side of St. Peter's with your ticket in hand when the time came for the 11:00 audience. Reggie, bless him, that big-hearted atheist, was so refined in his sensibilities as to not only not withhold these discoveries from Wilde but to hurry back to the hotel to bring Wilde news of them. Indeed, he'd appeared breathlessly inside their room that afternoon, as if he'd run the whole way up the stairs. Who knows, maybe he had. The man had no athletic prowess, but he was only twenty-nine. Wilde, meanwhile, had been lounging across his bed, trying to read the poetry of Gabriele D'Annunzio without falling asleep.

"If you show yourself on the Piazza del Popolo tomorrow morning around eight," Turner said, "you may be able to buy your way into an audience with the Pope." At the word "buy," Turner's dull blue eyes twinkled, as if this were the best joke anyone had ever told him.

It seemed so preposterous an idea all Wilde could think to say was, "But how?"

Turner, thick hands alight, his heavy jowls broadening into a smile, launched into the whole story of his discovery. Typical, and so very charming, of the man. Reggie never let ten words do the trick if one hundred-and-ten could. When Turner was finally done, Wilde still wasn't sure that his friend wasn't pulling his leg, setting up a practical joke, telling a fib to get his arse out of bed at a barely civilized hour. But Wilde couldn't resist finding out. "Then tomorrow I will be there," he said.

And so he had. It was indeed a thoroughly inhuman hour, more for Wilde than for Rome, but he had managed to arrive on the Piazza del Popolo not just on time but a half-hour early. He even willingly joined the hurly-burly elbow thrusting and hip turning and shoulder wriggling of those assembled as they struggled to earn or keep their place in a line that organized the moment someone spied the Cardinal's carriage. For his part, the Cardinal spared barely any time on this exercise: a quick escape from the carriage, a single command to bring the line into order—*immediamente*—and then the brusque distribution of the tickets as an aide gathered the necessary cash from each person. When the tickets were all gone, the Cardinal turned back without so much as a "Bless you" or a smile or a word of explanation of what to do with the tickets now that they had them. He must know, Wilde thought, that they all know. The Cardinal simply spun on his heel and began walking back to the carriage. The driver opened the Cardinal's door, he stepped up, the door was shut, and the curtain pulled. Within moments, the carriage was headed back to the Vatican.

Wilde was participating in this pursuit of a blessing partly in the spirit of a lark, but not entirely. Certainly he considered it good fun—after all the righteous vituperation he'd felt directed at him from all corners of the moralistic world—to get a blessing from the most distinguished man in the Christendom. But he also had a more pressing reason for wanting to do so. One that he had confessed to Reggie before they even arrived in the Eternal City. Wilde had not felt right in his body for some weeks now—an aching feeling that while hard to pinpoint seemed physical in nature, more specific than spiritual malaise or romantic downturn. He knew what those felt like. Its origin was somewhere inside his head but it continued into his neck and even the right-hand portion of his chest and shoulders. Sometimes he thought he felt it as low as his calves. It was worse on some days and virtually nonexistent on others, but never completely gone from his consciousness, except when he was asleep or drunk. More immediately worrisome was a rash that had developed on his right cheek. Bright red: an ugly, irritable stain. About two inches long and more than a half an inch wide. As if someone had slapped him recently and his face had still not recovered. But no one had slapped him recently. No one had ever slapped him, not even in prison—there they resorted to more brutal measures. Yet there it was: the stain.

When Turner, first arriving at Wilde's hotel room in Paris, had seen the rash, he'd been unusually alarmed. He wondered openly if Wilde had eaten something wrong. Wilde couldn't think of what that could be, since he didn't eat much of anything anymore. Not unless someone else was paying. Then Reggie speculated that maybe Wilde had rubbed against a wrong sort of plant. Something alien to Paris.

"Plant?" Wilde had guffawed. "On the Rue des Beaux Arts? On the Rue Bonaparte?"

Turner, his blunt nose curdling like a bulldog's, did not appreciate Wilde's sarcasm. But he quickly hit on another answer. "Are you keeping yourself clean, Oscar? Does this fleabag place even afford you a bath? Instead of giving you champagne maybe Dupoirer could take your clothes to the laundry."

"My, that's a kind thing to say to someone after you see them for the first time in months," Wilde had protested. Nevertheless, for Turner's sake, that afternoon he washed thoroughly in an old laundry tub Dupoirer provided him, taking care to scrub his face as busily as he could. It made no difference. The rash remained.

Now, hundreds of miles from his Paris hotel home,

inside the Gregorian Chapel, only feet from Pope Leo XIII, Wilde did not know what he should expect. In his modern heart, he knew it was rank primitivism to expect that a blessing from an old man in a robe would relieve his sickness. But in the same heart he knew that he was superstitious as a pagan, and he liked himself that way. Wilde believed utterly in signs and omens, portents and divination. He believed in natural powers broader and deeper and older than logic; and if pressed he would admit that he thought that a man, or a woman, could access that power with the right words, the right efforts, the right state of mind. It wasn't for nothing that he'd often told Ross that if he were to be any kind of Christian it would have to be a Catholic one. More than any other, the Catholic Church recognized paganism's essential truths—even as it tried to steal them. After all, why the inordinate Catholic emphasis on ritual? On mystery? On magick? And all of that was true, except that Wilde also knew he really wasn't a Christian and couldn't be; not yet, at least. But he hoped he could remain the pagan he was and still entertain the idea that a smiling eighty-nine year old with a cross around his neck could summon miracles through a bit of Latin and a raised hand.

As the Pope stood ready now to start whatever this blessing was, Wilde was shocked to find that he was holding his breath; his pulse was running; the blood was banging at the top of his forehead as if the middle of some carnal excitement. But, no, it was just anticipation. It was expectation. It was... belief. When the Pope extended an arm, Wilde saw the gathered men and women bow their head; so he did as well. He kept it bowed as Leo spoke his holy words, in a Latin cruder than Wilde would have expected for a man who'd been a priest for sixty-two years: "I bless you in the name of the Father and the Son and the Holy Ghost. If you suffer from infirmities of the body, may they be healed; if you suffer from tribulations of the spirit, may they be calmed. And may the Lord God, for the rest of your days, renew you and mount you up as if with wings of the eagle."

When the words were done, Wilde continued to kneel as Leo passed along the line of them, one by one, laying a hand on each: onto a shoulder or a neck or a crown or a hand. When the pontiff came to Wilde, Wilde could not keep himself from looking up into the old man's face. It was then he was stunned to see the passivity in those dark blue eyes, the motherly gentleness. Wilde's own eyes teared; he was afraid he might weep. The Pope smiled at him and then touched the rash on his cheek—that exact spot—with his papery hand, his fingers were so light and Wilde could barely feel them. Yet the touch felt warm all the same; heated by holy fire. The single moment seemed to go on for minutes; and then the pontiff, as if newly and differently exhausted, moved haltingly on to the next person.

When Wilde made it back to his hotel room that evening, the first thing he did was move to the mirror. For hours he'd felt an odd tingling sensation on his face, and he could not help but think he knew what it signified. He turned the gas lamp in the room on full and leaned toward the glass, but it wasn't necessary to get close. The change was immediately obvious. His rash, so red before, had dulled to a burnt brown tone—not too far from the color of a declining sunburn. And the mark, Wilde was certain, was now both skinnier and shorter. Not more than an inch long.

He turned to Turner, prostrate on the farther of the room's two beds. "My god, Reggie, it worked. I mean, it's working."

Turner looked up at him with impatient, exasperated eyes. Had he really been that trying a companion at dinner? He'd been more talkative, certainly. More opinionated. More contentious. It didn't help that the day up to that point had made Turner unusually cantankerous—while Wilde had wandered the neighborhoods of Rome, almost delirious from the Pope's touch, Turner had been rudely treated by a shopkeeper and later set upon by gypsies—but Wilde couldn't help himself. Thrilled by the day's developments, he'd gone on and on with ideas for Turner's column, when he hadn't given half a thought to newspaper columns for years, not since he'd edited The Woman's World back in the 80s. When they'd left the restaurant he'd made Turner loan him money for a new pair of shoes. (After all, his current ones barely kept the rain off his feet.) Maybe worse, he'd made Turner buy himself a new hat. The Tyrolean Reggie liked to flaunt, especially away from home, was perfectly ludicrous for an English society man, and he'd told Reggie so. "I am not a society man," Turner had responded. "I write about society men." Wilde had the incontrovertible comeback

ready: "To know them you have to be one of them."
It was a succinct formulation of the strategy Wilde had
governed his whole life by—until March, 1895. And it
was hard to argue that from a purely literary standpoint it
hadn't worked, even given the events that followed.

Turner had frowned drastically, but pulled out another handful of lira and bought a top hat Wilde liked.
"If you're going to make a statement," Wilde said, "it
might as well be an elegant one." Turner shrugged and
looked wistfully at the Tyrolean, which Wilde was now
clutching out of reach, like exhibit A. When the day had
begun, the last thing Wilde had anticipated was arguing
with Reggie Turner over headwear. But something about
meeting the pope had given him a new optimism. About
what, he didn't know exactly. But did that matter?

"What's working?" Turner said now from his bed,
as if barely able to stand to another word.

"The blessing. The pope. My rash is disappearing."

Turner sighed. "It's not. I can see the mark from
here."

"I know, but it is not as large as yesterday, and the
color is different."

Turner stared harder, gauging the size of the mark.
"Looks about the same to me. Maybe it's the light in the
room."

"It is not the light in the room. Furthermore, if you
would come here and look you would know I am right.
And need I remind you that it was you who so kindly
rushed back here from the Via Paolina to tell me I could
have an audience with His Holiness?"

Turner dropped his head to the pillow and emitted a sadder, more tired noise. Flat on his back, he stared dismally at the ceiling. "So it's 'His Holiness' now?" He spoke it with quiet resentment, but not quietly enough.

"What did you say?"

"Nothing." Turner put both fists over his eyes and dug in. Then he stopped, blinked, and rolled toward Wilde. He stared, no expression on his face. He rolled back. "I accept your statement."

"No, you don't."

"I just said I did."

"You just don't want to get off the bed."

"I don't want to have to look at your face anymore."

Wilde laughed. He laughed hard and long and wide. He wondered if he should let twenty-nine year old, bodily exhausted Reggie Turner stay there while he, forty-three year-old Oscar Wilde, newly blessed, hunted down exotic male companionship on the streets of Rome. In fact, he decided, that's exactly what he would do.

The next morning, Wilde was out of bed forty-five minutes sooner than the day before—Turner, in the other bed, was stone cold asleep—and he made it to the Piazza del Popolo a full thirty minutes earlier, so early he was one of the first hovering there, waiting for the Cardinal. In fact, he was the second in line to receive a ticket. The next day, Wednesday, he was first in line. By Wednesday evening, the mark had shrunk to about a quarter inch in length and was no more than the width of a shoestring. Best of all the color was now a faint pink, so pale it nearly merged with the natural color of Wilde's skin. And the mysterious pain on the right side of his body had so measurably decreased that Wilde no longer noticed it. Even Turner had to admit he was looking better. Although Turner—who could not under any circumstances accept the proposition that a blessing received by a religious man could overturn the imperatives of biology—credited the improvement to the Roman air and the Roman water. When Turner offered this opinion, they were seated outside at a brilliant trattoria just off the Via Urbana, catching not just lunch, but eyefuls of handsome Roman men.

"You and I both know," Wilde countered, " that the air of this city is famously polluted, even dangerous. People have caught ill and died because of the Roman air. And the only thing Roman water would do is give me gastrointestinal pain."

Turner shrugged, determined to be unconvinced. "So maybe it's the Roman fucking then."

Wilde clapped his hands. "Very good. I only wish it were so. Truth is, rash or no rash, I've had no success on that score. Though I have tried my best." He raised his glass of wine, as if in salute.

"Oh, poor baby," Turner said. "And in the process, I'm sure, spending all the lira I give you."

"Of course, what else would you expect me to do?"

Turner turned unexpectedly pensive. He looked down at his plate of mussels, and then up again. "Not a thing, dear. I would not expect any other thing at all."

Wilde was not surprised by Reggie's resistance to

his enthusiasm for these papal visits, even given the fact that Reggie was the one who set him up in the first place. Nary a person Wilde knew would accept the premise that Pope Leo XIII had performed a miracle cure of a skin rash; no one except Robert Ross. For that was one of the insolvable mysteries of Robbie: Somehow Ross had remained, even during the periods of his most flagrant sexual profligacy, a practicing Roman Catholic. Not just practicing but devout. And not just devoted to the show of it, the part that had long attracted Wilde—the sonorous rhythms of the Latin language and the feminine delicacy of the windows; the physical thrill of incense and statues and shadows; the elaborate performance embedded in every ritualized Catholic moment—but the faith itself, the idea of the organization and its elaborated dogmas, of Petrine succession, of an orderly afterlife governed by a caring but rule-enforcing God. Wilde could not comprehend this about his friend, but he knew that only by accepting Ross's faith as genuine could one really know the man at all. But Robbie was the eccentric among Wilde's current stock, depleted as it was. There were plenty of non-practicing, once upon-a-time French Catholics in the group, and a few stern would-be-if-not-actually Protestants, both of the French and English variety; but largest of all was the contingency of atheists, including Turner, who, to top it all, was not only atheist but Jewish. A very modern fellow indeed.

On the dawn of the fourth, and last, day he could receive the Pope's blessing—they were leaving Rome the next morning—Wilde was first in line for a ticket. He thought he saw a flicker of recognition in the stolid eye of the cardinal, but it earned him not a bit of conversation from the man. Wilde didn't know what to do with himself. He was too agitated to want to go back to the hotel and try to sleep, so instead he caught a cab straightaway to St. Peter's Square. By 8:30 he was standing in front of the side entrance closest to the Gregorian Chapel, the door that in three hours or so would be opened for him so that the last part of this magical healing could take place. What he would remember, and tell everyone about, for the rest of his life.

Unfortunately, it was colder than any of the other days. Roman winter was revealed. An ungenerous wind blew in and around the square, attacking the side of his face, the skin under his chin, the hair on his head, the exposed flesh of his hands. He'd been in such a hurry to make it to the Piazza del Popolo that morning he'd accidentally left his hat and gloves in the room. Wilde considered squatting by the door, crossing his arms around his knees and huddling with his own girth to outlast the wind. But then the guards would surely think he was a tramp, maybe even a mad one, and chase him off, ticket or no. So instead he stood straight, as tall as his height could allow, put one hand inside the other and closed his eyes. Through concentration, he thought, he would remove himself from his body; he would move his living awareness out of his brain, out of the limits of his physical being, somewhere just off the edge of his shoulder, where it could keep watch over his shivering body and reunite with it if a final crisis happened. Otherwise, he would linger bodiless, viewing St. Peter's with the invisible eyes of his unfrozen, unknowable consciousness.

This worked for almost two hours, but then the rest of the day's group arrived. There was loud chatter and impatient words, calls for the guards to let them in early so they could get out of the wind, swearing at a world that just by the fact of its turning and its climate could bring about such evil breeze. At rest inside his consciousness Wilde sighed; then he rejoined his body. He was instantly cold, the shock so intense he stumbled in place and fell against the wall of the basilica. Every bone in his body was rattling, trying to stir his blood. His lips may not have been blue, but they felt like it. He felt like he'd been buried in ice for centuries and only just recovered. He heard one voice after another snicker at him in Italian: "Look at the fat one"; "No one told him about January in Rome?"; "He could have brought a hat." Wilde was so shocked by the sudden renewal of his moribund being he could do nothing but sit and shiver and believe he was about to die; until at some point he heard a familiar machine-like cranking noise and the door behind him opened with a start. Suddenly, he was surrounded by pressing bodies all wanting to get inside. He was kicked. He was kicked again. Someone cursed at him. Wilde closed his eyes and awaited the end, not exactly unhappy at the prospect. Then he felt hands beneath his underarms, and a muscular god was pulling him to his feet.

"Do you have a ticket?" a rough voice spoke in only serviceable Italian funneled through some drastically different European accent. "Or do I need to expel your culo from the Square?"

Wilde panicked, fearing that with all the rough and tumble the ticket might have fallen out of his overcoat pocket. It might even have been stolen during that long stretch when his mind had existed blissfully outside the borders of his body. But, no, there it was, the little slab of rough textured paper. He gripped it hard between his thumb and forefinger and extracted it hurriedly before the guard could carry out his threat. He turned to see a big-shouldered young man with a smooth, white face, thin, clipped mustache, and precise brown eyes staring at him as if he were a villain. The guard wore the same soft round cap as the others, one that practically buried his hair line beneath its mass; too the same ornamental uniform: an ocean-blue jacket with two stripes of red down the front that extended all the way to the hem and rimmed the whole garment; knickers the same oceanic color but accented, from the calf down, by black and red striped stockings that just covered the top of black leather shoes.

Upon each jacket stripe was embroidered in yellow a pattern of shapes; not ecclesiastical necessarily; no, how could they be? This was no priest but one of the Pope's Swiss guard. A hired soldier. Wilde thought to ask the guardsman how his uniform came to have such a beautiful design, such expansive style. Then he thought maybe he should ask how the guardsman himself came to be so beautiful; or at least so strong. But then he saw the ponderous leather belt circling the guardsman's stomach, and the sword hanging there. Instead of asking anything, he just held out the ticket and said "Qui."

"Not me," the guard barked as he thrust a thumb over his shoulder. "Him."

Then Wilde saw another guardsman waiting inside the door, this one blonde with unhappy, pooling green eyes. He also saw that all the other ticket holders had disappeared. If he did not act fast, he might not get a seat for his last papal audience. He might not get his blessing. He scurried to the door, gave his ticket to the blonde guardsman, and stepped inside. A second later, the guardsman swung home the metal door, calling to someone outside, "You are not legitimate. His Holiness will not see you." Then he secured the creaky bolt, locking Wilde inside.

As soon as Wilde entered the Gregorian Chapel, Leo appeared, accompanied by the usual retinue of younger men— a collection of chamberlains and priests—who served as his assistants for the day. On his second trip to the chapel, Wilde had been both surprised and not to see that one of these priests was his old flame and tentative lover, John Gray. While at Reading, he'd heard rumors of Gray's conversion to Catholicism. Then, a year or two ago, Ross had informed him of Gray's revelation of a priestly calling. Wilde had been amused. John Gray called to the Roman Catholic priesthood? That hardheaded child of working-class Protestants, that proud, self-made student of poetry? When Wilde had known him, Gray was as determined as Wilde to claim and hold your attention, to push his verses into your face, to hear you compliment them. He was also more convinced of his own beauty than anyone Wilde had ever met, even more than Bosie Douglas. And he'd had sexual desires nearly as urgent as Bosie's. This John Gray was being summoned to the priesthood; he with the superhumanly delicate chin and poignant nose, feather soft brown hair, womanly auburn eyes? This man who took hurt so easily and forgave only with great difficulty? This unisexual who had served as the actual model for Dorian Gray?

He had predicted Gray's calling wouldn't last. And yet two days before, who had been among the Pope's attendants but John Gray, dressed in a black cassock, his beauty still evident if beginning to take on a worn, early middle-aged look. In Gray's alarmed stare Wilde saw that the man recognized him; also that Gray did not understand Wilde's presence in the chapel. And that was all right, because Wilde didn't understand it himself. Wilde tried to hold Gray in a look, but Gray glanced hard away. And he refused to meet Wilde's eyes for the rest of the brief ceremony. Seeing Gray step slowly off with the other attendants, drowned in black, and then disappear through the doorway behind the altar, was like watching a ferocious and elemental pagan spirit slip into some ground hole to live out of sight for a millennium.

On this last day, however, Gray was nowhere to be found. Leo was here, as frail and benign as always, but moving even more slowly and mindfully than usual, and with obvious pain on his face. Wilde wondered what was wrong with him. There was no way to know, and no way Leo would tell anyone here. It was their ceremony, intended to relieve their pains, not his. For all Wilde knew, Leo's new discomfort was the result of taking, like a master yogi, all of their individual pains into his own body and removing those pains from the faithful. The only question, Wilde asked himself, was whether Leo was strong enough to withstand those pains and whether, like a yogi could, he would be able to convey them by act of will out of his own skin and into nonthreatening nonexistence. Wilde was not sure that was part of Leo's magic. He was no Indian master, only a Pope. Wilde knew what would really cure this pontiff: a comfortable hotel room, a hot bath, a glass or three (or five) of champagne. Would Reggie mind paying for those?

When Leo finally stood before them in the usual place, he was breathing laboriously and frowning a look of concentration at them. He did not smile as usual; he did not raise his arm in a quick, casual greeting. He did not shout "Benevenuto" or "Non è una bella mattina?" Instead, he made his hand form the sign of the benediction and, with a grimace, started into his Latin prayer. When he was done, he dropped his right hand like dead paw into the cup of his left. He looked at the group with an expression that Wilde was tempted to call confusion. Then, suddenly and without warning, his eyes cleared and he showed one of his characteristic face-breaking smiles.

Wilde saw again the man who had issued the bold encyclical that in no uncertain terms spoke of the miserable lives of the working classes and the duty of governments worldwide to ameliorate their putrid living conditions, who dared speak of a "natural justice" more permanent than market forces, more imperative than the profit motive. *If through necessity or fear of a worse evil the workman accept harder conditions because an employer or contractor will afford him no better, he is made the victim of force and injustice.* To be the leader of an institution that had benefited and continued to benefit so gratuitously from the largesse of the richest of men and the starkest of capitalists, and yet speak out so publically against the interests of those men in favor of the powerless masses those men employed, was an act of righteousness so pure Wilde knew it could only have come from a man of divinely refined soul. The encyclical was something Jesus could have written.

The pope's smile lingered there for a moment, but then it collapsed. Leo frowned again and appeared unsteady on his feet. Wilde could not tell if the man actually knew where he was, who these people were before him. His gaze was full of black alarm. One of the assistants took a step in the pontiff's direction. Then Leo blinked. He shut his eyes deliberately and reopened them. Once more, his gaze was clear. He nodded, then slowly turned a quarter turn and began to walk in front of the row of the kneeling devotees, but without pausing before each one as he usually did to say a word or lay on a hand. He seemed to just want to get away.

Because of the delay at the entrance, Wilde occupied the last space on the left. As the pontiff walked past, ignoring Wilde, his shimmering, snow-white cassock only inches from Wilde's fingertips, Wilde could not help himself. He reached out and took a handful. "Padre," he said, under his breath. Leo was brought up short. He stood as straight as he could, his eyes wide at the audacity of this kneeing layman. Wilde released his grip, just as the pope opened his mouth as if about to say, "Unhand me, you miscreant." Then as he looked at Wilde's face, his gaze softened into something like pity, or even affection. He brought his right hand around and laid it upon Wilde's cheek. "*Dio ti benedica, mia cara,*" Leo said. Then the pope smiled. Wilde blushed; he lowered his eyes. The old man dropped his hand and continued walking, down to the main corridor on the north side of the building and then up, as if he intended to go out the same door through which Wilde and the others had entered. The small army of assistants rushed after him.

* * * *

At dinner later, Wilde could not stop talking about the moment when the head of the Roman Church stopped and smiled at him in particular, him only; had laid a hand on him alone. He kept repeating it over and aloud. "Me, Reggie. He stopped for me." His cheek had started tingling the moment he felt the pope's hand, and it had not stopped tingling since, not even hours later. The cheek had only grown warmer, even toasty, as if flush against an oven. "I can feel it. The blessing. It's finishing off my brand."

"Your brand?" Turner said. He coughed out a laugh.

"The brand on my cheek, the wicked mark. My wickedness."

Turner laughed again, softer, even concerned. "You are not wicked, Oscar. None of us are."

Wilde didn't even hear. "But is it gone? Can you tell?" The whole afternoon in Rome he had tried to spy his cheek in the windows of the shops they passed, but he could never see it clearly enough—and Reggie refused to say anything about it at all. Apparently, he would have to wait until they were safely ensconced again in the hotel room.

Turner drew a slow, sad smile. "Dearie," he said, "you know your cheek is perfect. It always has been."

CHAPTER SEVEN

Paris. February, 1900.

He was sitting at the meager writing desk, with its scratched edges and worn varnish—possibly some other hotel's castoff that Dupoirer had laid his bargain hunting hands ahold of—not writing but smoking what was proving to be a very bad Nazir. He'd paid Charbonneau, the clerk downstairs, a whole louis to find blonde cigarettes somewhere on the Rue Bonaparte. Charbonneau came back entirely too soon and wearing a guilty look. He passed the pack of Nazirs into Wilde's hands and hurried away from the door as if afraid he would be whipped. As soon as he lit one, Wilde understood why. The cigarette had gone sour, almost rank. There was no way this could be a newly purchased pack; if it were it must have come from a shopkeeper who kept cigarettes around for two years. Probably the clerk had begged an old pack from a friend and stowed the louis somewhere on his person to use for a gin or an absinthe later.

Wilde decided to let it go. He would not complain to Dupoirer. He would not upbraid Charbonneau himself. He knew that no matter how much he might castigate or plead, the man would never admit to his crime. "They are new," the clerk would say. "They are absolutely new. Right this minute. You can ask the man at the shop himself. He will tell you I bought them." Charbonneau, who had a gift for both exasperation and dissapointment, would put on such a look of such wounded vanity that

Wilde would be made to feel ashamed for his doubts. No, there would be nothing to be gained from the confrontation. Wilde also knew that if he went to the tobacconist friend of the clerk, that one would swear that of course Charbonneau had just bought them, and that he himself just received them into his store from a supplier. And yet, there was no fooling Wilde's taste buds. Stale was stale. Old was old. Spent was spent.

He kept smoking.

Gently he brushed the tips of his fingers against the rash on his cheek, that recalcitrant barb that seemed to have a mind of its own. Worsening and then improving and then worsening again; worse now than it had been for days. It had been only six weeks since he'd knelt before the Holy Father and received that man's blessing. Only six weeks since all had been right with his skin. What had happened? Not three days after his return to Paris the rash had reappeared, and then the low-level, singing body aches that had finally seemed to dissipate by the time he and Reggie had caught a train out of the Eternal City. Could he be allergic to Paris? No man's body would resist Paris. No man's body would try to fight it off. Why would any body want to? What he needed to do was stop making guesses and pay for an actual doctor. Either that or pay to see the Pope again. But he couldn't possibly afford that. And there was no way Reggie Turner would.

It was the height of both civilization and of humanism, Wilde decided, to assert that a person could cure a skin disease merely through the power of belief. Although for Wilde it had been as much a question of penance as belief. Or rather the purification that the penance could bring on. He had no doubt that the curative in Rome worked because he'd been willing to submit to the inconvenient routine of all those return visits, day after day, waiting in line for a ticket, pressed by the other, more animated devotees, then standing outside the basilica for so long just for the sake of those few Latin words and the feeling of the old man's hands against his cheek. And so it was with his present smoking of the Nazir. While it might seem odd to an outsider to characterize smoking as an act of penance, it certainly was at the moment. He could have thrown down the pack in justified fury, stomped down the stairs to confront Charbonneau while there was still time, threatened to talk to Dupoirer about it and have the sour, duplicitous clerk fired if the louis was not returned. He could have done all that, but instead, he sat perfectly still, lightly puffing on this very bad cigarette; holding the pollution in his mouth to make sure he really tasted it. In the meantime, inside his soul he tried for a condition of perfect forgiveness and loving kindness, holding at bay the longings and sufferings and expectations and frustrations of this earthly coil; molding through force of will his inner person into something approaching... bliss.

His enchantment was interrupted by a knock on the door. It occurred to him that maybe Charbonneau had had a touch of conscience and wanted to return his money, but when he pulled open the door he saw instead a boy dressed in clean but ill-fitting pants and a shirt too large for him. His loblolly ears were a force unto themselves and his loose brown hair would have looked quite wild if allowed to grow longer. His gaze meanwhile was a pestering, smoky green. The boy stuck out his hand. In it was an envelope.

"Letter," the boy said, in French.

"You're awfully young for a postman," Wilde said as innocently as he could.

"The man downstairs told me to bring it up."

Wilde smiled. Too afraid to bring it up himself. He nodded, reached into his pocket, found nothing. The smile disappeared. He grabbed the letter and said thank you, hoped the cowardly desk clerk had at least paid the boy for his trouble. Chances were, though, that Charbonneau had told the boy the gentleman upstairs would offer him something. It was why the boy agreed.

"I appreciate your help... really," he said, pushing the words like an inappropriate gift in the direction of the expectant boy, hoping they would be enough to satisfy the occasion, but knowing they wouldn't. Which is why his next action was to close the door.

Before he even read the name, he could see from the handwriting that the letter was from Ross. Wilde sighed warily. Robbie might have been one of his first male lovers and most loyal friend, but he was also, sometimes, a hectoring pain in the bum. This could be anything, Wilde knew. Anything. It could be good. Quite good, in fact. Or it could be very very bad. All he knew was that it was something.

Oscar,

Of course this matter is entirely between the two of you, but I feel obliged to pass on news I heard last night. Douglas has inherited £20,000 from the old man. What he must have done to wile his way into Queensberry's good graces again I hesitate to even consider. But it's done. Forgive me for trying to advise you, but there seems no better time than now to press your case. If he, and she, hadn't made the promise to you in the first place there would be nothing to consider. But they did. And now it is time for them to pay. Time for him to pay.

Besides, your request need not bankrupt him (if Bosie is capable of behaving even the slightest bit responsibly with this money). Even as little as a £1000 would put you on a footing you could live with, for now. And his willingness to consider this would go a long way to removing their moral debt to you as well. (I realize that it can never be fully removed, no matter how much they give.)

But you must press him now, if you mean to do it at all. Because there is no knowing how quickly he will spend the entire sum if left to his own devices. I expect very quickly. I know you know what I'm talking about. I hear he has already moved to Chantilly and has grand plans. I'm sure he does.

I will send you his address as soon as I know it. Or you probably could uncover it yourself just as easily. Surely Bosie has friends in Paris who still keep track of him????

Just ask him to meet you in Paris. You need not tell him why. Tell him it is an urgent matter between the two of you. Curiosity alone should compel him to come.

Good luck in the ensuing battle. He will surely resist your request, so you will need to keep at him, keep reiterating his family's promise, and their moral debt. His too. Bosie's moral debt.

Surely even Bosie is not so sordid as to be unmoved by that consideration.

Robbie

* * * *

Turning the corner at the Avenue de l'Opéra, intending to head north, it was actually difficult to walk despite the fact that the night before he'd slept better than he had any right to expect, that he carried his cane, and that he'd already braced his nerves with a glass of Armagnac at a café three streets back. He wore the best of his suits, the only one that evidenced no sign of stain or tearing, the one with the least obvious end-of-life smell. The one he reserved for those times, even now, when it seemed important to impress. He'd used the last of his current resources to get his shirt pressed and his shoes shined—and for the drink, of course. He would not eat later in the day and probably for the next one as well, unless he could find a café or restaurant willing to extend him credit. Virtually no chance of that. And he had to hope that Douglas would be willing to cover the cost of whatever they consumed during this meeting. Surely they would consume something. This was too significant a conference for them to simply gab and leave. Certain diplomatic—to say nothing of Parisian—protocols would need to be respected.

But Wilde couldn't know. He couldn't know what Douglas was planning exactly—assuming Douglas himself even did—he couldn't know if the boy had guessed in advance what he was here to tell him and what that might mean. Bosie might come primed for battle or for reconciliation; but Oscar well knew from all his years of association with Lord Alfred Douglas that no matter what Bosie came primed for he was capable of changing his mind in seconds.

Ahead of him lay the busy business of the avenue, including, blocks away from where he presently stood— bloated and unsteady on his feet—the intersection with the Boulevard des Capucines, on the other side of which sat the Café de la Paix. That was where Douglas had agreed to wait for him, after specifying that he would not visit Oscar at his "atrocious" place of residence. Oscar had never eaten at the famous—and expensive— café, which sat on the bottom floor of the Grand Hotel, although Louis Latourette and Ernest La Jeunesse and Jean Moréas and several others had said kind things about the place. He'd started the morning hoping he would finally have the opportunity to take a meal there. But now, standing on the street, close enough to spy the café's actual location, Wilde wasn't sure if his stomach was in good enough shape to handle anything more than a stiff drink. Probably after the meeting was concluded he would be ravenous, no matter what kind of answer he got from his old lover. But he was nothing but nauseous with tension now. As he stood and wavered and squinted, he thought that he ought to be able to see the amazing sunlight of Bosie's hair, the exquisite sculpture of his forehead, the needy intensity of his eyes, even from this far away. But of course all he could see was colored awnings, chairs assembled on the sidewalk, shadowy bodies leaning or bending or sitting. He was not close enough yet for a truly clear view. He couldn't just stand here. He had to move forward if he ever wanted to see.

Then there was Douglas, alone at a table near the outer edge of the assembly, a glass of something next to his elbow and staring into a book. Wilde felt himself take a quick breath of surprise—and not just because he never expected to see Douglas again—but for the evident change in him. He had last seen Bosie—how long was it now?—a mere six months—and yet here the man looked so remarkably different. There was still the waifish face; and the pronounced, almost elfin, hooked nose; and the slight, skeletal build that even in his twenties had made him look like a schoolboy. But now, on the cusp of thirty, Bosie's hair looked darker, closer to pure brown than blonde; for his coat he'd traded out the pin-striped dandy outfits he once favored for one that was strictly black, though tight fitting; and he'd given up the rakish boaters for a sober gray homburg. Presently the hat sat on the table in front of him, and Douglas's hand rested nervously on top of it, as if needing to be ready at any moment to jump up and run, properly attired. Good god. The beautiful young poet, this impulsive little boy, was all dressed up like a country squire taking a day in the city. Since last they'd spoken, Bosie's new book had appeared. From an English publisher: Grant Richards. *The City of the Soul*, he had called it. Bosie had been kind enough to send Wilde a copy, along with a polite note. *You heard some of these poems in process. I thought you might be interested to see them in their final forms. AD.* He had not read the book yet. He couldn't bring himself to. From others, he'd heard both good and bad. He hoped Bosie wouldn't ask him about it.

His heart was charging too badly. Wilde let out the breath, took in another, more regular. He told himself, I'm meeting a friend at a café. It was a much less monumental idea than I'm meeting my former beloved, the man who ruined me. Yet it was still monumental. His legs moved; he proceeded forward.

He hadn't been out with an actual friend in almost a month. The last time was an evening with George Alexander in mid-January. Before that an accidental run-in with Latourette, an old Oxford associate, outside of the Calisaya. In the month since, he'd meandered into this café or that and tried not to order anything he couldn't conjole someone else to pay for. Or he'd whiled away hours window-shopping, imagining what he might have bought if he'd actually had a legitimate reason to stand there. It was a way to make a day go by. Once he was standing in front of a patisserie, scrutinizing the petits fours, when he was startled out of his reverie by two pushy English women. They claimed that he'd been biting his fingers with longing, but he remembered doing no such thing. In his mind, he'd been merely observing, taking in another of the uniquely Parisian delights. The two women humiliated him by insisting he let them buy him dejeuner at the nearest café, a meal he tried to recompense them for with conversation, but it came out over urgent and forced, almost slap happy, with not a whit of cleverness. Worst of all, the lunch was bad. As soon as he could, he hurried away and prayed never to cross their path again.

Now who else was before him but Alfred Douglas, the one who, it could be said, had started it all. In some ways Douglas—even after all he'd done or refused to do—after their very long and very complicated history together—was Wilde's only real friend, even if at the same time his worst. Douglas had never gone to jail or turned up bankrupt or lost any children over the scandal, but he'd been hurt by it all the same: implicated, despised, put at odds with his father, made to flee his home country for months on end. Bosie had been, and was, Wilde's partner in all that happened. That still meant something; it ought to mean something. Even if today Bosie was a man who would probably not buy him a meal.

But it had not always been that way, Wilde thought. He must always remember—for the sake of both fairness and hope—that it had not always been that way.

The sun was hot above the summer-green stretch of lawn, but not hot enough to blister. This was southern England after all, not Rome. And late June rather than merciless August. It helped too that an occasional breeze rose off the Thames; it helped even more that the pair of them, atop a bed sheet stretched over grass, damp from their latest dip into the river, were nude and spread-eagled before it, literally escorting its winds into their being. It helped that the tallish front of this early-Victorian estate blocked human views of the piece of the lawn where they lay, enticing them to unwind into the kind of pure pleasure they needed and deserved. Earlier they had put in four hours of reading and writing and then reading their new writing to each other and at last hurrying to adjust their new writing while the other's suggestions were fresh in their ears. Immediately after came lunch, replete with at least a glass too much wine as well as more beef and cheese and pears and confectionary than their bodies could readily absorb. Then, in the boozy, bloated, honey-rich weariness of mid-afternoon came this present excursion across the back lawn to enjoy the sun and each other.

Douglas had rented the house at Goring-on-Thames, supposedly for Wilde's sake, from late May through the end of July. Then Douglas had unexpectedly shown up two weeks ago, for the stated reason of celebrating his "escape" from Magdalen college—he'd officially withdrawn after the college expressed its disfavor for his not showing up for his Greats examinations—and for memorializing his entrance into the world of professional gentlemen. The stated reason Wilde had holed up there—fifty miles removed from his wife and family—was to finish An Ideal Husband, *a manuscript he was tardy in delivering into the hands of three distinctly interested theatre managers. The success of* A Woman of No Importance *had shown that Wilde was no West End flash-in-the-pan, no one-offer. In fact, it was rumored that he could become the next theatrical celebrity, ready to unseat the likes of Sydney Grundy and W.S. Gilbert as the king of the London comedy. Wilde was only too happy to accept these accolades, and any consequent income, except that he must first complete his next play.*

What the stay at Goring had become, however, was less an isolated retreat than a combination boys' camp and writing school for Bosie, with Wilde as the resident headmaster and schedule keeper, and an alarmingly regular horde of visitors as guest lecturers/

late evening revelers. They were full days; full to overflowing. Too many hours of windy, high-minded opinion-swapping and aesthetical pontificating, too many days spent pronouncing at full volume Shakespeare and Jonson, Philip Sidney, the bawdy half of John Donne, and even that earnest Puritan John Milton, whose words were too delicious to withstand: Of Man's First Disobedience, and the Fruit / Of that Forbidden Tree, whose mortal taste / Brought Death into the World...; *playing parts, putting on voices, stretching out vowels and boot-heeling consonants like guttersnipes; too many hours arguing or laughing or giggling instead of writing; too many cigars; too many cream-covered dinners with excessive desserts, prepared by the actual French chef Bosie had found in Kensington and dragged along with him; too much Burgundy red, Russian vodka, and Scotch whiskey; too much ill-played singing in the wee dark hours of the Goring morning; too many nighttime whooping wading parties; too much drunken fucking; too many days waking late and hungover and not keeping to schedule.*

But there had been today, and the schedule they had assiduously kept, the words they had produced. And there was this too: the sunny silence on a lawn beside a river, their heads back and their eyes closed, with an English breeze tonguing their Thames-wet bodies, lapping them up. It had been, Wilde considered, a just about perfect day, perhaps the best of his life. And there was a sadness in that. Because if today was the best day of all, there could be no better, no matter how long he lived. He reached over, eyes still closed, and grasped Douglas's slender hand; he felt the younger man's fingers, as smooth and delicate, and nearly as sensitive, as a woman's. He loved the sensation of that hand. He could not hold it and not feel completely at ease.

"That was a very fine piece you wrote this morning," Wilde

murmured. *"Your best yet."* He could not help but turn his head and observe Douglas through narrowed eyes: the pale, skinny body; the ribs; the masculine nipples upon the flat plain of his chest; his pointy hips and blonde pubic hair; the smooth but evident muscles in his upper legs; that legendary face with the precise angles and long dark eyelashes that any woman would kill for.

Douglas, however, neither turned his head nor opened his eyes. Instead, he waited several seconds before speaking, and when he did it was with uncharacteristic languor, as if he had just woken out of a dream. Maybe he had. *"Which piece do you mean?"*

"The sonnet—for your brother."

Douglas nodded slowly, a smile weighing lightly on his lips. *"Thank you."* Then he sighed. Then: *"He's a sad case."*

"Francis? How so?"

Douglas opened his eyes; he met Wilde's gaze. *"I know you think that I am reckless, Oscar—"*

"Do I say that?"

"Come on, now. You think I'm reckless."

"I think you are daring."

"To you that means reckless."

"It does?" Wilde thought about this for a moment. He could not decide whether or not he agreed. *"I think you have extraordinary courage. The courage of your desires. The courage of abandonment. I wish I could say the same for myself."*

Douglas chuckled and squeezed Wilde's hand. *"I would say that about you. After all, between the two of us, who is taking the greater chance?"*

Of course Wilde knew what Douglas was saying. Wilde was married—a father—while Douglas was completely without entanglements; Douglas could hide if necessary behind the bastion of his family's social position, what with his Marquess of a father, once a member of the House of Lords; whereas Wilde was almost entirely a man of his own invention: an alien from Ireland, his place in London society earned through the sweat of his brow, the haughtiness of his affected accent, and the uncompromising clever- ness of his conversation. So was it true that he was putting himself at risk? Wilde did not imagine so. He was simply too well known now. Even the Queen knew his name—or so he'd been told. He was in demand at any dinner party that mattered and the author of more than one play that had made a producer rich. He could call his own shots, set his own hours. Taking a chance? Being Oscar Wilde, he felt certain, was defense enough against chance.

"I don't know, Bosie. I don't know about that. But we were talking about Francis."

Douglas's look changed: from dreaminess to worry. His brows knit. He pulled his hand away from Wilde's and studied the older man's face as if expecting to find written there the answer to a question he had not yet put into words.

"Of course you know he is Rosebery's secretary."

"Indeed. It's quite an honor for him. An honor for your whole family—to be so trusted. And it is a service for the na- tion, I'm sure. The man could be Prime Minister someday; perhaps soon."

Douglas did not reply right away, but was pursing his lips, evidently holding fire. "Yes," he finally murmured. "Soon." Then: "The thing is, there are services he performs—I mean for Rose- bery—that no one knows about." He focused his gaze on Wilde. "That no one must ever find out."

"Are you saying what I think you are?" Wilde asked.

"I am."

Wilde looked at the river: the blushing, twinkling, eddying bulk of it, sliding along without a single worry. "Well," he said, "who among us hasn't heard the rumors about Rosebery."

"Yes, who?" Douglas said in a squeezed voice, and Wilde heard instantly the note of pain there. Pain and naked fear.

"I understand what you mean by Francis's recklessness. It puts him at some peril, doesn't it?"

Douglas nodded wistfully. "What will happen to my brother if one of Rosebery's enemies finds out, if they can offer conclusive proof? What will happen to him? He has placed himself in quite a compromising position. He has placed Rosebery there too."

"No, I think Roseberry did that to himself, Bosie."

"Of course, but... it's still reckless."

"Yes. All right. I suppose that's the truth."

"And I worry about him." Wilde heard the distinctive warble in Douglas's voice. He could see the start of a shocking tear in the boy's eye. In Douglas's eye, a tear.

"You are a beautiful soul, Bosie. Do you know that? Have I ever said that to you? I have long and deeply admired you; and I have enjoyed you. I have taken you. But I also love you; and it is your soul I love most of all."

Douglas smiled: a sad but profound expression. Beautiful and guilty. Then, as if by an act of will, Douglas turned it to a smirk. "Oh, belt up, Oscar. I had no soul before I met you, did you know that? I've always said that to Mother: 'I hang about with Oscar Wilde because he has shown me what I can be.'"

"That's ridiculous," Wilde said.

"It's true. I was nothing but a sod before I met you."

"A sod? You? Really?"

"Yes. Really."

"Well, for the record," Wilde said, "to me you are nothing but a beautiful boy. And a pure angel."

Now Douglas's smile glowed, like a toddler's. He grabbed Wilde's hand and kissed it.

But it was not true that Douglas was only a beautiful boy, and Wilde knew it, especially after these weeks with Douglas at Goring. Douglas was also a literary talent, possibly a first-rate talent. But like all young talents, at the moment his gift was mostly a matter of potential. He was aspiring rather than arrived. But for whom wasn't this true at age twenty-three? Wilde's job was to see to it that Bosie's native talent flourished completely and eventually. But how to do that, how to make sure of it? With Douglas, Wilde knew, it all started with confidence. Douglas needed a confidence bordering on petulance to pull off any kind of work, any kind of attempt. About sexual matters Douglas was not merely arrogant he was practically a tyrant. A beautiful blue-eyed despot. A swaggering, big-pricked Nero in the bedroom. No wonder he never failed there. No wonder he always took what he needed. But it was different with poetry. With poetry, Douglas was merely feeling his way around: reading and learning, playing with gestures, some charming, some dreadful. His palpitating fear of incompetence was apparent whenever he read his work aloud. Why not, Wilde thought now, pay the boy a powerful tribute, hand him an amazing gift, one that could only make his confidence soar?

"You know, Bosie, I've been thinking."

Douglas shot him a scandalous look. "Yes...?"

"Stop. For once can you get your mind out of your willy?"

"You've never minded it being there before."

"True as that may be, I have something else to discuss. Something actually important."

Douglas frowned, suddenly concerned. *"All right."*

"I've been turning over in my head the possibility of commissioning a translation of Salome *into English. I mean my* Salome, *of course. It is about time, after all. It nearly killed me to see its performance forbidden here. But there is no reason that the play should just languish in Limbo forever. I cannot stand for that. It is, I hate to admit, my favorite of everything I've written, and I cannot stand that the public is not allowed to see it. So if a performance is off-limits I will just have to make certain it is published. In English. So English men and women can read it."*

"You said 'commissioning a translation.' Don't you want to do it yourself?"

"I could. I could. And maybe it would be a passable translation. But I fear I am too close to it—I mean my French original—to properly handle it, take it apart."

Douglas nodded: once, several times. *"All right. Yes. And why are you bringing this up now?"*

Wilde smiled, held fire for a single, purposeful moment. *"Do you think you would be up for the job of translating?"*

Douglas's jaw dropped; his mouth hung open.

"You have the necessary sensitivity to language," Wilde went on. *"Such sensitivity. And just as important, you have the necessary sensuality of outlook to do justice to the play's contents, to its message."*

"Me?" Douglas could barely get out. *"You want me to be the sanctioned translator of your* Salome?*"*

"I do."

"The translator, as in the person whose name would be right next to yours on the title page?'

Wilde chuckled. *"Precisely. Right next to mine."*

Douglas was so stricken—with something like joy, or maybe it was terror—that he looked pale, even deathly so. "But Oscar, you know that I am not even a university man. I never will be, not now."

Wilde waved an arm. "You are merely following in that hallowed tradition of Swinburne: i.e., the permanent undergraduate. The diploma means nothing. I have one—and I tell you, it means nothing. I was Oscar Wilde before I earned it. I remained Oscar Wilde after I did. I remain Oscar Wilde now. You are, always have, and always will be Bosie Douglas. And that is quite good enough for me."

Douglas kept staring in disbelief, as if expecting that at any moment Wilde would retract the words. But Wilde was not going to retract his words. Never. Finally, Douglas shook his head. "Of course, I accept your commission. And I cannot thank you enough. It would be an honor. The highest of my life."

If anything Wilde was happier with this turn of events than Douglas. Wilde did not know if he had ever felt so pleased with a decision as the one he had just made, the offer he had just extended, which was not even on his mind while they traipsed across the grass, bed sheet in hand. But it might, he realized, be the most beautifully perfect gesture of his life, far more beautiful than any of his numerous words. Because it had helped make a person; it had helped nourish another man's talent.

Maybe it was his beaming inward satisfaction, or maybe it was the effect of his body drying, or maybe it was merely the fact that the day had transitioned yet another minute deeper into June, but the afternoon felt crisp on his skin of a sudden, on the far side of warm. He propped himself up on one elbow and said to Douglas, "What do you say that we celebrate our new partnership by taking another dip in the river?"

Douglas stood: grinning, hale, and boyish. His hands expectantly on his hips. His willy hanging down between his thighs: long and fat and juicy as ever. Not far at all from Wilde's lips.

"I say that I take you up on that," Douglas declared. "Now catch me!" And at that he took off like a bullet, like a baby, for the water, his lean buttocks flashing white. Wilde laughed and stood too, if more slowly. No, he couldn't catch Bosie. He'd never catch dearest Bosie. But he sure wouldn't mind trying.

Douglas's head shot up, as if an alarm in his spine had gone off at Wilde's approach. He locked eyes—those nervy, daring blue beacons—with Wilde and did not change his expression. Bosie didn't smile. He didn't grimace. He didn't blink. He might have been staring at a fly that happened to cross the air in front of his table. Douglas slipped the book into his coat pocket, too quickly for Wilde to see any title or notice anything about its shape.

"So you really did want to meet," Douglas said.

"I did."

"Sit down." Douglas's tone was closer to a command than an invitation, a command delivered to someone you believe is about to make an embarrassing scene.

"May I order a drink?" Wilde asked as soon as he was seated.

Douglas shrugged with one shoulder. "Why are you asking me? You can order as many drinks as you can pay for. It's none of my business."

Wilde blinked; he looked away. He did not signal

for the waiter.

Douglas took a theatrical sip from his glass. It looked like brandy. Then he settled into his chair, leaned into its back. "What do you want, Oscar? Why contact me now, insist on a meeting?"

The moment had come. It was time for the plunge. Wilde rubbed a hand across his lips. "I have heard something from Robbie."

Douglas rolled his eyes. "Oh, Robert Ross? You mean that supercilious automaton? What claptrap is Ross making now? What does he know about anything?"

Wilde sat still; quiet; he let the accusation fly unanswered into the air and then gone.

"He's always been envious of me, you know. He's always wanted to be me. I don't know why you trust him."

Wilde spoke carefully. "You served us both tea, Bosie. At your flat. Remember? It was a beautiful afternoon."

Douglas shifted in his seat. "Because he was keeping his mouth shut that day, for some reason. I don't know why. I didn't know then."

Wilde nodded slowly. He wanted to ask if Douglas had written any more sonnets, if for no other reason than to soften the mood, but he knew that would get him nowhere. He tilted his head to the left and observed a short, broad woman trying to step up into a hansom. She was with a man, but the man inexplicably had entered the cab first and was now just waiting for her instead of helping. The cabbie, meanwhile, stood at the rear of the vehicle, his bulky black frock buttoned all the way, not looking at her, his expression impassive. None of them, not even the woman, seem to find this arrangement unusual. She lifted her left leg again, found the low hanging step, and surged. But she only was able to pull herself halfway up before she lost either heart or strength. She fell backward, losing her grip, and wound up a pile of disheveled dress and coat and hat. With a word from the man, the cabbie flicked his long whip at the horse's rump: a single, gentle slap. The horse began to walk. The woman remained where she was.

"So what is this about?" Douglas said.

Wilde came back. "What?"

"This." Douglas gestured: an abrupt, haphazard, almost violent motion.

For a woozy moment, Wilde thought Douglas was referring to the woman. "In fact it's about you."

"I don't think so."

Wilde took a breath. "Your father and his inheritance."

Now Douglas practically hopped from his seat. "How is that any business of Robert's? How is it any business of yours?"

Wilde paused. "I had hoped that would be obvious."

"Hah." He threw his head back. "Really. Fancy that. Obvious."

"Bosie, we've talked about this before. You did promise me. And your mother too. She too did promise me."

"And she gave you money twice, almost three hundred pounds put together, if I remember correctly. Or are you choosing not to count that?"

Wilde struggled to maintain his calm. He looked at his hands resting on the table like a child's at supper. "The affair cost me £3600, almost seven hundred of which was your father's own legal fees, which became my responsibility. You know this."

"I know she gave you money. That's what I know."

"But she promised—both of you promised—to reimburse me for the full cost. After all your father did to me, all that he took away."

"So I'm not supposed to spend any of father's money on myself, is that it? I'm supposed to turn it over to you? Even though he gave it to me. Even though he detested you. He reviled you. Even though I—not you— worked terribly hard to repair my relationship with him. And it was terrible, Oscar. The man was half out of his mind and not in the mood to forgive. But I remained patient, and we worked through it. I did that. My father and I came to an understanding; a love actually. My father loved me. He always loved me. That's the long and short of it. As misguided as his actions were, they were driven by love. And now—well, mercy—he would be outraged if he heard I gave you even a farthing of what had been his."

This was the first time Wilde had ever heard Douglas characterize Queensberry's pursuit of a legal case against him as an act of love. But he managed to swallow that sentence and remain calm. Somehow he managed to stick to his script.

"It was promised to me."

"It was never promised. It was talked about. It was discussed. It was an idea my mother considered, like so many other ideas she has."

"It was not an idea. It was promised. By both of you. You and she practically swore on a bible. You wanted to restore what I lost. That's what you said. Together."

Douglas sat back in his chair, flustered and almost out of patience with the conversation. Wilde reminded himself to be careful how hard he pushed.

"Promises. Promises. Listen to yourself, Oscar. You sound like a child. And you were always supposed to be the elder statesmen of our partnership. You were supposed to be the lion while I acted the part of the impetuous child. Now you are the child. Practically an infant. Whining at me about words that were spoken years ago. Words that weigh no more now than the wind. That mean nothing more to me than you do."

"Apparently not," Wilde said grimly. He was stung, devastated, but he refused to cry. He would not show a single tear. Because that was just the sort of victory Douglas would relish.

"Listen to yourself," Douglas teased. "'Apparently not.' There once was a day I would have been afraid of that tone. Afraid of your disapproval. Now you just sound pathetic." He drank a sip more of brandy. Then he decided to polish off the glass. "If there's anything I'm afraid of now it's Robert Ross misrepresenting me, as he has a long habit of doing. That's what I should be afraid of. You're probably under the impression, from Robert, that I'm sitting atop a pile of gold and smoking a pipe, like some worthless gentleman of leisure, like the friends of our fathers and mothers. But that's not what I'm doing. I am putting my money to use, and my life to use. Unlike you, I am doing something substantial with it."

Wilde knew to what Bosie was referring. Since his letter informing Wilde of Bosie's inheritance, Ross had written with more news. Douglas was not spending his newfound wealth on anything that promised a secure return but in the most fatuous manner possible: on a stable of racing horses. But that wasn't all. There were all the other expenses one would expect with Douglas: gallons of wine; a wardrobe extensive enough to afford him a new costume daily; a library that went well beyond the arc of his decidedly middlebrow tastes. If you don't talk to him soon, Ross warned, he won't have anything left to give you.

"I was doing something useful with my life until your father made sure I went to prison."

"You charged him first. You tried to put him in jail."

"You wanted me to put him in jail! You begged for me to continue."

This was such an old discussion. Even as Wilde said the words, he knew they were pointless.

"Your decision, Oscar. Always yours to make. You didn't have to listen to me. Besides, you knew how vindictive papa was."

"Are you going to blame me for your father's mania?"

"It sounds like you're trying to blame me."

Wilde sighed. The young man was impossible. No, the boy; the boy; because, Wilde was disappointed to realize, that was what Bosie had remained, despite the country squire ensemble. "Of course not. Of course not. But—"

"It's like you're blaming me for your having fallen in love with me."

Wilde cringed, stricken. So many different regrets and frustrations—plain heartaches—overwhelmed him at once, but at the center of them, like a scarecrow upright in the middle of a hail storm, was one thought: But you were always in love with me; weren't you? For years this had accounted to his own personal Apostles' Creed: The young Bosie, rough scholar and aspiring poet, entranced by the dazzle and accomplishment and beauty of the older man, had fallen in love first. At their first meeting—their very first meeting—he had sent barbed hooks into Wilde and refused to let go, refused to take no for an answer on all sorts of matters, not just the most obvious. Because Bosie's need was just too strong, his fascination with Wilde's allure utterly complete. Kin to an obsession. But truth was that it was all so long ago now—that time before prison—that time of his independent life, it was hard for Wilde to trust his own memory.

"You were an invert before you met me, Oscar. Let's not forget that. Let's not make up a story wherein you were the loyal, devoted, clean-living, straight arrow husband, and I happened along to corrupt you."

Wilde began shaking his head, slowly. For what he

wasn't sure. His head just moved. Maybe to ward off this punishing attack.

"You were tired of your wife. In fact, you detested your wife. You detested her body and you detested her mind. And you detested her morals. You were sick of her wanting you to be happy with a conventional domestic life when you were not at all domestic and about the least conventional person in England. Around the time you met me, if you recall, you were chasing the willy of a friend of mine; but instead of catching his, you caught mine."

Was this true? Good god, Wilde wasn't sure now. The willy of a friend of Bosie's? Now whose willy would that have been? What Wilde remembered is that he met Bosie when Lionel Johnson brought him to 34 Tite Street for a party. Surely, Wilde had never chased Lionel Johnson's willy—or any other part of him—not that ferret-faced, disconsolate mess of a closeted Uranian. A gruesome man, a man completely without charm. But who then? It could have been anyone, came the sighing thought. There had been so many. Wilde could not deny that once he stumbled out of his vows, once he discovered that indulging himself with young men need not be fantasy only but an actual course for his life, he had become a sexual bedlamite; indulging himself rather than denying. Because, after all, after the first occasion of sin, what do the others matter?

Even so, there was something wrong about Bosie's characterization. It was too coarse and reductive a summary of what for Wilde had always stood as the most important encounter of his life. The one that determined everything that came after. So whatever came before, whatever urgency propelled him accidentally into Bosie's presence that first time, made no difference. It had no existence. Or, rather, its existence belonged to an Oscar Wilde no longer alive, not the Wilde, years later, sitting at this table at a café on a windy Paris street on the left bank.

Wilde found his voice again.

"Of course you didn't make me. I never said that. I am not saying it. I'm talking strictly about the legal case, the one your father pursued. He did it to wreck me, and to separate us. To make it impossible for us to be together because I would so disgraced, so broken, so bankrupt." And it worked, his head screamed, but he kept the thought to himself. Look at us, sniping at each other. Exactly what Queensberry wanted had come to pass. "Your mother and you, recognizing this, promised to make amends. Both of you together promised. Please don't tell me you don't remember that."

Bosie's answer was to grow hot in the face. "I'm tired of being made to feel guilty by you and your measly coterie of peasants and hangers on. Give it up. And tell Robert the same. You're out of prison now. You are free. Go live. Go write. Don't blame anything more on me. I have a life. I get to live that life as I choose. You go lead yours."

"I wish I could."

Douglas shook his own head, a look not of defense but ultimate disgust. He picked up his glass of brandy without looking, saw that it was already finished, and so set it back down again angrily. He reached into his pocket and extracted some francs, cast them on the table. A blow-off gesture, Wilde thought at first, crumbs to a starving dog. Then he realized that Bosie was merely paying for his drink. Apparently, this encounter, and his chance, was almost over. "I should tell you that the money father gave me I am putting to use in the most practical investment available. I am making for myself a new identity. One I intend to capitalize on as soon as I can."

"Capitalize?" Wilde was genuinely curious what he meant by that.

"There's a veritable lake of wealthy American women up in Chantilly. Divorcees. Widows. Heiresses. And they like the way I look. They like the way I dress. They like who I am. It won't be long before I will be in a position to make my pick out of the bunch. And I can guarantee you I will pick well. And when I pick I will be settled for life."

"That's what you want? To marry a woman you can't stand in order to gain access to her money?"

"Isn't that what you did?"

Wilde started. His arms moved, his head moved, his hands. Why no; that wasn't it at all. In the beginning—in the beginning—he'd simply liked Constance. He'd been fascinated with her and her many fine qualities which even now he had to admit: her idiosyncratic thoughts, her kindness, her pools of reserve and patience and self-acceptance; the lack of triviality in her nature, when so many women of her class and circle were nothing but trivial. Cute playthings for him to toss about, turn over, and spear through the loins with pointed flirtations. No, in fact, Wilde had certainly convinced himself he was in love with Constance Lloyd. Because he was, in one way or another, according to his fashion. As for her fortune, he had not been sure about that at all. When he proposed to Constance, he did not know exactly how much she—and therefore he—stood to inherit. And it didn't much matter, because back then he had ultimate confidence in his ability to turn his talent into gold.

"I'm not sure our situations are comparable," Wilde said.

Bosie would have no more. It seemed that anything Wilde said, no matter in what tone of voice, was an irritation. "Base line, Oscar: I don't have any money to give you. Even if I wanted to. I have too many fixed expenses in Chantilly. Far too many."

Wilde couldn't help but crack a smile. "I'm so happy for your happiness."

"Oh, give it up. You're a free man. You can't ask for much more than that. And you're still Oscar Wilde—if you want to be. You still have your name."

"My name. My name? Are you crackers, Bosie?"

"I told you, I'm not going to be made to feel guilty. Not by Robert Ross. Not by Frank Harris. Not by Reginald Turner. Or whoever else now belongs to your self-styled army of obsequious slaveys. I am going to live for me for once. I'm going to spend the inheritance as I need to—for me. Try owning a stable of horses and see how quickly the money goes."

"I'm sure it does," Wilde said. He thought of how quickly his own money went whenever Bosie was around. Junkets to Spain. Junkets to Rome. Junkets to Algiers. Gifts. Dinners. Clothes. Bottles of wine. Evenings at the theatre. Nights in the arms of gigolos. Who paid for all of that? And who had wanted them in the first place? Whether they had been his own choices or Bosie's it didn't much matter, because the fact was such expenses were the price for keeping Bosie around. And Wilde had known that all the way down to his toes. Bosie hadn't needed to demand anything specific, because the demanding, consumptive nature of his personality impressed itself on one automatically, without consciously trying. Wilde knew he had been too obliging—far far too obliging—but he didn't know then, and he still didn't, what other choice he'd had.

Finally, whether Bosie had fleeced him or if he had fleeced himself, it was all water under the bridge. What he had now was his miserable, bankrupted existence. And he needed Bosie's help. He had hoped, hoped more than anything, more than for even the money, that Bosie would want to help; not out of obligation, not from the force of legal argument, not from any threat, but out of actual love—some abiding, immovable affection. Because Douglas had once loved him, Douglas should want to help him. Now that he could.

"You have left me bleeding, Bosie," Wilde muttered into his elbow.

"Not at all," Douglas said. He pushed back his chair and stood up. "I've simply left you."

PART TWO

CHAPTER EIGHT

Paris. March, 1900

Coming back across the Pont de la Tournelle, he felt the cold and the lingering wetness of the day sink into the bones of his fingers. The sky was dismal: an avalanche of gray. Meanwhile, the March wind was on and off active, as if playing with a notion of torture. There was nothing he could do, however, except to keep moving, keep walking. Sooner or later he would reach a place he did not need to move from.

Wilde had gone to take in the exhibits at the new Grand Palais, because it had been recommended by Dupoirer, and because it was free on Tuesdays. But the palace's doors had been closed and locked without explanation. It occurred to him to knock, but then he realized not only the futility but the ridiculousness of the gesture. So he'd simply turned and walked back the way he came. It would be a long trek to his hovel of a room. Too long, at least by his standards, if not the standards of the average Parisian. Parisians walked farther and harder than Wilde had any use for. At this point in his life what he needed most were Paris's comforts and its kindnesses and its excesses and its vaunted (if not always demonstrated) liberality.

He had not felt right in his body for several weeks. Since his unsuccessful meeting with Douglas at the Café de la Paix, new symptoms had come on, heightening the now familiar aches he'd been worried about in Rome.

Three or four times he'd experienced actual vertigo, his brain both airy and in pain, the world dipping and fluctuating before his eyes like a sine wave. He'd had to take to his bed for more than a day at a time to get over each attack. And while once recovered he could resume his old, listless rounds more or less intact, he felt constant muscle soreness. Like what he'd felt in Rome but worse. Tighter. Constant. When he got out of bed in the morning—a normal morning without vertigo—his ear throbbed with a worrisome, peculiar pain. He'd suffered an abscess while in Reading, and he wondered if somehow it could have returned. But it was not just the ear. Some days he hurt all over, on every side, top to bottom. When he finally managed to push himself out of bed, he hobbled around as stiffly as an old man with gout. On an almost daily basis he considered not getting out of bed at all, in order to deny the humiliating stumbling act.

A bath sometimes helped. Coffee and something to eat. Champagne helped most of all. It was impossible for him to feel distraught under the influence of champagne. Somedays he would down an entire bottle before heading out to meet the day. And the walking helped, reluctant as he was to admit it. The sore muscles and stiff joints softened after a while, although on days that his ear hurt, it just hurt. No amount of walking would take that away.

As he crossed the Seine, with the whole of the city spread out for him in every direction, he thought of the substance that was Paris. The physical fact of it. Its logic; its sequential, mathematical grandeur. He liked to think that he did not need Paris's long blocks and its exacting organization; he did not need for the boulevards to intersect at such regular intervals with its lesser major streets, or for its side streets to run north and south or east and west with such reliable infallibility. Because he liked to think that he was a man perfectly indifferent to walking in Paris, a man who was more than happy to take a hansom; who at any time, actually, would prefer a hansom to a walk. But of course hansoms cost money, and when there was not a friend nearby, he was the one who had to pay for it. Which on this day was impossible. So he walked, or rather—as he liked to think of it—treated his joint pain and his looming vertigo with physical exertion.

He wished he were someplace warm with a drink and a delightful, clean-faced boy for company. Or failing that with a faithful ally from England like Reggie or Robbie. But Robbie was established in London for the season, and Reggie had gone back indefinitely after their Roman foray. Neither would travel to Paris anytime soon. Frank Harris was too busy making junkets to Monte Carlo to make sure the manager of his restaurant didn't rob him blind; that and bothering Wilde to hurry up and write the first act of the play they'd talked about the previous summer. But he was done with writing, and Harris, at this point, should know that. Harris's last ditch notion that they write a play together—Harris offered to do the yeoman's work on the project, if Wilde would just deign to write the opening act—was as impossible as it was touching. The discussion ended with Wilde tepidly agreeing to the plan provided Harris pay him £50 for the concept they discussed, an old one Wilde had tossed about in 1894 but done nothing with. He'd then gone and laid in a stock of champagne with the £50 and proceeded to forget the conversation altogether, at least until Harris starting bothering him with letters and the occasional stopover on his way back from Monte Carlo.

Maurice Gilbert was still in Réunion. When he'd first arrived on the island in August, Gilbert had sent a letter explaining that his company might only stay until November. A month later, he'd written to say that the army had changed his mind. Once more, their assignment was to be of indefinite length. "And they will not even tell us why!" Gilbert complained. Of course not, Wilde thought. That is what it means to be in the army. And in prison.

For a while after the painful run-in with Douglas and Gilbert at Nogent, Wilde had barely been able to summon the boy in his imagination. His mind actively resisted any effort, probably because that picture of Bosie reaching for Gilbert's willy would have been too much to take. Then, after a time, he had tried again. He had tried because he was lonely and because he knew Douglas was absent from Paris and because he was faced with these considerate notices from Réunion, and out of allegiance to their formerly exclusive love affair. But now, after several months without a letter from him, with no idea when or if he would ever come back, alas, Maurice Gilbert seemed just... gone. And as for Bosie... Lord Alfred Douglas wasn't worth considering anymore. He just wasn't. No, all that Wilde had at present, that minute, was the late-winter Paris chill, this bridge, and his miserable old body, such as it was. That would have to be enough.

As he reached the end, he spied a young man seated on a wooden stool that angled slightly westward, toward the Île de la Cité and Notre Dame. An easel stood before him that held a sizeable piece of canvas in a stretcher frame. Wilde could only see the back of the canvas and the squirrely concentrated expression on the face of the young man. With his cinnamon red hair and fair skin and dusting of lingering freckles, it was a safe bet that the man was not French. English? Quite possibly. Scots? Let's hope not, Wilde thought. Besides, in his experience he had not seen many Scots with cinnamon hair and freckles. The man could, of course, be Irish, although one was far less likely to meet an Irishman than an Englishman in Paris, even less likely than it was to meet an American.

An American? Might that be what he was? Wilde looked again, more critically. With a bastardized group like the Americans it was hard to recognize them with a single glancing appraisal. One had to be close up, to watch the assertive motion in a person's shoulders, the spring in his neck, the cold, doubting cockiness in his eye. These were the features that gave away an American. And then when the man opened his mouth... Well, any idiot could tell an American then, even if the man was speaking French. Maybe especially if he were speaking French.

Americans of a certain class, Wilde knew, regarded a Parisian sojourn as a veritable social requirement, not dispensed with except for reason of bankruptcy. Wilde had met plenty of them so far in his stay here. He couldn't say they were all dreadful, though many of them were. But for their dreadfulness and even their naked philistinism there was the crucial benefit of their more guarded attitude toward him. The English—unless they were actual friends of his—he never talked to anymore, so certain could he be of their disheartening rudeness. With the Americans it was at least still worth the chance.

He's certainly earnest, Wilde thought, as he studied the face of the young man. And that would be typical of Americans. Also typical of artistic Americans in this city. Nowhere in the world but Paris could one find such a tidal pool of aspiring New World pups, angels of young people with the determination of miners and the dreams of billionaires. They set up their easels on whatever bridge or street corner they chose; in every one of the city's six-dozen museums; and in each of its parks. So determined; so hardworking: bent over their canvases, pushing their brushes like swords. Always working. It would have been heartbreaking if it were not at the same time so noble. Too noble for him to criticize. He had not that hardness in him anymore, if he ever did have it.

Wilde stared the young man in the eye as he passed, but he received no stare back in return. Too bad. The wave in his hair was endearing. As was his short, upturned nose; rather like Robbie's nose, what had always been his best feature. For certain, this boy was pretty enough to waste some time on. But alas, the fellow remained genuinely engrossed. A couple yards farther on—on the other side of the painter's back—Wilde stopped, turned, and faced the canvas. He was too curious now about what he might see; what was so beguiling that it could hold a young man's wavering attention to the point.

The painter was indeed composing a view of the cathedral—a capable if not exactly startling rendition—although the cathedral was not, at that moment, what he was fussing with. Instead, he kept running his brush through river water that formed the lower quarter of his painter: the turgid, gray winter face of the Seine. The young man was busy reworking the color of that water with brush stroke after brush stroke, layering in a variety of new shades: cloud white; mud brown; a slurred combination of blue and black and yellow that looked something like purple set on fire and turned to ash; an erratic, nonsensical alarm of orange. Nothing that the young man added, however, made the water any more realistic or more enticing to look at. His gray was gray; but not firm or dark enough; not substantial. Which is not to say that what the picture needed was more darkness. No, Wilde doubted that would do the trick. More dark wouldn't make the river water look any more alive but only like a darker kind of dead thing. Either way the water would carry no momentum. Something was incomplete—or plain wrong—in the young man's method; something was not clicking. But from Wilde's limited artistic experience—he was an amateur ink-on-paper sketcher—he could not say what that was. All he knew was that whatever the young man had tried so far wasn't working. What existed on the canvas was not the wintry

Seine but slate-toned sludge.

"Water," Wilde said, in English.

The painter started and turned. "Pardon? Did you speak to me?" His eyes—a murky, mineral-flecked brown—studied Wilde with the same hard ferocity that he'd just focused on the painting. Meanwhile, with his first spoken word the painter had given himself away. Wilde had been right: American.

Wilde tilted his head a quarter inch and reconsidered the painting. He opened his mouth as if to speak, then squinted. "I would never have thought that spending an afternoon scrutinizing river water is a good thing."

"Scrutinizing?"

"Isn't that what you're doing?"

"I thought I was painting it." The American stood up then to address Wilde full on. He gripped his palette and brush tightly, as if afraid Wilde would try to remove them. He was of medium height, shorter actually than most Americans he'd met, but with a healthy breadth to his shoulders and a kind of rangy sinuousness he associated with ancient Greek wrestlers and English footballers. Quite a specimen, actually.

Wilde wasn't quite sure what to say in response to the American's last statement, so he just said, "Yes." He saw the muscles in the painter's neck stiffen defensively, as if he had received an insult. The American was outfitted in an ordinary shirt, businessman white, relatively new, and black trousers that looked suspiciously unblemished. Perhaps his parents, who surely must be bankrolling this European lark, were wealthy enough to buy him a new wardrobe each week. But in that case, Wilde wondered why the young man had not purchased a coat to guard him against the cold. Wilde had his own overcoat on, raggedy though it might be, and he still felt chilled to center of his being. How could this young man just sit there and go on working?

"That does appear to be popular occupation," Wilde said, "especially in this country."

The painter shrugged and went back to work. "It is a part of the landscape," he said.

"I think you should draw a blue line—or a gray one—and let it go at that." The painter wheeled and studied him again. "It does not even have to be a straight line. I will grant you a curve. But, really, you'd be better served foregoing all this newfangled frenzy over atmosphere."

"How byzantine of you," the young man said.

"Exactly."

"You're not kidding, are you?"

Apparently he was supposed to have been kidding. Wilde felt the scrim of a distaste forming on his tongue; then he reminded himself that every young painter here, no matter what his nationality, would have the same attitude as this American. Apparently, it was in the Paris well water. "Not at all. I am decidedly not kidding. In fact, you will learn that I never kid anyone anymore. So trust me when I say that I find it a complete waste of time for a painter to be fussing over the particulars of water. It is only water. It is not as if it carries an attitude toward one. Or toward anything."

"I would disagree."

"Of course you would. Almost any painter would these days. But there are other painters to model oneself upon."

"Yes, ones that lived 400 years ago."

"Does that make them wrong? Or irrelevant? Does time alone invalidate a person?"

"We've learned a thing or two about representing water in 400 years. That's what invalidates them."

"Have we? What have we learned? Tell me. Please."

The American paused, turned his eyes away, thought hard about the right words to use. He thought so hard Wilde almost fell in love with him, right then and there. "I would say we've learned about the expressive nature of worldly things."

"Expressive?"

"And to resist the tyranny of the line."

Wilde felt himself smile. He hoped the young man would understand. He did not mean the smile as a rebuke, not at all. It just felt so good to be standing here before an earnest, handsome young man and toying with ideas. "One could argue that the 'line' is our only vestige of hope against the heathens. It is only the line that separates us from chaos. As for the expressiveness of worldly things, I have not yet seen and never will, any inanimate object or a force of nature—or even an animal, no matter how beloved—with a fifth of the expressiveness of the human face."

The American's expression clouded with something like anxiety. Or maybe it was just disapproval. "I have nothing against the human face."

"You were making jest with the Byzantine painters a few seconds ago, but I challenge you to find anything in nature as penetrating as the look on the face of St. Bartholomew in the painting by Giovanni di Paolo. Or, let's take it out a century or so. Surely nothing in nature is as subtly knowing as the eyes of Catherine de Medici in her portrait by Clouet." Now the young man looked confused. "François Clouet. The French portraitist. He painted all the royals four hundred years ago. You mean you've not seen a Clouet?" The American shrugged. "You'll not see any bit of 'worldly things' as charmingly ingenuous as the face of his Henry III. It's not that far from here, you know. The painting, I mean. Thirty miles or so, at the Château de Chantilly. You really need to go see."

The American nodded, once, as if he were telling Wilde that the name of the place was now marked in red in his mind.

"Every one of those paintings, especially the Giovanni, is absolutely dictated over by the line. They cannot escape it nor would they ever want to. And not a single one gives a fig about showing us water."

The young man's brows crossed, an affecting expression. "So you don't like water," he said testily. "That's obvious."

Wilde laughed. "The water is just an example of what I mean. In truth, I do not really care that much about how our modern painters fool with water. Although it does seem to have become an obsession with them. Rivers. Fog. Steam. Rain showers. Pond clouds. If they're so intent on water, I say let them imitate the medievals: a few jags, a few curves of line."

Wilde saw something shift, and then something else dawn, on the painter's face. Clear as a breakaway sun.

"Are you Mr. Oscar Wilde?" the painter said.

Wilde winced. "I am." Without meaning to, he brought his hands together in front of his body, as if to guard against a kick; but otherwise he stayed his ground.

"You saw me painting on this bridge this afternoon and took me for a man of the world."

"Actually I took you for either a nincompoop or a person with an inhuman resistance to cold. Why are you not wearing a jacket of any kind?"

The American laughed: full-throated and warm. "Wrong on both counts. I'm just a shopkeeper's son from Winnipeg."

Wilde was surprised. He'd not met a Canadian yet in Paris, not counting Robbie Ross, of course. And Ross was nothing but a uniquely liberated Brit. Surprise or no, Wilde went undeterred. "Hasn't anyone told you that March is not when you paint en plein aire? Every painter I know is working in his studio, enjoying the benefits of warmth. You are the only one brave or foolish or ill-informed enough to try to withstand the Parisian winter."

Now the Canadian smirked. His brown eyes lit with a yellow tint of pride. "Winter is what I suffered through for the first seventeen years of my life. Paris isn't cold, just annoyingly damp. And living in London taught me more than enough about weathering the damp."

"London?" Wilde asked. The Canadian nodded.

"How long?"

"Three years."

Another surprise. Most New Worlders retreated long before three years had passed. "Fair enough. The truth is, when I saw you out here painting in the cold I took you for a man willing to suffer anything for his art."

The painter lowered his head, as if abashed. "Thank you."

"Thank you," Wilde said.

The head came up, uncertainty and evident discomfort in his eye. Wilde braced. "I didn't know you were in Paris, Mr. Wilde."

"For now. For as long as I care to be."

"Why Paris?"

"Since you know my name maybe you should tell me yours. Then we can continue the conversation on even ground."

Brief, embarrassed smile. "Sorry. It's Eugene Johnson."

"How long have you been in Paris?"

"A year."

"Really? Three years in England and a year in Paris. You should know better." Wilde smiled gaily, to add to the jest, but then he realized at once—how could he have forgotten?—that this Eugene Johnson had been in England while he was in Reading prison, and when he got out. This Eugene Johnson might have been one of the people in Victoria Station that day, staring at him as if he were a three-headed zebra. "And what did you think of dear old England?"

"It's old. Which is why I'm in Paris now."

"Paris is old."

"Yes, but it does not feel old. In fact it feels completely new."

Wilde bowed, not unshowily. "So we agree. You asked me 'Why Paris?' To that I can only respond, 'Why not Paris?'"

"Yes," Johnson said, nodding. "I concur." He looked at the bridge beneath his feet for a moment, then up at the water. Except he seemed not to be looking at the water but at a certain question in the air. The skin was tight on the sides of his face, and his small, diamond shaped ears were pointed back. His eyes ticked as if counting off possibilities. A sudden rush of pedestrians—their faces closed, their coats heavy, their footsteps purposeful—passed on his left. He watched them for a few moments. A delaying tactic. "I guess what I really mean to ask is why Europe. I mean for you. When I lived in England I heard people wonder why you stayed for your trial and your verdict. They said everyone knew you were a goner. They all thought you would run while you still had the chance. So why choose to go to prison instead of fleeing England only to flee England when you are free and legal again?"

Wilde felt himself sway as if under the effect of the cloud-fueled breeze. Except there was no breeze at that moment, only an accusation that really wasn't one, a question that was friendly but could not help but to disarm him. His head went light and the blood pulsed through his skull like black spots. His ear stung with a pain he thought he had successfully left behind that morning. "I cannot give you an answer, except to say that at each turn I made the decision I felt I wanted to make and that I must make."

Johnson nodded and said nothing more about it. A moment later he turned around to face his painting once more. He examined it for a moment, then ran his brush through a pool of black paint on his palette.

"Thank you for listening to my palaver," Wilde intoned. "Please feel free to paint the Seine in whatever manner you think best."

Johnson offered a little shrug.

"I am much alone now," Wilde added quietly.

"No, Mr. Wilde, it's been my pleasure," Johnson called out, a bit too loudly. He smiled once, without looking at Wilde; a mandatory expression it seemed, but of course it wasn't. It was not mandatory these days for anyone to smile at him. Then Johnson proceeded to add more color to the river.

"May I talk more with you?" Wilde asked. "May I stay? Or would you prefer—"

Wilde saw Johnson's upper body freeze. Then the man relaxed slightly: a conscious act, an act of will. "I'm sorry. I'm supposed to be through with this by this evening."

"Some other time, then?"

Johnson said nothing for several seconds. Then: "Well, I am sometimes on this bridge. But not very often." That was all.

Wilde waited. He waited. He heard for the first

time in this conversation the river move beneath them. He felt the wind pick up again and clatter against his cheek, strong as in autumn, strong enough to cause a burn against his exposed skin and start a teary wetness in his eyes. He blinked, but it didn't help. The blinking made no difference at all. All the world, including the young man's painting, had a river gushing through it.

CHAPTER NINE

Paris. May, 1900.

"*C'est ridicule!*" Wilde exclaimed. Then slower and louder again—C'est-ri-di-cule—as if this were the only way Frank Harris could understand even rudimentary French.

Harris was obviously surprised and possibly angered by Wilde's vehemence, coming as it did after ninety minutes of discussion already. Harris's eyes widened; his brows lowered. Then with an erratic movement he picked up his napkin from his lap and wiped his mouth. He stared at the cloth morosely, as if examining the quality of the weave or some questionable residue he'd just removed from his lips. His head came up, but he instantly looked away, as if in search of a waiter—but there was none, and there would be none.

They'd lingered too long already at their sidewalk table at the Café Marocain, longer even than Parisians do. They'd lingered so long no one was eating lunch anymore. They'd seen the rush of people returning to their shops and their offices and their libraries and their factories after having devoted two hours to a midday meal. Drowned in out-of-season overcoats, or wearing frocks, some even carrying umbrellas; a din of sudden bodies emerging onto the narrow Rue des Saints-Pères. It had rained the night before, but morning had brought only a fog and then a drippy mist, both of which had cleared out well before lunchtime. The result was a cool afternoon with a smell as of winter lingering too long and a scrim of precipitation on the street; but this had not kept the Parisians from their dejeuner. Nor from their sidewalk tables. They'd eaten and eaten, and lingered and scrutinized and chatted. Then, come 3:00, they'd all scurried back to their places of employment.

Wilde and Harris, meanwhile, had kept on at the Marocain. Not to chat. Nor to scrutinize passersby. No, their business was pressing and too knotty to resolve quickly to either man's satisfaction. They'd stayed so long that when they'd asked the waiter for another bottle of wine, the ugly little man had tried to run them off with word that the café was closing in preparation of the evening service. Harris, peeved, had paid the bill in order to get rid the French irritant—a round bald head and flaring brown eyes, a thick set of shoulders inside his immaculate white shirt—to make him leave them alone so they could continue their conversation. Or their negotiation. Or their disagreement. Well, call it what it was: their argument. Harris had paid the bill and then remained there, pointing and pressing his case, determined not to leave until Wilde had accepted his view of the situation.

Which Wilde would not; not even if they stayed here for a fortnight.

"It's just not done, Frank. I know you are not a man of the theatre, but I think that even you can appreciate how absurd it is to think that you can take some other artist's idea—perhaps a few of his thoughts about setting, and a bit of his characters—and then write a play of your own with them. It won't work. It's a preposterous notion. Not if you want to produce a play that's any good."

"In that case, why did you encourage me to write it?'

"I did not encourage you."

"Why did you sell the idea to me?"

Wilde waved his arm, a loopy, light-headed gesture that he was not sure succeeded. In fact, here Harris had a point. "If you're foolish enough to buy it from me, why should I not sell it to you? It was your initiative, remember."

"To encourage you to participate in the creative process. Which you said you would."

"Hah!" Wilde tossed his head back, almost as showily as in the old days. Problem was, now he didn't have the hair for it; the thrown head did not make nearly the same dramatic statement without the hair. "That's on you, Frank, not on me. That is your old idiocy. I told you over a year ago that I am not going to write again, and I meant it."

Harris's face went grim; his hazel eyes never looked darker, never blacker. "As I recall, that was not what you said when he made our arrangement for this play. Here. Last August. Our arrangement was that I would write acts two, three, and four. You, when you felt up to it, would write the opening. That's what we agreed to; that's how we left it. That's what I got for my £50."

"Yes, that is what I said. To get rid of you. To get you off the damned subject. But I was not, and am not, going to retreat from what I told you in La Napoule."

"So you were lying."

Wilde sighed. He was so tired of this luncheon, of this debate, of these bad feelings toward an old ally. Harris had no idea how more complicated he had made Wilde's life by going ahead and writing the stupid play; the play that had been nothing more than a fancy, a topic of casual conversation between them eight months ago, when Harris had stopped in Paris for a visit. During that bantering and speculative discussion Wilde was not about to admit to Harris that he'd sold this same idea to half-a-dozen others already; and safely too, because not a one of them would ever actually produce the thing. Not even that fellow Roberts (Harold? Herbert?), whom Leonard Smithers, his English publisher, had found for him when he explained in a letter how hard up he was; not even Roberts, for whom he'd drawn up an entire four-act outline and written several paragraphs of character notes, because Roberts had agreed to pay him £250 instead of the £100 Wilde usually charged.

Roberts wouldn't produce the play. Wilde had known it from the second he'd sold it to the man, without even knowing Roberts himself. Because writing a play, an Oscar Wilde play no less, was far more difficult than any of these amateur theatre enthusiasts imagined. Frank Harris had paid him only £50—£50!—and now, in comparison with the harmless, forgettable Roberts—who was happy just to own an Oscar Wilde outline—Harris was set to ruin everything. For the length of this luncheon Harris had insisted that he would finish the play himself if Wilde didn't agree to do so. Talk about blackmail. Forced to either write what he no longer had the heart for, or to watch a butcher like Frank Harris mutilate the subtleties of his concept. It was absurd. It was insanity. The simplest course would be to admit to Harris exactly how often he'd sold the concept already and then watch as the journalist and would-be playwright abandoned, with abject disgust, the project altogether.

But Wilde could not admit what he'd done. Could not admit that this was the real reason he was arguing so vociferiosly against what Harris was set to do. Dear old converted-American Frank would only come at him with the worst sort of American-style righteousness. And Wilde no longer had the stomach for that, if he ever did.

"All right. Fair enough, Frank. For the record, what I recall saying is that I would consider writing an opening act, not that I would absolutely write one."

"No, that's not what you said. You said when you were up to it and ready, you would do it."

"Well, I'm not up to it. I will never be up to it."

Harris sighed painfully and pressed back into his seat.

Wilde raised a hand. "No matter. I do not care. If you want to believe that I lied to you, then believe it. Because you will believe that no matter what I say. And if it makes you feel better to believe it, then fine, please do. But understand that that is really not how I see the whole affair."

"I cannot fathom," Harris said, as if nailing his sentence to the wall of the café, "how you could possibly see it any other way."

Without warning, Wilde's brain swooned for a moment and then it cleared, but suddenly his ear hurt again—quite a bit—enough to encourage him to spit his response at Harris. "The way I saw it—and the way I see it—is that I could never imagine you would be so foolish as to think you could pull it off."

Harris blinked; his words stuttered in their rush to come out. "What's so foolish about it?"

"Have I not made that clear enough already? To try to put flesh on the bones on some other man's notion?"

"Shakespeare did it. Regularly. Name me a single play of Shakespeare's in which he is not making use of some preexisting story. Some other man's preexisting story. I bet you can't."

Wilde rolled his eyes: carefully. He could not risk another swoon. Of course Frank Harris would bring Shakespeare into the argument. Wilde could have predicted that amateur move. From Wilde's experience, people brought Shakespeare into any discussion to prove anything, from the price of cheese to the divinity of kings. Shakespeare was like a second Bible for the semi-literate.

"Do you really need to be so predictable? Shakespeare's age was another epoch compared to our own. The Elizabethans might well have lived in a prehistorical millennium. You might as well tell me that Euripides worked with other men's ideas; that's how long ago Shakespeare is to us right now."

Harris showed a grim smile. "Euripides did work with other men's ideas."

"Stop. Just stop it. I'm talking about the now. I am

talking about modern men and a modern theatre. It's the worst sort of form in the modern theatre to take another man's idea, the idea of an actual dramatist, and attempt to make it your own. It's bad form—plus, it's just bad."

Harris ticked. "What do you mean?"

"You don't think you can possibly write anything good, do you?"

"I think I have already written something good. Good enough that Mrs. Patrick Campbell would like to star in it. Good enough that she insists I stop waiting around for you to compose the first act and write it myself. 'A play is not a patchwork quilt,' she said. 'You don't take separate parts and try to needle them together.' That's what she said was bad form."

Wilde sat back again. The discussion had just about exhausted him; and his ear was starting to throb in that uniquely hot, piercing way; and he had yet to win his point. "There is no accounting for taste," he started. "Besides, I don't know Mrs. Patrick Campbell at all. Who is she anyway?"

"The latest new star. Her name is Beatrice but she prefers to go by Mrs. Patrick."

Wilde waved the information away. "Like I said, I cannot judge her. What I can judge—because I know you all too well—is that your heart is not in the theatre. And that can't but make it very hard for you to know what to do when you try to write a stage play. In order to write an effective stage play you must have a long history of actually seeing plays staged. You must love to see plays staged. You always attended the more celebrated productions, Frank. The ones everyone else did. But that was all. I never saw you at any of the rest; the more daring and eccentric ones; the ones that actually made the most difference. I, meanwhile, practically lived in the West End. I don't think I missed a single opening for ten years. I have the stage in my blood. Can you really say the same?"

Wilde could see Harris sitting up, gathering himself with an evident cockiness and a pert smile, as if he had expected just such a reply; as if he had done his homework, industrious American that he was, and was now ready to use it. Harris glanced into his wine glass for a moment and then held Wilde's gaze. "I seem to recall you telling me, quite a long time ago, that when you were writing your first play for George Alexander that you shut yourself up for a fortnight with a library of modern French plays as your company. You read through them all ravenously; and that's how you learned your métier."

"Yes. So? I don't deny that. One should read plays. Everyone should read plays."

Harris raised his arms in exasperation. "What do you think I've been doing all these months, sitting on my hands? I've read everything I could possibly get a hold of. I put aside everything else. I could barely tell you a thing about world affairs just now, or even the politics of England."

"That's sincerely too bad, Frank. Because world affairs is your métier."

Harris sat back as if struck. He began to shake his head, with the same expression and the same rhythm as if he were talking to someone addle-brained, or a two-year-old. That was it. Wilde had had enough. He had just offered Harris a genuine compliment. He had meant it as one. And Harris had gone and rejected it. His ear was starting to pulse, maybe with the rhythm of his anger. Now Wilde wished they could order another bottle of wine. No chance of that. The ugly waiter was probably not even working anymore; probably he was home soaking his feet.

"I see no point in us wrangling anymore about any of this," he tried. "The point is that apparently you are on the verge of finishing a play and then mounting a production of what is essentially my work. I cannot imagine you, as a novice playwright, will have any success with the thing—but that is immaterial. The fact is that you can't go off and write a play of mine without my permission, not without paying."

"I paid for it already. Fifty pounds. Last August."

"Fifty pounds," Wilde said and just let the fact hang in the air.

"Yes, fifty pounds. What of it? It was cash money, delivered on the spot. I pulled the bills out of my pocket and handed them to you. I don't recall you having any problem with it then. You seemed very happy to have the money."

"Of course, I was," Wilde said softly. "Of course." He remembered the week quite well, actually. Robert Ross's visit had preceded Harris's by a few days. He and Robbie had gotten into an argument, rare for them; Ross had cut short his visit and returned to England before Wilde could ask him for a bit more allowance, on top of Ross's usual monthly contribution. All Wilde had left in the world then was a few francs. For two days he walked the streets of the left bank, hoping to run into someone who would buy him a meal. But he met no one. Then Frank Harris showed up, eager to give him £50 for the sake of an old and sorry concept. Frank Harris had actually held out £50 in paper bills and begged him to take it.

"But it's a pittance, can't you see that?" Wilde said. "If you're so set on actually staging this thing you should give me half of what you make from it. Now that would be something. That would be fair. But fifty pounds? It's a pittance for an Oscar Wilde play."

Wilde could see anger gather again in Harris's cheeks; it began to funnel down the firm lines of his jaw, ready to explode onto the point of his chin. He knew exactly what Harris was about to say, as if the words were printed on a sign above the man's shoulder: It's not an Oscar Wilde play. It's my play.

At that moment, from only yards away on the Rue des Saints-Pères, coincident with each other, came a shout from a man's voice and shrieking whinny of a horse; also the sound of shifting of cargo in the back of a wagon that has been brought to a sudden halt. Both Wilde and Harris looked to see what looked like a workman—based on the condition of his boots and the terrible shirt he wore—supine on the damp street, without a coat, still alive but looking dazed and barely conscious, while the driver of the wagon was standing up in his seat shouting recriminations. *"Idiot! Imbecile! Ce qui ne va pas avec vous ? Faire une habitude juste marcher dans une rue sans regarder?"* Idiot! Imbecile! What is wrong with you? Do you make a habit to just walk into a street without looking? The driver, a thick-cheeked man in a bowler, sat down then, huffing and steaming, eyes darting, still vivid. He stood up again. "*Ne savez-vous pas que vous aurait pu blesser mon cheval?*" Don't you know you could have hurt my horse?

It was not clear at all that the man lying in the street understood, or even heard, what the driver was saying. One of his legs moved. Maybe an arm. Three or four people surrounded him and leaned over, blocking Wilde's view. One of the people moved, and Wilde heard the sound of a cheek being slapped. The slapper yelled: "*Restez au courant. Ne pas dormir. Vous pouvez ne jamais se réveiller.*" Stay aware. Do not sleep. You ma y never wake up.

Others on the street started pushing in order to see what was going on. Then the group surrounding the fallen man shouted for everyone to let the fellow get some air. Reluctantly, bodies moved back. Then the fallen workman was pulled onto his feet. Wilde could see that he was blinking. He was breathing. But his dark hair was a splayed mess, his threadbare white shirt was soiled with wet and mud from the street, and his face was pale. He looked as if he would collapse to the ground the second they let go of him. He squinted once, then glaced with amazement at the horse. He offered a ragged, dizzy smile. Wilde wondered if the man was drunk. Either that or knocked out of his head. Then Wilde saw the man shake his shoulders, as if with a chill. He said something in a quiet voice to the taller and beefier man keeping a hand under his left arm. The beefy man nodded and let go. The man who had been struck stayed standing. Apparently he was not about to fall asleep forever. At this point, the wagon driver—who was seated again, silently stewing—made an obscene gesture to the struck man, who reacted not at all, except to look confused.

Wilde turned back. He saw that Harris's face had changed. The rising and pointed anger had bled away. Now Harris looked only enervated, and maybe even saddened. "Tell you what I will do, Oscar." Harris reached into his coat pocket and brought out a billfold. From it he extracted three bills. Wilde could see right away they were not francs but British pounds. "For the right to use your idea, and out of the goodness of my heart, I will give you another £50 today. And when the play opens, if it ever opens, I'll pay you still another £50. And that will settle it. Is that all right with you? Is that enough? Can we call that a deal?"

Wilde hesitated at this turn of events. He saw the bills in Harris's hands. He didn't know what to do. Given the current state of the franc, and the state of his wallet, those pounds represented considerable spending power for him right now.

"Come on, Oscar, please?" Harris said. "I'm tired of arguing with a friend. I don't enjoy it at all. And, besides, look, when I'm done paying you, it will be three times what we agreed upon last August."

Wilde knew how many others would surely protest when they saw something called Mr. and Mrs. Daventry, written by Frank Harris, open in London that autumn. He knew he owed it to Harris to warn him. But that would extend this already over-long and distasteful discussion, perhaps by several hours. And likely he would also lose Frank Harris as a friend. As well as these £50. He glanced one more time at the bills.

"All right, Frank. Truth is, I don't like arguing with my friends either. So I'll take your money. And I guess that will settle it, after all."

CHAPTER TEN

Paris. September, 1900.

Though his whole head was singing with the ache that had started in his right ear, he pushed through another bitter sentence. He squeezed the body of the pen and, as he wrote them, bit off the words in his mind like portions of a sour root: *If you deny this demand of mine, I will be forced to reconsider everything kind I have ever thought or said about you. Every word I have spoken in your defense. All the times I have deflected criticisms lobbed at you.* He paused. He winced. He pushed through the next, angrier sentence: *I certainly will not allow you to simply ignore me, as you ignored my last letter. It is outrageous, Frank. Outrageous for you to just leave me here, in bed, in continuous pain, alone and without a penny. While you, unbelievably, have made a great sucess, thanks to my idea.*

Wilde knew too well Harris's reasons for staying away at present, and for not responding to his previous letter. Harris had dutifully paid off the last £50, in person and ahead of schedule even, but that was before the play had opened and two subsequent developments: first, the surprise success of Mr. and Mrs. Daventry, which was filling the Royalty Theatre most every night, despite whispers that Harris was not the actual author but only a front man for the disgraced Oscar Wilde; and second, the emergence, as soon as word of the new production spread, of every person to whom Wilde had previously sold his Daventry concept; at least a half-dozen souls who came out their gopher holes and began badgering Harris, accusing him of an infringement on their justly procured rights to the property.

Harris had posted from London a furious screed, accusing Wilde of having knowingly committed fraud and complaining that instead of earning him a richly deserved income stream, the play was costing him thousands of pounds, as he was forced to purchase back the rights to Wilde's concept from a whole host of assorted laggards and would-bes who apparently owned it before Harris did. *If you had just told me the truth I would never have gone ahead with the production. Why in blazes did you not simply tell me the truth? I am not sure I can even call you a friend any more, Oscar. Because a friend does not do to another friend what you have done to me.*

Wilde had no sympathy for Harris. He was not surprised by Harris's anger, and he did not enjoy the fact that a man he'd long known and even cherished was so amply exasperated; but that was another matter than feeling guilt. Wilde knew the financial realities of hit shows in London as well as anyone. Whatever Harris said, he doubted that it actually cost the man "thousands" to acquire rights from the others. And if the play continued to draw the kind of audiences it was currently, Harris stood to make many thousands more above what those rights were costing him. *Mr. and Mrs. Daventry* would not and could not bankrupt Frank Harris. Meanwhile, here he was languishing in Paris, living hand to mouth, with his ear in such a bad state he'd all but stopped getting out of bed. Finally the situation had so infuriated him that ten days before he shot off his own screed, demanding that Harris, considering Wilde's need and his extraordinary contribution to the play, offer him a percentage of the royalties. In only that way, Wilde argued, could he be fairly compensated.

And then Harris had decided to ignore him. Which is why Wilde had been left with no other choice than to try yet another letter, on this of all days, with his ear hurting like a son of a dog. *You can complain all you want about my "outright fraud," but what would you do when you run your fingers through your pockets and pull out nothing? Do I ask you to live on nothing?*

The more infuriating aspect of the whole affair was that Frank Harris was not a playwright. He did not now, and never would, have the refinement for the job. Harris was all about worldly action and public bluster; he was about making arguments, winning arguments, and retiring rich with yet another skinny young girl in his bed. Harris, friend and good heart though he was, had no subtlety; he had no ear for the secret lines of communication between human beings, what forever went unsaid though at the same time loudly proclaimed; what went unexpressed except through metaphor and dodge. He had such a tin ear for the discrepancies in manners that it had been impossible for Wilde to imagine him ever penning a comedy based on manners, though Harris certainly had it in him to write a bold review of someone else's comedy after the fact. But then Harris had gone and done it. Done it well enough to have a hit on his hands!

If you would just agree to what I suggested in my last letter, to give me a cut of the royalties—not even that large of one; say thirty percent—everything will be solved. You will be formally off the hook; I will no longer hound you; and for once during my stay here I won't have to scrounge for my dinner. I can even hope to get this terrible ear of my mine fixed, which for the last month has presented such trouble as I would not wish on anyone—even you, my scoundrel thief, my blustering plagiarist.

All right, so "plagiarist" might be a bit strong, but in his current mood Wilde didn't care. It was an uncharitable letter to a friend who had once done his best to keep Wilde both alive and free, but Wilde didn't care about charity; he cared about pain. He cared about having enough money to pay whomever he had to to get rid of that pain. The pain had become so intolerable that two weeks earlier he had written to the British embassy for a recommendation of a physician. The embassy had offered their own doctor, a young Frenchman named Maurice a'Court Tucker. Tucker had examined Wilde but so far taken no real action, except to impose his relentless cheerful company upon Wilde almost any day of the week, whether Wilde wanted it or not. Neither had Wilde paid him. Meanwhile, the pain had only gotten worse, turning so bad that now champagne almost did no good; at least until Wilde had drunk so much he passed into a soggy black stupor and snored so loudly that the occupant in the next room had complained to Dupoirer and thus was moved. Wilde didn't know how many rooms Dupoirer had with which to shift unhappy tenants. But he was also just about out of money for champagne. What Dupoirer gave him free of charge didn't begin to cover his medical need.

I am thinking I may have no choice but to try opium as my next self-styled treatment. I know you would disapprove, but then again you are not exactly affording me the highest medical care, are you? So far the doctor I employ has figured out nothing. He has also fortunately declined from sending me a bill, but the day of reckoning is near.

Without warning, the door to his room opened. As if summoned by the devil, in walked Doctor Tucker. This marked the eleventh time in nine days he'd come to Wilde's hotel room. So far, the thirty-year-old physician was more valuable for his stark black hair and restless eyes, his unblemished hands and rowdy laugh, than for his diagnostic skills. But at least he claimed confidence in the prospects for Wilde's recovery. Wilde was not certain he should believe the man, but for now he'd decided he would. Because, after all, what would be the alternative.

Tucker stepped to the center of the room and began talking. Wilde noticed he had not brought a doctor's bag with him. So, once again, this visit was for conversation and information only, not for treatment. Wilde almost fainted. When would he receive actual ministration? "How do you feel?" Tucker called out, in English. "Do you feel any better? Were you able to sleep? Did the *médicament* help?" The evening before the doctor had given Wilde the slightest dose of morphine, barely any at all, but enough apparently for his purposes. Also, apparently not enough to matter. But Wilde had appreciated the effort.

"It did not, doctor. I think you need to give me more."

Tucker frowned, his brows coming down low over his eyes. Wilde could see naked puzzlement there. "I'm afraid I do not understand," the doctor said. "And frankly, I am beginning to worry."

"You're beginning to worry?" Wilde dropped his letter and his pen and the book he had been using as a hard surface. Surely leftover ink from the pen's nub was spoiling the bed cover, but he could not bring himself to care about such things anymore. By the time Dupoirer decided to bill him for it—and chances are Dupoirer never would—he'd be dead.

"Yes, I am. I admit it. If this were a simple matter of an infection, time and your temperature elevation— you know, the *fièvre*—should have cleared it up."

"I don't have a fever, doctor, although my head is indeed on fire. It actually feels as if I am drowning inside. Drowning from water that is scalding hot."

Tucker nodded slowly. A thought moved across his eyes, then passed. He made one noise, then another. Clearly, the man had not even a hypothesis for what was causing Wilde's symptoms. Not even now, after nine days on the job.

"I did tell you, did I not, that in prison I suffered an abscess in this ear? The doctor there looked at it and treated me. Don't you think it could be the same now?"

"I have looked, and I do not believe that is what you have now."

Despite his discomfort and his agitation, Wilde kept himself from saying, How much do you actually know about it, Doctor? He congratulated himself on his gentlemanliness and wished Tucker would reward him with more morphine. He wondered, out of nowhere, about that Canadian boy he'd met at the Pont de la Tournelle. How much he had complained about pain then— but how much better he'd felt! Just sore and achey, not on fire, not drowning. He wished he had met the boy again, but he never had. Though since then he'd passed over the Pont de la Tournelle probably forty times. Eugene Johnson had simply disappeared. Back to Winnepeg, perhaps. Never to be heard from again.

"So what is wrong with me, then?"

Tucker brought his right hand to his chin; his left hand cradled his right elbow. His expression migrated from puzzlement to a dark and solemn consternation. Finally, his gaze left Wilde's face and focused instead on the floor.

No injured ears down there, Doctor.

"I am afraid," Tucker started, "that I see no other recourse than surgery."

This was sudden. And Wilde was fairly certain he did not want Maurice a'Court Tucker slicing up his ear. "You are sure about this?"

"I am sure yes. We can, you see, relieve the... the... *pression*; on the inside, you know? There is surely fluid, perhaps much. We can release the fluids and set your ear clear. And then after it is healed we can hope you recover. It is at least a step toward a solution."

"So you intend to just cut out my pain?"

Quick, nervous smile from Tucker. "Plus ou moin."

"And it's that simple?"

"Simple?" Tucker offered a shrug. "We can hope. But we cannot know until we open your ear and look."

Wilde was warming to this idea. Cut out his pain. Was that possible? He was not sure he even cared. Besides, even if it was impossible, what was the worst that could happen? Could he die during the operation? So much the better.

"All right, so when do you want to do this? And at what cost to me?"

Based on Tucker's new sour expression, the second question was for the doctor a distasteful one. "Cost? Who can say until we open you up and look inside? I do not want to mislead, you understand." Tucker must have noticed the barbed look in Wilde's eye. "Okay, yes, however, I see how you may need a general estimate. So, let us say that we do what I expect and the cost is thus along those lines—"

"You keep saying 'we.' Is that merely an affectation, or are you telling me that someone will assist you with the surgery?"

"Assist?" The puzzlement again. Wilde wondered if he needed to use the French word instead, but assist seemed a fairly basic concept, one that any second language speaker would have had to master almost immediately.

"Assist you. With the surgery." My God, did he have to do a pantomime for this nincompoop?

For no apparent reason, Tucker laughed. This was frightening; also inappropriate. "I see your misunderstanding. I comprehend. No, I am not the surgeon. I am not a surgeon."

"So who is the surgeon?"

"I do not know that yet. I will have to see who is available."

"Available when exactly?"

"Tomorrow, of course."

"Tomorrow? You want me to undergo surgery tomorrow? *Un jour a partir de maintenant?*"

"Does this frighten you? If yes, we can wait. I understand."

"No. We will not wait. I am not frightened, and I want you to cut out my pain."

"Of course. So I will return tomorrow with the surgeon, and you will have the operation, and you will pay him."

"Pay him? But how much?"

Tucker startled. "Oh, yes, exactement. The general estimate... So then let me say 3000 francs."

"3000."

"Oui."

Tomorrow?"

"Yes, of course."

Wilde sighed and leaned back against his pillow. Down there below somewhere was his stranded letter to Frank Harris, complaining about his impoverishment. His ear was soaring and pulsing now—high and hard and scorching beats—while the middle of his head billowed and bellowed. He was really not sure he could stand another second of it. He was tempted nearly every moment to find a knife and remove his whole head from his neck.

"In that case," he spoke slowly, trying to line his words up right, "we cannot do the operation tomorrow. Not a chance."

CHAPTER ELEVEN

Paris. October, 1900.

Though it was a full six hours earlier than the hour he normally would force himself to sit up in bed and accept that he could sleep no more, Wilde sighed, leaned forward, and scooted back until he was supported by the headboard. It was pointless to try to rest anymore. He had not rested the entire night. It was not for lack of fatigue that he hadn't slept. Indeed, Wilde felt as tired as he'd ever felt in his life: his eyes burned and felt scratched as if with sand, the insides of his head were gluey and red, his cheeks were drooping. I must look utterly dreadful, he thought. What had him awake now was simple pain. Because of the surgery scheduled for this morning, Tucker, during his check-in the night before, had cut Wilde off from morphine for one evening, a tremulous decision that left Wilde in tears, begging the doctor to reconsider.

"No, no, no," Tucker had replied—Wilde had noticed and begun to resent his habit of triple word repetition—"the surgeon will surely give you something before he cuts into you. We do not want to worry about whatever that is mixing with the morphine."

"Let it mix. I don't care. What's the risk? That I sleep even better?"

Tucker laughed as if Wilde had said exactly the best

joke he'd ever heard; then he began to pack his physician's bag.

"What if I don't sleep?" Wilde exclaimed finally. "How can you expect me to sleep without morphine?"

Tucker had considered this question seriously for a moment and shrugged. "To speak truth, Mr. Wilde, I don't expect you to, and I don't see how it much matters. Whether you have slept or not, the doctor can perform the surgery. And he will give you something to make sure you are not *conscient*. So you will definitely sleep after he gets here."

"But I'll be a wreck, a shell of myself," Wilde tried, knowing exactly how pathetic such an answer sounded.

"When haven't you been a shell of yourself," Reggie Turner had said with a suggestive smile. Turner, who'd arrived only the night before, had come back early from a trip to Egypt as soon as he heard about the surgery.

"Shut up, Reggie," Wilde shot back, regretting every syllable even as he spoke them. "You know nothing about my morphine."

A small, patient look on Turner's face. "I know more about it than you think. And I believe the doctor is right. The last thing we want is for the surgeon's sleep medicine to mix with the morphine and put you six feet under ground before he's even had a chance to save you."

Wilde had no reply; at least not he cared to give. After a minute, he muttered, "Surgery is a lot to live up to. Especially for me."

Turner smiled. "When hasn't Oscar Wilde been a lot for you to live up to?"

Wilde shrugged. True as this may have been, it was irrelevant. He'd never had surgery before.

Tucker had taken advantage of the interruption to say goodnight. Soon after, Reggie went upstairs to the room he'd let from Dupoirer for the week. "As long as you're set for the night," Turner chirped. Wilde was not set, not at all, except to endure hours of filmy hot pain, but instead of guilting the friend who'd gone out of his way to be in Paris just now, Wilde merely sighed and said, "I am certain I will survive. Just turn down the lamps if you will."

Any hesitation he'd felt about the surgery was gone, demolished by the two weeks it took for him to raise donations to cover the cost of the surgery and by another round of this oceanic pain. Now, on the very day of its arrival, he didn't care if Dupoirer himself took a knife to his head—as long as someone did it and the knife was sharp. For the greater part of his life Wilde had avoided doctors, even when he could have afforded them with no difficulty. He preferred to breeze through whatever ache or soreness he might have felt, relying instead on the traditional medications of cocktail, bath, and prayer. It was not as if he had doubted any physician's skill—he was the son of a physician, after all—but he objected to their necessity. I'm still young, he had said at twenty-eight and thirty-three and thirty-nine. Not until prison had he learned that one's body, if pushed beyond its ken, could respond with non-negotiable demands, demands that could only be answered by a month in an infirmary or the ministrations of a professional. At present, the only restriction on his care was economic, not spiritual, but this block had been overcome when George Alexander and Paul Fort and Pierre Louÿs and Jean-Joseph Renaud and Jean Moréas and Ernest La Jeunesse and a few others whom those men had contacted had agreed to chip in to cover the cost of the operation.

Tucker, meanwhile, had, as promised, located the surgeon: one Paul Cleiss. A superb knife man, Tucker had exclaimed. An artist! Tucker had said it so aggressively that Wilde feared the opposite might be true: that Cleiss was a hack whose only qualification was his willingness to chop a body on the cheap. Or it could be that Tucker was trying to capitalize on certain mind-body connections, to play them in Wilde's favor. It would be just like a French doctor, and like a Frenchman, to assume that one's attitude toward the event—one's belief in it—could positively or negatively affect the success of the event itself, and of its aftermath. Perhaps this had something to do with France's tradition of Catholicism, with its emphasis on mystery. In non-Catholic Britain, Wilde knew, a cut was a cut, an operation an operation. Either your physician knew what he was doing or he didn't; and if he didn't, it did not matter what you cared to believe; you were headed to your doom.

For the moment, Wilde would commit to neither way of thinking. He would judge Cleiss when he saw the man, when he took stock of his face and neck and bearing: how his shoulders sat on the top of his body and how straight was his back. He would look at the man's hands to see if they looked sufficiently supple or if instead they looked like a butcher's hands. No matter what, though, the operation would take place. It would take place even if Cleiss were a left-handed baboon with a blue nose, red eyes, and a puffy orange arse. The pain had become that bad.

On the other hand, it was possibly a good sign that Tucker seemed to be gaining in mood and confidence every time Wilde saw him. The doctor was nearly 100% certain that a single operation would resolve the matter: let loose the fluid, relieve the pressure on Wilde's inner ear, eliminate the pain, and set up a full recovery. As soon as the wound from the operation healed, Tucker said, Wilde would feel as good as new. By no means would Wilde permit himself to believe what Tucker said just because Tucker said it. He'd been sick so long, or what felt like so long. It felt like he'd been in severe pain for seven years, even if in truth it was more like tolerable pain for seven months, followed by a month and a half of torture. If nothing else, cutting into his ear would get the immediate discharge out. It might give him a week of relief before it went bad again. And at this point, Wilde was more than willing to beg money from half-friends and suffer the invasion of a surgery if it gave him even a week of peace.

Immobile as he'd become, the operation was to be performed in his hotel room, with Wilde lying flat in his own hotel bed. He couldn't imagine Cleiss was too happy about this arrangement, but according to Tucker, the surgeon did not mind. As Tucker put it: He is such a master he can cut into you no matter where you are. Cleiss would bring along a nurse as an assistant. So no fears if there is a surgical emergency. The nurse can help.

Another person to pay, Wilde thought. Then: Surgical emergency?

"Will you be here for it?" Wilde had asked Tucker during his visit, the night before. Tucker might be of questionable expertise—he might even be a complete rube—but he brought optimism into the room; and that is what Wilde needed more than anything now.

"Me?" Tucker had said, surprised, as if—despite his near constant attendance for the last three weeks—such a development had never occurred to him, was not even remotely thinkable.

"I know you have other patients," Wilde countered. Tucker's face twitched, and the doctor glanced away guiltily. "Oui, oui, oui," Tucker said quickly. "Many patients, all over. Second arrondisement; eighth arrondisement; nineteenth arrondisement." He ticked them off on the fingers of his left hand, like a toddler learning to count. "So, unfortunately, no. I cannot come tomorrow for the surgery. But you will be in excellent hands. And I will stop in later to check."

"How much later?"

Tucker offered a difficult shrug. "Who can say for sure, one day before? Later. After the operation."

Wilde could not thank Reggie Turner enough for coming to Paris as he had, but as he thought about it, alone now in his room, with only the stale morning for company, he doubted Cleiss would want some layman lingering near while he cut open that man's friend. Likely Cleiss would exile Reggie to the lobby or even to the street. Wilde's only company during the operation might be a surgeon he'd never met and a nurse who did not yet have a name. Wilde considered whether he should ask Dupoirer to send Charbonneau over to Nortre Dame to buy him a string of rosary beads—anything that might substitute for a hand holding his own while the doctor cut into him. He almost decided he would do that, but then he realized he was out of money.

Before nine, Reggie arrived, full of the cheerfulness Wilde would expect to see from a gentleman taking cocktails at five but not from a sober person a couple hours past dawn.

"So life exists at this hour, does it?" Wilde said.

"It does for me."

Wilde grunted.

"I seem to recall that you rose terribly early to see the pope."

"I don't know who the pope is. Tell me."

"Oscar."

"I am never up at this hour in Paris."

"What about Oxford? Surely you saw a sunrise or three at Oxford. Some all night foray? Maybe an early morning study session?"

Wilde jeered. "I never needed to study, Reggie."

"I don't believe that."

"It is what I tell people. It is my legend. But it's true that I studied little."

"Like I said, I don't believe it. I went to Oxford too, remember."

But Wilde would not retreat. "I read widely. I studied little."

Turner smiled. "So, in other words, what others call studying you call reading."

"Hardly. I read what I wanted to. I'm a curious person, Reggie. I always thought the most efficacious strategy for an education was to follow one's curiosities."

Turner gave him an ironic look: all forehead and eyebrows. "You've certainly done that."

"We all have!" Wilde waved his hand back and forth between them. There was no need to specify what "we" he was referring to. "And, besides, if I ever did deign to study it would not have been at an hour like this one, fit only for ghouls and nursemaids."

Reggie chuckled. "All of Paris is awake, Oscar. They're roving the streets."

"Let them. I won't."

"Well, you can't today in any case." Then Reggie's tone turned serious. "If you want to try to sleep now, go ahead. I'll answer the door when Cleiss comes."

"Very kind of you, but I doubt I would sleep now if I could not all night long."

"Try."

"I won't be able to."

"Try for my sake." A lippy grin this time.

Wilde managed a wrecked and weary sigh. "So that's how it is, my friend. Very well. Very well."

And then, without warning, his ear in as much

pain as ever, with Reggie Turner as his company, Wilde snoozed. The next thing he knew a warm hand was pushing his shoulder. He opened his eyes to see Turner, who was pointing to the other side of the room. Cleiss had arrived with his carpenter's bag of equipment and a nurse in tow. "Ten o'clock," Turner said.

Just as Wilde had anticipated, the sight of Reggie Turner, and the explanation that he was here for the sake of the surgery, caused the surgeon to raise an officious eyebrow. It was ridiculous really. No one on earth could look more harmless than Reggie Turner—a thick-nosed gent with broad features, forgettable tan-brown eyes, a comedian's forehead, and a grandfatherly moustache that separated the bulging top of his face from his regrettably weak chin. Indeed, no one on earth was more harmless than Reggie Turner. But of course this would not matter to a medical man on a mission. At the doubtful look from Cleiss, Turner politely excused himself to the hallway, putting aside a confrontation. The nurse carried three bags of her own, so that she and the doctor formed a kind of elephant's procession into Wilde's small room. What was all this baggage for? He'd thought this operation was a simple matter of letting some fluid out.

Cleiss, a formal man with a stern brow, round eyeglasses, and a neatly maintained little moustache, set his bag down on the floor and stepped over to the bed. He knew enough to stand on Wilde's left side, where he could be heard. He bent his head slightly and spoken in stiff but correct English.

"Mr. Wilde, I am, of course, Paul Cleiss." He stretched out his hand. Wilde had no choice but to shake it. Wilde was discomforted to find out that the hand was strikingly cold—even though the day outside, according to Turner, was warm. "I am the surgeon to complete the operation today. "

Wilde wished again that he had the rosary beads. "My pleasure," he said, with no pleasure in his voice at all. There was no point in faking.

"And my assistant this morning will be Mademoiselle Camile Allard." He motioned to the nurse, who stood unmoved just inside the door, still gripping her two large leather bags. Dressed in a long black overcoat, at the lower edge of which a pair of roughened black boots could be seen, her dark hazel eyes more consternated than uncaring, a faintly lost expression on her face, Camile Allard could be any working woman one sees on the streets of Paris on any weekday. Who knew? Maybe that's exactly what she was. Maybe she'd been borrowed for the morning from some fish seller's stand or a crew that cleaned apartments or a café that had just finished serving that day's round of breakfast. She might be eighteen or twenty-eight. Her hair was dark but not exactly black. Once Cleiss said her name, Allard looked Wilde in the eye and nodded slightly. Maybe he was wrong, but he thought he spied—for the most fleeting of fleeting instants—a look of sympathetic amusement on her face, perhaps even the beginning of a curling smile. Wilde hoped this was true. It reassured him to think that the assistant to the man performing his operation might have intuited the great cosmic joke his life had become, with this operation only the latest in a series of meager punchlines. *Someone might as well smile about it before I die.*

Cleiss straightened; he held his back in place now with an almost regal stiffness. "So this is how we will proceed," he began. "Mademoiselle Allard will prepare the region around your ear... for the cutting. And she will prepare the bed to receive the blood." Wilde swallowed at the open utterance of that word. "Meanwhile, I will set out my knives for the surgery. When all these things have been accomplished we will administer the chloroform... so to put you to sleep."

"Chloroform?"

"Yes."

"Is that not what people have used to kill themselves?"

Curt smile. "Some persons, yes. Those intent on self-abuse. But it is used too in surgeries of this type. There is no reason to fear. It has been commonly employed in this country for decades."

"And it will keep me asleep?"

"Yes."

"And you've used it before?"

"Several times."

Clearly, Cleiss was not going to brook any resistance. And Wilde had no intention on staying awake while a stranger stabbed into the side of his head. *Bring on the chloroform,* he thought. *Bring it on, unto death.*

* * * *

A gluey gray light stung his face and hurt his brain, so he closed his eyes. But the image of pain as a physical entity resided at the center of his mind and try as he might he could not blink out that image by thought alone. Where had this hurt come from? What did it think it was doing? This was a new and alien pain, unlike the constant, muted throbbing from the right side of his head that had bothered him for weeks. This pain was sharp and entirely central, as if a walnut had been inserted into the folds of his brain and was sending out signals in all directions, brutal as lightning shocks. He rolled his head to one side, kept his eye closed, and realized he was nauseous. Worst of all he was so thoroughly out of available energy—not the same thing as exhaustion—that he did not know if he was capable of aiming his vomit toward a bucket or a crapper, assuming one was even available. If one was available, the mechanism was useless; because he had no energy to stand up and walk to it. Rolling his head to the side of this surface was the most he could do. He realized with the thought that he did not even know where he was. He only knew that he was supine. In all the world, this was all there was to know. When he next tried to open his eyes he saw a second's worth of dizzyingly active wallpaper, vibrating at him its pattern of scattered and inelegant blotches. The pattern made his nausea worse. In the moment, his stomach surged and seconds later he felt the burn of rising bile in his throat. He managed to roll all the way on to his left side. He dipped his chin and opened his mouth and expected a stomachful to immediately charge out, except very little did: only a string of greeny, elastic bile with eccentric flecks of brown and red. When he opened his eyes again, a figure was leaning in to him. A man he'd never seen before: maybe thirty, with brown eyes, an impressive moustache, and a tall forehead rounded on top. The man's left hand was on Wilde's shoulder. Wilde's chin was resting in the mess he'd made.

"Oscar?" the man said. "Are you still among us?"

It seemed to take Wilde several minutes and a Heruclean effort, but eventually words came out. "Who are you?"

The light was too bright, too invasive. He shut his eyes. When, after what seemed a long time, he opened them, he saw the strange man again. More about him registered now: a fleshy lower lip, avuncular cheeks, the honest expression that reached all the way to his eyes. "You know who I am," the man whispered with an accent that sounded English. He put his hand on Wilde's shoulder again and smiled. "How are you feeling now? Any better?"

Wilde opened his mouth and planned to say something cogent, maybe even cheeky, something on the order of "I still don't know who you are." But all he got out was the "I" before he heaved all over again, without warning; his back snapping, his head jutting forward, his stomach squeezing inside him like a hydraulic pump. Then one more time, but with even less success. Only a few strings of saliva found their way out of his mouth. The space on the sheets next to his left cheek felt damp. And it smelled.

The next time he opened his eyes, the man with the moustache was back, examining him with a new, almost maternal concern. The man's hand was on Wilde's side now, not for the sake of comforting but to hold Wilde in place until this fit, or whatever they should call it, passed.

"Don't be embarrassed," the stranger said. "Doctor Cleiss said this might happen. It's just a reaction to the chloroform. That's why they told you not to eat this morning."

Had he been told that? Which morning? And had he done what they asked? Who would have told him this, anyway? Cleiss? Wilde did not know a Cleiss. What kind of name was that for a Dubliner? And how did this jowly Englishman know so much about it? What was the jowly Englishman doing in his parents' house? And if a doctor was in the room, why was the doctor not talking to him instead of this kind but apparently useless stranger? Wilde's eyes drooped. At some indeterminate time—it might have been a second later or two hours—they sprung open again. The mustached man was still there, but his look now bore some determination.

"All right then," the man said. "Let's clean you up." He pushed on Wilde's side with his left hand and easily rolled Wilde over so that once again he was on his back. "Cleiss should be here soon, along with the nurse. But I don't think they would want you to be lying in that."

The man went away, and Wilde once more closed his eyes. He felt a coarse rubbing sensation around his mouth, his chin, the left side of his face. He opened his eyes. The man was beside him again holding a gray towel

Wilde almost recognized. The man rubbed compulsively at the space of sheets next to Wilde's head, ferocious to make them dry again, make them neat.

"Thank you, Reggie," Wilde said.

Turner shrugged. "Can't let you stink of honk when the doctor comes back. He'll say I wasn't doing my duty."

"Your duty?"

"A joke."

"What time is it?"

"Three o'clock."

Wilde managed a nod. That seemed about right for waking up from an operation. But then he realized something. "What is the day?" he said.

Turner chuckled. "Same day. The doctor carried out the surgery this morning. Just feels like weeks later, I'm sure. You'll be groggy for a while more, the doctor says."

"Tucker?"

"Cleiss."

"Who's Cleiss?"

"He operated on you, you fool. And he gave you the chloroform. This morning. He was here with his nurse."

Wilde, after considering it for a moment, did indeed recollect a woman standing in his room in a long overcoat. Was that the nurse? He'd had so few women visitors for so long, whereas in his old life his social community had been predominantly women: those spenders of their husbands' money, those organizers of dinner parties, those advocates of the theatre and of the opera and of temperance. He missed them. Missed their essential difference. But hadn't there been something different about the woman in the dark overcoat? He couldn't remember. He thought harder and realized he could not bring a clear picture of her face to mind, only that dark coat. Had the woman in his mind now actually been Death and not a nurse; Death lingering near his bedside to see what would come of this operation? And if so, where was Death now? Waiting in the hallway? Hiding under the bed? His eyes were open and apparently he was still breathing. Maybe that was his answer.

"Where is Doctor Tucker?"

"He stopped in. On his way to the embassy."

"He did?"

"He did."

"I don't remember that."

Turner laughed. "You were unconscious."

"Sounds terrible."

Turner emitted a low, careful noise. "I don't know. Only time will tell."

"Will Tucker come back?"

"Do you want him to?"

"Yes, very much." Indeed, this was true. In the moment, Tucker felt like a good luck charm that he had not recognized and thus had misplaced.

"That's fortunate because he's coming back tonight to say hello. And again tomorrow, he said, along with his wound dresser, to check on the incision."

"Oh," Wilde said. Then several seconds later: "I'm

glad." His eyes drooped. He still felt so tired, which he could not understand. He'd been sleeping so many hours already, and it was, according to Turner, only mid-after-noon. There were wide gaps between his thoughts in which the only thing that he heard inside the cavern of his brain was a low buzzing, like the soft burning sound of a gas lamp. He'd never had such slow thoughts. Never in his whole life had his thoughts been slow.

"You took me to Rome," Wilde said.

Turner gave him a long look. "Glad to hear that you remember our little journey."

"It didn't work."

"Was it supposed to?"

"Of course it was. Why go otherwise?"

"It made you happy, Oscar. You were happy to be there."

"I never found anyone to kiss."

Turner laughed, brightly. "Oh, dearie. I guess not. But this is the first you've admitted it."

"Is it?"

Turner nodded.

"Well, I didn't. I should have kissed Pope Leo. That would have made the newspapers." Wilde's expression changed: mild confusion. "Is Leo still alive, Reggie?"

"The pope? Of course."

"How old is he?"

"I don't know. Old. Ninety?"

"Ninety? My god." Wilde shook his head slowly. How did a human being live that long? He really could not understand. He couldn't even imagine.

"Is Robbie still alive?"

"Of course Robbie's alive. He would have come, but he knew I was here."

"Good," Wilde said, nodding slowly. He really had thought in the moment that maybe he'd gone decades ahead, and Robbie had passed.

"What about Bosie, is he alive?"

Turner looked stunned. "Douglas? Yes, Douglas is alive, Oscar. Why would you ask such a thing?"

Wilde shook his head. He did not know what answer to give. He shook his head again. "How am I going to pay all these people, Reggie?"

"Who?"

"Everyone."

"That's for another day."

"What?"

"Each day has enough worries of its own."

Wilde laughed, a loopy sound that forced its way painfully out of his throat. "Did you just quote Jesus?"

"Did I?"

"I think you did. The Gospel of Matthew." He couldn't stop the weird laughter; it kept cutting up his words and making him lose breath.

"Imagine that. A good Jew like me."

"Good Jew?"

Turner smiled. "A Jew like me."

"I don't know, Reggie, but I think that is supposed to represent the end of the world."

"Good Jews?"

"Christian Jews."

"Is it?"

"Something like that. Ask me again tomorrow, and maybe I'll be able to remember."

Another chuckle from Turner. "All right. Tomorrow, Oscar."

"Yes."

"For now sleep."

"Sleep?"

"For now sleep, dear. It's what you need."

"It is, isn't it?"

So he did.

CHAPTER TWELVE

Paris. October, 1900.

If anything, Tucker was more exuberant than usual: his small face wider somehow, the lips of his smile stretched farther, his dark hair glinting with an urgent black brightness. "I told you I would come and I have," the doctor shouted, in English. He stood in the hallway outside Wilde's hotel room. Beside him was a man Wilde had never seen before. A Frenchman by the looks of him: what with his almost olive skin, gloamy eyes, and characteristically weak Gallic hairline. Too, he wore the mangy mustache seemingly required these days of every Frenchman, and a dank look that suggested broad skepticism. What was unusual about this man, though, especially for a Frenchman, was his height. Wilde guessed he might be as tall as six-feet-five inches. Taller even than Wilde himself.

"And you are no longer in bed," Tucker continued, just as loudly. "I take that to be a good sign."

Wilde wasn't sure. Was it a good sign? Could he really say he was feeling better? The facts were that Reggie Turner had departed an hour earlier and would be gone for the better part of the day, doing some investigative work for the Telegraph. To keep Wilde company, Turner had left behind a book of bawdy French verse, a loaf of bread, and a bottle of burgundy. Turner had offered to cancel his appointment and stay, but Wilde told him not to. He could lounge in bed, read, sleep, eat, drink wine, and try to ignore his operated-on-yesterday ear just as well with or without Turner in the room. And it was true that one day later the ear did feel different. Not as clotted, not as stocking-jammed. The center of his mind was still a woozy jumble—residue from the morphine Cleiss had given him before he left—and there was no doubt of the fact of the tight new pain at the incision line. But the throbbing, oozing, hot-colored discomfort that had filled the entire right side of his head for weeks had diminished; at least to the extent that he felt able to move off the bed, to open the door when the doctor knocked. As long as he did not move his head too much or too suddenly, his head felt all right.

In fact, it was the second time that morning he'd been up. Earlier, realizing that Turner had failed to provide him a red wine glass, Wilde—with only a robe for a cover and his hair a flying mane—had stood at the door of his room and shouted until Charbonneau sent his son up. Apparently, the boy had taken to recreating in the hotel's lobby, and apparently Dupoirer did not care. Wilde paid the boy what few coins he had to borrow or steal a burgundy glass. The boy happily agreed, except that what he brought back was a glass for sherry. And an ugly one at that. Like father, like son. There was nothing for Wilde to do but let it go. "Très bien," he said, and even offered a smile as a tip.

He had been thoroughly enjoying the book of verse—it went surprisingly well with a glass of Burgundy—and reveling in his reduced level of pain when he began to notice a leaking sensation at the incision line.

Instinctively, he brought his hand up and touched the ear, but felt of course only the bandage. He was tempted to pry a finger underneath and feel what he could, but managed to resist the urge. Tucker was coming, so he said. When the doctor came he would able to inform Wilde about this new leakage. He would tell Wilde whether or not he should start to worry. Wilde held his fingers to his nose, expecting—or hoping—that in touching the bandage some information about the condition of his ear had transferred to his skin. He sniffed. Only the vaguest, barest scent of rot. But rot indeed. He did not know what to make of this development. He drank another glass of Burgundy and read on. Then Tucker had knocked, forcing him up a second time.

"I hope it is a good sign," Wilde said presently.

"How can it not be? How can it not be?" Tucker turned to the man beside him and gestured emphatically. "Mr. Oscar Wilde, this is Monsieur Philippe Hennion, the wound dresser I told you about yesterday. Monsieur Hennion, *je vous présente Monsieur Oscar Wilde.*" From his formidable height, Hennion gazed down upon Wilde and offered only a languid nod of appraisal. Wilde had to wonder if this man too, an assistant to a second-rate embassy doctor, knew about him.

"Monsieur Hennion will attend to you every morning, changing the dressing and examining the ear. Later, he will report to me. If necessary, I will come to your room myself, but that, right now, for each day will be what is called an 'open question'; yes? I will come as often as necessary: several times a day or maybe not at all. But

Monsieur Hennion will attend to you every morning."

"For how long?"

"Until the wound is healed, of course."

"And that will be?"

Tucker offered a shrug. "Who can say? Not too long, I expect. And at that time you should start to feel much improved. This getting out of bed will be nothing. You will want to walk, to swim, to go the opera."

Wilde smiled at the doctor's enthusiasm, but the expression made the incision hurt so he stopped. "But what if after the wound has healed my ear still hurts?"

Tucker frowned, brought his hand to his chin. "I cannot imagine that happening," he said. "Sincerely, I cannot. But if so it would be a cause for concern, yes."

"Another operation?"

Shrug. "Who can say? I would rather not predict."

In other words, yes. Without intending to, Wilde slumped, even as he stood there. His shoulders dipped, stomach sagged, lungs lost air. "Because at the moment, doctor, it's not feeling entirely normal."

Tucker waved the concern away. "Of course not! One day ago your ear was being cut upon." He imitated a motion a sawing motion, one used by a person laying a knife into a loaf of bread. "Of course it does not feel good in this moment! There will be many days before it feels normal. But eventually, yes."

Wilde nodded. He appreciated the optimism, but at this point he could believe much more willingly in that bottle of Burgundy.

"Now, please, return to bed, so you can rest the ear

and I can inspect." Tucker turned and spoke in a squall of French to Hennion. Wilde could not help but notice that in Tucker's translation of the facts he had made the case far more positive than it deserved. In Tucker's telling of it, Wilde was suffering now from an "unusually small amount of pain for so soon after a major operation." Wilde would have spoken directly to Hennion to refute that summation, including the "major operation" bit— how many major operations get done in a hotel room— but he knew exactly how impolite that would be. Plus he really just wanted to get back to bed.

Once he was settled, Hennion approached, with Tucker in tow, drawing close to Wilde's right side. The tall man leaned over and examined the dressing applied the day before by Cleiss's nurse. He made a noise.

"What?" Wilde said. "What is it?"

Silence. Was Hennion talking something over with Tucker and he just couldn't hear?

"What?" Wilde tried again. He started to turn his head, but Tucker interrupted with a friendly warning. "No, just hold still, please. Hold still. There is nothing to worry about. Monsieur Hennion needs to remove yesterday's bandage." What the hell was Hennion grunting about then? What could he possibly have seen before he even removed the bandage?

Wilde quieted and Hennion began, his hands moving with startling delicacy. The tips of his fingers barely grazed the side of Wilde's head and while he worked through the motions slowly there was never an awkward pull or unseemly force used on the bandage, which seemed to slip off as readily as if obeying a command. The whole time Wilde was braced for a shock of pain—his teeth remained gritted and his eyes almost shut—but before he knew it the bandage was removed and he felt the gentle air of the room against his ear.

"So," Tucker said, "now let me look." One immediately positive sign: Wilde heard Tucker well—not as well as his left ear could have, but much better than he did two days before—as if ton of blockage had been evacuated from his ear canal and it was nearly a smooth passageway to the inside. Tucker leaned in. Like Hennion, he made a noise, but it was a lighter, more warbly, more speculative kind, an erratic countertenor compared to Hennion's worried-filled basso.

"Yes?" Wilde said.

"Very interesting," Tucker said. "*Très, très, très... interesant.*"

"Please tell me."

Tucker stood up straight, apparently done. He walked around to the center of the bed so that he could address Wilde directly without making the patient turn his head. "The ear is clearer than before, I think. You have lost a great deal of *fluide*? You are able to hear now from this side, yes?"

"That's correct."

Tucker practically blistered with joy. "This is superb, an excellent reason for hope. I would anticipate that in the coming days you will feel better, not just in the ear but in all ways."

"Are you sure?"

"You know of course that one can never be sure in medicine. The human body is a rare and mysterious machine. Of your recovery, though, I am hopeful."

"You saw nothing that troubles you?"

A new look on Tucker's eminently changeable face: a suppressed grimace that came out as a hard, flat look, one that kept his mouth in a straight line. "Well," the doctor began, "there is a bit of new wetness at the incision line. It appears to be pus."

Inside himself, Wilde grew still. Pus was not something that struck him as traumatic, but given Tucker's last reaction apparently it was not a good development.

"But really," Tucker said, "this is to be expected with a new cut."

Also with a damaged ear.

"Pus is actually preferable to a clear liquid. It indicates an eventual recovery. There may be a bit of an infection, though I see no obvious signs of one. I anticipate that more pus will accumulate and then stop. And as your incision heals, the pus will disappear. And when you are fully recovered from the operation, your life will be your own once more."

Wilde burped out a grim chuckle. "Since when has my life been my own?"

Tucker paused, blinked, his expression stuck as if he had to translate Wilde's statement multiple times before any workable meaning arrived. Then he stretched his arms out to his sides. "I am speaking medically, of course."

"I know that," Wilde grumbled. "What about this

infection, though?"

"I do not know if the ear is infected or not. That was merely a supposition."

"Shouldn't you know?"

"With the human body knowledge sometimes is not immediate."

Wilde almost laughed. That sentence contained more in it than Tucker could begin to know. He wondered if he should try to talk the doctor into writing poetry. Problem is, the man lurched into poetry only when he was not trying to be poetic.

"Even so, what can you do about this infection?" Wilde asked.

"We may not need to do anything, if there is only the pus. As I say, the pus is a good sign. But if you insist"—Tucker motions became more energetic, anticipatory; Wilde might even call them joyful—"I could wash the ear with carbolic acid."

"Acid?"

"It is the proven way."

"Of what?"

"Retarding infection."

"Acid?"

"Only if you wish. But I am happy to perform this service."

"What do you wish?"

Tucker smiled broadly, like a comedian with a punchline. "Full recovery, my dear Oscar Wilde."

Wilde groaned. "I do not think I want an acid wash on my ear. Not right now."

Tucker bowed with exaggerated graciousness, but the comic gesture only annoyed Wilde. "Unless," Wilde said, "you really do think that will solve it and the ear will then be free to heal normally."

New look of concentration from Tucker. "I am not sure the wash is necessary. Because I am not sure the ear is infected. But it would not be a problem to perform; and it would cause no damage. None at all. A bit of pain, yes, but no damage. If you decline, it may still be okay. The pus, if that's what it is, is considered a good sign. It means the ear will heal slowly but will heal. Within a week or two you should feel completely sanguine about taking a walk outdoors. Go to a café. Go to a garden. In fact, I would recommend that you actually do those activities. At a certain point the plein air should speed the healing. As well as pick up your spirits, which is perhaps the more important consideration."

That seemed like a very tall order indeed. Picking up his spirits. And in two weeks he would be roving the Paris sidewalks again? In the moment, in the bed, with his ear bleeding pus, this seemed like a fantasy.

"So" Wilde said slowly, "you really think two weeks? That's all?"

Tucker smiled: that same old too-easy expression. "Again, who can say with the human body? But it is possible."

"And Monsieur Hennion will come for those two weeks?"

"Yes. Everyday. And he will report back to me. I will come frequently as well. It is always a pleasure."

Wilde nodded. It was so simple a formula he couldn't believe it: pus and then healing. Two weeks of modest discomfort and then health. Walking through the streets of Paris, scrounging up drinks in a café. Might he finally find out what Maurice Gilbert was up to, now that the boy had left the army? Might Bosie come down from Chantilly for a visit? In two weeks, could he actually take a drink with Bosie Douglas and ask if he had found a wife yet? Was it that simple a matter?

"So I guess that is it," Wilde said. "We wait and see."

"Not exactly. You have not told me what to do about the acid."

"Acid?" Wilde thought that he had.

"Do you want that I wash your ear with the acid or not?"

Wilde almost laughed at the look of longing in Tucker's eyes. Apparently it was not everyday—if ever at all—that the doctor was permitted to wash a patient's ear with carbolic acid. Wilde tucked his smile away.

"I will decline the acid, Doctor. But thank you. I am sure you are right that it is the prescribed method. But just now I will spare my ear that pain."

Tucker frowned, once. He brought his hands up as if to initiate a fistfight, or something. Then he nodded and said, "It is as you desire. It does not matter. Either way, you will get better. I am sure of it."

CHAPTER THIRTEEN

Paris. October, 1900.

The first few mornings, Wilde tried to tip the wound dresser. Each time Hennion politely declined Wilde's money. The fourth time Wilde tried, with more insistence than ever, Hennion reacted angrily, snapping at the patient with a precision born of hurt pride: "This is my job," he said in taut French. "Not a hobby. Doctor Tucker pays me." As if Wilde was suggesting that Tucker had somehow manipulated Hennion into working for free.

After this exchange, Wilde gave up trying to tip, but he remained curious about this wound dresser. Such a collection of contrasts: large and yet delicate; attentive and yet stern; silent and yet with much apparent knowledge. One morning, about a week after Hennion had started coming, a morning with no sighs or low-level muttering, no expressions that suggested it was useless to hope for complete recovery, Wilde asked Hennion straight out if he had a family. Wilde knew it was violation of their protocol, but he couldn't help himself. The arrangement—the man coming to his hotel room day after day and touching Wilde's ear while barely saying a word—had become oppressive. Even depressing. It was discomforting for him to try to carry on a conversation when he couldn't monitor the other man's expressions, but for Wilde this was infinitely preferable to no conversation at all.

"So, Monsieur Hennion," Wilde started, "Doctor

Tucker tells me you are married."

Silence. "Yes."

"Any children?"

"One."

"Boy or girl?"

"A girl, yes."

"So she's a girl?"

"Yes."

"Ah."

Silence.

"And your wife... does she work too?" Wilde would not think of asking this question of a British husband, who would surely be insulted by the insinuation of poverty. But one thing he enjoyed about the French was how much more direct he could be with them, on all matters of life.

"My wife works outside our home," Hennion answered, slowly, "but she works as a mother to the girl as well. This is an important job."

"Of course you are right. I did not mean to suggest otherwise."

Silence.

"And what is the company where she works? What kind of job?"

"She is a laundress."

"Fascinating," Wilde said, though it wasn't. The laundries, it seemed, employed half the young women of Paris. The other half worked in brothels. "And is she large like you?"

"Like me?"

"Yes."

"My wife is a woman, monsieur. She cannot possibly look like me."

Wilde chuckled, even though he was certain Hennion could not be making a joke. "I don't mean like you exactly. I am merely wondering if she, like you, is tall. You are tall for a Frenchman, Hennion. I know you know this."

"My wife cannot be tall. She is a woman."

"French women are never tall?"

Pause. "No."

"Really? Never?" Wilde considered the statement. While everyone knew the French could never match the towering Dutch, or even the English or the Germans, he found it hard to believe that in the entire country no woman managed a man's height. Didn't such anomalies happen everywhere?

For several moments, Hennion considered the question again, finally amending his previous statement to, "I have never seen a tall French woman."

Wilde reveled. The man was an intuitive logician! Realizing that the absolutist proposition he had just espoused could not be proven correct unless he could claim to have personally witnessed every single living case, Hennion immediately refocused his proposition so that it fit the narrower base of his experience. Brilliant. Deft. And utterly instinctive.

"So," Wilde said, "your wife is short."

"Yes."

"Pretty?"

Wilde sensed Hennion's embarrassment; also his disapproval. "She is my wife, monsieur."

Wilde laughed. "Yes, of course. Although I'm sure she is also very pretty. Most wives are." Other men's wives. He was thoroughly enjoying this conversation—even if Hennion wasn't—this chance once again to charm; best of all, the chance to finally know the quiet man.

"So your wife is short and she works as a laundress."

"Yes."

"Also as a mother."

"Yes."

"And what is her name?"

"My wife's name?"

"Yes."

"Josette."

"Josette. Simple. Efficient. I like it. It is the name of a good woman." Hennion said nothing, just carried on with the dressing. "And your daughter," Wilde tried, "does she have a name?"

Hesitation. "Yes."

"What is it?"

Greater hesitation, bordering on uncertainty. Finally: "Adélaïde."

"Really? Adélaïde? That is exquisite, Hennion. Adélaïde is one of my favorite French names. That is the truth."

"I'm glad."

"She must be a charming girl, perfectly beautiful."

"She is five years old."

"Of course. So much the better!"

Wilde could feel Hennion immediately react: not well. The wound dresser withdrew from the conversation with a frostiness bordering on disgust. Repeated attempts to draw him out were met with silence. Wilde didn't understand. He'd only been asking about the little Adélaïde. His charming little five-year-old girl.

Oh.

The comprehension came at him—all at once, a tidal surge. And then he felt nothing but hopelessness, as pure as he had not felt in a long time, as bad as when he first entered prison. From those days, he recognized the feeling: the abject loss, the withering embarrassment, the disbelief so profound it registered as bodily shock; more than anything, the abiding wish that he was dead. Gone. Except his entry into prison was so long ago now—five years—and he was supposed to be a free man now. He had served his time and paid his legal debt. He was supposed to be in the clear.

He'd only asked the man about his daughter.

Could Hennion really believe that someone like himself was asking for that reason? Or did this reticent, competent wound dresser—the one sent to him by a licensed doctor—just assume, like everyone else did, that if a man was guilty of one corruption he might be guilty of any?

"I have finished your dressing," Hennion said, not without a hint of malice. "I must go to another appointment." He stood, gathered his things as usual.

Wilde said nothing. Another appointment. Maybe Hennion did have another appointment; maybe. But it didn't matter. Wilde stayed exactly where he was and watched as the bulky Frenchman stalked to the door and then left without turning to him or so much as offering a goodbye.

CHAPTER FOURTEEN

Paris. October, 1900.

The door opened shyly. From his position on the bed, his back supported by as many pillows as he could keep in place, Wilde saw the slow motion yawning, as if a breeze had entered from downstairs and then pushed gingerly against his door. For seconds, this was all he saw: the door to his room hanging open and no one coming in. He set down his book beside him—a new biography of Michelangelo, in Italian, that Reggie had found somewhere in the city and thought Wilde would appreciate. However, the author, one Corrado Ricci, demonstrated no genius in his own native language; more like the lumbering earnestness of a bank manager rendering a financial report; which was the last thing you might expect from a man moved to write about Michelangelo. Italian was Wilde's fifth language, and his least studied, but he suspected that even he—at least in his salad days—could have written better Italian than this Ricci. For a few seconds, the thought occurred to him to try to rewrite the biography, just to show how it could have been managed. Less a translation than an elevation. But it was only a moment's impulse. He quickly realized how absurd the idea was. What would he ever do with the revised manuscript?

"Hello?" Wilde called. Then, as if in response to a magical incantation, into the room stepped Robert Ross. "My god, Robbie, was that really you who opened the door?"

Ross, trying on a sly smile, said, "What, do think I'm a ghost?"

It was only then Ross took in the room. Wilde saw the disappointment on his face; more than that, the soul sadness. Wilde knew exactly how terrible this room was that fate had assigned him to. So did Ross. Robbie had seen it before, but not recently, not without such an evident dinginess and ill-patient odor. If anything, the room was growing dirtier and more fetid every week, though Charbonneau cleaned here as he did the other rooms, and though Wilde moved infrequently enough to make any mess. The room contained fewer pieces of furniture than when Robbie last visited: one bed, one narrow chest of drawers with the paint nakedly peeling off it, and one chair with uneven legs and no cushions. The writing desk Wilde had asked Dupoirer to remove, since he had no reason for it anymore, and it only made the small space more crammed. There was the same window, but usually Wilde kept the curtain pulled across it so that the only illumination was of the sallow, incomplete kind, coming from one of two gas lamps affixed to the righthand wall. The flame from the working one was bare, half-strength. The other gas lamp, as of August, didn't work at all.

The carpet on the floor was colored a mucky crimson that had absorbed decades of stains, spills, stinks, and street-dusty shoes; and Wilde could not swear that in his tenure more stains had not been added. In this one regard, the dingy light was a plus: visitors could not make out just how degraded and soiled was the floor beneath their feet. The hideous wallpaper, meanwhile, featured the same dizzying array of colored blotches that never quite added up to figures and, besides which, was coming apart from the wall in several spots.

Ross completed his survey. When he stared again at Wilde, it was with a heartbreakingly fraudulent attempt at normalcy.

"No, not a ghost," Wilde said. "In fact, I can't think of anyone else I'd more like to see right now. This is genuine magic. You being here, just now."

Ross cracked a sidewise smile. "No magic, Oscar. You sent that dreadful telegram."

"I did?"

"Terribly weak? Please come?"

"That wasn't dreadful, it was the truth."

"You don't look too bad right now."

"I don't feel too bad right now."

Same smile from Ross.

"Don't look at me that way, Robbie. I really did want you to come."

Ross nodded. "I know. Reggie told me."

"Reggie?"

"He telegrammed me too. Said you were absolutely desolate. Down and out from the surgery. I thought I should come over right away." Ross paused, tilted his head, as if to get a more critically enhanced view of his friend. "Except you seem almost normal at the moment."

Wilde smiled. "Looks can be deceiving. The ear has healed from the surgery, but on the inside something is still amiss. No one seems to know for sure what exactly or what to do about it. Doctor Tucker warns me that another surgery may be in my future. But for some reason I do feel better today. I really can't know why. But I'm grateful I can read—such as it is." He waved at the disappointing Michelangelo biography. Ross noticed but didn't ask. "But if I were you I would not go around telling anyone I am back to normal. I can hear out of my right ear better than I did yesterday. But even after my surgery there have been whole days when I almost hear nothing. For some reason the surgery didn't work the way it was supposed to. Tucker can't say why, and all his wound dresser did was grunt at me. But even so, the doctor may decide I need cutting into again."

"But you're not in pain. I mean right now?"

Wilde shrugged. "The pain today is more muted. But it's still there. It's still a soprano, but instead of releasing an aria onstage she's in her dressing room practicing scales."

Ross smiled sarcastically. "Sounds beautiful."

"I don't recommend it. She's awfully flat at the moment, actually. But she keeps trying. So you better speak up."

Ross chuckled and came over. He laid one hand flat against the bed. "How are you, Oscar? Really?"

"I'm dying, Robbie."

"Don't say that."

"I'm dying. I have to say it, or else I will be terrified."

Ross nodded slowly, exhibiting a shamed look. He glanced at the wall on the other side of the bed, the thin side table and stiff chair there—anywhere but Wilde's own face. Wilde wished Ross would just say whatever it was he wanted to say. What was the point, now, of hiding anything, of keeping thoughts, no matter how morbid, from each other? It had always—always—been a singular part of Ross's charm that Wilde could say anything to him; think out loud along the most preposterous or self-centered lines. Robbie heard it all and never judged. So why should he hold himself back from a similar freedom?

Or weren't they the same kind of friends anymore?

"That's—that's just," Ross began, "not something that one is used to hearing."

"Now you're the one who sounds terrified."

"No." Ross shook his head firmly. "Not terrified. It's just that when I came and saw you... you looked like the old Oscar... lounging and reading. I thought maybe..." His shrug added a period to the sentence.

"Robbie, no matter what happens to me I will have to die at some point. Inevitably there has to be a funeral. Some year. A good Catholic like you should know that." The mild attempt at a jest went nowhere. Ross's face was as blank as if he hadn't heard. Wilde kept trying. "In any case, I don't expect I will outlive this century. The English would not stand for it. In fact, I think I'm singlehandedly responsible for the failure of the Exhibition. Did I tell you that? I went with Reggie when he was over here in April. It had just opened. We were both looking forward to it. I still got around pretty well then. I put on my good coat and my passable shoes. I wore a cravat and a pocket watch and a homburg. I walked around with my cane like an invading god, or a magistrate, and I did it on purpose.

The Exhibition, after all, is where Europe meets."

"Yes. And so what?"

"The English, that's what. The English couldn't stand it, seeing me happy and obviously not in prison. So they went away."

"Come on, Oscar. All of them?"

"I am not lying to you. I saw nothing but shock and dismay on every one of those pale northern faces."

"How can you be sure they were English?"

"What a question. Twenty-three years in the country doesn't count for anything?" Ross shrugged. "Besides which, never ask an Irishman how he knows the English. You might not like the answer you get."

Ross gave off an annoyed shrug. "What do I care if you insult the English?"

Wilde moved a hand. "The point is I knew who they were, and they knew who I was, and they couldn't stand it. They will not stand for me anymore. They wanted me dead in the first place. You know that's true."

"Some of them wanted you dead."

"Almost all of them wanted me dead." His voice went louder and more hurt-filled than he had intended. It was amazing, even to himself, how the resentment still burned.

"All right," Ross relented, "but even so, who cares about the English and their wants? That can't make you sick. That can't keep you from getting well."

What a difference, Wilde thought, between the observer and the observed; the well and the not.

"It has made me sick, and it has kept me sick. I

should think that would not need proving." Again, the shame on Ross's face, the momentary shutting down. So out of character from his usual positivism. For the first time that Wilde could remember, Ross seemed at a loss. Poor Robbie, he doesn't know what to do with this truth. "I am dying. Please just accept that. Because if you do not, I will have to keep reminding you, and that will ruin our fun."

At that, Ross smiled meagerly. A brave attempt, but the pain was full in his eyes. He scratched his head and blew out a dejected stream of air. "I've heard reports about why the Exhibition Universale failed. No one said anything about Oscar Wilde. Mostly they talked about how expensive it was to put on, and that the tickets were out of reach for much of the public."

"I do not deny any of that. But what I say is true nevertheless. If you go down there today you won't see the English. You'll see plenty of Frenchmen and maybe some Belgians. Some Germans and Dutch and Spaniards. But no English. Word got out. I scared them off."

Ross smiled. "I wasn't sure if I even cared to see The Exhibition, but I'll guess I'll have to now. Maybe I should take you."

Wilde chuckled. It felt good—physically healing—to hear the noise from his own self, to hear that particular eruption in his chest. "That's right. Let's finish the deal. Scare away the whole continent."

"Why not? The thing is set to shut down next month anyway."

"Ah ha! So what you're saying is that I opened it,

and so I should close it. Perfect." He saw that Ross was examining him again: the quiet, circumspect look, the lingering sadness. "It's not the end of the world, you know."

"What?"

"Death. My death. The universe will go on. You will go on. Reggie will go on. And Frank. And even dear old misguided Bosie. Don't get me wrong. I will miss all of you terribly. I will even miss the world, strange to say. Miss it more than it realizes. More than it deserves. But—also—I will be all right."

"I won't," Ross said.

"Psssh. I would not expect such romantic rubbish from you, Robbie. Of course you will go on. You are too busy a person not to. You give yourself too much to do, even when you don't have to. And when you stop—when you're actually, finally done—then you will see me again."

"Is that what you believe?"

"Isn't it what you believe?"

Ross shrugged. "I suppose. Some days it's hard. But, yes, I do believe it."

"One of us has to, for god's sake."

They both smiled. Then Wilde said: "What I think is that we will pass every day in our porphyry tombs, catching up just like old friends do. You will tell me the news from London, and I will tell you the news from God. And when the trumpets of the Last Judgment sound, I will turn to you and whisper, 'Robbie let us pretend that we do not hear it.'"

Ross laughed, a good but shocking noise, because it so rarely came out of the man. Realists like Ross tended

not to laugh very often, leaving that expression for lu-
natics and poets and children. Wilde, who counted himself in all three of the latter camps, had never stopped
laughing—until he went to prison. There was absolutely
nothing to laugh at in prison.

"More says hello."

"More? Oh, yes. Of course. Tell him the same for
me."

Ross studied him for a moment. "He promises to
come... before too long."

"Yes, before then, let's hope."

Ross, as if pricked by something, took a few steps
away and then back. "I should tell you, Oscar, that I can
only stay for three weeks."

"Three? Why? Have you decided to go back to
your journalistic hack work?"

Ross smiled. But what might have been intended as
a wry expression only came out as haggard. "No, it's my
mother. She's moved to Nice, you know."

"Yes, you told me."

"She has asked me to come see her soon. She
claims to not feel altogether herself lately, whatever that
means. I guess I need to find out. So I've promised to go
down early next month. On or around the tenth."

Wilde nodded distantly. He couldn't help but think
of his own mother—and the loss of her. More than anyone else in his life, more even than Constance, Jane Wilde had insisted on believing the best about him; even
as the very worst rumors—worse even than the truth—
began to circulate; even after his two trials started. But

then she had had to live through the indignity seeing her baby son openly reviled and insulted: in major newspapers, in street conversations, in public speeches, in parlor room back talk. Everywhere. When she died he was only halfway through his prison sentence. She could not even know if he would live long enough to endure it. For the longest time, Wilde's working assumption was that he had killed her. Yes, she'd caught bronchitis, and she was seventy-five years old, but Wilde was convinced that it was no viral disease, or at least not only or primarily that, that had killed her. Her son's fall from grace had made her give up hope in living; that outcome alone had guaranteed that something would kill her; sooner rather than later. Bronchitis was merely the circumstantial murderer. It was Wilde himself who had done her in. Why else had the officials at the prison put him on suicide watch when the news of her death arrived? They were evil those men, but they knew exactly what they were doing. If he'd had the means, Wilde would have certainly killed himself. With no hesitation.

"That's good of you, Robbie. You should go to her. You're a good son."

"If I was a good son I would be there now."

Wilde nodded. "You are also a good friend. And in that case, I am very happy to have you here."

"You look so much better," Ross said after a moment. "I mean compared to what Reggie said."

"What did Reggie say?"

"He said you looked like you might not last the week."

"Rather impolitic of him. Completely unlike Reggie."

"Doesn't matter. I'm glad he was wrong. You look so good I'd like to take you out to a café this minute."

"Thank you, Robbie. But I think I should stay inside and stick to dying." He hadn't meant it as a barb—only a bad joke—but he saw a new incision of pain open on Ross's face. So he added: "Perhaps we can bring the café to us. Make a supper here. Invite all the good people we know in Paris. There must be two or three of them left."

Ross looked at him—and the room—doubtfully. When he spoke it was slowly and without conviction. Obviously he hadn't gotten over that last "dying" remark.

"Other than Reggie, who is there?"

"Who? Well, more than you know, my friend. Reggie, yes. For sure." He glanced at the Michelangelo book, considered saying something, then didn't. "And Willie's wife—former wife; I mean his second wife—is here. Lily. With her daughter and new husband. It's a stopover. They're on their honeymoon."

"They brought the girl on their honeymoon?"

"I think someone in Paris is going to show her around for a few weeks, while they go to Venice."

"Ah. Better."

"She married again, almost immediately, you know. Her husband is a lovely and possibly brilliant man. Somehow he is Portuguese and Dutch and British all at the same time. I haven't figured it out yet."

Ross nodded. "I heard. Alexander Teixeria de Mattos."

"Do you know him?"

"I've met him. But I know more about him then I really know him."

"It's not clear to me how they met. Not through Willie surely. Teixeria seems far too refined."

"No, I would bet Willie knew him. Your brother knew everyone."

"My brother offended everyone, you mean. And he let them down."

Ross shrugged. "Tramping on the dead, Oscar," he said in a low voice. Then, shifting: "Actually, I expect Lionel introduced them."

"Lionel?"

Ross looked at him, disappointed. "Johnson."

"Oh, of course. Lionel. Lord, Robbie, sometimes I think my mind is going to rubbish." It sounded in his voice like a clichéd, a cover-all excuse, but in fact he'd felt in the last few minutes a rush of fatigue; his consciousness growing swampy and muddled, newly aware of pain in his ear. A more localized, singing pain. The soprano had moved backstage. He'd only awoken two hours earlier, from a soggy, champagne assisted sleep. But if this supper part was to come off, he would need to nap first. "Lionel Johnson. That explains it very well, actually."

"Explains what?"

"Nothing. I don't want to prejudice you."

"Prejudice?"

"Wrong word. I do not mean it. Too negative."

"Wrong word for what?"

"Influence. But, no, that's too general."

"Good god, Oscar, what are we talking about?"

"Rather then, let us say, determine your observations."

"Of what?"

"Of him."

"Who?"

"Lily's husband."

"But I've met him already."

"Forget it please, all right? Please? We keep talking, and there is a party to organize. And I think I have to rest too. Can we say that an early supper will begin in this room in two-and-a-half hours? We can invite you, me, Reggie, Lily, Teixeria. And the daughter: Dolly."

"What is she like?"

"I've only just met her the one time, and she mostly just made faces. But I am told on a typical day she is a holy terror. Quite the individualist."

Ross smiled. "Imagine that from a Wilde."

"She is my brother's daughter."

"And your own niece."

"I was never a terror, Robbie. No matter what people think."

Ross chuckled lightly. Then at once his brows slanted sharply. "How do you suppose they will find out about this party?"

"You will tell them."

"And where do I find them—I mean Lily—in order to do that? I know Reggie is at the Regina."

"That's easy. I shall tell you. Lily and Teixeira are

staying at the Intercontinental." Ross looked impressed. "Yes, this new man is quite the change from Willie."

Ross nodded. "Obviously."

"They should not be far from Reggie."

"Let's hope," Ross said. He started for the door. "Of course, I can't know they will be in."

"They'll be in. They are all here in Paris just waiting for news of me."

Ross smiled. "All right, then. So it's a date. I'll also need to scare up some food."

"There are several restaurants nearby that could make up something for you. I don't think I will be eating. But I will enjoy watching everyone else eat."

Ross frowned. "You're not eating?"

"Not today. I don't feel it. Maybe later. You know, the ear seems to have a direct line to the stomach."

"But you said you felt better."

"I did, didn't I?"

"You should eat something."

"I will happily indulge in champagne."

Ross frowned. "I said eat."

"Champagne. Make sure you bring back several bottles."

"I think you should eat something. And maybe hold off on the champagne. Reggie told me how much you were indulging."

"Dying, remember?"

Ross threw his hands in the air. "Then what's the point, Oscar?"

"The point is to bring good people together. The

point is to dispel the darkness. If just for an hour."

Ross nodded sadly. "Yes. Of course. All right."

"Talk to Dupoirer, if you can find him. He'll recommend a place. He may even be willing to pay. He's said a half-dozen times that he wants to buy me supper. Unfortunately, his hotel is too rancid to employ a decent kitchen." Ross offered a squirrely look. "Otherwise, he takes excellent care of me."

Ross glanced at the carpet and the chest of drawers. He looked back at Wilde with snagged expression. "Yes, I can see."

By 5:15 the group of five plus one was assembled; seated—or rather crammed—at a table and chairs Dupoirer had lent them from his own apartment downstairs, along with a tablecloth, silverware, and glasses. Ross placed the table in the only available space in the room, a foot or so beyond the end of Wilde's bed. The fare was simple, what the staff of the Trois Citrons could doctor up on short notice: omelets with gruyere and chives, pan-fried baby potatoes, a salad of mixed greens and walnuts. Two bottles of champagne. Wilde didn't ask Ross whether Dupoirer had donated the meal as a celebration of his return to lucidity, or whether Ross himself had had to quietly eat the expense. Ross, Wilde knew, was getting along in London, but just barely.

After being more or less chased out of the newspaper racket, Ross had determined to survive solely on the monthly allowance from his mother. He refused to let who he was and what he did with his body contradict with his source of income. He'd been getting it for years now; and while his mother's allowance was enough for a single man to live on comfortably in London, Ross was by no means sitting on a fortune, especially considering that he'd agreed to send Wilde £150 a year. Craftily frugal, Robbie was always able to cover his own expenses—he never complained of being hard up—but Wilde knew that he could not have planned on footing the bill for a dinner party. Wilde decided to merely lay still, lap up champagne, and not ask how the food had been paid for, safe in the knowledge that if Ross himself had paid for it Robbie would never tell.

Meanwhile, Wilde had not lied about Dupoirer's kindnesses. The hotel proprietor had been as generous, and as reasonable, as any guest could hope. If he hadn't been able to remove all of Wilde's worries, at least he had not made them worse. Wilde never entirely understood the nature of Dupoirer's generosity. The man did not seem to be unisexual—at least there was no evidence Wilde knew of—and when Wilde indirectly pushed Dupoirer for an explanation—by singing high paeans to his generosity, and with as Irish tripe as he could muster—the most he ever got from Dupoirer was the comment that he was "eager to come to the service of genius." Very difficult for Wilde to complain about an explanation like that.

Wilde decided that maybe Dupoirer was one of those men who had always aspired to a certain kind of celebrity, or at least a communion with celebrity, but after ending up as the owner of one-star hotel on an unsightly side street, a disgraced Irish writer was the only celebrity he had a chance with. Of course, it did not matter, in the end, why Dupoirer did what he did. What mattered was that he had saved Wilde's life. Wilde knew that there were still many persons in and around the city—not all of them American or English transplants—that wanted nothing to do with him whatsoever. Who regarded him as a villain, as a criminal, and most likely as a damned soul. Dupoirer, meanwhile, had not only given him a room and paid off his debt to the Marsollier, he had chased off curiosity seekers countless times with bald lies such as 'Mr. Wilde has gone off sightseeing in the south,' or 'Mr. Wilde has changed his lodgings to the Hotel du Louvre.' It was no exaggeration to say that Dupoirer had rescued Wilde's final days from unmitigated disaster. After all, one could not die in Paris without a room to sleep in. Not if one hope to maintain even the roughest semblance of one's former self.

Ross uncharacteristically hung fire for much of the meal, casting cautious glances at the other four, the nervous host who at the same time had taken on the job of caretaker for the sick man in the room. Wilde half-expected that at any moment Ross would stand and wave a stern finger at the door. Can't you see that Oscar is tired? If you care anything for him, please leave. Of course, Robbie would never do that. He was far too even-tempered to deliver such a scene; plus, Ross knew that Wilde wanted this party. The whole time, Wilde tried to send mental messages to him, to tell him to relax. It doesn't matter, does it? No matter what happens next, we all know what is going to happen.

Lily, who had turned forty the year before, looked tired and even bothered, certainly distracted when she entered the room, as if she and her husband, or perhaps she and her daughter, had fought the whole way over from the Intercontinental and then had had to simply stop the argument—no resolution achieved—when they reached Wilde's door, which only set the bad emotions flying in and around and about them all, with nowhere safe to go. Wilde thought that her thin hair needed tending to; and that her walking coat was uninspired, even dowdy. Her husband did not display any particular anger or bother, just the same fastidious sharpness of look and walk and expression. As he had been the first time Wilde met him, Teixeira was dressed to the hilt, in an elegant dark suit and a high collared shirt so stiff it must have starched to within an inch of its life. The whiteness of the shirt made a dramatic contrast with the tanned tone of his Portuguese skin. His face was closed and quiet, and yet his small round eyeglasses glinted fiercely, as if with a repressed and even dangerous energy. As soon as he entered he began glancing around the chamber, taking it in: the furniture, the windows, the curtains, the man still supine on the bed who was observing him every second. Dolly, meanwhile, seemed to Wilde exactly as she had the other day when he first met her: bored and slightly militant. After a while, she stopped listening to the adult talk and began to explore the small space, forcing her mother to keep calling her back to her side. At least until they could finally sit down at the small table and get started with the business of eating.

The heroic one at the supper was Reggie Turner who, God bless him, acted as if this affair was just an Oxford summer tea party. He laughed on purpose; he told a joke, he related anecdotes about his neighbors on St. Leonard's Terrace; he discoursed about a novel he'd like to write. Lily, for one, was completely taken with him. Even Dolly, who mostly kept up a sour and doubtful aspect beneath her shiny dark cap of black hair, seemed to like Reggie. But who didn't? Turner won everyone over the moment he opened his mouth. Wilde had witnessed Reggie charm so many young maidens and the mothers of those young maidens and even the married sisters of those maidens—especially those married long enough to have lost all illusions about their husbands—while men with more money, more glamour, and distinctly better bloodlines became invisible to them. The remarkable thing, the endearing thing, though, was that for Reggie it was never an act. The man was naturally warm, naturally curious—literally about anything—and for a writer unusually outgoing. Wilde supposed this must be a necessity for a journalist. Reggie did not have to put on a disguise in order to charm; Reggie was charm itself. True charm, Wilde knew, always being tied to selflessness.

This, of course, had been his problem. Back before his downfall, he'd enjoyed a reputation as being the most elite of social men: a wit without parallel; a polish so thick one could practically lick it off him. He was known as the one necessary guest for any distinguished dinner party. You simply did not try to throw such a party without being assured Oscar Wilde could attend. As a result, whole

weeks passed before Wilde had to buy his own supper—
or, worse, eat at home. It was not a little like being a king.
But when Wilde saw how quickly people turned on him
during his time of trouble; and how many of those same
people had refused to turn back, he realized the truth of
the matter. All those hosts and hostesses had not been
so much charmed by but afraid of him, and thus when
he had his downfall they were all quietly applauding. In
contrast, if Reggie Turner were ever sent to prison for
gross indecency, half of London society would weep; the
other half would be outraged. They might even storm
the jail. No one disliked Reggie. Not the husbands and
fiancés he made look like dullards; not the ex-boyfriends
whom he finally had to break from for one reason or
another; not even the conservative newspaper men who
gave speeches and printed gossipy editorials about an
unnamed but "unnatural and despicable corruption festering at the center of our most renowned palaces of
learning." Somehow they never blamed him, one of their
own inky kind, for that corruption, despite the fact that
it was at Merton College that Turner first experienced
sodomy and, upon experiencing it, initiated one or two
others as well. With Reggie Turner all was permanently and irrevocably forgiven. Wilde never begrudged the
man that. Instead, he marveled. He counted it as one of
his remaining mercies of his life that he could still call
Reggie Turner a friend.

"How are you finding the literary life?" Reggie
asked Lily, leaning so close to her he practically spoke
into her ear.

Lily smiled, abashed but also pleased to be put on the spot. "Oh, it's fine. Alexa goes about his business quietly. I try not to disturb him."

"So I should have said: 'How is the literary wife?'"

She smiled. "That I am. But of course I have my hands full with my daughter."

Turner glanced at Dolly who, chewing uncertainly on a forkful of omelet, shot her mother a sharp look.

"I don't know," Reggie said, "she looks like a real dear."

"I am a dear," Dolly said, and the table laughed. She looked around, confused, even annoyed. "I am, if you actually know me."

"Isn't that true of everyone, though?" Reggie said. "We're all dears; no matter what mistakes we make."

"I don't make mistakes," Dolly said.

Reggie guffawed. He was enjoying this patter. "I don't imagine you do. You are obviously too smart for mistakes."

Dolly raised her chin and looked at her mother as if to say, See, what have I been telling you?

Lily responded with a meager smile. "In any case, my days are full."

"Mr. Alexander over there won't let you peek into the books?"

Now Lily stole a glance at her husband, who was sitting across the table from her, scissoring through a baby potato with slow scrupulous care, as if worried his fingernails might get dirty. It was not clear to Wilde if he was even listening to the conversation. Ross, meanwhile,

distracted and tired, sat back and observed them all mute-
ly, content for the moment to let Reggie carry the day.

Lily pushed a strand of hair over her ear. The gray,
Wilde noticed, was far more prominent then when he'd
first met her in the mid-90s. That was no more than six
years ago, when she was merely the latest girl Willie had
taken a fancy to. But what a six years: Willie moves in
with her. Then Wilde himself becomes an internation-
al disgrace. Lily becomes pregnant and endures a cata-
strophically difficult eight months before—a month
ahead of schedule—she gives birth to Dolly, who nearly
dies in the first week of her life. Later, Lilly suffers three
pregnancy scares and during one of them takes so much
henna powder she is almost hospitalized. She agrees to
marry Willie though reporting to others she that she no
longer loves him and possibly never did. Willie's drinking,
always bad, gets worse, and he stops writing. Her daughter develops a reputation as a wild child and is mostly dis-
invited from family functions, which causes Willie to riot
against his own mother. Drink finally kills Willie at age
forty-six. Then Teixeira de Mattos, whom apparently she
has known platonically for years, proposes. She accepts.
Even if Lily had not reached forty the year before—the
gentle, harmless aspect of her face molting into plain-
ness—all that she'd lived through in six years would be
enough to turn any woman's hair white.

"It would need to be a very quick peek," Lily said.
"My husband is quite hawkish about his work. Also hard
to fool."

Turner sat back with mock horror written on his

face. "You make him sound like a monster." Teixeira sent Turner a not-amused look before cutting into another potato. So apparently he had been listening. "Well, instead of a peek perhaps," Turner tried, "you could manage a criminal grab, carry away the document to a safer place, for spying."

"It's probably safest to keep it right where it is," Lily counseled. "I really don't mind. Willie didn't like for me to ask him any questions about his writing either. I learned that quickly enough."

Teixeira put his knife and fork down; he lifted his head. His mouth was set in a thin-lipped line. "That is because the man didn't want to admit that he had not written anything."

"Hello there," Dolly cried out to Teixeira. "You don't talk that way."

Teixeira paused long enough to level a cold stare at the girl. "I will talk that way Dorothy, if it is the truth. And it is. And your mother knows this." Then to Wilde: "I am sorry, Oscar. I do not mean to offend."

"You stop it," the girl responded, pointing a fork at her stepfather.

"I'm afraid it's my fault, dear," Turner broke in, speaking to Dolly. "I mean I got us on this subject in the first place. Your mother and her husband were simply trying to enjoy a meal with Uncle Oscar before I butted in. So if you want to point the utensil at anyone point it at me." Then he smiled avuncularly at her, and her face lost its hard edge. She put the fork down, flummoxed and chastened.

"Don't worry, Alexander," Wilde said. "You really cannot offend me where my brother is concerned. There's nothing you could say in this room that I haven't told myself already—or told him."

Teixeira nodded, visibly relieved.

"Besides, with only one of my ears functioning properly, I only hear half of what you say."

The group laughed, and now everyone looked relieved.

"Very appropriate, Oscar," Turner chided, "since that's the most anyone's ever listened to you."

Nervous chitters from Lily and Teixeira. Obviously, they didn't understand. Reggie, noticing Wilde's improved state, was trying to summon an earlier time, when such spirited give and take between friends was the stuff of life. His comment, coming in the form of an insult, was an act of nostalgia. But it would be too much trouble to explain this to Lily and her husband; so Wilde didn't try.

"Which ear?" Dolly said. She was staring at him with glossy speculation; penetratingly, like a scientist studying a new species of fish.

"This one." Wilde put a finger to his right ear.

Dolly stood and stepped over to the bed. For a frightened moment, Wilde thought she might touch him. "Hello!" she shouted into the damaged ear.

"Dolly, now stop!' Lily shrieked, and Teixeira looked newly horrified, but Turner seemed perfectly amused by the girl. Wilde took his cue from his more sanguine friend. "Thank you, Dolly. I think you may have cleared out my ear for good."

The girl wheeled and glared at the table. "See?" She stalked back and launched a newly confident attack against the omelet.

"And so tell me, Alexander," Wilde asked, after a large and useful sip of champagne, eager for a new topic, "what are you translating now?" Teixeira was clearly unprepared for the question, especially from a man whose life was supposedly set to end any day now. He let his fork fall to his plate and made sure to finish chewing. Then he raised his hands and started gesturing with the movements that punctuated every one of his sentences.

"Actually, I am between projects at the moment. My translation of Jozef Israëls's Spain has only come out this year. I was busy until the last moment with that one."

"So nothing in the works?"

"No, I'm afraid."

"But you say you are between."

"Yes. I am."

"Between means there must be something on both sides of you."

Jagged half-smile from Teixeira: there and gone again. "Yes, of course. This is correct."

Wilde waited. When the man didn't respond, Wilde said, "What is behind you is the Israëls's book. What is on the other side?"

For a second, Teixeira went white, then recovered, understanding. "I see, yes. Sorry. I am deciding between two possibilities, actually. Two different memoirs. I will certainly do one; I may do both. Either those of Chateaubriand or Paul Kruger."

Wilde groaned. "I think if I were you I would stick with Chateaubriand."

Teixeira nearly leaped out his chair at this implied insult to the former president of the South African Republic. "But Kruger is such a fascinating character! So many contrasts! He was a thoroughly modern man who not very long ago held an important position in the governments of our world, and yet at the same time he had the feudal spirit. He only read one book. His entire life, one book."

"Which book?"

Teixeira seemed surprised. "The bible. Of course."

"Of course?" Wilde remarked. "Why, I thought you might say The Iliad or Medea or Lysistrata."

Or The Art of War," Ross interjected dryly.

"No," Teixeira said, disappointed. "He was not that modern."

"Technically, you mean ancient," Wilde started, "but I know exactly what you are saying. I've long felt, as far as I can remember, that the Greeks and the Romans—and the Chinese too—have more to say about the time we live in now—and maybe about all time—then Christianity ever does or can."

"That spoken by a Christian," Ross said.

"Am I Robbie? Certainly I am a devotee. An admirer. But am I a believer? I don't think I know."

"'I do believe, Lord,'" Ross quoted. "'Help my unbelief.'"

"Touché."

Turner fumbled a nervous sigh. "If you two papists are going to start slinging the Word around, I might have to leave."

"Me too," Dolly said.

"Papists?" Wilde said.

"Not yet," Ross said.

"But no, but no," Teixeira cut in. "Don't leave. This, you see, is exactly it." His hands were demonstrating again; his voice rising higher, the round eyeglasses glinting as much with boyish enthusiasm now as with literal light. What a change from the tense, glancing man who had entered the room earlier. "The world we exist in is one of conflict—or perhaps negotiation—between exactly those two clients: the Jewish and the Greek. Everything we Europeans look at or swear to or tussle over is on account of the Jews or the Greeks. Because we cannot, as a European people, decide, there is nothing but disagreement. Even killing. And too even as individuals we hate ourselves, because we cannot decide each of us for ourselves between those two poles."

As the translator spoke, his voice ascending so high Wilde would actually label it fey, Wilde glanced at Lily, hoping for clues. But all he saw on her face was perfect impassivity, as if she'd witnessed her husband's mannerisms and affectations—and his arguments—too many times already to even notice them anymore. So, she does not yet know, Wilde thought. Or she has not let herself know. Like Constance all those years, insisting that her husband had too strong of an independent streak to be confined to ordinary domesticity. And on top of that,

Constance would say, he is kept astonishingly busy with trying to line up actors, directors, producers, and publishers. So busy there's simply no time leftover to stay in his own home. Or sleep with his wife. That so many glittery beautiful young men and known unisexuals were regularly included in her husband's social circle Constance chalked up to coincidence and, as laughable as it might seem, to his ability to withhold repugnance toward others he knew lived in sin. Wilde had actually heard her say to someone, at some dinner party, before things became bad between them: Oscar is a man of superhuman tolerance, and of profound Christian forbearance for the weaknesses of others. You have no idea. Oh yes, they did. Everyone in their circle knew about Wilde and his weaknesses; they knew about that one hanger on, in particular: Bosie Douglas. Everyone knew the truth about him and Bosie; everyone except Constance. Until it became impossible for even her to deny anymore.

Wilde looked at Turner. Reggie, though he'd only just met Teixeira, would understand what he had been getting at in that conversation with Ross. Reggie was too quick not to see it. But rather than playing a game of smug glances at Wilde or Ross, Turner was listening to the translator with almost excessive interest: his eyes alight, his face full of marvel, his mouth partly opened as if ready to squawk with appreciation. Kruger's years of military service in South Africa. Kruger as Vice President of the Transvaal. Kruger riding a hot air balloon over Paris. Kruger helping to end the Boer War. Reggie was always so good. Not just a good listener but plain good.

Here was a man Reggie didn't really know blowing exuberant air about another man who sounded even more dull than Wilde expected; and yet Turner was determined that Teixeira go away thinking he had entranced them all. No wonder so many people in London happily and inadvertently provided material for his gossip column. They trusted Reggie Turner completely. They would trust him with the secrets of their lives. And the truth was that even though the column was gossip, Turner chose not to report a great deal more than he did report, to the eternal relief those he consulted.

Wilde looked at Ross and saw that Ross was looking at him. Or, more precisely, frowning—with obvious concern. Wilde shook his head, a motion too small to be noticed by others. *Please stop worrying about me.* His gaze found out, Ross turned his head back toward Teixeira, and Wilde saw that even then Ross couldn't listen to the man without being distracted by the finicky movements of Texeira's wrists, the flecking signals he made with his fingers, the elongated hollows of his cheeks as he roared through his appreciation for the former South African president. Now Ross wore a face that Wilde could only think of as skeptically amused. Wilde stared at Ross until Ross stared back. Wilde sent a message through his eyes. Robbie gave up an eighth of a smile and tilted his head Teixeira's way, a return message. So Robbie saw it too. Wilde nodded.

He realized then that the rest of the company was looking at him, and not with very much pleasure. "So what are your thoughts these days, Oscar?" Lily said, a distinctly new and sour tone in her voice.

"My thoughts?"

"You seem fairly silent, and yet Robbie here says it's the best you've looked in weeks. That's why we're having this party, isn't it?"

"I know he says that, so maybe it is actually so." Wilde finished his glass of champagne and signaled Ross for a refill. Ross frowned but obliged. "I'm afraid," Wilde continued, "I've not had much chance for thoughts recently, not waking ones. When I'm awake I'm either out of my head with the doctor's morphine, or in too much pain to entertain a single cogent idea."

Lily raised her eyebrows. "In your sleep," Teixeira asked, "does the pain subside?"

"It does, and thankfully even my mind returns. I entertain elaborate phantasms. I like to think these are acts of imagination and not pharmacology."

A sign of a smile from Teixeira. This man, Wilde thought, should smile more. It would make him infinitely less tedious. "Your dreams, you mean?" Teixeira said.

"Yes, my dreams. I have wonderful dreams. I dream I sup with the great deceased."

Turner chuckled. "I am sure you're the life and soul of the party, Oscar."

"We do have very interesting conversations."

"Willie used to say such things," Lily said, breathily.

"Really?" Wilde said. This was a genuine curiosity; it did not at all fit his usual picture of his brother. "When?"

"On his deathbed."

The room grew quiet and newly tense. Lily, who'd lowered her head to her plate, looked up and then around, embarrassed, aware of the accidental import of what she said but unable to retract it. Coincident with Lily's look, Wilde felt a shocking new deposit of pain bloom in his ear. Within an instant it spread outward, backward, and downward so that it resonated close to the center of his being, as bad as before his surgery. Then he heard a tone, not like any tone he had heard before, whether natural or manmade, a humming that burned and felt hard and bronze at the same time. The odder thing is that this tone, this audible sound came not from anywhere near his ear or around his ear. Instead, it seemed to come from inside his own mind, settled there with preening inertia. Wilde closed his eyes. It was easier to endure the misery if he did not to see faces at the same time—dumb, healthy, living faces; faces not in pain. And then he felt a surge of familiar nausea, what often came over him during pains of any kind. His vision, even with his eyes already closed, went dimmer. The champagne glass fell through his fingers. He forced himself to open his eyes, and as a result was assaulted by a vision of gray-faced bodies in bulky suits standing and moving without sense; whether toward him or away he could not tell, and it didn't matter because none of them could help him.

CHAPTER FIFTEEN

Paris. November, 1900.

It was crisper than he expected for a late autumn day, even in Paris. A chill burrowed itself through the folds of his coat and then hunkered down against his shirt. Here on the Rue des Beaux Arts—outside the Hotel de l'Alsace—he took a long, slow look at the sky and wondered if it would be worth it, this adventure, no matter how much he'd complained to Ross about seeing nothing but the inside of his hotel room—its terrible wallpaper and shoddy furniture and dirt-in-the-corners atmosphere—no matter how much better he'd felt and looked that morning. His collapse at the supper party days before had proved to be a meaningless setback, not indicative of any malignant change in his condition. He'd slept for several hours, with on and off periods of half-lunatic consciousness. Tucker had come as soon as Ross could get hold of him—which was not easy in the evening time—and pronounced that as far as he could tell there was nothing different about Wilde's condition, nothing he noticed at least. He should feel better soon. Let him rest for a couple of days. But after that, if he feels like it, take him out. Probably it would be good for him. Perhaps we have all just waited too long to force him out into the open air.

Two days passed with no visitors—by design—except for Ross, who maintained a constant surveillance, a chair pulled near the bed, his head bent over a book; and for Reggie, who spelled Ross for long stretches each day. Lilly and Teixeria had left for Venice. Dolly was being entertained elsewhere in Paris.

Then just that morning, Wilde awoke feeling even better than on the morning of the supper party; also antsy and physically impatient with any more of his imprisonment. Ross was plainly surprised, perhaps even dismayed by Wilde's announcement. But nonetheless Ross immediately suggested they let a hansom and take a ride through the Bois de Bologne. Wilde could not resist the notion. He had not been to the Bois in probably a year, and besides it seemed the one inevitable place he must go if his health allowed. For who knew if he would ever be able to go again.

But he had not been prepared for this shuttlecock of a cool wind, the unforgiving flatness of the hard blue sky. Paris had turned cold of a sudden. Even so, he still wanted to go. Wilde closed his eyes, raised his chin, let the sky descend and the breeze ascend, chilling his cheeks as best as—or as worst as—they could. Then he would decide.

"Oscar?"

The air, he declared, was good. How could it not be, compared to the sickly climate of his room, rank with hopelessness and lost causes. Books never to be written. Forgiveness never to be had. Love not to be realized. This air was fresh. This air was not doctored. This air was free to roam.

A hand was touching his elbow. "Shall I signal for the cab?" Slowly, Wilde opened his eyes and saw the face of Robert Ross, one of his first lovers, who, in the weird alchemy of a lifetime, was still here, at the end, when so many others had disappeared. Looking into Ross's small precise face, Wilde could see past the well-tended moustache and smoothly shaven face; past the hair, failing though it might be, that he'd carefully combed into position; past the perfectly knotted tie; and realized that Ross was tired. And maybe more than tired, he was scared. Scared to overturn Doctor Tucker's orders, but more scared of all the unforeseen that could happen as a result of exposing a sick man to the elements. Wilde knew that Ross would have been all too happy if he'd refused the suggestion of the Bois de Boulogne. If he had his druthers, Ross would have denied the suggestion himself. But Robbie loved him too much to do that.

Maybe he'd been too willing to talk about death with his best friend. Maybe he'd let his own fear get carried away. In his determination to shove aside the growing panic, the despair, the ever-increasing accumulation of regrets, he'd talked about death so much that Ross expected him to pass out at any moment. Someday, Robbie, but not today. Not this day. Not with the Bois awaiting me.

"I'm not going to die, Robbie," Wilde said. Ross's startle and the confusion were apparent. "I mean today, with you here. I would not do that to my oldest friend." Relief relaxed Ross's face for he first time since he'd crossed the threshold of Wilde's hotel. Then Wilde saw something else that was encouraging: the return of what he knew so well, what he'd missed: Ross's barbed irony, his sense of embittered play.

"Thank you for telling me, Oscar. Now I won't have to piss in my pants."

Wilde laughed out loud, so hard his lungs almost hurt. Then Ross raised an arm and waved at the street. As if by magic, a hansom immediately rattled over and slowed to a stop. The driver, decked out in cold weather attire—billowing top hat, heavy frock, and thick gloves—looked at them expectantly.

"*Bois de Boulogne, s'il vous plait,*" Ross said.

The driver nodded without a word, as if he'd known all along what Ross would request, because he'd heard the same instructions dozens of times that morning; as if there were no other place—in Paris and on that day—for anyone to travel to.

* * * *

It made a difference, of course, when they were finally rushing along through the park in the cab. Images from the Alleé des Acacias flipped past his open eyes: the broad, tan expanse of the dirt avenue passing underneath them; the tall range of green, still vibrant trees off to the far left; the dozens of the other cabs with their cheerfully gabbing passengers and mute drivers. Noises ambushed his ears, both the good and the bad: the dry quick sound of the wind; the infernal rattling of the cab's wheels; the cloppity commotion of dozens of horses' hooves; the occasional shout from a passenger in one cab to a passenger in another; trivial Saturday morning salutations. At the first the stimulation had done his heart and his body good, even the cold had, but quickly Wilde felt overwhelmed. His dying skin felt chilled; more so every moment. Worse, he who had been shut up against human society and left to work out his own salvation in the stale quiet of a hotel room, could not help but see all this human clamor as a kind of pollution, something that if he were not careful would drown him. He shuddered, involuntarily.

Ross looked over at once, his expression wary. "How are you taking it?"

Wilde raised a hand, but he wasn't sure why. He opened his mouth. He tried to say something; he wanted to say, Don't worry. It's nothing. I am fine. But he couldn't make the words come out. Like a senile ninety-year-old caught between the impetus to speak and a flawed mechanism for bringing words to his tongue, Wilde found himself in a mental desert, lacking the precision for recollecting phrases or the urgency to make new ones out of nothing. What finally came out of his mouth sounded something like "worto."

"What?" Ross said and wheeled in his seat for a closer inspection. "What are you trying to tell me?" Except for the rule against champagne, Wilde had tried to follow doctor's orders. Even today, this trip. It was doctor's orders. And yet here was Ross, the friend come to help him, terrified he'd only made matters worse. Wilde tried to shake his head; maybe that could count as the confirmation his words wouldn't allow. But he didn't like how shaking made his head feel. In fact, just a few seconds of the motion set his inner brain spinning, dancing as if on spindly and drunken legs. Then his mind was fully engulfed in a dizzying vertigo: too light, too thin, too unstable to hold on to so much as one word or one thought or a single reason for anything. The daylight struck his eyes like some lighthouse illumination, foaming painfully yellow; the noise of the carriage and the horses and voices struck him anew and struck him louder, exaggerated as trumpets. He was forced to close his eyes. He wished he could close his ears.

"Oscar?" Ross said. "Oscar?"

"Robbie," he forced out, word after singular slow word, "I feel giddy."

Ross practically shouted, as if Wilde had just admitted to murder.

"I believe..." Wilde managed, but no more.

"We should go back, shouldn't we?" Ross called.

Wilde did not know what to say. Yes, of course, going back would be the logical thing to do. Probably they should never have set off in the first place. Probably he should never have left his bed. But there was something about the vividness of this vertigo, something so bright in the texture of the light that had broken up his vision, and so particle-hard about every sound striking his ears that he suspected that soon he might never see or hear from this place again, soon he would not be able to see or hear a thing. Wouldn't it be better to draw this ride out as long as possible, to gather from it whatever he could, make it as meaningful as a last experience is supposed to be? It was now or never, after all. Life or death. This is what he decided he would tell Ross, just as soon as he could get his eyes open and his mouth; his tongue around words. But then he heard Ross abruptly turning in his seat and banging on the side of the hansom.

"Driver, stop the cab. We must return to the city. My friend is sick."

PART THREE

Paris. November, 1900.

"Why don't I remember this?" Wilde said slowly, the words, numbed and bodiless, forced out of himself instead of spoken. Even to himself, even considering the numerous glasses of champagne he'd finished earlier, Wilde's speech sounded wrong, as if his tongue, instead of affording the mellifluous verbal music that had once been his stock in trade, had grown thick in his mouth and occupied the area as inconveniently as a carcass.

"Because you're scared and you're tired," Ross said. Robbie glanced at an unusually somber Turner, who stood even closer to the bed, on Wilde's right, only a foot away, and who now studied the quilt with a combination of fascination and soul-terror. Reggie, impossible to fathom, seemed in the moment too terrified to talk. "And I think Doctor Tucker gave you too much morphine last night."

Wilde felt his head move: big lobby motions, back and forth. "No, Robbie, he did not. He gave me what I needed. What I need." Wilde paused and licked his lips, waiting for the right words to fall from the roof of his mouth and bounce up, off his tongue. "He—I mean Tucker—the lovely man—the happy doctor—"

"What?"

"I need it. The morphine. To sleep."

*

Robert Ross's face was close and yelling. "How much champagne did you drink this morning, before we came?"

For some reason, his friend's words did not line up in a tidy order, did not run straight through his ear to his mind. Instead they broke and fell apart, bounced over his chin to land on his chest. But he took a stab at an answer.

"Only one bottle."

"Only one?" Turner said, his arboreal eyebrows flourishing.

"Honest to god," Wilde said.

"So you're done for the day, I suppose?" Turner added, softly.

"Done?"

*

Ross flailed. "How long have you been doing this?"

"Doing what?"

"Two bottles of champagne a day."

Wilde didn't understand. Hadn't his friends noticed that he liked champagne? Hadn't he been drinking it the whole time they'd visited with him?

"Sometimes I drink three."

*

Ross pointed to the dresser, and with an effort Wilde followed the motion to its indicated end, to what rested there: one of the hotel's ugly porcelain serving trays.

On the tray was half a baguette, and a couple wedges of white and gray cheese—barely nibbled on. This was very odd. Wilde not remember seeing any bread or cheese in his room previously. Nor did he feel the sensation of food in his body anywhere. Only liquid.

"Did I eat that?"

"You ate some, yes," Turner said quietly. "We wish you'd eaten more."

*

"Where is Reggie, Robbie?"

"He went out."

"Out? Where?"

"He's out. I'm here now. He'll be back later. He'll be back tomorrow."

"He's out?"

"He's out, Oscar."

"But I feel him here."

"He's out."

"I feel him here."

"No."

"I feel someone here, Robbie."

*

Wilde sighed. He felt the air in his lungs reverberate like a beaten skin. "It's such a sad sad story."

"Which story is that?" Ross asked.

"You know about my play, right?"

312

"You don't have a play, Oscar. You haven't had one for years."

*

"Have you talked to Frank since his play opened?"
"Frank and I run in different circles, Oscar. You know that."

Wilde nodded, but the movement, even a little of it, made him feel as if his head were about to fall off. Apparently he must hold his head in a single position, no matter what. He wasn't sure he could manage that.

*

"It's not just Sedger."
"What?"
"Who has a case against him."
"Against whom?"
"You know."
"I don't."
"Were we not just talking about Frank?"
"Frank Harris?"
"Yes, Robbie. Frank Harris. Were we not just talking about Frank?
"You were talking about Frank yesterday, Oscar."

*

The roof of his mouth felt dry. So dry. Not the

bottom only the roof. He made motions with his jaw. He felt his jaw opened and close, but his mouth became no wetter. Maybe he only imagined the motions.

*

Ross opened his mouth to speak, a question in his eyes; but then he stopped. His face was clear. The question gone. He let out a calm, quiet groan. "How many others?"

Wilde hesitated. "Maybe three or four."

Ross eyes widened. "Three or four?"

"Maybe five. Maybe six."

Ross slowly shook his head. "For how much?"

"Oh. Same thing. £100 each. Except for this man Roberts. A lovely man."

"Roberts who?"

"Hmm?"

"What's his full name?"

"Who?"

"Roberts."

"Oh. Well, I don't know. Smithers found him for me."

"Smithers? Why?"

"Hmm?"

"Why did Smithers find him for you?"

"Oh. Because I asked him."

*

He hadn't spoken in several seconds. Of that much, he felt confident. But what had he been speaking of before he stopped?

"Can you ask that again, Robbie?"

"Ask what?"

"Your last question."

Something discernible changed in Robert Ross's eye. There was a hardening in his upper cheeks.

"How much did he pay you?"

"Who?"

"Roberts."

"Roberts? Oh, he paid me £250."

*

Wilde felt someone else move. Someone not Robbie. He managed to move his head slightly to the right. There was Reggie. Reggie was back, sitting in a chair, taut against the bedside. So good of the dear man. But he had the worst, diarrhetic expression on his face. And those lurid eyebrows were arching again. But, a second later—it felt like a second later—Turner was smiling: an illicit kind, the kind one knows one shouldn't show but can't help it. Ross, meanwhile, just made a clicking noise.

"That is a problem," Ross said.

*

"So," Turner said, with an undercurrent of playfulness, "now you're saying that you pay for your champagne through fraud."

"Yes!" Wilde exclaimed. We was so glad that his friends finally understood. He had not been sure, in his state, how accurately he was communicating. Apparently, accurately enough.

*

"Of course," Ross started, "you could have simply written the play yourself; that way you would have made the most money of all."

"We are so far beyond that point, Robbie," he said tiredly. "You need to understand how impossible that is now."

*

Wilde almost fainted against his pillow. In the moment, he felt a black presence stand up in the corners of his vision, then lean over, as if to get a good look at his face. Wilde shivered. All the way up and down his back, even on his neck to the very tip of his skull, he felt a chill. Is that how it was to be? Is this how it would come, in front of his friends, just as one of them is about to abandon him? But then the figure stepped back. Just as Wilde, in his mind's eye, was set to turn and look the figure in the face, it slid into the murk behind him, without any definite reckoning of its size or shape or proximity. He opened his eyes, realizing for the first time that he had closed them at all. He saw Robert Ross and Reginald Turner studying

316

him: not with fear, but more like ordinary anticipation.
Then he realized. They had no idea about the dark figure.
They had no idea it had come that close. They were simply waiting for him to respond to Ross's last question. But
he could not remember what that was.

*

Ross strode directly to the door and opened it. Wilde, from his pillow, studied Robbie's face the whole time.
Whatever was out there in the hallway, Ross was seeing
it. If it was indeed the black figure, Wilde would be able
to read it on his friend's expression. But wouldn't that
mean the figure would get Robbie first? Another sadness
to add to his others? Then Wilde heard a man, an actual one, speaking in the hallway. A voice Wilde thought
he recognized. Ross nodded once. He put his hand in
his pocket and brought out some coins. He extended his
hand through the doorway, gave one or two of the coins
to the man, and then took something from him. Something paper. He thanked the man and shut the door. Ross
looked at what he was holding in his hand—a letter. Wilde saw Ross give a tiny shake of the head, as if to chase
off a bad, stray thought. Then he came straight over to
the bed and handed the letter to Wilde.

"The clerk brought this up for you," Ross said.

Wilde saw the squirrely, impatient cursive on the
envelope and recognized it at once. His heart moved:
a sloppy flopping motion that bore wet, urgent echoes
from almost a decade before. "Bosie," he whispered.

*

"I got fifty pounds from Bosie!" Wilde yelled. "Look, Robbie. Bosie sent me fifty pounds."

"Yes, look," Ross said.

"What a dear boy. What a beautiful soul. I knew he loved me." Fifty whole pounds. And just when he had told Ross and Turner that they needn't worry, because he had no money for champagne today. Well, he had the money now! He could pay for three or four bottles—and then the three of them would celebrate Bosie's largesse. It was kind of a miracle, wasn't it? And best of all is that the miracle came from his very own beloved. Dear dear Bosie.

"That's good of him, Oscar," Turner said. "I must admit." Turner directed a looked at Ross that Wilde registered as careful. But he couldn't possibly know what that meant. Of course it was good of Bosie. It cheered Wilde to see his friends realize this. Who, after all, was better than Bosie? And it did mean Bosie loved him again. What else could it mean? Or had Bosie always loved him? Hadn't Bosie always loved him? Even when they were children together? Wait, were they children together? How long had he known the man? Suddenly Wilde couldn't remember. All he knew was that he had a check for fifty pounds in his hands, and it came at exactly the right time. He was smiling now and Turner was looking at him, the top of Reggie's suddenly bulbous forehead motioning wobbly fashion, as in a funhouse mirror. Now that was odd. Wilde stared at Turner until the motion stopped and his friend's head went back to normal.

*

"Where's Reggie?"

Ross, unfathomably, sighed. "He's out, Oscar."

"No, he's not."

"I'm telling you he is."

Why was Robbie sounding so cheeky all of a sudden? He'd only asked the question.

"But I feel him here."

"He's out."

"But I feel him here."

*

"Where are you going?" Wilde said.

Ross stopped, sighed. He turned back. "I am going to Nice, Oscar. My mother lives there now. And she is very ill. And I promised I would visit her. And Reggie will be here any minute. That is what he promised.

"I am ill, Robbie."

Ross sighed. He lowered his head.

*

Wilde lurched off the pillow and sat up straight, a naked fear electrifying his spine. No, not just fear. Knowledge. "What if I die, Robbie?"

"You won't."

"Everyone dies."

"You won't. Not while I'm in Nice. Tucker was just saying, just yesterday, that he thinks there's a chance you'll completely recover."

"Tucker is an imbecile."

Wilde saw Turner smile gently; so he knew Reggie must share this view as well. "You don't know what kind of pain I'm in, Robbie. Maybe this is the pain one feels before one dies." He hadn't believed this until he said it, but now that he'd said it he believed it wholeheartedly. Because it made sense of the elusive black figure. When was the last time he'd seen it? How often had he? He couldn't remember. But it was not here now. Not now. Not this present moment. Maybe, Wilde considered, the trickster was playing hide-and-seek with him until Ross left, and the second Robbie stepped on the train, out of touch, out of reach... Wilde came all the way up off his pillow, and, straining, sat up in bed. He stretched his arms out toward his oldest friend, who any minute now might step out the door and leave his life, in every sense possible. "Please don't go, Robbie. Don't leave me here."

*

"Robbie," Wilde started. He was not sure where the sentence was headed or where it would arrive, only that he wanted to begin it, only that he had to begin it, in order to make sure that it landed somewhere, even if with wobbly knees and vertigo and no balance. "When you get to Nice . . ." He paused, but seeing the look of expectation on Ross's face he knew he had to say something soon.

"Yes?" Ross said, almost with all of his good old jauntiness.

"Look for a spot."

Ross's eyes darkened.

"A spot for what?"

"For us."

"For us for what?"

"You know."

"I don't, Oscar. Really." Now Ross was talking quickly and with annoyance. Or was it fear? "What are you talking about?"

"To lounge. To linger. To sip champagne and look at the sea. I mean, of course, once I'm all better."

Ross smiled slowly. He looked at Turner, who was also smiling. Something passed between the two men, but again Wilde could not read what it was. Nothing bad, it seemed. Nothing bad at all.

*

Footsteps. Slow, slurring steps. But more. More than minutes ago. More than days.

"Reggie, this is Father Cuthbert Dunne. I found him at the Passionist rectory. This is Reginald Turner, Father. He works for *The Daily Telegraph* in London."

"*The Telegraph*, eh?"

"Indeed. You know it."

"Yes. Yes, I do."

Silence.

Who is speaking?

*

"Reggie's been keeping an eye on Oscar whenever I have to go out. In fact, it was Reggie who summoned me from Nice. Just in time, apparently. I only arrived this evening."

"Yes," the priest said. "Just in time." Then: "The man has close friends, I see."

"He does," Turner said, but nothing more.

*

"I think I'll leave you two to this, if you don't mind," Turner said. "I'll be upstairs. Call me down when you're through. Will you, Robbie?"

"Sure thing." Pause. The door opened. The door closed. The silence carried a new, strained texture. He wished he heard cooperation.

"We've rented a room on the third floor. In order to be as available as much as possible... For Oscar, you understand. We never thought we could keep him from dying, you know. We never had that illusion... We just wanted to be close."

"You do not need to justify the room," Dunne said. "It's not any of my business."

*

You say he can hear us?"
"He can."
"How do you know that?"
"I know my friend, Father."
"Mr. Ross, he appears to be unconscious."
"He isn't. I know my friend."

*

Ross's footsteps surged past the priest. Wilde heard him draw close, lean in. Robbie's voice in his left ear. The good one. "Oscar, I've brought a priest. Don't you want to be received—finally?"

*

"That's a yes," Ross said.
"If you say so."
"I say so," Ross said.

*

"Has he ever been baptized into another church?"
"That I can't tell you."
"Why not?"
"He never acted it."
"So no then?"
"That I can't tell you."

A long, bristly, impatient sigh.

"He's dying, Father."

"What about the parents?"

"They're dead."

"I mean, what religion were they?"

"Anglican. Technically. That's what Oscar told me. I don't know if they practiced. I tend to think not."

"Even the laggards will get their dopes baptized. Usually."

"I suppose so. But I really can't swear to that in his case. Can we get on with it, Father, please?"

A measured silence. It sounded like calculation. "If you are really not sure, I can give him a conditional baptism. That should cover it."

*

"Hurry," Ross said.

*

"Oscar Wilde, if you are not yet baptized, I baptize you in the name of the Father"—droplets of water struck Wilde's head and his naked chest—"and the Son"—another bit of the palmful—"and the Holy Ghost."

*

"I've seen him before, you know."

"You have?"

"Once. Long ago."

"Where?"

"Dublin. I was just back from China and heard that he was lecturing at Trinity. About his trip to America."

"He gave many of those. That's how I met him, actually."

Silence. It grew longer. And louder. Then: "He certainly looked different then."

"Didn't we all, Father?"

"Much thinner, almost rawny. But quite the peacock in that suit of his. Almost a fancy dress, that outfit. And the long hair, so long. He moved like he was posing. And he talked like he'd been born in Kensington Palace. Didn't appreciate that, if you can forgive me for my saying, Mr. Ross. It was that accent of his more than anything that drove me away as soon as the affair was over."

A difficult silence. How he wished he could enter it, end it.

"I would have advised you not to take too seriously any accent of Oscars. He had a talent for them. He found that they put people at ease."

"It didn't me."

"Perhaps you are not like most people, Father."

Silence.

"Probably not."

*

"Shouldn't we offer him the sacrament of Penance?"

Robbie's voice: so thrilled he was almost gushing. Robbie.

"He's in no shape for that, is he? And technically it isn't necessary. Purification is implicit in baptism."

Ross was breathing. "Shouldn't we offer it anyway?"

*

"Perhaps you could tell me—tell us—some of his sins. We could ask Mr. Wilde to raise his hand, as he did before, to confirm the truth of what you say. And then again, one more time, to assert his desire for forgiveness for those specific sins."

*

"We're doing it for you, Oscar. We are going to set you up for your final ride. I will tell a few of your sins to the father. The ones I know about, at least." Robbie chuckled, a forced sound. "Then we will ask if you admit to these sins and if you want forgiveness for them."

*

"Is he still listening?"

"He's listening."

"Is he still? Listening?"

"He is."

"Is he? How do you know?"

"I know."

"You know?"

"I know, Father."

*

"One more," Robbie said, after a pause so long Wilde could read the pain in it. "A kind of love for men that the church regards as shameful."

"Shameful?"

"That's what I said."

"Do you mean sodomy?"

"The love of one man for another can take many forms, Father."

"Why, of course."

"Then let's leave it at that."

Silence.

"Fair enough. Could we at least name the sin as 'an unnatural desire for physical contact with other men'?"

Nothing. No sound. No agreement.

Hurry.

Then Robbie muttered a bitter word about "nature."

"What?" the priest asked.

"Yes," Robbie said, tight-lipped. "Whatever you say, that way." Robbie's assent sounded like crumbling words, barely ejected, as if he were speaking through a mouthful of biscuit.

"Mr. Wilde, do you confess to the sins Mr. Ross has outlined?"

"Yes." Robbie's voice: a strangled whisper, as if surprised and disappointed at once. How could Robbie be surprised, after all that has happened? And would Robbie really want him to dishonor this theatre?

*

"He can't speak the Act of Contrition, Father," Ross said, as if he'd only just thought of it. "How do we proceed?"

"Technically, he just needs to be contrite. He only needs to desire the Lord's mercy. And he's communicated that to us."

Silence.

"And," the priest continued, "he needs in his heart to promise the Lord to not commit these sins again in the future. To make an honest effort to avoid them."

"Afraid there's very little chance of him ever sinning again. Even if he wanted to."

"Obviously."

"You aren't going to give him a penance, are you?"

A surprising sound: a priest's laughter. "What would you suggest?"

"I think he's suffered enough penance already; five years' worth."

"All right. I must say I agree with you."

*

"On to Extreme Unction?" Robbie said, the giddiness—or perhaps it was only relief—uncontainable. He was getting what he had wanted for so long but never wanted to force. What they both were afraid of?

"It would seem appropriate," the priest replied. "Given the circumstances."

"Yes. Of course. Yes." Was that sadness in Robbie's voice? Sadness come back.

"But, I must say, three sacraments in a row. Mighty unusual. A record for me."

A soft noise from Ross. "Let's set a record with Oscar."

*

Hurry.

"Hurry, please, Father. He might be weakening."

"He is?"

Hurry.

"Hurry, please, Father."

*

Pages turning in a prayer book. Pages stop turning. A figure—a figure standing—on his right leaned down, leaned over, leaned over top of him. He could smell the breath. He could hear the words.

*

"O Lord, Jesus Christ, Most Merciful Lord of Earth, we ask that you receive this child into your arms..."

*

"Go on, Father," Ross said.

Silence.

Hurry.

"I don't... I don't..." Something was above his head, an inch over his mouth."

"What is it?" Ross said.

"I would rather not make a mockery of the sacrament."

"What mockery? What do you mean?

"I don't hear him breathing."

"No."

"I don't."

Sudden shuffling. Robbie's body close.

"He's breathing."

"What?"

"He's breathing."

"Where?"

"What do you mean where? He's breathing."

"I don't..."

"Do it."

*

A thumb hard against his forehead for the second time. Viscous liquid dewing the heat of his skin, pooling but then moving, toward his eyes.

*

"By this sign thou art anointed with the Grace of the Atonement of Jesus Christ, and thou art absolved of all past error and freed to take your place in the world that He has prepared for us."

*

"I was worried," the priest said. "I was worried—you understand—that before I could anoint him that last time—"

"Oscar is still with us," Ross asserted. "He still hangs on. For now, he hangs on."

*

"He's remarkable, isn't he?" the priest said.

An Expensive Luxury

Paris. 3 December, 1900.

The procession was to start at nine o'clock in front of the Hotel d'Alsace. It was only a modest gathering of persons who had assembled at that hour, dressed in uniformly grim expressions; drowned in the top hats and overcoats and veils and black dresses and wool gloves needed to withstand the new winter chill. The sky above them looked cumbersome, a collection of dim gray clouds, clotted and gaining weight, backed into each other and holding still, blunting any conceivable sunshine and intimating snowfall. The air contained that tell-tale winter-heavy smell and tangible wetness. It felt like at any instant it might thunder.

At the moment, however, not a one among those gathered studied the sky. With a few exceptions, each man or woman seemed contained inside the border of his or her own pain. They scratched their freshly washed faces; they examined newly shined shoes; they softly slapped their palms together. For an instant, they might turn and mutter a low syllable of mourning to some other mourner standing nearby, but the other would never react. There would be no indication that the muttering had ever reached the other's ears. And neither would the mutterer speak again.

Robert Ross was there, and it was he, the only one, whose eyes darted from person to person, taking them all in; also the street itself, from the hearse to the nearest intersection; from the lamppost to the street sign affixed to the second floor of the hotel. Rue des Beaux Arts, it read. His gaze moved urgently and nervously from place to place and person to person, as if it were his sole duty to make sure Paris itself was outfitted correctly for the ceremony of this day.

Reggie Turner was there, his arms crossed over the front of his body, his head lowered, his face fixed in a look of dire immolation. No one spoke to him, not even Ross. And if anyone came near him they were careful to give him broad quarter, as if he gave off some repulsive force as dogmatic as a magnet, when in fact they were simply trying to render the man his privacy.

Jean Dupoirer was there, his moustache waxed and his thin hair oiled, his new overcoat purchased only two days before in anticipation of this occasion, as perfectly fitted to his form as was possible in Paris. The purple stain on the side of his face was more muted a tone in the bland winter light than it was inside under a lamp; it matched the muted expression on his face. Beside him stood his clerk, Jules Charbonneau, a thin man with a narrow, vaguely agitated aspect, who glanced at his employer as if awaiting instructions. Charbonneau—who manned the front desk of the hotel on most days, and who also cleaned rooms and tended to any emergencies that arose with guests, including requests for items like cigarettes and bibles and umbrellas—finally turned away and stared at his shoes as if bored.

Phillipe Hennion was there, silent and gloamy, in a frock, a bowler, and walking shoes. He kept his hands in his pockets, only occasionally speaking out the side of his mouth to a short, plump woman standing next to him. She—who displayed, beneath a broad brimmed black hat, a full head of dark, wavy hair—might nod but otherwise said little to him; the only time she became animated was when addressing a young girl who stood there holding her hand and looking mildly lost.

Doctor Maurice à'Court Tucker was there, and though he made a point to remain in their vicinity, Tucker spoke nothing at all to Hennion or the woman or the child. Instead he kept his smooth face raised into the cold, with a solemn and vaguely confused aspect, especially when a shiver overtook him and he shuddered across the breath of his shoulders and down the length of his spine.

More Adey was there, looking older than his thirty-four years and far sadder: his dark, deep-welled eyes, the first sign of gray emerging in his new beard, the manner in which his upper back and shoulders curved like an octagenarian's, although this was merely a habit of his, a way to compensate for his height. He could have been mistaken for a man of forty-five or fifty, and in his conservative brown suit and waistcoat as a vacationing banker or out of favor Oxford don, perhaps a member of the Conservative Party, rather than what he was: an art critic and aesthete and political nihilist. Adey hovered near Ross silently, as if were that man's legal deputy or a *chargé d'affaires* whose services have been rendered meaningless since the ambassador arrived. He kept a concerned eye on Ross, and was never more than the five feet away from him, but said nothing. It was not widely known then that they had become a couple—well before Ross left England to visit Wilde in Paris for a final time—and Ross preferred to keep it that way. Though he had been so kind to Wilde while Wilde was in prison, bringing him books and writing him letters, circulating petitions for his release, Adey had seen very little of the poet following Wilde's permanent move to Europe, and so he knew none of the French men and women who had played a part in the drama of Wilde's latter years. Surely it must have been this reason to that he stood by silently and let Ross direct the affair.

Maurice Gilbert was there, his eyes red-rimmed, as if from a bout of just-exhausted weeping, his cheeks so drawn and slender as to have entirely lost the boyish fleshiness they exhibited not even half a year earlier. Now his chin appeared more square than rounded, his neck more attenuated, and his shoulders more firm. Yet all these characteristics, instead of making him seem healthier and more vigorous, put one in mind of illness. Every other minute or so, Gilbert would look around as if for someone to share his sorrow with, but finding no one he fell back into his own remorse.

Frank Harris was not there. With the success of *Mr. and Mrs. Daventry* in London, he had sailed in mid-November to New York, looking to negotiate with potential producers of an American staging. The negotiations fell through when these businessmen heard from sources in London that the play had actually been written by Oscar Wilde. As much as Harris protested, as strenuously as he tried to explain the exact provenance of the source material and what he'd done with it, even offering to produce his own drafts of the play, written by his own hand, the producers would not budge. "No one in this country," he was told one day over luncheon at Keen's, "will want to pay hard cash to see anything imagined by that deviant." Before Harris could say a word, the producer came back with, "or anything they think might have been imagined by him." Harris had just gotten finished with a particularly demoralizing meeting and returned to his hotel when he found a telegram sent by Robert Ross from Paris telling him that Wilde had died. A crossing could be accomplished in a week at best. As soon as he found out about the funeral arrangements, he telegraphed a florist in Paris.

Two French men and two women, who might, all of them, been in their middle thirties, and who seemed unattached to anyone else, stood among them. They were dressed in decidedly rougher fashion from the others, even from Hennion and his wife, with shoes that had been either not well cared for or made to suffer through long days of work and coats that had been made to suffer through one too many Parisian winters. They looked on impassively, as if observing a stage play they had not paid for but had decided to stick around for regardless, since it cost them nothing.

The driver of the hearse sat in his place at the front of the wagon, his gloved hands casually holding on to his horse's reins. Except for his blazing white shirt, he was dressed all in black: trousers, shoes, low peaked top hat,

and a serviceable frock, more warm than stylish but sufficiently dignified not to steal notice from the fact of the
coffin resting inside his wagon; which was the sartorial
mission, after all, of any hearse driver at any funeral. The
driver stole repeated glances downward and to the side,
checking for the signal that must sooner or later come
from Ross. Other than that, he did nothing but stare at
the back of his horse, as indifferent to the occasion as a
passerby.

The coffin resting inside that hearse was an ornate,
lavishly decorated, and richly lacquered box, featuring
panels of three different types and tones of wood—
black oak, chestnut colored maple, and dark cherry—and
glinting gold-plated handles. One of the most expensive
and unusual coffins available, it had been ordered and
paid for—Robert Ross discovered when he tried to purchase a casket himself—by an anonymous donor. As brilliant as it was, the coffin could, almost by itself, make up
for the lack of real sunlight.

Alfred Douglas was there too, standing before the
coffin as if frozen in place, his shoulders back like a soldier, his neck stiff, his hands joined together in a pose
of respectful waiting. The cashmere coat he wore was so
spotless it must have been brand new; same for his silk
top hat, and black trousers, and black leather shoes. But
at the moment, Alfred Douglas seemed as unaware as a
groundhog of what he was wearing. He was aware of
nothing but the fact of the coffin resting in the wagon
of the hearse. He stared at the box with a look so hard
and so pestering he might have been trying to set it on

fire. Occasionally, one person or another would touch his shoulder or speak a word into his ear, but Douglas responded as if he never heard the word or felt the touch; that is, not at all.

At or around ten minutes after nine, Ross gave a nod to the driver, who turned back to his horse and slapped the reins. The horse took its first step, then another; the wagon gave a start and then its wheels began to roll. At this bit of action, Douglas stirred. When the wagon had moved ahead ten feet or so, Douglas trotted to catch up, to remain the exact close distance to the vehicle he had maintained all along. And as the hearse—pulled with experience slowness by the driver's dutiful horse— moved closer to the Rue Bonaparte, then took a left turn there to head south on that street, then continued steadily for several blocks until it reached the Boulevard Saint Germain and there turned left and finally found its way to the front door of the Church of Saint Germain des Prés, Alfred Douglas managed to stay closer than any of the other mourners, his step more determined than theirs and his head most firm.

The funeral service was scheduled for ten o'clock. It took several minutes after the hearse was parked for the pall bearers—Ross, Turner, Douglas, Adey, and Dupoirer—to carry the coffin into the vestibule and for those five gentlemen, as well as the others who had walked in the procession, to find seats. Ross, for one—who had tried his best to keep the funeral quiet, fearing a resurgence of the anti-Wilde claptrap of years before, especially from parishioners of the Church of Saint Germain des Prés—was shocked and confused to find scores of persons inside, some he knew but many he didn't, people who dared the sudden cold and the threat of snowfall to pay respects to his friend.

Included among the scores were five middle-aged women of indistinguishable nationality, who huddled in a pew near the front, their shoulders bent toward each other, their faces brimming with anxiety. Not a one of them did Ross recognize, and it was frankly astonishing to him to witness the extent and the evidence of their pain. Occasionally one of them would cover her face with her hands, and every few minutes a member of the group would grip another, as if this were necessary to remain conscious. Ross considered going to them to ask if they needed assistance; but he decided to leave them be.

In attendance too were Anton Babineaux and Edouard Salvage, two young men who played the trumpet and the trombone, respectively, in a quintet that performed nightly at the Calisaya, an "American-British bar" on the Boulevard des Italiens. Before he became too ill to go out anymore, Wilde had frequented the Calisaya and made a game of attempting to seduce Salvage, a temptation Salvage had no trouble resisting—he was, after all, thoroughly involved with the group's piano player—but Salvage enjoyed the game anyway. Present too was Louis Latourette, an old Oxford associate of Wilde's who occasionally lectured at the Sorbonne medical school and once, after meeting Wilde at the door of the Calisaya had walked with him for hours, back and forth over the bridges of central Paris. Seated near Latourette, though they did not know each other at all, was Stuart Merrill, the American expatriate poet who had once circulated a petition of support for Wilde among writers in the United States; also his wife, who while person after person filed into the church kept her eyes and mouth closed, maintaining an aspect of repose that could have been meditation.

Several other writers were present as well, including Ernest La Jeunesse, the literary critic who had occasionally kept Wilde company on his treks through the Latin Quarter; Paul Fort, the symbolist poet; Pierre Louÿs, who had made a name for himself by depicting lesbian eroticism in his fiction and poetry; Henri Davray, who two years earlier had translated *The Ballard of Reading Gaol* with Wilde's help; Sar Louis, an aspiring playwright who had once approached Wilde with the hope of translating *Lady Windermere's Fan*; and Jean Moréas, the transplanted Greek novelist who wrote almost exclusively in French. Also two painters: Léon Printemps and Theodor Pallady.

Teixiera de Mattos was inside the church, along with his wife Lily and his stepdaughter Dolly, the offspring of Lily and Wilde's older brother Willie. Lily and Teixiera had concluded their Venetian honeymoon and were on a train back to Paris when Wilde had passed. Now they waited for the funeral service to begin with an aspect that was at once rested, burdened, and embittered. Teixeira mostly remained stone-faced, save for his characteristically darting eyes; Lily, meanwhile, looked drawn and regretful. Dolly, though quiet, fidgeted badly.

Elsewhere in the crowd were four of the Passionist

fathers who lived at the same rectory as did Father Dunne and had heard his tale of Wilde's moving and shocking death; three street dwellers—a woman and two men—to whom Wilde had given money on several occasions and even let spend some nights with him when he lived in the Hotel Marsollier; a teenager named Nicolas Lévêque, whom Wilde had befriended for a span in 1899; and Eugene Johnson, an aspiring Canadian painter who eleven months earlier had met Wilde on the Pont de la Tournelle but never again, yet since had reenacted his conversation with Wilde so many times to so many people that friends began to wonder at its apparent significance.

There were several others in attendance too, yet unidentified, more people than space can allow or patience extend to be described in particulars, people not famous either to us or in their own day, people unknown to Robert Ross or Reginald Turner or Alfred Douglas or any of Wilde's old associates from London, but people there just the same, on that day, in Paris, at the Church of Saint Germain des Prés; people who for their own reasons and from out of their own histories wanted, just like Ross and Turner and Douglas and the rest, to recognize one man's idiosyncratic and affecting greatness. Since time and patience cannot permit us to enumerate their particulars, we will simply mention them in passing and move on.

The first row of pews, however, was reserved for those closest to Wilde during his life in London and/or his death in France: Robert Ross, Reginald Turner, Alfred Douglas, Maurice Gilbert, Jean Dupoirer, and More

Adey. The service began several minutes late, to no one's surprise and no one's concern. That anything involving Oscar Wilde should start within an hour of when it was supposed to was something of a miracle.

One of the vicaires at the altar—there were three, along with Father Cuthbert Dunne—spoke the Latin of the funeral mass. While persons of any faith—or no faith, for that matter—were welcome at the service, when the time came to distribute holy communion only those baptized or converted into the faith were allowed to receive. These included Robert Ross, Alfred Douglas, Maurice Gilbert, Jean Dupoirer, Henri Davray, Sar Louis, the four Passionist fathers, and about a third of those whom we have suffered to reference only in passing.

****

At the grave in Bagneux, a shower of flowers and a variety of wreaths were on display. These included one from "The service de l'Hotel," one from More Adley, one from Reginald Turner, the one ordered by Frank Harris from New York, one from Arthur Clifton, one from Louis Wilkinson, one from Harold Mellor, one from Mr. and Mrs. Teixiera de Mattos, one from Doctor Tucker, and one from Adela Schuster. The largest display, however, so large it was propped on top of a metal stand and thus stood apart from the rest, was paid for by Alfred Douglas. At the head of the coffin, meanwhile, Ross placed a wreath of laurels that he had bought and then personally adapted. To the outside of the wreath he affixed a small metal plate that had been etched with the words, "A tribute to his literary achievements and distinction." To have such a plate etched on such short notice had cost Ross significantly more than the wreath itself. But he did not stop there. Inside the wreath he tied slips of paper with the names of those who had been kind to Wilde while he was imprisoned or after his release. Some of the names included were: Frank Harris, More Adey, Arthur Humphreys, Max Beerbohm, Reginald Turner, Arthur Clifton, Adela Schuster, Harold Mellor, Alfred Douglas, Ada Leverson, and Rowland Strong.

The burial rite began a few minutes after 1:00. While the day could certainly not be called warm—especially with the December wind that blew over the top of the graveyard—the snow that threatened at nine had never materialized. Indeed, the palpably moist and heavy atmosphere, those ominous barometrical indicators and hints of thunder were gone. The air was drier, and overhead the bunched, dark-looming spectacle had lightened considerably and begun to break apart. It was even possible to imagine that before night came on, a ray or two of sunlight would show itself, perhaps even the whole monster: whitely and cooly radiant in its clothes of winter.

Wilde's coffin, not yet lowered into the grave, was still visible to all. For the moment, it rested upon a network of boards laid over the hole. He could not be buried yet, after all, until the proper words had been sent, the proper ceremony completed. The graveside rite took only fifteen minutes and was delivered by Father Dunne, who—after the long vigil at the Hotel d'Alsace on the night of November 29, and all the additional hours spent there the following day, and further hours hurrying together a sermon for his Sunday obligation at the Church of Saint Severin, a duty Wilde's death had forced him to postpone, and the subsequent flurry of funeral preparations about which he had to school Robert Ross as well as assist the man in his negotiations with Father René Archambault, pastor of the Church of Saint Germain des Prés, who did not want to believe, even after Dunne confirmed it, that Oscar Wilde had died a Catholic— looked thinner and grimmer and decidedly more wan than he had only three days before. To put it most simply, he looked at least five years older on the afternoon of December 3 than he had on the evening of November 29; but, on the other hand, it was the kind of aging that suggested not senility but increased wisdom, even beatification. Looking at the priest now, Ross had to wonder if Father Dunne had had anything to eat at all since that last, forced spoonful of pea soup on Thursday night. Or had it been for the Passionist priest, as it had for Ross, only cigarettes and coffee?

The acolyte, a delicate and rubescent youth with coiled brown hair, a womanly chin, and ears as smooth as the skin of a plum—a boy Wilde would have favored— with one hand held up the prayer book for Dunne to read from while with the other hand clutched a small bucket of holy water, within which rested an aspergillum. Near the close of the short rite, Dunne lifted the short instrument from the bucket and shook from the metal ball on its end a thin shower of holy water upon the coffin. He placed the aspergillum back in the bucket and said, in English, the final words of the rite: "May his soul and the souls of the faithful departed, through the mercy of God, rest in peace." Then the collection of people at the grave, regardless of their religious persuasion, answered, "Amen," a quiet yet affirmative sound that extended over the top of the coffin like a blanket preparing it, and them, for rest. In the moment, Father Dunne looked out at and around the gathering, bemused, as if he had forgotten they were there, as if he could not figure what these people were about. He nodded once and looked at his shoes, his hands crossed in front of him. The acolyte glanced at him uncertainly, leaned closer in, as if he intended to whisper to the priest, but then Dunne's head came up with a new vigor, a clear look in his eyes, and an expression that spoke of satisfaction at the completion of a righteous deed. The acolyte, as it turned out, whispered nothing at all, but seeing Father Dunne's face proceeded to begin packing up the priestly equipment.

Ross said to the crowd, "Thank you everyone for coming here today. It would have been a comfort to Oscar—it is a comfort to Oscar—to see so many of those whom he loved gathered around him." A couple people took initial steps away from the gravesite, so Ross raised his voice to finish his announcement. "While this cemetery will be a very comfortable abode for Oscar for now, most of you know that I'd like for Oscar's final resting spot to be inside central Paris, where he spent so many of his last days. When that happens, and Oscar is moved, I will tell as many of you as I can. Until then, I implore you to come here and visit him. We all know how little Oscar liked to be alone; so let us bring him plenty of company."

Nods all around, but no smiles, no lightening. Indeed, as soon as Ross stopped speaking the scene was overrun by a choking silence, a tension that resonated like anger but was not anger but something lower and sadder and more hopeless. It became too much for Father Dunne, who stepped toward Ross and murmured that he would have to get going. Ross nodded as if he expected this. Then he reached out to give the man a last handshake.

"You've been so kind," Ross said. "About everything. I don't think I could have found a more suitable priest."

Dunne went ashen of a sudden, as if mortified, and his eyes glistened. He looked at the ground and only with difficulty brought his gaze back up to meet Ross's. It was the least I could do for him," Dunne said. Then before Ross could say another word Dunne added, "Georges and I must be getting back. You understand."

"We all must be getting back," Ross said. With that he turned to the group a last time and said, "If you came here in one of the carriages, we will need to return to them. If you made arrangements with a cab, then of course your time is your own. Stay as long as you like." Ross held his gaze a moment or two longer, looking for sign that his words were understood and accepted, but no answer appeared to be coming. "Come on then," he said under his breath to More Adey, and the two men, heads down, started on a silent trek back over the cemetery lawn, toward the driveway, seventy yards on, where the carriages were parked. Father Dunne and the acolyte followed.

There was demonstrable reluctance from the rest of the group to move, but finally, regrettably, they lurched, the group of them, from the gravesite, like a crawling beetle with a missing leg. The coffin remained where it was, resting atop the boards, awaiting the arrival of the graveyard men, who would make sure later that the coffin was placed safely within the confine of the hole they'd dug and then doused with dozens of shovelfuls from the pile of dirt that stood only feet away. As experienced as they were, it would not take the men very long, nor would they be unduly excised by the work, which was a good thing, because four other coffins needed to be placed in situ the same evening.

When almost everyone had vacated the gravesite and begun to follow Ross and Adley, their hearts heavy with the reality of the loss they had suffered, their thoughts busy with too much for a single one of them to put into words—memories of Wilde's last days, and of his much younger days; recollections of reading the words of his poems or seeing a performance of a play; worries about how often they could actually make it to Bagneux, or even Paris, to see this grave, and not knowing what they should say if they ever did; the sentiments embedded in the burial rite and in the words of Ross's last announcement—the sound of a high-pitched shriek broke across the air and landed as sharp as a lancet inside the body of every man or woman. "Oscar," a voice was saying, "nooooo." All heads turned back to the grave, where could be seen Alfred Douglas on his knees, in his new clothes, on the floor of grass and graveside dirt, his hand stretched out toward the coffin, fingers reaching, as if the box represented a last form of physical rescue for himself, or perhaps some impossible spiritual redemption. But his fingers could not reach far enough to touch the coffin, so he resorted to the shriek which came and came and came—"It's not fair; it's not fair; it's not fair"— until it seemed that it would never stop coming; but then his words turned to tears, and his voice to a gasp, as his upper body heaved with lung-heavy spasms.

They watched Alfred Douglas for as long as they could stand to, but finally none of them could watch any longer; so they left the man to his own agony in a far corner of the provincial graveyard, beneath a sky now not quite so remorsefully gray, a sky now new, a sky increasingly, ever since morning, open to compromise with the living, only twenty-nine days shy of a new century; a century that, they could not yet know, would grow comfortable with so many different notes and varieties of thunder.

A Note on Sources

This novel arose from a long-standing admiration for the stories, play, and poems of Oscar Wilde; even more from an equally long-standing curiosity about his final years when, released from prison, he had somehow to make a new life out of the shattered remains of his old one. Most biographical sketches of the author mentioned that following his prison sentence he moved to France and then died three years later. But what happened in those three years?

It took several years—decades actually—for me to get around to answering that question. But when I did finally decide to answer the question for myself I realized I had an advantage that authors of historical novels do not always enjoy: a solid familiarity with the creative output of my subject, as well as lived experience in many of the places that would need to be depicted in the novel. With that as a knowledge base, I plowed into biographical scholarship on Wilde, both in print and online, for crucial details about his person, his friends, his family, his milieu. Every major character in this novel, even the priest who baptizes Wilde before he dies, is drawn directly from the facts of Wilde's life, and many of the scenes were suggested by the biographical reading I carried out.

Three sources were of special use. The first was Richard Ellman's still classic *Oscar Wilde* (1969), which for decades stood as the authoritative scholarly account of Wilde's life. These days, Ellman is rightly criticized for some peculiarly ham-handed, and simply wrong, statements regarding Wilde's sexual life and physical condition. But his Oscar Wilde remains an unavoidable resource for anyone interested in researching the author. Another extremely valuable source was Neil McKenna's more recent volume *The Secret Life of Oscar Wilde* (2003), which served as a useful corrective to Ellman, especially for suggesting exactly how exuberant and unapologetic was the homosexual life Wilde lived.

The last source I must mention here is Frank Harris's *Oscar Wilde: His Life and Confessions* (1916). Despite its title and what might have been Harris's original intentions, the book is far less an objective biography than it is a remembrance of Wilde from a devoted friend. But in this regard, the book proved quite valuable. One must be careful with Harris, as he tends to place himself at the center of the drama of Wilde's trials and later years. But the sympathetic picture Harris draws of Wilde strikes me as credible and was deeply influential to formulating my own idea of Wilde as a fictional character. I even borrowed bits of Harris's remembered conversations with Wilde to fill out the scenes in my novel in which the two are talking, debating, agreeing and, more often, heartily disagreeing. To say the least, *Oscar Wilde: His Life and Confessions* is a mixed bag of information, but for that reasons one of the most important sources I consulted.

John Vanderslice

CPSIA information can be obtained
at www.ICGtesting.com
Printed in the USA
BVHW01s2037080118
504682BV00018B/44/P